LEAVE THE KEYS

in the

Visor

Susie M. Bruning

susie.bruning@gmail.com

402-499-8779

88,000 word

To Aubrey,

Sorry I lost you in Target that one time and customer service had to intervene.

THERE IS NO SUCH THING AS FUN FOR THE ENTIRE FAMILY

--Jerry Seinfeld

My name is Natalie Calhoun and I've watched thirteen people die. *Thirteen.* It's a horrible number and I've been told not to count—the shrinks mumbling crap about low morale and suicide—but it's an impossible task since I watched my own mother die, her last seconds wasted in my panicked, futile efforts, making the woman who gave me life the first honorary name on my own personal death list.

I didn't talk about my personal childhood catastrophes since my job as a cardiologist entailed making life-or-death decisions. In other words, I was expected to save people. Making these decisions was easy, like solving third grade math with the answers written on the wall. I guess I'm bragging, but I am very good at it. Hospital staff hung upon my every word as if it were gospel or written orders from a high mandate. I wanted to laugh out loud at their careless, unwavering trust, but kept my mouth shut. No one questioned me. And with my past, maybe they should have.

It was a Tuesday. I was celebrating my thirty-first birthday with an espresso and a bag of Cheetos, sitting in the St. Matthew's doctor's lounge that was painted pastel blue, decorated with modular furniture and geometric-pattern green carpeting. There wasn't a single window, but the room had three ventilation shafts, circulating the odor of day-old tomato soup and tuna sandwiches. Discarded soda cans lay abandoned on tables and the trash overflowed with surgical masks and booties. There were homeless shelters in Kansas City with a better social vibe. My feet were perched on a table, showing my Christmas socks that I'd gotten ten years ago from my pseudo-stepmom Eve. They went well with my black scrubs that, like me, hadn't seen a wash in forty-eight hours.

My colleague Phil was leaning over and handling day-old sandwiches in a tepid mini-fridge, scrounging for one that wasn't tainted with salmonella or pickled relish. He was your typical Stanford-biochemistry-grad-that-had-settled-for-medicine guy. He was five-seven, weighed a buck-fifty, and drank strictly Americano coffees. He had round professor glasses that he shoved up into his black, curly hair when he was stressed, which was any time that irate families backed him into a corner demanding answers he didn't have. He was attractive in a dean of humanities kind of way.

Phil sniffed my direction. "I don't know who smells worse, you or the chicken salad. How long since you've been outside? Or taken a shower?"

Phil had serious issues with those who didn't take personal hygiene seriously. He always carried the lingering smell of perfumed talcum powder. He once relieved me of my day's consults just so I would see a woman who'd been using a dumpster behind a Chinese buffet restaurant as her living quarters for two weeks.

It was 07:05 AM. I'd been at the hospital for forty-nine hours and thirty-two minutes. I rubbed my hands over my face. "I've been here two days. Worked my 24-hour shift. Then Clinton's. His wife is due any minute." I leaned back, stretched my arms and pointed at the food. "If you wait another hour, they bring breakfast. Sometimes chicken noodle soup and turkey sandwiches too." I smelled a sour lemon odor and put down my arms. "And maybe egg sandwiches."

Outside, there was sound of laughter and a cell phone ringing. A surgical nurse opened the door, glanced around the room and said, "Sorry. I was looking for Dr. Klein?"

Phil said, "In CT," still staring at various bread items. She backed out of the room and shut the door. He grabbed a bagel and regarded me. "Really? Do you know the lunch specials too?"

"What?"

He shook his head. "Forget it. I'll wait. Don't want to vomit in the ER to start the day."

He leaned against the counter and pulled a white sheet of paper from his pocket. His finger moved down through a list of printed names. "Get me up to speed. 305?"

6

I cracked open the Cheetos and watched as artificial yellow dust settled on my white jacket. "305 had a stress test and is cleared to go home," I replied, looking at my own list and the handwritten notes. One of my nurses had drawn a large penis next to the guy's name. He was six-seven and had some of the largest hands I'd ever seen. I'm not going to lie, I had some personal interest there, but I also wasn't a urologist; all things below the sheets would remain a mystery.

"315?" Phil said, bringing me back to reality. Overhead, the operator called for security to the emergency department, which happened about twice a day.

I chewed on a fingernail, which was already bitten to the quick. "His cardiac enzymes and creatinine levels are high. He needs a stress test and a renal ultrasound." I tapped my lip, thinking. "Maybe a pysch evaluation. He went apeshit in MRI."

Phil laughed. "OK, tread lightly there. Intensive?"

"There's consults on 644, 645, 652 and 671." I paused. "And 678. You know, *that guy*." I tried to appear contrite. I wasn't. "Sorry."

Phil eyed me. "Shit. Isn't he dead?"

"Not yet."

Phil's voice took on a child's whiney tone. "Wasn't he like, *dead-dead*? Two days ago? Dissection, congestive heart failure and his kidneys trashed?"

"Family's wavering. Wanted a full code at the eleventh hour. His *dead-dead* status went to *half-dead*. He's got ten drips going, including three pressors."

Phil said, "Good God. Why didn't they just let him go?"

I shrugged and didn't answer. If you did, you were immediately pegged as an outsider, a novice, or plain idiot. People lived, people died. Families wavered. Everyone found it hard to

7

make the final decision. As cardiologists, we were past the drama—most days were no different than the episode of Lucille Ball and the chocolates on the conveyer belt, all of us hustling to keep the pace with the overwhelming number of patients thrown at us.

I picked up my bag and kept my arms close, keeping any unpleasant smells from leeching into the air. My phone pinged with an incoming text. I disregarded it because I was officially off duty.

Phil peered up from the list. "So you're actually *leaving*?"

There was a trace of mockery, but I didn't bite. "Yeah."

"You and Trevor doing anything tonight?" he asked.

"I doubt it." The phone chimed again and I reached into my pocket, switching it to vibrate. "I went ahead and picked up Chris' clinic for tomorrow."

He shook his head. "You've lost your mind."

I shrugged. "Nah. He's got plans. I don't."

Phil stared, his face tight. "You should make plans, Nat. Do something. Anything. You're always *here*."

My phone hummed, rattling inside my pocket. Phil asked, "You going to answer that?" as the overhead speaker called a "code orange" in the ER. He looked up, muttering, "Wow. The natives are rowdy this morning."

I slid out my phone and took a quick glance.

Trevor: We need to talk.

Trevor: Hello?

Trevor: Hello?

Phil continued, "Crap, Natalie, haven't you've picked up enough shifts? You could take off . . ." and counted on his fingers, "for a month."

8

I nodded. It was true. In recent months, I'd covered shifts for half of the cardiology group and taken call for the others; practically all of them owed me favors.

The door opened and there was movement in my periphery as I saw a vascular resident sliding past me, his eyes darting away when I caught him staring. He tripped, getting away from me. This wasn't an uncommon occurrence; I was something of an anomaly because I was the only female in the cardiology group, but most of the whispering conjecture and gossip centered around the sizable scar that ran from my ear down into my neck, ending in a gruesome pile of scar tissue that peeked out at the juncture of my right shoulder. The tissue had a military-field-patch-up-job appearance about it— angry and red, crisscrossed with indented lines—as if chemo- radiation had been used to kill it. I'd thought about having a cosmetic surgeon fix it, but my brother Tommie had convinced me that scars were the topical timeline to a person's life. By getting rid of it, I'd be tearing out a piece of my personal scrapbook. I suppose that thinking was directly linked to him being in the military too long. He was always saying interesting stuff like that, so I kept my scars. It was a fearsome reminder to all staff to give me at least five feet of personal space.

Phil watched the guy as he moved to the other side of the room. He took a step closer and whispered, "Just thought you should know. Malcolm's still interested. If . . . you know . . . things . . . well, you know."

Malcolm Carter was a neurologist, just like his father and grandfather. He probably came shooting out of the womb with a stethoscope around his neck. The three of us had started together at Stanford medical school, when we were fresh grads and still showed up in starched, ironed clothes. He was a good friend, but made me uncomfortable because he'd become a professional of crossing personal boundaries. I scoffed, shoving Cheetos into my mouth. "Give me a break. Malcolm's with that nurse on the fifth floor. Everyone knows."

Phil laughed. "He said he's keeping his options open. For you."

9

I groaned. "Gross." I caught the resident listening and narrowed my eyes in his direction. The poor guy dropped his orange juice and it splattered against the wall.

Phil shook his head. "Quit scaring the kids. They complain about you in staff meetings."

I ran a hand through my unruly blonde hair that I kept in a pixie-cut suitable for work and tucked it behind my ears, which only enhanced my appearance of surfer-girl-from-California, except for my heinous scar. I mouthed the words, *Don't care,* and smiled. As a farewell, we knocked knuckles. I wished him luck and walked out, heading for something other than pumped, regulated air and weak sunlight that filtered through sealed windows. I silently prayed that my car would start. I pulled off my scrub top and stethoscope, which left me in a t-shirt and black scrubs, hoping I passed as a regular visitor. I walked through the lobby, past concerned groups of families, and exited via a long sloping hallway strewn with wheelchairs and boxes of medical supplies that led to the physician basement parking. It was supposed to be a privilege, but felt similar to walking into a morgue due to the dank, cold temperature. A smattering of cafeteria staff took their break in a shadowy corner; some of them smoking in violation of hospital policy. My 2002 Subaru Outback sat wedged between Phil's Range Rover and an Audi SUV.

As I opened the door and slid into my car, my scrubs caught on the torn nylon seats that I'd repaired with duct tape. I hung my stethoscope around the manual transmission. Seeing the many luxury cars, I felt a deep longing to own something that wasn't purchased off of Weird Wally's Used Car Lot. The only thing my checkbook afforded right now was a Kia Soul—a vehicle marketed with commercials using animated rapping mice cruising downtown to appeal to the sixteen to twenty-four age group. I was months away from finishing a cardiology fellowship and the financial boon that came with it, but I'd also managed to acquire a whopping five hundred thousand dollars of student debt. Add in my mortgage, I was close to hitting seven hundred thousand. The sum was easily compiled when I'd completed my college degree at Wellesley, wasted a full year in pharmacy school, before dropping out and

10

attending Stanford medical school, with a cardiology residency and fellowship to follow. I had the kind of debt that made a person think about faking their death and moving to Mexico to change their identity.

Due to my financial liabilities and personal apathy, if you caught me somewhere outside the hospital, there's a good chance you would've pegged me for a woman who did part-time personal training or worked at a Starbuck's. I could have been your hippie neighbor that sold Himalayan salt lamps as I walked down the street in a pair of loose pants, Birks, and a Minnesota Vikings hat shoved on my head. My life was two warring universes; I was simply in one or another, with no overlap. Whereas the snap decisions at work were like grabbing toilet paper—automatic and necessary—my own personal life was a vast swampland of indecision and vague insecurities, bogged down with a heaping dollop of laziness.

In matters concerning my personal life, I had all the tools, but refused to use them. I was no different than a gifted three-point shooter, refusing to come into the basketball game until the final seconds, and only if the team was ahead by twenty points. At the ripe old age of thirty-one, I still called my dad or brother when nagging personal problems snuck up and tapped me on the shoulder. I didn't expect answers from them, but used them as a touchstone, for which, maybe, I might find my way back to the person that I was at work. The person I could have been in my own life, with the right instruction or persuasion.

If I were normal.

Which I wasn't.

* * *

Coffee in hand, I drove out of the parking garage, through security gates and was headed south on I-76 outside Kansas City, shoving a banana into my mouth, when I called my dad, Martin. He worked from home doing accounting and taxes for several large construction companies.

"Hey," he said, "Happy Birthday!"

11

I rolled up my windows to hear the conversation, but the car's suspension rattled enough that I yelled to be heard. "Don't remind me."

He adopted a very dour voice, "Happy Birthday."

"Stop."

"OK. How about this? I think I'm going to Scotland!"

"Whad," I said, working past banana goo in my mouth. "Weally? When yoo guws going?"

"No. Just me. Not Eve." Dad said.

"Huh?" I asked, confused.

"Just. Me."

Surprised, I dropped my cell phone in that black hole between the seat and console, where things disappeared for years, next to petrified French fries and fuzzy, sticky coins. Swerving, violating at least three state driving laws, I grabbed for the phone. I heard his muffled words, "Eve is going to Quebec with a friend." Wedging my hand in the crevice, I retrieved the phone and a discarded sucker stick, which I threw to the floor. Dad said, "I've decided to do my own trip. By myself."

Eve had been my mom since I was ten. Initially, she'd lived across the street and worked in the middle school cafeteria. When my mom died, she'd stepped in when things had fallen apart and never left. She and Dad weren't married, but after twenty years of cohabitation, they might as well have signed the paperwork and made it legal. Eve was consistent as a north winter wind, possessed the unfortunate square body of a German matron, and had taken over the maternal responsibilities of our household when it'd been reduced to rubble and ash. She'd touted discipline like an army sergeant, but showed us love by encapsulating us in her sheer bulk, as if squeezing us to death would take the pain away. She'd raised us as well as she could, which is to say, she kept us from killing one another in our teenage years. With no children of her own, she'd

12

been out of her depth. At that time of our lives, we'd taken on the wild personalities of feral animals. Tommie had been the worst; acting like a rabid dog, acting aggressively towards anyone who got close for no explainable reason. I wouldn't have blamed her if she had thrown us out by the third week, locked the doors and made us take up residence in the garage with the cats.

I wiped my hands on a Starbucks napkin, pushed the banana peel into the empty coffee cup and threw it to the floor, where it would stink up the car for the rest of the day.

Dad asked, "Natalie, you there?"

"Huh?"

Was I? It was hard to tell. The week had been a proverbial wrecking ball, knocking a hole so deep into my psyche that I could fit a basketball team and their mascot into the middle of my chest. My problems were accumulating at a rate I couldn't keep up with. My troubles with my live-in boyfriend Trevor had escalated to a point where most nights, I was sleeping in the doctor's lounge and keeping a stash of clothes in an overnight locker. I'd stake out my own house to see if it was safe to spend a couple hours, shower and eat, before leaving again to avoid face-to-face contact. Making matters worse, I'd come out of the house several days ago to find out that my ancient Subaru wouldn't start. Once I'd popped the hood, it was obvious to see the missing sparkplugs and cut battery cables. I lived in a rough part of town, but it was a strange act of vandalism.

"How's Trevor?"

I didn't respond because I really didn't know.

"Busy?" he asked.

"Yeah," I replied.

Dad really didn't care, but was being polite. No one in my family thought Trevor would make it to the finish line, including me, especially since recent lively texts from him suggested I was a regular Hannibal Lector of relationships, eating my own heart, until there was nothing left.

"So, Nat," Dad said. "You think I can do it?"

"What?" I asked. The engine light on my dash had gone from an intermittent blinking to a steady red.

"Nat? You listening?"

"What?"

"Scotland."

"Yes!" *Land of the green, home of the kilt.* "Umm . . ." I took a moment thinking about my dad travelling alone at sixty-eight. He wasn't your typical twenty-year-old-deciding-to-solo-backpack-across-country type, smoking weed and listening to reggae. He had several serious cardiac issues and hadn't left the country in ten years except when Eve had convinced him to take a Mexican cruise—the type of vacation where everything had been paid for and within arm's reach. His travelling alone to Scotland conjured images of him driving on the left side of the road while navigating by a map and swerving to avoid hitting sheep. What if his defibrillator fired? Or the paramedics showed up? I could see a scenario where well-meaning health professionals threw up their hands in despair because he refused medical treatment, even though he lay on the ground like Phil had told him to until the events passed, as sheep sedately walked around his body. Even worse, I saw him on a decrepit ferry service in the Atlantic Ocean and someone accidently knocking him overboard, never to be heard from again. At a bare minimum, you need a companion to scream out when the shit hits the fan just so other people know that you've been thrown into deep waters. I sighed thinking about all the nightmarish outcomes.

"I heard that sigh. And it makes you sound like Eve. I'm telling you now because I wanted your opinion before the *whisper campaign* starts."

"Whisper campaign?" I echoed, while swerving to miss a construction cone exiting the interstate.

14

"Every time I want do something out of the ordinary, the whisper campaign starts and then the next thing I know Eve is shutting down the whole thing. I just wanted to ask you if you think I can do it. Alone."

Truthfully? No.

His idea of a "solo trip" was a notion borne of thin ice, escalating temperatures, and possibly dropping into the deep end. He had no business going to Scotland by himself. The whole venture needed to be shut down immediately. Or someone needed to go with him. Someone other than me; I had no time for a family vacation in the midst of twenty-four-hour-work-days and escalating financial burdens.

But how do you say no to a father who set aside all concerns to raise three children? Who bought you a motorcycle when you were fifteen so you could cruise around your small midwestern town because he refused to buy you a car? Who does that for a teenage girl? Are you crazy? I laid it over on its side and burned the skin around my ankle on the muffler inside of a week. He sent money on a regular basis when collegiate fiascos left me lacking for funds and showed immense patience when I called three different times, in three different states, each time telling him that my car was leaking a different color of fluid. The last time I'd been in Utah. He'd carefully explained the blue-green fluid was coolant and the radiator had a hole, and "Congratulations!" I'd worked my way through every single possible color of automotive fluids.

"Why are you going to Scotland? Can't you do another cruise with Eve? Something simple?" I asked, hoping to install some sense.

"You mean sedate."

"I mean safe."

"Stale."

I sighed. I hated it when he beat me at my own game.

15

"I want to go to the Hebrides," he said. "Maybe the Shetland Islands as well."

"What? What's the Hebrides?" I pronounced it He-brides, like it was a venereal disease; he corrected me. I said it incorrectly again to just get on his nerves.

"Stop it. I know what you're doing. The Hebrides are a group of islands off the western coast of Scotland."

"I never heard of it."

"Of course you haven't."

"What's that supposed to mean?"

"You're not as smart as you think you are."

I ignored the comment because it was true. "Why isn't Evie going?"

"She's going to Quebec for *leaf-peeping*. Can you believe that? I am not going to my spend money to stand around and stare at leaves and wildlife. I can walk out the back door and do that." Eve was one of those academic master gardener people, reciting Latin names of flowers as she walked amongst them like a Julia Childs of the fauna. I humored her one day with a companionable walk through the garden because I wanted to score her Buick to go to a party. Within five minutes, it was so annoying I'd wanted to shove daisies down her throat. *Bellis perennis,* my ass.

"Ask one of the boys. They'll go." I was referring to my brothers, who were both older; one lived in Minnesota and the other in London.

"I guess I could. Would they be interested?"

"Probably not," I said. "Just ignore them if they say no."

We both laughed. Sean, the middle child, was an actuary for an insurance company and used numbers like the rest of the world used ketchup. One of his most annoying traits was that he recited statistical odds in everything, in the midst of any conversation. My oldest brother, Tommie, a college swimming star, had been in ROTC and eventually recruited into military special ops. He was now an assistant to a high mucky-muck Colonel at the London embassy, with vast travelling experience because of his job.

"Listen, no one goes to Scotland by themselves." I took a sip of coffee and spilled some onto my shirt. "It's just . . . lonely and sad."

He laughed. "Please, I've never needed anyone's company."

It was true; he really didn't need me or anyone else. Unless CPR was necessary, which brought us back to the problem of him travelling alone to an isolated international destination, which was the exact definition of Scotland—a vast landscape of endless green, heather, castles and Celtic lore. And Culloden. The Scottish version of our Gettysburg; a bloody massacre where approximately a thousand Scottish clansman lost their lives at the hands of the English in about sixty minutes. I had something of an obsession with Death and had become an expert on his most destructive and beautifully creative work, seen at Gettysburg, Somme, and Antietam.

Was it macabre?

Well, yes.

Death and I had become acquainted early in my life and he'd been following me around ever since like a faithful dog. I welcomed his presence and made permanent his company by carefully crafting a career that demanded him as a necessary sidekick. In my most hectic and stressful moments, when chaos was the most defining thread and the world slowed down like squeezing time through a pinhole, if I squinted hard enough and looked into my peripheral vision, I could see Him.

Yes, Him.

Death.

Sitting across the room, waiting patiently. For me.

Did that make me crazy?

Probably.

My career was decorated with life and death and the evasion of it. Over the years, the rigid lines of medicine had blurred and changed direction, making many things seem possible. In my over-taxed, sleep-deprived, cross-wired mind, I'd crafted Death's image; he was a tall, emaciated man of about seventy years. He wore a porkpie hat, plaid shirt and had a small notebook tucked in a front pocket, hiding a wrinkled packet of Lucky Strikes, like a racetrack gambler past his prime. He kept a toothpick stashed in the band of his hat, and when I was especially tired or stressed, I would spot him pulling it out and placing in his mouth, leaning back in a chair, chuckling, as all I attempted was for nothing. I worked hard, but I knew that no matter what, some of my patients would eventually be written down in that dark ledger.

And I guess if we're laying all of our "loony" cards on the table, you should also know that my own name had been written down in that tablet of his and hastily scratched off. For the time being. Because of this previous, almost fatal encounter, I wore the permanent jewelry of his handiwork and this connection made us very close.

"Natalie, what do you think?" Dad said, interrupting my thoughts. "You think I can do it?"

"I don't know. Let me think," was all I could say.

2

My family always wondered about my choices in men. The truth was, after finishing college and then another ten years of advanced schooling, I'd come out of a long educational wagon ride to find myself almost thirty, with all decent men swept up by women who had had the time to chase them and get a ring on their finger. Those women hadn't been buried in books, attempting to maintain their sanity in a career that was dominated by men. I'd become a man to survive, and consequently, the men in my life had included me, but not dated me. It was a side effect I hadn't realized until it was too late.

As I finished my residency, it became clear the fish pond had become decidedly smaller and one had to fish at the deepest levels to come out with anyone close to compatible. Trevor had been funny and smart, but not a perfect fit. I hadn't been in a position to be picky because I usually chased off most men within fifteen minutes due to my horrible conversation skills that mimicked a frenetic combination of Stephen Hawking, Rodney Dangerfield, Denis Leary, and SpongeBob. I had a MENSA-level IQ, but the mouth of the sailor. When I did go out socially, I laughed too hard, spoke too loudly, and drank beer and whiskey until I slurred words or fell off my barstool. Most men found this, at a bare minimum, tedious, and the least tolerant, like running me over in a car still wouldn't quiet me down. For most, I simply wasn't worth the effort. Trevor dealt with it by just concentrating on football, and stayed with me because I had an uncanny ability to crunch statistical probabilities and decipher Vegas betting lines to come up with true winners. For him, I was a lucky rabbit's foot that could not be thrown away.

Even though we had nothing in common, both of us had stayed with the relationship because we'd spent so little time together. By the time he'd moved in and started his mad scientist tinkering, I'd lacked the fortitude to get him out—which sounds like *you're fine with the food poisoning because you're too lazy to complain about the strange taste of the hamburger.* In the last several months, we'd defied each other relentlessly, arguing every time we were together. I'd spent the last week devising a plan to get him out of my life.

When I pulled into the driveway of my house, I noticed the spotlight over the front porch and garage was still on even though it was early morning. My dilapidated Craftsman was in a Kansas City neighborhood just east of Troost Avenue, which since the fifties had been a hotbed of racial tension, but was a convenient twenty-five minutes from the hospital. After moving in, both of my neighbors had cited high crime statistics and insisted on the increased lighting for my protection. They touted memberships to the NRA. I told them I was pretty good with a scalpel. I hadn't seen them much after that.

My phone buzzed with the incoming text:

Trevor: I can see you outside. Why are you just sitting in the car?

Nat: Quick peeking out the window. It's creepy.

Trevor: News flash. It's even creepier to sit in your car and stare back.

When I finally walked through the front door of my tiny bungalow, I'd been missing from my household for fifty-two hours. Fifty-two hours sequestered in an environmentally controlled, secured setting, where hardly anyone knew my first name and spoke to me only if absolutely necessary. It was, at times, pure bliss. And now, against my better judgment, I'd left my personal work haven to return home to Trevor, who was probably waiting to tell me that he was leaving.

I found Trevor feverishly packing items in the box-sized living room—cramming belongings into garbage bags like it was Armageddon and zombies were about to bust into the house. I looked behind me to just make sure nothing was lingering in the yard.

"It's about time," he said, throwing a full trash bag to the ground and picking up an empty one. He was using the leather couch to pile all his belongings; it was my only piece of furniture not from

20

Goodwill or Craigslist. It was a strange compliment to the stacked crates being used as side tables. He said, "You can't hide at the hospital forever," and walked away into the bathroom.

"I can try," I muttered, as I took some of his bags and put them in the alcove by the front door.

"I heard that!"

I ignored him and walked to the galley kitchen to find a bottle of red wine. It was eight AM, but I poured myself a healthy dose anyway. At that exact moment, Trevor came striding out of the bathroom carrying essentials and threw them in a grocery sack. A bottle of shampoo fell to the floor. Twice. Trevor gave up and threw it into the trash, which toppled over with the weight.

He turned and said, "Really, Nat? Wine? The morning shows aren't even over."

"Maybe it has to do with the fact that I've been up *all night*."

Trevor stopped his packing and stared. He had the same look as those ER docs after a bad accident in which they lacked the ability to patch back together the mangled bodies. He said, "You and me. I can't do it anymore." He pointed between us. "It's not working." Trevor was a bit of grandstander, so I sat down and started drinking wine. He barreled on, waving his hand in grand emphasis, needing no input from me. "You're never home. You're completely absent. From me. From this relationship. From *any* relationship for that matter."

"OK. Got it."

"No. I don't think you do. You've been hiding. For days." He looked over and caught me mid-sip and shook his head. "More like weeks." He walked over and took a quick look out the window, checked the front yard and pulled the curtain shut. He turned towards me and put his hands on his hips, as if an important message was about to be imparted. "To be honest, I feel like one of your chickens."

21

I choked on wine, sputtered and wiped my mouth. "Excuse me? Chickens?" I fought the urge to laugh out loud. I'd heard comparisons to many, many things, but never chickens.

"Yes, chickens," he echoed.

"Poultry?" I asked, adopting a confused face.

"What? I'm talking about chickens."

"Right," I said. "*Hens*." I knew I was pouring acid on a wound, but I couldn't help myself.

"*Chickens*!" he screamed. "Chickens! Stop it. You're missing my point."

"I guess I am. You lost me at pullets."

Like a living thermometer, Trevor's neck turned red, making the slow migration up to his face. He picked up a glass and spat, "Really, NAT! You want to play games now?"

Inhaling air through his nose, garnering some kind of mental fortitude, he put the glass back on the counter as if it weighed ten pounds. I watched him do it with some disappointment. It was no secret that I circled conflict as if it were a fire I couldn't get close enough to, even if it singed me so badly it stung sometimes.

"I am having a serious conversation!" Trevor shouted. "Can we discuss something without it going sideways?" He picked up a kitchen towel and wrung it in his hands.

I filled my glass to the very top of the rim and leaned over, slurping like a five-year-old. Not the most adult behavior, but it matched the occasion.

"Are you even listening, Nat?" Trevor said, returning to the previous job of gathering household items—many of which I'd purchased before he moved into the house.

"Is there a point to our breakup," I scoffed. "Over *chickens*?"

"It's just a perfect example of why we need to end this." He regarded the toaster sitting on the counter, found it suitable and put it under his arm.

I took three healthy swallows of wine. "I'm confused. Are you comparing yourself to a chicken? Or my emotional state to that of a chicken?" It would have been a first, even for me. "I'm a bit confused."

"Listen, Natalie. It's not just about *chickens*. It's that childhood story you tell about the chicks. And the refrigerator." He pulled out several beer steins and put them on the counter.

I groaned. "Seriously? You're bringing up *that* story? To use as an argument to break up with me?"

Trevor turned, placing his hand on a blender. "Yes. I am."

What Trevor was referring to was a childhood story of mine that my family lovingly termed the "Poultry Purge." I was raised in a rural area. One of my jobs was taking care of chickens, including the daily task of gathering eggs, which I detested. Those nasty old gals would eyeball me, knowing I was there to steal their personal goods and would time their head-bobbing efforts to peck at my hands. I was a belligerent nine-year-old who hated the job. One day, on my way out to gather eggs, my mother warned me that one of the hens had been lying on some eggs for a long time. She told me to leave them alone. I went on my merry, caustic way, gathering every single egg in the hen house. I was the poultry grim reaper.

An hour later while my mother was having her usual Saturday morning coffee with friends, a distinct chirping could be heard. One person suggested that barn swallows must have gotten into the chimney. Flashlights were procured, but no birds were found. When my mother opened the refrigerator to get more butter for the cinnamon rolls, the horror of what I had done become fully evident. The hen had been sitting on those eggs for a full twenty-one days and those poor birds were hatched into a very dark, cold world, in which they succumbed quickly to the hostile environmental conditions. What was an ideal temperature for milk was death for the fowl. The chicks all died within the hour. Tommie called me the "frozen butcher" for weeks.

"So one moment in my very young life is the crucial point to the breakup of our relationship?" I asked, tired of this conversation. Tired of everything.

"Do I need to remind you that you tell it at parties for a laugh?"

This was true. It went over like hot cakes after the first round of drinks were finished. "It's a very funny story."

"It's not. You killed baby chicks. And you told me that you never cried. Not once."

Had I really told him that I hadn't shed a single tear? Maybe early on, when I was trying to impress him with my hard-core farm attitude. How was I to know that he was a card-carrying member of PETA?

"The point is, Natalie, you don't show emotion. *At all.* I keep waiting for it. Hoping to see it surface. True emotion. Are you even capable? You run on autopilot. You didn't care for those chickens, and you . . . you . . ." *drum roll please,* "you don't care about me." He paused for dramatic flair. "You killed this relationship, just like those chickens."

He waited for some kind of reaction. I finished my glass of wine. "Is this about the ring?" I asked.

"Stop it, Nat. Your diversion strategies won't work. It's about a lot of things. Not just the ring." He sighed. "You know, for someone who knows so much about the inside of hearts, I don't think you have one at all." He gathered up a few final items and walked to the front porch.

I followed, holding the bottle of wine. "That's it?" I asked. "I'm a chicken killer and you're leaving?"

One of the neighbors stopped to watch the spectacle. It wasn't often that someone yelled, "chicken killer," without it being a march on a Tyson processing plant.

"That's it, Nat. I'm done."

I rolled my eyes. "You mean *finished*."

"What?" Trevor asked, turning back.

"Nothing."

"What'd you say?"

I sighed. "Finished is the right word. We're *finished*." Just like a suicide bomber, I walked into the situation with enough verbal ammunition to make sure the whole thing exploded. The words came out on their own accord. "If we were a cooked chicken, then we'd be *done.*"

Trevor screamed, "For God's sake!" as his hand reared back. We both stared, waiting for the final outcome. Grinding his teeth, he dropped his arm. Spitting the words, he said, "I am *so done* with you. Done!"

He turned and dragged his bags behind him, headed for his car. He'd left the pans, taken his laptop and the toaster, and six of the beer steins. Apparently, he was planning on living on beer and toast.

I yelled from the front yard, "Hey! Did you mess with my car? Take sparkplugs to keep me home?"

"What?" He seemed affronted, as if keeping me home was the last thing he would want. "Of course not. Why in the hell would I do that?"

"Well, someone did."

Trevor surveyed the run-down houses and deserted street. He said, "Well, it wasn't me." He opened the car door and mumbled, "I'll come for the rest of my stuff after football season is over."

25

"Football season?" I asked, confused, walking to his car. It was a very arbitrary amount of time. He wasn't a professional athlete, with a grueling travel schedule, but an IT software engineer who thought he had a knack for household electrical wiring.

"I have things to do until then," he added, being evasive. Trevor did fantasy football and placed bets, but only on college football games.

"Are we talking the college play-offs or the Super Bowl?" I asked, trying to find humor. "Or did you join the Powder Puff League?"

He slid behind the wheel, ignoring me. Before slamming the door, he said, "Grow up, Natalie. Not everything is for a laugh."

I walked back to the house and turned off the porch light, flinching as the hallway light came on instead. Trevor's presence wasn't going to fade anytime soon. In his mad scientist "I-can-fix-it-even-though-I'm-not-an-electrician," he'd turned my house into a Little Shop of Electrical Horrors. Every flip of the switch had me awaiting the next wiring snafu.

An hour later, with another bottle of wine in my hand, I flipped on the kitchen light and screamed when the garbage disposal went off, manically chewing on a spoon that had fallen in the drain. The utensil was thrown into the air and back into the sink. I stared, trying to get my heart to slow down, checking to see if, in fact, I'd peed my pants.

Happy Birthday to me.

*   *   *

Twenty-four hours later, I was back on the interstate, headed to work, shifting the Subaru into fifth gear, shoveling ibuprofen into my mouth and repeating the previous day's events, including making a phone call—this time to my brother Tommie. I needed to convince him to accompany Dad to Scotland. He lived in London and had travelled to most parts of the world. If he went, I could be completely free of any parental obligations or worry. Any snag or

26

derailment, Tommie would have an answer. He was the oldest child and capable of handling every kind of "Holy Shit!" situation. Tommie had spent time in Jakarta, China, Vietnam, Korea and Thailand. With that kind of international experience, Dad could stumble into a Bosnian landmine field and still possibly return with both legs.

Tommie declined immediately.

"What the hell?" I said. "You can't say no."

"No." He cleared his throat as if just waking. "By the way, Happy Birthday."

"It was yesterday. Thanks for remembering, asswipe." Tommie and I had never let responsible adult behavior get in our way of a juvenile conversation.

"I did remember, but I was in the middle of a thing." I heard giggling in the background and Tommie shushed the person.

I groaned. "Seriously?"

Tommie expelled air and there was the rustle of sheets. He said, "Hold on," and then whispered something to his companion. This was followed by the sound of running water and the clink of glass. When he finally came back on the phone, Tommie explained that after spending two weeks at his vacation home in Philippines, he had no vacation time to spare.

"So, you really can't go?"

"Listen to me carefully. *Noooooooo*. Can't he wait? The brass are being stingy with R&R."

"He wants to go now."

"So take him. Just don't kill him."

"I'm not going. I'm a cardiologist and needed here. Saving lives."

Tommie snorted. "I'm in the military and saving the world."

"I think your crew is doing their best to destroy it."

"Look who's talking."

My panic was rising. "Listen Tommie, someone has to go. And I can't. But Dad wandering alone in Scotland and touring every whiskey distillery is akin to hiring a pyromaniac to work at a fireworks stand."

Tommie laughed and said away from the phone, "No babe, that's sour. No, not that either." I heard a sigh of frustration. "Nat," he said. "Yes, *that one.*"

"Should I call . . . after lunch?"

"Call Sean."

I said nothing as I clutched the phone in a death grip.

"Nat?"

Ideally, Sean was the perfect choice; my serious middle brother that had a shining history of befriending foreign exchange students and wowing the eighty-plus crowd at church with his flawless manners. He'd surpassed every expectation, including graduating valedictorian and summa cum laude, while Tommie and I had blown them to smithereens by attending keg parties and wrecking cars, causing Eve to be diagnosed with several cases of stress-induced shingles.

Tommie had a hard-core military background that supported conservative politics, while I favored the free-range liberal politics that comes from going to an institution that once burned bras. Since Sean went by the numbers, seeing everything in black and white, he took pride in dismantling everyone's views as if they were easy children's crossword puzzles. It led to vicious shouting matches around any table that sported food or drink. Tommie thought I was spoiled, while Sean said I was an irresponsible mooch. All of these things were true. Sean often muttered to Eve that although my career was "upwardly mobile," I was "running nowhere" with my personal life.

I didn't disagree with Sean's views, but I argued with him for formality's sake. I called him a stooge, a non-thinker and a cog in the system. Due to this family history, family gatherings were calamitous drunken affairs as petty belittling and fighting ensued between mouthfuls of food. Tommie and I engaged in two-against-one situations in which we picked on Sean, attacking from all sides—a type of middle-school behavior where popular kids targeted an outsider. Eve attempted to stop it as she prepared the turkey at the holidays, sometimes crying into her fourth glass of wine.

But to ask Sean, I would have to call him. Talk to him. Be nice to him. As young children, Sean and I'd been inseparable. As adults, we barely took the time to phone, only seeing each other at the holidays. There was a brutal history between us that we couldn't shake. On the day my mother suddenly died of an aortic aneurysm, the two of us had been the sole witnesses to her last moments. We'd been ten and eleven respectively, Irish twins, and mere children with no idea what to do. I'd acted; Sean had not. I'd run for help, as he stood frozen against the wall in shock. Later, after her death and the resulting events, something broke between us that could not be right again.

Instead of discussing what happened, we covered it with a Band-Aid and ignored it, until it was a festering wound within the family. In the years to follow, we turned on each other, resorting to derisive humor and belittling to deflect everything, including our own feelings. We followed our father's lead by putting on brave faces and soldiering on, which was perfected to an academic level.

The cutting flippancy became a concreted part of my personality, as well as Tommie's; both of us choosing careers— medical and military—that included a large amount of death and surrounded us in people who acted the same way. After years of watching people die, of watching my mom die, I had no guidelines for what was appropriate humor or not. I was similar to a teenage boy making penises jokes; I used it as the grease-and-battering-ram to get through awkward and terrible situations. Sometimes it freed me from awkward moments; other times I was lucky I wasn't dismissed from school after scathing complaints.

After my mother's death, humor kept my family together, but also kept us very far apart. Conversations were kept at a superficial level—afraid that if we dug too far, we might end up in a discussion of substance. Nothing could have saved my mother, but I'd never stop thinking that we'd failed her either. As a cardiologist, I was attempting to undo that moment, to amend a wrong—the past was a possible future waiting to be made right again.

"Natalie?" Tommie asked.

"Yeah."

"You're out of options. Call Sean. It's fourth down and you gotta punt."

"Stop with the adages. You sound like a retired ESPN announcer."

"Ok. How's this? You're screwed. Call Sean. See if he'll save your ass."

We agreed to see each other soon—which wouldn't happen—and I ended the phone call. I parked next to Phil's Range Rover and walked through the underground tunnel, lit by dim floor lighting, barely missing housekeeping staff that was hauling garbage. My phone vibrated with an incoming text.

Trevor: My membership to Draft Kings has been cancelled.

My short-fused rage simmered to a high boil.

Nat: YES

Trevor: You thought I wouldn't notice?

Nat: The whole point is that you would notice.

30

PAY YOUR OWN BILLS!

Trevor: Do I need to remind you how little I make? Give me just this one thing.

Nat: Do I need to show you how much I'm into the government for? They send agents to my house to remind me that my first child will be sold into Russian labor camps.

I headed towards the hospital's front lobby and the coffee shop for a triple espresso to cure my insatiable headache when my father called.

"Hello, darling," he chirped over the phone.

"Wow, you're chipper." I said, "You evade Eve's spinach smoothie this morning?" while sidestepping a woman pushing a wheelchair who seemed intent to take out my left knee.

Eve worried about Dad's health, making kale and banana concoctions that he poured down the sink when she wasn't looking. After his pacemaker and quadruple bypass surgery, Eve had taken Dad's whisky and Doritos, and replaced them with V8 juice and Veggie Straws. It was a source of constant bickering between them.

"Exactly. We're celebrating right now."

"We—?" A page for Dr. Simmons blared overhead, which wasn't unusual, but I could hear it through my phone as well. "Where the hell are you?"

"One guess."

I rounded the corner into the main lobby, crowded with staff and visitors alike. Past the gift shop that sold candy and flowers and amongst the throng of people waiting for coffee, Phil and Dad stood in line, waving at me. I hung up the phone and walked over. Both smiled mischievously, as if their collusion was a thing of supreme comedy.

"Ha-Ha," I said. "You're both so cute." I narrowed my eyes at Phil. "We'll talk about this later."

"No need," Phil responded. "Eve suggested a travel check-up and I agreed. We're conducting it right now. Over coffee. You can join us."

"Travel checkup? In the coffee line?" I shook my head at Dad. "You're not going anywhere until we can find someone to go with you." The line moved forward. "I'll call Sean."

"Already tried," Dad said. "Yesterday. He's busy. Something about the upcoming wedding."

Sean had surpassed all odds by finding Liz, a woman who'd agreed to marry into the Calhoun family even after we attempted to deep-fat fry a partially thawed Thanksgiving turkey, turning it into a giant flamethrower, starting the back porch on fire.

The barista motioned with her head and I held up three fingers. Phil held up two. My father looked back and forth in confusion. "What's that? Code?"

Phil shrugged. "Shots."

Dad's face brightened as he looked over the counter.

"Of espresso," Phil clarified.

Dad muttered, "A shame," and said to the barista, "I'll take a glazed donut and one of those mocha Frappuccino's. With whipped cream and sprinkles."

I put up my hand, stopping her. "That'll be a granola bar and black coffee," and sent off a quick text to Trevor:

Nat: You need to fix the household wiring "problems" you created.

The response was immediate.

Trevor: Not my "problem."

Phil said, "At least give him a croissant."

"A bagel," I replied.

"Danish," Dad volleyed.

"Stop it." I said, looking up from my phone. "Banana bread."

"And we're back to the fruits and veggies," Dad muttered.

"*Wedding planning*?" I asked with derision. "The groom doesn't do anything. Liz is probably over the moon doing all the arrangements."

The woman handed us the coffee and my father took a sip, cringing as he burned his mouth. "That's just what he said."

We moved to the side, awaiting our espresso drinks near a large piece of artwork that depicted many circles and squares in a wash of sea blue. It was supposed to promote peace and healing, but reminded me of a high school geometry lesson on acid.

"Well then, Eve is your last option," I said. "Tell her to put a hold on her Quebec plans. The leaf-popping can wait several months."

"*Leaf-peeping*, you minx," Phil said, "And it's *seasonal*."

I glanced at Phil. "Since when are you an expert on leaf-preening?"

"I'm gay and it's required reading."

"That's so 1980's Laura Ashley queer," I said.

"You're gay?" Dad asked, mystified. "*Like all the way*?"

I hit him on the shoulder. "The smoothies are making your head soft."

Phil laughed and grabbed our coffees from the counter. "The halfway thing makes dating difficult, Martin."

Dad shrugged, "I was just kinda hoping . . ." looking to me.

I sighed and muttered, "Unbelievable," as I typed another text to Trevor.

Nat: Switching on oven vent is turning off refrigerator.

"If Phil was an option, I would have married him straight out of medical school," I replied.

Phil said, "Ah, hon, I would never come between you and Trevor's eternal love," and gave me a sideways smirk. Dad spit coffee that landed on the floor. I stepped out of the way, refusing to acknowledge the inane conversation because I was engaging in a more ridiculous one on my phone.

Trevor: I suggest canned goods, chips, and items with high preservative levels, which is your diet anyway. As well as baby chicken.

"How about one of those packaged travel tours? With transportation and hired staff?" I asked, changing the subject.

"They herd you around like a flock of birds!" he said, indignant.

"Folks, let's not panic," Phil said, taking a sip of espresso. "Nat can go."

Dad and I stared in confusion as the barista yelled my name.

I blurted, "What?"

"You can go," Phil repeated.

"You know I can't," I replied.

"She can?" Dad asked.

34

"No. I can't." I emphasized. "*I can't*," looking directly at Phil and narrowing my eyes. "The call schedule is already set."

Phil sipped his double expresso. "You've been cleared. I got the travel dates and the scheduler made the changes. Everyone owed you favors anyway."

"What? No," I said. "That's not possible. The guys would never agree to it."

"I told them you'd be gone for two weeks," Phil said, smiling. "It bolstered their enthusiasm."

"No," I said, shaking my head.

"Oh, yes!" Phil beamed, raising his arms. "You're going to Scotland!" and shimmied his hips.

Dad laughed, saying, "Great! We're all set," and took a large bite of the gluten-free banana bread. His eyes bulged as he coughed, spitting a gooey, regurgitated mass into a napkin. "Sorry," he said, embarrassed. "But it tastes like plywood."

*   *   *

A month later, my phone rang in the wee hours of the morning after a fourteen-hour shift and three complicated interventional catherizations. I fought off pillows and sheets to find the phone on the floor, hidden beneath dirty scrubs. It was three weeks before leaving for Scotland and I barely understood what was being said.

"Hey, it's Sean."

After experiencing family tragedy and too many nights on call, I sat up and said, "Huh? What's wrong?"

"It's decided. I'm going."

"Sean?" I croaked.

"I'm going. To Scotland. I just purchased a ticket."

"What? What about wedding . . ."

"Planning?"

"Yes."

There was a pause. "Not needed." Silence. "Liz can do it."

I said nothing. My brain wasn't functioning. Maybe it was due to the fact that I was sleeping in a bed and getting real rest.

"Nat?"

"Yeah?"

"I'll text you in the morning. Go back to sleep."

"OK." It felt similar to a hazy dream, so I did exactly that. Except the next day, a barrage of strange emails and texts came rolling into my phone and the dream turned into a nightmare.

* * *

Text messages:

Sean: Which route to the western isles are you taking? I need to book the smaller flights in and out of the islands.

Natalie: From Edinburgh to the northern isle with an airport. Whatever it is.

Sean: You don't know the name?

Natalie: No. Is this a test?

Sean: Yes. You fail.

Sean: Who's in charge of this three-ring circus?

Natalie: Dad?

Dad: Natalie?

Sean: Forget I asked.

*   *   *

Text messages:

Sean: The last leg of the vacation is to Wales? Flight number please. And why are we going there?

Nat: It's a county.

Nat: Country.

Nat: Kind of.

Sean: Other reasons?

Nat: Royalty meets you at the airport and towns have names that are five syllables using only consonants. It's like they all got drunk and named the place.

Dad: I hear they have great trout pissing.

Nat: Jeezus

Dad: Kissing

Sean: Pucker up Nat.

Dad: FISHING!

Sean: I'm in.

*   *   *

Text messages:

Trevor: I'm so confused. Did you know that Michigan State was given a 10-point spread? How can a team blow it so badly?

37

Nat: There's money missing from my house. Please tell me that you did not break in my house to steal money and pay off YOUR debts.

Nat: Trevor?

Nat: Hello?

*   *   *

Email from Sean Calhoun

To Natalie Calhoun; Martin Calhoun

Subject: Hebrides / Car rental

Since Natalie is doing nothing to organize this fiasco of a vacation, I need driver's license info from both of you. License number and expiration should suffice. Just paid a 30-pound deposit on a car rental for the Hebrides. Or at least I think I did. Could not understand a word the guy said, so for all I know I just bought thirty ewes. Either way, I've got 30 of something waiting for us in Benbecula.

Sean

*   *   *

The morning of our departure for Scotland, Dad showed up thirty minutes early. We were flying out of Kansas City into Chicago, where Sean would meet us, and then we would all board a plane for Dublin and catch a final flight into Edinburgh. Dad rang the doorbell and stood outside, dressed in jeans and a pressed blue cotton shirt. I opened the door, looked around and said, "Where's your bag?"

There was a small black duffel at his feet; something about the size of one I took to the gym. He looked down and pointed. "That's my bag."

38

His luggage was representative of something a mobster would stash his car-boost tools or put the head from a decapitated body. Not only was it tiny, it hung limp, because it was only partially packed. "That can't be your bag," and kicked it. "We were only joking about taking two pairs of underwear."

"Funny," Dad said, as he picked it up and stepped inside. Dad's usual packing strategy was to put together whatever he might need in a bag and then remove half. His goal this time was to remove ninety percent, and then ten percent of that.

My suitcase sat next to the front door, where it landed after I'd let it fall down the steps, cracking the drywall.

Dad stared at the bag. "Seriously?" he asked. "That thing is as big as a bathtub."

"Is not."

He laughed. "Yes, it is. And probably weighs the same. Have you put it on a scale?"

I couldn't fit it on a scale and I wasn't able to hold it while standing on one either. Not without help. "They allow more weight for international flights," I said defensively.

Dad was still laughing as he walked into my kitchen to make himself a cup of coffee. "I just hope you can carry it, because the rest of us are not going to help."

I thought about the usual size of a European rental car. I had some concerns about my monster bag fitting, but I was not going to voice them. It was packed and I was not taking anything out. It was a matter of pride. We would have a car and I needed to look better than I usually did, which was sweatpants and ripped t-shirts I'd had since college.

We each made a cup of coffee and loaded the car. Dad and I had a leisurely drive to the airport and a quiet flight into Chicago. We both read and took small naps. It was all very civil and relaxed. When we landed in Chicago, I turned off my cellular roaming, since

I hadn't paid for international service and I didn't want to receive a single text in the next ten days. I planned to check my emails if Wi-Fi was available and respond to them only if it was outright necessary. As the stewardess gave instructions for departure, I took my first hard look at the flight schedule. Staring at the fine print, reading it three times, I inhaled air that wedged in my lungs like an orange and refused to come out.

Three months ago, I'd skimmed the itinerary and made sure we started in Chicago and we ended in Edinburgh, which was all that mattered. I handed it to Dad, pointing at the bottom. He peered at the lines for a full minute, before muttering, "Oh boy."

Dad had booked the trip on-line, put together by Expedia or some other web-based program. The computer had spit out the details, Dad had paid and neither one of us had bothered to check the small, inconsequential asterisk at the bottom. On the computer screen, it would've been in bright red, except Dad was colorblind and didn't see it. He'd printed it off and sent it to me. Without a color cartridge, the text ended up being a light grey. The indiscernible line explained that we had been given exactly one hour between our arrival at O'Hare's domestic gate to get all the way across the airport and board our next flight at the international concourse.

ONE HOUR.

I hit the full-fledged panic mode, because the concourses couldn't have been any further apart. Disembarking, staring at signs, we couldn't find the hidden escalators that took you to the trains that eventually transport you to the other side of airport to the international concourse. Even though we were still *at* the airport, when we stepped foot on the train, we had *officially left* the airport and would have to go through security all over again. I pushed Dad like he was an old mule, complaining when he wasn't carrying the weight he should have. I was always three steps ahead as we trotted along. The throngs of people were a moving obstacle course that we poorly navigated; Dad ran into travelers, barreling into their backs because he stared at his feet to keep from tripping. I yelled to be

40

heard over the flight announcements, but due to his poor hearing, Dad didn't hear me anyway.

Looking over my shoulder, I almost took out a small child tethered by a dog leash to a father holding two bags, who was practically dragging the kid. I regained my balance and glanced across the way, seeing an unmistakable porkpie hat and Hawaiian travel shirt. I did a double take. My friend Death waved, tipped his hat, and slid his arm around the shoulders of an obese woman struggling . . .

"Hey!"

I stumbled into the back of a kid wearing loose sweatpants and Beats, almost knocking him to the ground. "Hey, man! Watch where you're going!" he yelled.

"Sorry, sorry," I said, picking up his hat. I looked back, but there was only a son holding his mother's arm. Dad stopped and stared with a questioning look as other passengers plowed into him. I shook it off, saying, "Thought I saw someone I knew," and checked it off as anxiety.

We made it to our gate just as they were calling the second wave of passengers to board. I saw Sean standing by himself, an agitated look on his face. Tommie and I had been gifted the coloring of our mother, which was pale skin and blonde hair, but Sean had wild dark hair and blue-gray eyes. It was the result of a mutant, recessive Irish DNA hiding in the shadows, sneaking in when no one was looking. Tommie was a solid mass with model good looks. Sean was whip-thin and angular, like the silhouette from a Victorian novel. This landed him on the cross-country team but did not win him awards with the cheerleading crowd in high school.

When Sean finally spotted us, he sighed and muttered, "Predictable. Even odds," regarding our lateness. I didn't respond as I tried to remember the last time I'd seen Sean, and realized it'd been over a year. Or was it longer? He appeared pale and thin, his jeans hanging loosely from his hips. In a moment of panic, I tried to recall the name of his employer or other basic facts, and couldn't, which I found embarrassing. Tommie and I talked by phone or emailed

41

incessantly, and he sometimes showed up on my doorstep for an overnight stay before he flew off to strange locales. Sean only made it home for the holidays, which I sometimes missed due to my job. Truth be told, Sean was an unknown entity to me now. After my mother's death, sides had been picked and Tommie had chosen me. This left Sean the odd man out—frozen into a private group by himself, constantly looking in, but never gaining admittance. It was a cold truth that left me feeling uneasy as we approached.

We're not a family of huggers or kissers and have personal space bubbles so large we bounce off each other without touching, so we all muttered hellos, stood in line and waited our turn to get on the plane. Dad and I had seats together, and Sean had snagged one right behind us. Once boarded and my luggage stowed, I saw that a gift had been placed upon my seat.

"What the hell is this?" I said over my shoulder, as if Sean had handed me his dirty underwear. "This can't be from you." There was zero chance of it being from anyone in my family. Dad didn't give gifts, but gave money to others to buy them. Sean once bought all of his Christmas gifts at the local hardware store; mine had been a hot pink Hanes sweatshirt, a size too small, and Dad had been given a vice of such an enormous size that it could've been squeezed around my head. I'm still not sure that wasn't its original intent.

Sean shrugged. "It's from Liz. Something to help with the long flight."

"Oh," I said with suspicion. "Tell her thanks." Sean nodded and continued thumbing through the movie possibilities. I unwrapped the package and prayed for a book or something disposable. Even though Liz wasn't officially family, she was, at times, the best of us; the most sensible and especially kind in remembering people with little gifts. The rest of the Calhouns were like war survivors, staring at one another and grunting out responses only when necessary. When it came time to be gracious, we often looked the other way and pretended it'd been washed out of us in the interrogation process.

42

I tore away the gift-wrapping to find a padded, hand-sewn, cloth package. I thought, *Amish cherry pie? Homespun Chapstick Organizer? Miniature Chinese checkers?* My disappointment was rising. I hated games and Liz loved them, always forcing us to play charades at Christmastime. I had no intentions of playing Cribbage or some other annoying Victorian game during the flight.

Opening the package by a small button and elastic loop, I found an organized package of perfectly lined, small vials of clear liquid.

Clear liquid. Small vials.

I shut the package and cradled it between my legs. In those first few seconds as my deranged mind cranked its slow gears, my immediate thought was that they were portable containers of explosive Nitroglycerin. This is exactly how my brain worked; I immediately went to the terrorist plot plan, before anything else. I was holding a liquid explosive device that was packaged in a parcel that looked like a mini tampon holder.

My disturbed mind went further: Liz was really a terrorist and I had been blindsided by the happy, domestic façade all these years. I looked around and made sure no one was watching. I clutched the hazardous material tighter in my crotch, and thought, *I'm going to be just like that underwear bomber that lost his nuts in the failed terrorist plane bomb attempt, except my va-jay-jay is going to be the final casualty.* In a final act of survival, I thought I could possibly throw them into Dad's lap and pretend they were his, if it came to a decision of who was to be thrown off the flight.

I peeked again; opening it so that fellow passengers might think I was examining my tampons. Because that's a normal thing to do—evaluate how many tampons you have before a plane takes off. Upon closer inspection, I noticed each vial was labeled with concise handwriting and were properly identified as aromatherapy scents: peppermint, clove, tea tree, etc. A sane person would have sighed in relief, or even laughed, but I was not normal. My hands started to sweat. I fumbled with the small package, because it wasn't a bomb.

It was something inherently, devastatingly and catastrophically worse.

Five minutes before takeoff, I was holding tiny glass tubes of concentrated, intense scents in a small, enclosed space. The air on the plane was recycled and all these people would be trapped with me, for eight hours. I was a clumsy person. The possibility for total disaster was extremely high. I mentally sketched a scenario in which the entire contents of this case was mashed in the bottom of my backpack and the intense, intermixing aroma went flooding into the plane, where people choked and gagged, holding hankies to their faces, while others vomited into sickness bags.

Liz was a massage therapist and a full-fledged convert to "alternative medicine." During the holidays, she would chase me around with sage and green chai tea drinks that appeared to have suspended semen inside. Unfortunately, she'd chosen to marry into the Calhoun family. We were solid believers Mercurochrome could fix almost anything broken or bleeding; it was a nasty red liquid that burned like hydrochloric acid when placed on open wounds. "The burn factor" was considered the true indicator of bacteria killing potential.

Sean peeked through the crack and smirked. "Liz says to dab them on mid-flight." He laughed. "For serenity."

"Huh? Where?" I asked, mortified.

"Use your imagination."

"Not funny."

"I thought so."

"What if they break open?" I asked, panicked.

"I'm going to deny that I know you."

Dad looked up from his Wall Street Journal, "What are you two yacking about?"

I muttered, "Cooking spices."

There was a star by peppermint, because according to the list, it could alleviate headache and nausea, but also cause cardiac arrhythmia, known as atrial fibrillation. I'd never heard of this particular side effect; cardiac journals didn't investigate essential oils. I pinpointed the place on Dad's chest where his pacemaker/defibrillator was implanted. He had gotten the device right after an episode of his heart going into a deadly arrhythmia, accelerating into the 200's. Eve had called me in a panic and we'd transported him via ambulance to St. Matthew's. Phil had managed his care after that, since it was against corporate hospital policy to treat one's own family.

As the stewardess gave instructions on how to properly manage oxygen masks, I imagined myself accidently crushing this parcel, Dad leaning over and gasping for air, while the soft calming smell of peppermint drifted in the air. I could also see myself pulling an AED off the wall and yelling, "Clear!" all because I'd unleashed the "aromatherapy package" on the world.

I left the vials of disaster in the pocket of the seat in front of me, out of sight from inquiring stewards and possible flight Marshals with handguns.

3

Emails:

From Natalie Calhoun

To Trevor Smith

Subject: Immediate Concerns

Trevor,

By the time you read this, I'll be somewhere over the Atlantic. I am travelling with Sean and Dad to Scotland. Please refrain from breaking into my house and taking money from "hiding places." Or anything else. Whether you consider it or not, it is PRIVATE PROPERTY and I can call the cops.

Nat

* * *

From Trevor Smith

To Natalie Calhoun

Re: Immediate Concerns

Nat,

My current living situation has not quite worked out the way I had hoped; a conundrum of evolving catastrophic events, financial limitations, and employment non-disclosures. I was hoping I could supervise your domicile while you are on your sabbatical and work on electrical issues as re-payment for services rendered.

-Trevor

*   *   *

From Natalie Calhoun

To Trevor Smith

Subject: I am not an idiot

Trevor,

Remember my Chemistry and English double major? The translation to that mess of an email is that you have been sacked, thrown out of your apartment and bet too much on the Michigan-Michigan State game, am I correct? You can stop with the three syllable words. Monosyllabic conversation is fine. Let me help you. NO!

Nat

*   *   *

Eight hours later, we arrived in Dublin. Wispy clouds hung over rolling hills, and green pastures cascaded into forever. Four years earlier, I'd travelled here; I could remember the dark, drunken night in Killarney, the historic, renovated hotel, Guinness's and a full can of Pringles, which the bartender claimed was a true Irish dinner. We walked out on the tarmac and felt the cool breeze hit our faces and the jet fuel sting our noses. Inside the terminal, we squinted in the fluorescent lighting and bumped shoulders due to jetlag. I got a small amount of money and headed for hot coffee and decent food. The lines were long and I stood staring at congealed examples of what food they offered in a glass cabinet. Sean told me to hurry because our next plane was due to take off for Edinburgh in the next hour. It seemed a moot point, because he was always telling me to hurry.

47

I was on vacation; I wanted coffee. No sooner had I paid though, Sean was running towards me and screaming, "Hurry!"

"Hurry, now? Or hurry, in just a bit?" At the hospital, we had five different levels for "hurry," depending upon your tone.

"Hurry now," he said, "They're boarding."

"So that's a super hurry now?"

"Nat! Come on!"

I grabbed the coffees and ran to the gate, trying my best not to spill the precious liquid. We ran to a sub-basement area, where just outside, one of those buses with barely any seats would take us to our plane that sat somewhere stranded on the tarmac. We hustled to the ticket agent and handed over our passes. We were the last ones in the deserted room.

"You have to dispose of your coffee," the agent said.

"What?" I asked, clutching the coffee to my chest.

She smiled and it was a perfect example of what a customer service smile should be: glossy and fixed, exuding good will, with just enough steel to reinforce that they'll roll you to make you behave.

She said, "The coffee can spill. We don't allow it on the transport bus. For safety reasons." It was a rolling monologue that'd been repeated a thousand times over.

"This isn't McDonald's," I responded. "I know the risks. I won't sue." I screwed my face into a rather precocious look and she laughed. I pointed at the coffee. "It has a lid."

"I realize that," she answered with some sympathy. "But it's the rules."

I took an enormous drink, scalded my mouth, and threw the entire coffee into a nearby trash. It was a caffeinated travesty. Sean intended to drink every last drop and waved me on. "I'll just be a moment."

I boarded the bus. Long minutes passed as we sat unmoving on the tarmac. Tick-Tock-Tick-Tock. People craned their necks and checked their watches, wondering what was keeping the bus from driving to the plane. I looked over my shoulder, hoping to see Sean round the corner, but he failed to show for a very long time. When he finally got there, his face resembled a renegade possum, pinched into a tight frown with his eyes bugged out.

"Where have you been?" I hissed. People were staring, wondering whom the problem child was. I kept a suitable distance between us, so no one knew we were in the same party, never mind the same family.

Sean gathered himself, his wrath simmering around the edges of his eyes. Years of sibling experience told me that I was about to get chastised. "When you threw away your coffee, it spilled across the floor."

"What?" I asked, confused. "I threw it into the trash."

"There was no liner, idiot. None. The liquid hit the bottom of the can and seeped across the floor. There was coffee *everywhere*. I stayed and helped them clean it up with towels."

Of course he did, the bastard, because he was the good middle child who got awarded best behavior in school. Sean was the one that kept Tommie and I from making disastrous decisions when we thought duct-taping mailboxes and throwing toilet paper into trees was passé. In his tone, there was a middle child's insolence; a remnant of the years when we had all been spanked by our father and Sean had simply been rounded up in the process, even though he had little to do with it.

"Oh," I said, shrugging, nonplussed. "Sorry. How was I supposed to know?"

"It was a *mess*, Natalie," he hissed. "All. Over. The. Floor."

49

We hadn't gotten to Scotland yet and I was already causing problems. I pulled the scent bomb from my pack. "A drop of frankincense then? To calm down?"

* * *

Emails:

From Trevor Smith

To Natalie Calhoun

Subject: Positive thinking

Nat,

I realize you changed the locks, but it's my estimation that I can really do some good with your house. Had some issues with getting into the house, but I will replace the window in the back. With Navy's coach Meyer using the triple option offense against Houston, and somehow managing an unfathomable win, my own options have become very, very limited.

-Trevor

* * *

We arrived in Edinburgh and stood in a long line with other passengers waiting for a taxi. The sidewalk was mobbed with numerous people, many of which bumped into our shoulders as they passed by. A man stood coughing and I refrained from spraying him with concentrated tea tree oil to convince him to spew his germs another direction. As I attempted to walk to a coffee stand, Sean grabbed me by the elbow and jerked me back, saying, "Later."

"You're a killjoy."

"Cleaning up coffee once a day is enough," Sean said, as a loud motorbike roared by.

50

I shrugged. "Same day, different country. My coffee crimes are behind me." I started to walk off, only to have him drag me back again.

"We're on vacation," I said, pulling my arm from his grasp. "Do I need to resend the memo?" Nearby, an elderly woman removed a tiny white dog from a crate. I watched as it walked over and peed on a suitcase. The woman pretended not to see, staring the other direction.

"I'll be on vacation once we get to the B&B," Sean replied.

Against my will, I stood with my family. My right hand twitched every time I looked over to the line of happy customers getting lattes. When it was our turn, the three of us headed to the back of the taxi to load our suitcases. When the trunk was opened, I made sure my bag was the first one thrown inside.

"Seriously?" Sean said.

"What?" I asked, feigning ignorance.

Sean grunted as he repositioned my bag, then placed their two smaller bags in satellite around mine, like mine was the enormous sun, and theirs were Mars and Pluto, which isn't really a planet any more.

"See? It all works," and I got in the back of the car.

*   *   *

The bed and breakfast was a stately place with large Corinthian columns, right next to the botanical gardens. There wasn't anyone on the streets, except for pairs of elderly couples walking dogs or possibly going for the paper and coffee. The houses were grand stone edifices with the kind of manicured appearance that requires yearly maintenance and money—including brightly painted doors, brass knockers and wrought iron fences. I took a deep breath and smelled something similar to honeysuckle, or maybe it was the rosemary essential oil container leaking in my backpack.

51

The taxi deposited us onto the sidewalk—the driver feigning a hernia when he lifted my bag. He laughed. I didn't. I grabbed my behemoth bag and dragged it across the sidewalk to the elaborate fencing that surrounded the house. We opened a gate and walked into a contained flower garden, but hesitated as we approached the front staircase. As with other overnight international flights, jetlag was digging its claws into my head and refusing to budge, slowing my thought process.

Initially, I'd emailed the homeowner and proprietor, Tannis, telling her we'd be there early. She responded that would be fine and would be waiting for us, but she was an unknown entity in a foreign country. It seemed strange to be standing outside, awaiting entrance into her private home. I could have stayed there a monumental amount of time without moving—flowers blooming and insects buzzing around my head.

Sean looked to me, motioning with his head. I nodded back, telling him to shove it up his ass and take the initiative. Dad sighed, walked up and rang the doorbell. Immediately, there was a cacophony of dog's barking and small feet peddling in circles inside the door. I could hear an inner door opening and the sound of a latch, and a woman's voice telling the dogs to settle down.

The door was opened by a woman I assumed to be Tannis. She greeted us warmly as the dogs circled at her feet. She was a petite woman, with graying hair, glasses, wearing a denim skirt and sweater. She looked up at the sky and said, "You have some sun!" which I took as an anomaly. She smiled at us with what I would later come to know as the "Scottish smile." One part bonny hopefulness, one part, "Crap, here come the Americans." She asked us to enter and inquired about the flight. The dogs sniffed at our feet and gave up when we all appeared not to be carrying treats or raw meat in our pockets.

We were ushered into a front hallway, where there was a multitude of shoes, Wellies, umbrellas, and other paraphernalia meant to keep off the rain. It was a large old house, with two columns painted a deep red and a large front room containing a wide staircase that doubled back upon itself to the second floor. The house was formal and grand, rising two levels in the front hall. It had a homey feel with dog beds and other incidentals on the staircase. Four open doors off the front room gave entrance into what appeared to be living rooms and a kitchen, or a gaming and tearoom in another era. We all stood there, dropping bags and making noises, as if she'd taken us off the street for charity. A gray tabby cat sat on the staircase and a housekeeper vacuumed with an old Electrolux canister. The woman gaped, staring at my scars and slammed the vacuum into the stairs, almost knocking over a vase containing bright red Rhododendron blooms. Tannis gave her a look and she shuffled away. I remember Eve clipping a similar flower, placing it in my hair, whispering, "*Beware*," a small giggle, "*mischief.*"

"So," Tannis said, clapping her hands, "You're here for the day."

We all nodded, shuffling our feet like kindergarten students on our first day of class.

"What's the plan?"

All the travel preparation had gone into the Hebrides and Northern Scotland. I'd treated Edinburgh as an early stopover. Part of me had hoped just to sleep and drink, not unlike the plane ride. Once on the flight, Sean had brought up my lack of planning and we'd scoured a map, devising a plan. We realized that Edinburgh could have been a vacation in itself, with historical sites, art galleries and restaurants, but we settled on the historic Royal Mile being enough for one day. We told Tannis this and she gave a few suggestions.

That bit of introduction finished, she said, "So, who wants which room?" Another cat wandered into the room. A calico this time, with a paunch suggesting he ingested marbles part of the time.

I shrugged, unconcerned. As long as there was some kind of bed, I really didn't care. I had a long history of being able to sleep almost anywhere and so did Dad. After my mother had died, we'd all become night owls, trading rooms or beds, sometimes in the middle of the night. Tommie didn't necessarily want me crawling into his bed because I couldn't sleep, but he never made me leave either. For

53

this trip, Dad and I planned to share a room whenever possible for economy's sake, as long as there were twin beds and enough "Breathe-Right" strips to keep his snoring at bay.

"Whatever," I said. "Lead the way."

Tannis pointed up the stairs. "There's a room up there, across from ours. And there's a bedroom in the basement. Well, two actually."

"Oh," I said, "Two? Do you think we could have them both?"

Tannis stared at Sean and I. "Umm, sure," she responded. "Shall we look at the upstairs bedroom first?"

With her thick, Scottish accent, I didn't always understand Tannis. I only understood every third word and guessed the rest. Sean and I went up the stairs with her, and Dad stayed on the first floor, content to watch from the lower levels and keep the cats from attacking. She showed us an elegant room on the top floor, off the staircase, which was nicely appointed and had a view of the botanical gardens. She showcased this room as the best one. I wasn't interested; there was a double bed, which wasn't going to work for Dad and I.

I said, "Nice," as I stepped into the hallway. I turned to Sean, "You should take it."

What I failed to notice was Tannis' perplexed face—she looked at Sean, then me, trying to work something out.

I left Sean to situate himself and walked by a bedroom next door. There was a confusing, plethora of doors, similar to a holding facility in a prison. "Is this one available too?" I asked.

"Sorry," she said, watching Sean drag his suitcase into the room. "A relative is staying tonight."

"No problem. Why don't you just show us the basement rooms?"

54

The two of us headed downstairs, picking up Dad as we went. The steps into the basement were steep, concrete, and a "handicap accessible" nightmare. The weight of my bag pulled me downward and it took all of my strength to keep the suitcase from getting away and throwing me into a wall.

Tannis showed us the rooms—small, tidy and equipped with the essentials—and then went back upstairs. I dropped my bag and stood holding my arms to my body to generate heat. Now that I've been to Scotland, I understand the Scottish don't mind the cold. It's possible they have an extra evolutionary layer of skin that I don't. Or perhaps Americans have just turned weak in our Western comforts. Even though it was barely fifty degrees, Tannis had thrown open most of the windows. The basement felt eerily similar to a medical lab where they stored bodies awaiting autopsy.

"I can't do this," Dad said, rubbing his hands together. "I'll freeze."

We tried turning on the wall registers, but nothing happened. "I hate to ask her to turn it on," I replied. "Seems rude. I don't want to be the *whiny American.*"

"Well, then, give me *all* your blankets," motioning to my bed.

I made my first critical decision in the trip and marched upstairs. Tannis was puttering around the kitchen when I found her. "Hate to ask," I said, startling her. "I was wondering if there was a way to turn on the heat." I smiled, but it was forced. With the time difference and very little sleep, I felt like I'd swallowed a half bottle of Sominex and washed it down with two espressos.

She appeared confused; obviously the cold wasn't anything she ever considered.

I shrugged. "I guess we're a bunch of pampered Americans not holding up to tough European standards."

"I can turn on the electricity to the wall heaters, sure," she said. I'm guessing it was something she did once every five years in the rare occurrence of a cold snap.

I thanked her and turned to leave. She stopped me and asked if all our reservations were set for our trip north into the islands.

"Yes, I think so. We land in Benbecula and have secured a car with a local group there. North Uist, I guess? They're meeting us at the airport with a car." I laughed. "Sean did it all through email."

"Sean is. . . your . . . ?" she preempted.

"My. Brother," I enunciated with great care.

She giggled. "Ah, grand. It will be a pleasant trip. Goo' weather, I hear." She thought a moment. "Your rental? You remember the name?"

"The car?" I asked.

"No. The man."

"Oh! No idea. Very small affair." I didn't mention the sheep.

She nodded. "My brother lives there. Operates a farm. Also rents out vehicles to the tourists. Maybe him," she shrugged. "Maybe not. Many people do it."

I excused myself, going downstairs. The heaters turned on for the first time and Dad and I both cheered. After we put our things away, Tannis sent us off to the Royal Mile with instructions to get there by bus. Once safely moving in the right direction—almost accosting an eighty-year-old in our questioning—I made a comment about Tannis being nice, but confused, especially when figuring the rooms.

Dad said, "She thought you were married to Sean." He tilted his head in a manner suggesting this had happened before. "Wondered why you guys were sleeping separately."

56

Sean and I both grimaced and moved several inches away from each other.

We ventured to the Royal Mile, which was a historic district straight out of a Victorian storybook, complete with narrow, cobblestone streets, spires rising to the sky, and the buildings that had seen wars and disease come and go and still managed to survive. We found a restaurant along the lines of "Ye Ole Tavern," and went inside for food. It was early for lunch, but we were starving. Dad and I ordered the fish and chips. Sean got some kind of meat pie with smashed peas, which resembled baby food.

When the waitress sat a beer in front of my dad, I said, "So we're drinking?" peering at my watch.

"Yup," Dad responded, taking a large sip, mocking me.

"It's ten o'clock." I made no mention to the fact that both Sean and I were drinking.

"If you don't start in the morning, you can't drink all day," Dad said.

"You said you were only drinking one a day," I responded.

"Ah, right," Dad said, pretending interest in a chip. "Early one then," being evasive.

Two years previous, Dad's defibrillator had fired seven times. That was seven episodes of a small machine about the size of a woman's compact dosing him with thirty-five joules, which is similar to putting your hands on an electric fence while someone kicks you in the chest. The last two times had happened at Sean's house on Thanksgiving, while I'd been in Kansas City and on call.

Originally, Phil and I thought these episodes were being triggered by alcohol consumption. We cut down Dad's drinking to nothing, which was not well received. It was later determined the wires leading to the device were faulty, causing the device to fire "erroneously." With the new defibrillator, there'd been no incidents. Dad celebrated in grand style, throwing off the medical handcuffs and again partaking of his usual evening whiskey. Or whiskeys. No one knew for sure.

I raised my glass, "Well, cheers to Scotland, and big *Hip-hip-hurray* to falling off the wagon."

An elderly couple at the table next to us stared. Dad saluted them with a dark porter, and said, "It's all downhill from here."

After lunch, we walked to Edinburgh Castle and grimaced when we saw the long lines to gain entrance. Enormous groups of people poured from tour buses surrounding us; American, French and Asian individuals with tired looking guides waving a flag and yelling, "to keep moving."

I saw the lines and said, "I think I'll head back to Tannis' house to find a bottle of wine or whiskey. Whatever I can get my hands on first."

Sean grunted. "What?" He held up his arms, holding me off. "We're here. What's the rush?"

I was tired and being viciously attacked by hundreds of bugs, which surrounded my head. I swatted at them with enough vengeance that I appeared to be having an epileptic seizure. "Hello?" I said, as I ducked and weaved. "We're being eaten alive by mosquitoes."

A robust man in line ahead of us with small, circular glasses and pants hiked up to his belly button, turned and inserted himself into our conversation, saying, "They're not mo-squitoes," elongating the o in a way that made him sound Caribbean. "They're midges."

"Midgets?" I asked.

"Midges. They're *midges*," emphasizing the word like I was the most annoying person in the world. A friend beside him openly laughed and attempted to smother it, which only brought more attention to himself.

I stared. Not only was I fatigued and jetlagged, but I was being swarmed by people and insects alike. Essentially, I had the patience of a five-year-old in a candy store. The timing was very unfortunate for an unknown man to eavesdrop on our conversation and then correct me in public.

I squared my shoulders, my anger rising. "OK. *Great.* Strictly speaking," I held up my fingers to mime quotes, "we're talking about small creatures with tiny legs."

Sean muttered, "Oh, no." He turned to Dad and muttered, "Five to one she's losing it."

The man narrowed his eyes and blew air through his nose in frustration. "If you want to walk around misinformed, be my guest."

I guffawed because I was seriously considering throat punching a guy about tiny bugs whose sole purpose in life was to reproduce and drink blood.

Sean said, "More like three to one," attempting to push me away.

Sidestepping Sean, I moved closer and said to everyone in the area, but mostly to our bug expert, "Although I'd love to discuss the merits of *proper insect terminology*," I inhaled and paused to press the point home, "I find that my time is better served by having a very strong drink." I waved off the midges floating before my face. "That is, before my blood supply is sucked dry by the *midgets,* minus the t," emphasizing the letter in such a way that I almost spit on him.

Several people gasped, Dad shook his head, and Sean grabbed my arm and dragged me to the front of the line. He whispered, "I can't freaking believe you." Together, they walked me up to the next available ticket agent and handed over money.

"What?" I asked.

* * *

Emails:

From Robbie Durst

To Natalie Calhoun

Subject: Polite inquiries from a mutual acquaintance

Natalie,

     We do not know each other personally, but my name is Robbie. I've seen you at my bar, Risky's, with Trevor. I'm an old acquaintance of his, and I am writing to inform you that Trevor has some lingering financial issues that need urgent attention. He's disappeared and we found your email and phone number in a cell phone that he left behind. I don't wish to involve you in this manner, but I've been left very few choices. Please tell Trevor he needs to contact me.

Immediately.

-R

*   *   *

From Natalie Calhoun

To Robbie Durst

Re: Polite inquiries from a mutual acquaintance

Robbie,

    I am not with Trevor, in any way. Please cease and desist from contacting me.

Ever.

-Natalie Calhoun

* * *

Edinburgh Castle, situated on an immense hill to keep invading marauders at bay, had an entire community within its lofty confines. As the historical, royal Scottish residence, I marveled at the stables, the palace, and the rambling streets; the ability to build everything they needed in this one incredible place.

I walked into the room where Queen Mary of Scots gave birth to James VI and was astonished to see how small it was. People must have been shoulder to shoulder, staring at her vagina as she pushed out a baby. We walked into the Great Hall and I admired the weaponry on the walls, thinking about having a very large crown put on my head as I sat next to the "stone of destiny." I toured the room that held the crown jewels, touched lethal arsenal, and leaned over barricades containing cannons and gave panoramic views of the city. I had coffee in what used to be the horse stables and ate a scone. The sun shone and I felt warm and sated. I imagined what it was like to be nobility and live atop a very high hill and look out at your lowly subjects.

Sean wandered over and sat down next to me in what was called the Half Moon Battery. We watched as our father peered over the wall and inspected some of the 18-pounder cannons. There were men gearing up wearing grand military outfits and prepping a cannon. I watched them out of the corner of my eye.

"Trevor would have appreciated this," Sean said. "He goes for history, doesn't he? Why didn't he come?"

The sun went behind some clouds and it became chilly. I heard a woman announce that the militia reproduction and firing of the "one o'clock gun" would start momentarily.

"He couldn't. Busy."

Sean looked perplexed. "Doesn't he work from home part of the time?"

"Ah, yeah." I said, being vague.

61

Some of the fake military guys were loading guns and putting in yellow earplugs. They ushered Dad away from the wall and told him to stand with the rest of the tourists. I didn't care for loud noises, so I stood. Sean grabbed my arm and pulled me back down.

"And he couldn't get away?" he said, continuing.

"What? No."

"Why not?" The guys lined up in formation and bagpipes began to play.

"Maybe we should move inside," I said.

"Why?"

"Take a good look around, Sean. The military showed up for an early lunch. And they brought an arsenal."

The leader called for attention and the bagpipes played a mournful song that sounded like a dirge. To my dismay, people pressed in around us.

"You guys having trouble?" Sean asked.

"Trouble?" I asked.

"You know."

I stared. "No. I don't."

"Come on, you know," Sean said, waving me on.

"Oh, you mean with sex? Wow, Sean—"

"Nat, don't be gross."

"Gross?" I asked.

"The—"

"Sex, intercourse, screwing, fu—"

62

"Stop it! I meant the relationship," Sean said, flustered.

I could run circles as much as I wanted, but Sean was a dog on the scent. In a few seconds, he was going to cite all the statistics that proved the relationship was doomed from the beginning. He'd never approved and took any opportunity to say so when we were together. It was why I'd volunteered for the Christmas shift last year.

I said, "Yes, Sean, you might say we've had some trouble. Trevor broke up with me and moved out," just as the first round of gunshot pierced the air, causing me to jump and drop my coffee. I swore, "Goddammit," but gunshot covered my obscenity.

"Seriously?" Sean said, just as General Fancy Pants yelled, "FIRE!" and cannon fire blew out my eardrums.

"*Sweet Moses,*" I cried, holding a finger to my ear. "It was never going to work!" but I could barely hear myself talk.

Sean watched the gunmen, trying to time his words. "Did you chase him away?"

I held out my hands in disgust. *Oh, of course, it was my fault. It was always my fault.* "No!" I screamed. "We were terrible together." The men fired in tandem, and I almost fell off the bench. It rattled my chest and I felt air escape my lungs. "Oh my God, this is horrible."

Sean screamed, "The relationship?" between shots.

"The gunfire, you goon!"

I could feel the reverberation inside my head now; bouncing around like a marble in a wooden drawer.

"Why'd he leave?" Sean asked. I could barely hear a thing, except my heart beating in time with the cacophony of noise.

Then out of nowhere, several of the cannons fired in tandem, so incredibly loud, I thought a hole had been blasted through my body and taken off the side of my head. I yelled, "He thinks I'm a heartless wrench that operates without a fucking shred of emotion." I gesticulated wildly with my arms, "There! You happy?"

I sat there for a moment. Sean said nothing in return and stared. The world had returned to normal, but in my head, there was still the echo of gunfire. Beyond that, there was nothing but eerie silence. Similar to the cannons, it was deafening. Turning, I saw the entire brigade and congregated throng of tourists staring right at us, with Dad front and center.

I raised my hand and waved.

Dad waved back.

* * *

We stumbled on, all three of us trying to forget the public verbal catastrophe. At different times, I caught both Dad and brother giving me cautious looks. I pretended not to see. The last thing I wanted was some kind of watered-down sympathy. I realized that we were not even one day into our vacation and were already into deep waters.

We garnered some fortitude to tour the Royal Scottish Academy, but at five o'clock sharp, we hit the proverbial wall and could go no further. We limped into Tannis's informal living room and threw ourselves into antique tapestry chairs sitting next to neglected ferns. She dug out a dusty bottle of whiskey for Sean and found dark beers for Dad and I. I don't know if she wanted our company or not—we collapsed in her space and she took it in good stride. I sat in a wicker chair, near an open garden window with a gentle breeze. The cats slunk in and out of the room like discontented waitresses not doing their job, but hoping we would leave their establishment soon. We explained to Tannis that we wanted fine dining within close walking distance. She gave us directions to a nice restaurant four blocks away. We all sighed and Sean poured himself more whiskey.

Tannis asked, "So, how'd it go?"

No one spoke, and Sean and I refused to look at one another.

64

4

Emails:

From Robbie Durst

To Natalie Calhoun

Re: Polite inquiries from a mutual acquaintance

Natalie,

It appeared to me when I saw you that you might have had some past experience with pain. Maybe a lot of pain, if scars are any indication. Not that I'm one to cast judgment on another's appearance. Tell me, does Trevor have any kind of similar experiences?

-Robbie

*　　*　　*

At 4:45 AM the next morning, Dad and I stumbled out of bed and up the basement concrete steps with our bags. I missed the second from the top, rolled onto the first floor, barely hanging on to my bag to keep it from rolling backwards. We stood in the first-floor common room, next to the massive stairs that curled upstairs. Squinting, I couldn't believe that I'd insisted on the seven AM flight in order to get to the Hebrides as soon as possible.

Dad's face was blurry, from lack of sleep and too much wine the night before. He said, "Sean should be here by now. He's always the first one up."

I didn't disagree, but it was early and I wasn't really functioning at full speed. "He'll get up. Just give him time."

65

We sat on the stairs, side by side, our bags at our feet. It was silent, except for the rumble from the refrigerator that sounded like a tank gearing up for battle. I thought about searching for breakfast and considered the noise I would make. I imagined Tannis coming down the stairs, catching me as I rifled through her refrigerator, possibly taking items she had no intention of offering us. Breakfast was included in the price of the stay, but I think the amount of whiskey Sean had consumed the night before had used up our entire food allotment for the morning and the following week.

"No," Dad said. "You need to go get him. He's overslept."

I huffed. "I'm not going. I'm not even sure what room he's in." I shook my head. "What if I stumble into Tannis' room? No way. You go."

"I'm not going. I'm legally blind."

"You are not," I said.

"Right. Just old. You have to go," Dad replied.

"We're waiting."

"Natalie, someone has to wake him."

I didn't disagree, but I didn't want to go look for Sean in his private room. I stood my ground. For five seconds. Which is exactly when the cab showed up and honked outside.

"For Pete's sake," I muttered, standing and peering up the stairs.

Dad sat, waiting.

"I'm holding you accountable for any unfortunate circumstances that follow. And possible yelling."

He waved me off.

I used the railing to guide me to the pitch-black depths

66

upstairs. On the top landing, a small light dimly illuminated the space. I had a vague memory the upper level and the five doors leading to bedrooms beyond. I had some inclination where Sean slept, but that was little help when finding yourself in a dark box. I realized too late that I should have paid more attention. The whole thing was an impossible game show quiz; I knew Tannis and her husband were behind one door, the relative was behind another and my stupid brother was in a third. Five rooms, three occupants. Not only was I on some kind of deranged game show, the only prize I was receiving was a brother that I didn't want anyway.

In my fogged state of booze and time zone differences, the rooms to the left seemed a decent option. I was left-handed and naturally leaned that direction. I said a small prayer to the travel Gods, and then for good measure, I cursed Sean for putting me in this dire situation. I picked out the closest door and knocked.

Nothing.

I knocked again.

Nothing.

I stood back and peered around, blowing air out of my lungs, thinking.

Yeah. Nothing.

The foul language in my head could have seared the lacquer off furniture. Garnering my courage, I turned the handle and cracked open the door, just enough to see inside. My hands were shaking, causing the door handle to rattle. I spotted a window and dresser, lit by early morning light. I craned my head around the door, as my feet stayed planted in neutral territory. Leaning further, I saw a bed with a head of dark hair turned away from me, peeking out from beneath a large pile of white comforter.

Sean, thank God.

I cracked the door further and hissed, "Sean."

Nothing.

"Sean."

Nothing.

I looked down to the floorboard, which was the line of demarcation—from hallway to bedroom, from public to private. Neither of us was ten years old anymore. I muttered, "Crap," and tiptoed to the bed. I grabbed his lumpy shoulder and shook him. "Sean, get up. We got to go!"

Still nothing.

I grabbed a hold of the blanket. My intention was to freeze him out of his slumber, because holy shit, it was cold in there. The window was open and it was a mind-numbing, thirty-something degrees. I'd pulled the comforter down a few inches, when, out of nowhere, a hand reached out, grabbed my wrist and jerked.

I'm going take a brief moment to comment on physics. Don't get alarmed; it's nothing specific, like mass ratios or linear velocities. I was a small body at rest. My family's roots are Scottish-Irish, with a small dose of English to keep it interesting and controversial. We come from a long line of people who starved over the years and kept mobile because we were running from the enemy. We were built to run orders, not actually fight on the front lines. My hand was encased by another so large it had similarities to a catchers' mitt, or sometime in the far past, a hand that held a twenty-pound sword and pummeled men to death. It pulled hard enough that I lost my footing and careened forward—objects in motion tend to stay in motion, unless interfered by another object—where I landed on top of a body, wedging my right breast into a left shoulder, not unlike falling into an immense boulder that knocked the air from my lungs. I fell further to the other side of the bed, where an arm saved me from falling to the floor when it wrapped around me and pulled me tight. I might've swooned if the whole situation didn't resemble tackle football.

I was face-to-face, chest-to-chest with a slumbering giant, trying to regain my composure and free my arms. I wheezed out,

68

"Godzilla! *Let. Me. Go!*"

Green eyes popped open. Whoever this man was, he'd been sleeping. He was now fully awake, no different than one of those monstrous creatures in a dark cave, slumbering for hundreds of years, to be awoken by a stupid kid looking for gold coins. We lay body to body, his eyes moving, some great thought process trying to churn answers from clues that were not there. This is what I saw in his face as he worked out the details. *He did not know me. I was in his room. I was a girl. We had not had sex. He didn't think. I was not Scottish. I was foul mouthed and working my arms like a monkey caught in a cage. I did not look dangerous.* All these possible thoughts moved back and forth across his eyes as his sleep-addled brain fought to come up with answers. My only thought was *Holy Batman,* when my brain starting firing again and I realized that not only was I wedged into a bed with a strange, very warm man-bear, but this large individual was also naked.

We stared at each other for one more heart-stopping moment. Then he did the impossible. He curled his arm around my head and kissed me. *Kissed me.* Not a chaste peck, not a 1950's Fred Astaire lip-on-lip virginal kiss. This was a full-on-lip-lock-I'm-headed-straight-to-your-pants-and-suck-out-your-lungs-kiss.

What can I say? I hadn't been kissed like that . . . in *ever*. I kissed him back. Enthusiastically. He pulled me closer, wrapping a leg around me that had me in a full body embrace. I wrapped an arm around his neck and pushed my fingers into his hair. I have no idea how long the kiss lasted, but at some point, I was clinically hypoxic and needed air.

We broke apart, both of us out breath, staring at one another.

It was quiet for a two full seconds as he smiled at me—those green eyes narrowing in mischief. And because I was in another country, another time zone, another world, and possibly possessed, I smiled back.

God help me, yes, I smiled back.

I lay next to an unknown, naked Scotsman in the wee hours

of the morning that I'd just kissed. I decided I'd blame everything on either jetlag or an alien invasion as the eerie silence continued and neither of us moved. But at a molecular level, atoms shifted and slid left of center, similar to the quiet seconds before a level five tornado or the total pandemonium of a riot.

When the last single atom dropped off-kilter, causing the proverbial seesaw to unbalance, I heard Tannis whisper my name from the hallway. In alarm, I jerked back and the giant let go of me. I yelped, losing my balance, falling an impossible distance to the floor. He reached for me, but it was too late. He grabbed me just as I hit the cold wood floor, distending my arm in a painful way. Something popped and I screamed. He let go and pushed me like expelling a hooker that just worn out her welcome. He got to his knees, muttering, *"Sheet, sheet, sheet,"* while I hissed the English translation, "Shit, shit, shit," getting a full view of his expansive anatomy. He stopped long enough to notice his exposed problem, grabbed sheets and covered . . . parts.

I held up a hand and yelled apologies, "Sorry, sorry," as I backpedaled towards the door, saying, "Wrong room. Looking for brother. Wrong room," and crawled away. By the time I was to the door, I was crab walking, a second later, I was upright and running.

I plowed into Tannis, almost knocking her to the floor. Her hair was mashed to one side and her eyes were as large as saucers. I grabbed a hold of her to keep from falling. There was a small smile on her face that I really didn't appreciate.

"What's going on, love?"

"Wrong room. So sorry," I muttered, as I attempted to calm my breathing. "Give my apologies. To . . ." I looked back, "to the relative."

Tannis didn't say a word and pointed to the room next door. "That one might be what ye lookin' for, no?"

"Sure thing."

I ran into the next room and found Sean, who was turned

70

over in bed, his eyes red and puffy. "What's going on?" he mumbled.

"Get up. Now. We're going."

"What?" he yelled.

I motioned to his ears, indicating he needed to remove his earplugs. I said, "Get up!"

He pulled them out as his eyes searched the room, his hair standing up at odd angles. "What?" he screamed again.

"You overslept. We have to go," I hissed. "The cab is downstairs."

"What?"

"Get up! It's five."

"What? What do you mean it's five?"

"It's five AM. We have to go." I threw a pair of pants at him, which seemed ridiculous in light of recent events.

"Really? Five?"

I found a sweatshirt and tossed it at his head. "Oh, for God's sake. We're downstairs. The cab is here." I couldn't continue the conversation. It was like reasoning with a drunk.

I ran down the stairs and said to Dad. "He was asleep."

Dad was eating a croissant, still sitting on the stairs. "Told you so."

I stared at the pastry. "Where'd you find that?"

He pointed to the kitchen. "What'd you find?" a smirk on his face.

"Nothing."

He shoved half of the croissant into his mouth. "Didn't sound like it."

Sean came stumbling down the stairs, clothes wrinkled, hair askew, hauling his bag, and cursing under his breath. Tannis followed after, almost tripping on her housecoat. The cab honked outside. Sean wobbled from side to side, wiping sleep from his eyes. There were some distinct similarities between our group and the patients they ran through the emergency room in the wee hours of the morning.

"Let's go," I said.

"Why didn't you wake me?" Sean asked.

"I did."

"Not soon enough."

I ignored him and turned to hug Tannis, thanking her for the hospitality. Sean repeated my motions exactly. We walked outside and she followed, watching from the top of the stairs. We loaded everything in the back of the cab at our feet, where there were two seats facing forward and two seats that folded down and faced backwards. Right before pulling away, I glanced to the second floor and saw the giant standing in the window, his large pale chest in stark contrast to his dark hair, watching us go. I looked away, told myself it was Scotland and that we were headed north. I would never to see this guy again. It would be a story repeated for friends over a third drink.

"Why didn't you wake me?" Sean asked again, seething.

Dad gave me one of those *told you* looks and rolled his eyes.

"I did!"

"At five o'clock! At five!" Sean yelled.

"How was I supposed to know? You're always the first one up."

72

"I know. That's why you should have done it sooner." He said, disgruntled. "It was the worst night. I could hear Tannis' husband snoring through the walls. I couldn't sleep and went downstairs at one AM. It was freezing."

Dad and I didn't meet his eyes. It seemed bad sport to acknowledge our rather warm and comfortable evening.

"There wasn't a single afghan, blanket, anything. I froze to death, while those cats went in and out of open windows into the yard. I finally went back upstairs around three. There was more snoring. The whole place was an artic hole. Must have fallen asleep around four."

"On our way," I announced, all smiles and happy faces. "Maybe next time, don't even bother going to bed."

Sean gave me a withering look. "Maybe next time, wake me up. Earlier."

"Noted."

Sean scratched his head, trying to smooth down his cowlick. He'd buttoned his shirt wrong and his collar sat higher on one side. I said nothing.

"Was there yelling? Or was that a dream?" he asked.

"Dream," I said, meeting Dad's eyes and shaking my head.

Dad laughed out loud.

Sean said, "What?"

Dad said, "Look! They have Kentucky Fried Chicken here."

*   *   *

73

Emails:

From Trevor Smith

To Natalie Calhoun

Subject: Coming clean

Full disclosure: I made some unfortunate bets with a bookie named Robbie. My usual contacts weren't working and I had a line on several games that were a sure-fire way to win back some money.

And since when hasn't Alabama not come through in the last minutes? Always.

With the exception of this last week.

You're not going to believe this, but Robbie has become a bit threatening. You don't think they would do anything physical, do you?

-Trevor

*   *   *

From Natalie Calhoun

To: Tommie Calhoun

Subject: Issues

Tommie-boy,

Currently navigating Scotland with Dad and have no cellular international plan, so don't go texting me back with your "military grade phone that can text Zimbabwe" and charging me fifty cents per word. I wouldn't bother you, but I got ISSUES. Trevor issues. I think he's in deep with his bookie and hiding in my house to avoid them. And his bookie is threatening him, through me. You know anyone in the Kansas City area who can stop by the house and take a look? On the down low?

Nat

*   *   *

We walked into the airport at six AM; the place was overrun with travelers and serpentine lines that stretched to the doors. A panic bloomed inside me that the "sleeping incident" would result in travel problems. As luck would have it, our small airline company Flybe that was taking us to the islands only had a smattering of people. We'd booked tickets that headed north to Stornoway, in the Isle of Lewis, and then backtracked to Benbecula in North Uist.

To say that we walked miles to the end of the airport is not an exaggeration. If it had been a pioneer's trek across the western range, we'd been forced to leave extraneous possessions and the bodies of our dead behind as we schlepped along. Small in-country carrier groups were at the far reaches of the terminal, where there was only a door and some stairs, requiring you to walk onto the tarmac and up flimsy steps into the plane. The flight held about thirty people. We got one flight attendant, who wore the proper uniform, but took liberties with the scarf and shoes and knew half the people on the flight because they were there the week before. The pilot high-fived people and slapped the ass of a man that wore a Scotland rugby jersey. I didn't know whether this familiarity was enjoyable or disconcerting.

For all my hesitations, I fell asleep almost immediately. It seemed mere seconds when the pilot announced we were making our descent into Stornoway and to make the proper precautions regarding drinks, bags and bad tempers. We stared out the windows to find the concrete landmarks of Edinburgh had been replaced by islands and copious amounts of water. It was entirely too green for the eyes, as if someone had gone wacky with Photoshop. Debarking the plane, a cold wind smelling of salt and grass swept at my face and rolled through my hair. Rugged rolling hills of heath and rock surrounded me, with a backdrop of endless lochs. It was a forgotten fairy dreamland at the edge of the earth. I expected a Percheron horse mounted by a knight to go cantering over a hill, calling out a war cry, something similar to *Game of Thrones*, complete with enormous wolves and water giants.

The three of us stood there a moment while the air blew around us, through us. There was a scent of brine and the high-pitched call of gulls. The landscape was austere and remotely striking. I grew up in an area where open space was the only constant, with strong storms rolling over the plains and the call of coyotes at night. I've gone to large cities on vacation and enjoyed myself, but I've always had the nagging urge to get away, to find open air as soon as I could. In these Isles, I felt no similar tension. It was something close to home—the feeling of space and freedom.

Once inside the small terminal, we discovered a café and tiny shop selling wool items and whiskey. The workers at the airport all knew each other and called out "Helloo," as they came inside. There was the aroma of fresh coffee and sausage rolls, and the women handling security resembled homemakers more than TSA agents, wearing wool trousers with pinned hair, emitting small giggles as they passed items through the scanner.

Exactly one cup of coffee and sixty minutes later, we loaded the same plane and flew into Benbecula, our final destination for the islands. I was amazed at the numerous lochs dotting the countryside. It was staggering to a person who heralded from a place that counted rain in tenth of inches and turned into a parched desert inferno in mid-August. I looked at Sean and thought it was possible he was salivating and considering pulling on his hip waders right there. Sean occupied the seat in front of the rear-facing attendant and she'd eyed him suspiciously—we had no accents and were avid coffee drinkers, and were labeled American troublemakers immediately upon sight.

We landed at a small airport similar to Stornoway, with a terminal no bigger than a luxurious American sitting room and kitchen. Among the handful of people awaiting arrivals, there was a tall man with dark hair, work boots, and a baseball cap pulled low over his eyes. He scrutinized everyone like a criminal line-up at the police precinct. I'm guessing our American zeal must have been apparent because he immediately walked up to Sean, extended his hand and pronounced our last name of "Calhoun" with such a thick ancient accent that I felt swept back a good several hundred years.

Sean made some comment about our "American transparency" to induce a laugh. The man just stared. Sean introduced us and the man returned the gesture by saying, "Alec," and nodded towards a table with his head. Apparently the Scots weren't big talkers, but this man was a big guy; he was six-foot-four and weighed around two-forty. His feet were this size of concrete blocks and the table shook as he sat down. His cap had the bright red logo of the Wisconsin football team. I couldn't help it, I mentally recited the specifics: mascot, the Badgers, conference: Big Ten, previous season record: 11-2, before losing to Texas Christian in the Rose Bowl. Damn shame. Trevor had lost five hundred bucks on that game.

Alec produced a standard piece of white printer paper that had been folded several times. He laid it down on the table. When I peered over Sean's shoulder, I noticed several printed lines asking for name, address, cell number and driver's license. A fifth grader in computer class could have accomplished it.

"Wisconsin, huh?" I said and yawned.

Both Alec and Sean looked up from the paper, confused.

"The hat?" I asked.

Alec nodded and rumbled, "Hmmm," which I took as a Scottish yes. He asked Sean to write down his particulars, scratching behind his ear, finding a pen hidden in the recesses of his unmanageable hair. I assumed this to be our infamous sheep-chasing-rental-car-agent, and this was our rental agreement.

77

I asked, "That's it?" opening a bag of potato crisps that tasted distinctly similar to corn nuts.

Alec seemed confused. "Aye."

"No contingencies on hitting sheep or goats?"

Alec's eyes narrowed in a way that could only be interpreted as controlled frustration, bordering on anger. I don't know why I said it; I don't know why I said anything. Sometimes my mouth was on an adrenaline drip that could not be shut off. In the medical world, staff wrote it off as brilliant eccentricity, everywhere else I was considered a social oddity. Sean stared, concern written on his face, just like the time I suggested we build a fire in the barn to keep the horses warm.

"No," Alec responded, "Just need a number in case you guys take a wonky turn and plant it in a loch." He paused, looking outside. "And die."

"Ah . . . that happens?" I asked, worried.

The man gave us the barest of a smile. "No."

Sean barked out a forced laugh. He knew my history and parking a car in a ditch wasn't far from reality. Something about the comment annoyed me though. Alec needed to understand that I was the comic in this group. No one upstaged me.

Sean filled out the respective lines and asked, "Can we get her name on the contract to be a second driver?"

Alec scanned me from head to toe and appraised my worthiness as a driver and a woman. *"Yes,"* I wanted to say, *"I understand your hesitations. I'm very small compared to your gargantuan size, but I am sturdy and can drive a stick. I was a farm girl and killed chickens."* There were similarities between his glances and the eighteenth century arranged marriages, when a king sized up a girl's girth and possible childbearing possibilities for his son. In the end, my uterus and stature must have met standards because he said, "I guess you should just write your name by his."

"You guess?" Apparently my uterus was sub-standard after all. "My name?"

"Aye, by his," pointing to the paper.

"You want minor felonies as well?" I asked.

Beneath his thick hair, he had vivid green eyes that widened at my insolence, which made me happy.

Sean said, "Kicked in the head by a horse. Got issues. Don't mind her."

Alec said in a voice reminiscent of a Catholic priest, "A sin a sin, no? No such thing as minor. Even with felonies."

Sean guffawed. "No one is more informed about the gray areas in the law than Nat."

I leveled a look at him.

"Maybe driver's license number too, no?" Alec said.

I grabbed the pen from Sean and signed with a flourish, the men be damned. We all walked outside and found our father, who had been standing by the pier and surveying the area. The four of us walked over to an economy-sized Ford sedan.

"Ok," Alec said, "This is it," and handed the keys to Sean.

None of us said anything. As far as cars went, not only was it small, but I'd seen salvage vehicles with more spit and shine.

"You guys drive standard transmission, right?" Alec asked, rocking on his heels.

With a straight face, I said, "Nope."

A muscle twitched beneath Alec's left eye.

"She's kidding," Sean said, ratting me out, the bastard.

"Ok, then, off you go," Alec said, glad to be rid of us and walking away.

We all stood dumbfounded.

"Wait a second," I yelled. "What do you want us to do with the car when we're finished?"

Alec turned, confusion on his face. "Well, you leavin' from here, right? On a flight?"

"Yes," I responded.

"Just leave it," Alec said.

We stared, not comprehending.

Sean said, "Here? In town?"

"Aye," he responded, frustrated, waving towards the water. "Just drop it off here, in the parking lot and lea' the keys in the visor."

Dad snorted.

Sean said, "You sure?" watching some motorcyclists packing up their gear.

Alec shrugged, saying, "Lea' the keys in the visor. The car unlocked. I'll pick it up later." And he walked away.

It was official: We were off the grid.

5

Emails:

From Trevor Smith

To Natalie Calhoun

Subject: Forward progress, with some issues

Nat,

Since I've had some time, I commenced work in the kitchen to figure out the wiring snafu between refrigerator and wall switch. I disconnected the oven, disregarding the dishwasher. An overloading of the circuits caused an electrical fire in the heart of the dishwasher, which caused a water pipe to burst. There is both water and fire damage. I know this sounds scary, but I have a plan.

P.S. Most damage contained to kitchen. You can hardly tell the problems with carpet in living room.

Trevor

* * *

From Natalie Calhoun

To Trevor Smith

Re: Forward progress, with some issues

Trevor,

"This sounds scary?"

No. Not scary at all. IT'S A CATASTROPHE!

I've called authorities. Pack your belongings and leave or you will be thrown in jail. Get out of my house! Immediately!

-N

P.S. Robbie is looking for you. You need pay him. This is serious. Fix your "problems."

*　*　*

We drove to Lochmaddy, following road signs that were in both English and Gaelic, on narrow roads the width of paved golf cart paths. They were comical by Western standards, but taught us all white-knuckle-screaming-lessons on how to find "passing points" when another car would come careening at us at high speeds. The rental car rattled, had 95,000 miles and a wobbly clutch that felt like a loose bone joint on a geriatric patient. We agreed it was something left behind at the garage when someone had brought it in for repairs and decided they didn't have the money to pay for it. Since I had a 2002 Subaru with bad suspension, questionable heat and working cigarette lighter, I felt an immediate kinship with the car.

Lochmaddy was a small coastal village consisting of several inns, a gas station, a ferry dock and a smattering of houses. Situated on a sea inlet, with water lapping at rocky shores, it was a peaceful beginning after the noise and crowds of Edinburgh. I'd read some initial descriptions of Lochmaddy in 1616 as a rendezvous point for pirates. I figured if I was going to forget my heartless past and start marauding and pillaging new men, I'd been brought to the right place.

The Lochmaddy Inn was on the main street, next to the tourism center. We pulled into a parking lot with five other cars. There was a moment of silence as we all sat in the car and took a collective breath. There'd been five flights, a car rental with a manual transmission and questionable coffee to make it to this particular point. If that wasn't enough, we'd driven down the wrong side of the road on sidewalks, interpreting Gaelic/English road signs and narrowly missed sheep and other small animals.

We exited the car on wobbly legs and walked into the hotel to find the front desk abandoned. Large room keys the size of drink coasters hung on a pegboard, with a vacuum nearby and a sign that read, "Any inquiries should be made at the bar." I thought it a fine plan and considered making a plaque of the same order and placing on the front door of my house. Following instructions, the three of us walked single file down a narrow hallway towards the bar and to what smelled like grilled food.

I heard Sean mutter over his shoulder, "No matter what, we're getting a real breakfast. The Scottish kind."

The small tavern consisted of a corner bar, ten tables, and yesterday's special of fish pie written on a chalkboard. There was a panoramic view of the sea and the overcast sky through large windows, casting blue-gray light within the room. A middle-aged woman wearing jeans and a t-shirt stood behind a bar running a cappuccino machine, talking to another older woman with a vacuum nearby. They both turned as we walked into the room.

"What can we do for you, love?" the woman making coffee asked Sean.

Sean inquired about whether we could get our rooms this early, and if there was anyone around to do it.

"Oh sure, she's around. I'll find her," she said smiling, suggestively tilting her head at the other woman, giggling. "Don't know if you can get in the rooms, though. Still cleaning. Most likely."

The lady with the vacuum cleaner confirmed this as she muttered, "Hmmrph," and gave us a good looking over. "Couple of hours, yeah?" she said, as she took a sip of her coffee, enjoying her time. My kind of people; no reason hiding it, everyone needs a coffee break.

We ordered three coffees and our barista spoke about the area and where Sean could obtain a fishing license. "Oh, aye, you got to find the manager, at the Estate Office. He gives out the assignments, but already gone, along with the other fisherman. They make a regular morning thing of it here over coffee."

It became immediately apparent why Sean had picked this hotel and not the slightly more posh place up the street, and it wasn't for the price. I gave him a narrowed look and thought about his earlier email comment about "staying in a place *with salty men reeking of whiskey and herring.*" It wasn't exactly that, but The Lochmaddy Inn had seen better days. The hotel motto was "Once discovered, never forgotten," and it was possible that this slogan applied to some of the fixtures of the hotel; the carpet was thin and worn, the paint chipping in places and the staircase doubled back several times in a chaotic way from floor to floor, creaking and popping with each step. It was a gritty, coastal island inn.

We ordered breakfast, had several more coffees and plotted our day. Sean would secure a fishing license from the proper authorities and Dad and I would tour the local countryside. The waitress served us hot servings of two fried eggs, baked beans, grilled tomato and mushrooms. I even felt some benevolence towards the grilled tomato, even though I usually abhor any kind of whole cooked variety of it. After my Ireland experience, I passed on the black sausage. Dad ate the whole thing, saying, "Salty! Similar to sweetbreads, don't you think?" causing Sean to spit his into a napkin.

Leaving our bags in the car, we set out to find the Estate Office. It wasn't difficult; it was one block down the street. Mr.

MacDonald, the estate manager, sat inside a tiny office surrounded by framed and rolled topographic maps like an ancient Roman scroll maker. He gave us a firm handshake and Scottish hello and issued Sean a one-day permit.

That business accomplished, we walked towards the ferry office, which was the opposite way down the same street. Apparently, if it wasn't on the main drag, it wasn't needed. Our plan was to travel the next day to the Isles of Harris and Lewis for sightseeing, which required a ferry ride from North Uist to Harris to get there. When I read the guidebooks in a weak moment of organization, the information had been adamant about making ferry reservations before the vacation started, months in advance. I disregarded these warnings outright. When we showed up at ferry office, looking to purchase a reservation to Leverburgh on Harris Island, the woman behind the counter was all sad apologies, telling me that they were booked, unless someone cancelled. It wasn't passengers that were the problem; it was the car.

"Really?" I whined.

"Oh, yes, booked months in advance," just like the guidebook had stated. "Do you want to be put on a waiting list?"

Sean refused to meet my eyes, his anger visible in the way his finger tapped a fast beat against his leg. This was a revolving theme of conflict between us; him lecturing me about my disorganization and poor life choices, me not pay attention, and him enlightening and correcting me. Sometimes I did stupid things—even though I knew better—just to annoy him, no matter the consequences. Since the death of our mother, we'd lost the ability to civilly communicate past a basic conversation; the line severed and never fixed. When Sean agreed to come, I knew it meant we'd have talk and make real decisions. So far, it wasn't going well.

We grudgingly put ourselves on the list and strategized a secondary southern plan into tiny South Uist and then Berra, where a ferry was not needed because small land bridges existed. It was a dismal second option for our travels, but the only thing available without the ferry. Sean didn't speak a word as we walked back to the hotel parking lot. He opened the trunk to get out his suitcase and jerked at the handles, cursing, throwing all of them to the ground, like a mad housewife cleaning out a closet. Dad and I watched from afar, his anger a palpable heat wave. Sean took my travel backpack and threw it at my face. I fended it off with my hands.

"Hey! Easy," and threw it back.

He caught it with one hand. "Congratulations, Nat. Super job planning the trip." He tossed the bag again. This time, Dad put out his hand to catch it and missed. It fell to the ground between us.

"Stop it," Dad said. "We'll figure it out."

"*Figure it out*?" Sean said, scrunching his face. "There's no figuring." He gestured towards me. "We're going to drive around two tiny islands that no one cares about because Nat didn't open a computer and organize a thing."

"We'll get it sorted, "I said, "Quit treating it—"

"Oh, I'll treat it anyway I want," Sean said, cutting me off.

Dad moved towards Sean in a consoling gesture and stepped on my bag. There was the sound of glass breaking, which reminded me of a Jewish wedding, except no one was yelling mazel tov.

We all peered down. My brain clicked through several possibilities: *Make-up? None in the bag. Sunglasses? On my head. Coffee mug?*

A tumbler clicked into place when an odorous wave of something akin to five gallons of Life Savers smothered in Vic's Menthol Rub soaking in a barrel of Listerine saturated the air. Horrified, I pushed Dad with enough force that he fell backwards against Sean. I picked up the bag and screamed, "Get away. MOVE, MOVE, MOVE!"

Several families watched in shocked silence as I yelled, waving my arms like a person in the midst of mental breakdown. I screamed, "Peppermint, peppermint!" as parents grabbed children and went running towards the hotel. A toddler was pushed down in the melee and lay crying on the asphalt, until a parent came sprinting back, grabbed him by the collar and drug him to the hotel entrance. Sean and Dad stood stupefied, their mouths hanging open.

I ran to the water, throwing my wallet and phone to the ground, carrying the backpack as if it was an essential oil Molotov cocktail. Once at the water's edge, I dropped the bag in the water, stomping on it with my foot and held it below lapping waves.

I yelled over my shoulder, "Got it. No worries."

After five minutes of underwater submersion, I sniffed the bag and deemed it safe. I limped back to the men with one soaked shoe. When I got close, Sean asked, "Are you sure you don't want to call the bomb squad?"

"Just being careful." The parking lot was empty except for the three of us. "Ever consider what would've happened if they'd been crushed on the plane?"

"There are small children that'll need PTSD counseling now," Sean said.

"Blame Liz," I responded. "Who gives an aromatherapy scent bomb as a vacation gift?"

Sean looked away, said nothing and walked over to his small bag that was still sitting in the parking lot. He bent over as he extracted numerous pieces of fishing equipment. The suitcase was a bottomless entity, with what appeared to be an entire bait shop inside. On his knees, rifling through its contents, Sean pulled out hip waders, flies, floppy hat, some kind of military vest with five hundred pockets and bug spray. Items were lined up for inspection like we were homeless and he was considering our possibilities for survival.

My eyes slid to Dad, who was watching with avid interest. Of course he was. He was hoping for trade secrets so he could limit his already rudimentary clothing attire to five pieces and secure it all in a fanny pack. Sean had brought a small carry-on suitcase, but I

87

was sure eighty percent of it was fishing gear and the remaining twenty percent was actual necessities for dressing and hygiene. This worried me, in that we were only on our third day of vacation and I'd already seen clothes repeated after they'd been shoved into plastic bags after a rainy day and several muggy, overheated bars.

My shoe made a squelching noise as I stepped closer. "Is there any regular clothing in there?"

Sean pulled out some duct tape, not meeting my eyes. "Sure. Of course."

Who brings duct tape on vacation? I took a step back. "Like what? You can't wear hip waders to dinner."

"I've got a couple of t-shirts."

"Couple?"

"One extra."

"Heaven help us," I muttered, "I hope you two packed extra deodorant."

We drove to the designated fishing spot, going past our turn three times before spotting the unmarked road, arguing about it the entire time. The countryside was picturesque with lochs so numerous it was impossible to count—all of them with the possibility of trout magic. Dropping off Sean, we promised to return in five hours because we had no way of calling him. Sean grabbed his gear and readied himself for fishing greatness. As he walked off into the great unknown, I thought, *See you later, you wee scunner.*

* * *

Dad and I traversed around North Uist in the beat-up Ford. We'd been told by our local barista the coastline road was beautiful and there were several attractions roadside. With no agenda, no time schedule, the two of us scampered around the island. We stopped for some pictures, wandered cairns, and adjusted to driving on the wrong side of the road while the car made strange, grinding transmission noises.

The whole afternoon was made right by a little excursion into some Celtic Stones called the Pobull Fhinn. Hiking up to the ancient circle, we stood in its center for many minutes, which sat obtrusively in the heather like chipped teeth in a dinosaur's mouth. Without an obstacle or person to impinge our vision of the horizon or rocky landscape, we found perfection. It was quiet. It was pure. It was Scotland.

Thirty minutes later, we found a hotel and went inside to drink beers. This sentence could have been included in every description of the Calhoun family travels. *They went inside and drank beers.* The hotel had a terraced area that included a small garden and several tables. We sat outside, the only people in the place. I tried making a dinner reservation, but they were already booked for the night. Slightly disappointed, I ordered another beer and watched the breeze move through a cluster of Scottish bluebells at my feet. I could hear Eve's voice whisper, "*harebells, also known as campanula,*" as bees circled my face, attracted to the lingering lavender-eucalyptus scent still clinging to my clothes. I could have sat in the pub all night, but at that moment, my fisherman brother was wandering aimlessly around the heather, possibly lost, wondering if we might just leave him.

It wasn't a bad thought.

*   *   *

Dad and I had the radio blasting to a traditional Gaelic radio station when we arrived at the fishing drop-off point, the announcer informing us of sunny skies and thirty percent chance of rain. Sean stood alone in the parking lot. Not a good sign. He limped to the car and dropped his stuff.

I grimaced. "That bad?"

"No bites. Nothing." He glanced over his shoulder. "Lots of heather. He might have assigned me this area to just get rid of me."

I thought, *Wow, the locals are doing it too?*

Sean tossed his stuff in the car and crawled into the backseat. He slumped like a delinquent child whose parents had taken away his cell phone. I told him that we needed to check back with the ferry office for a possible reservation.

"Fine," he said. "But I need a beer. Quickly."

Whatever my evil tendencies towards Sean—and there were many—I still wanted him to go home with grand stories of catching fish in Scotland. No fisherman wants to tell friends about trudging through endless heather without a single bite. Our car ride to town was a quiet one. At some point, Sean, leaned forward and said, "What's that?"

I looked to the countryside. "Heather. Islands. Water."

"No, idiot. The light," and pointed over my shoulder. "On the dash."

The check engine light had started blinking five miles back, which really didn't surprise me. The car was a ratty contraption similar to my Subaru, and my initial reaction, when I'd seen the light pop on and off earlier, was to drive on until it could really make up its mind. I ignored a pesky catalytic convertor light for two years. I found it got easier with time. Of course, Sean was horrified when I verbalized this.

"At the bare minimum, we have to make sure there's oil in the car."

"Now?"

Sean made a sound similar to a goose being strangled and yelled, "Pull this car over."

"OK. OK," I said, realizing I might be taking the pesky sister act too far. I pulled to the side of the road, just past a small cottage where a man in matching upper and lower camo fleece was mowing his yard in front of a tidy white cottage.

90

I searched below the wheel and console for a button that would pop the hood. "I can't find it," I said, hitting my head.

"What do you mean you can't find it?" Sean asked.

"There's no button," I said.

"I don't believe you."

I gave him a look like he was the most annoying person in the world, which at that moment, he was. During parts of this vacation, I was reliving my childhood; glances, cutting words and snide remarks were working their way back into the conversation as if we were teenagers and fighting over the TV remote that only got five stations via the antennae on the house. I found it both refreshing and disconcerting.

Dad leaned over to help and I searched dark crevices for anything that appeared to be a latch. I pulled loose some wires from beneath the dash and realized I might be messing with the heater and let them go.

Sean got out of the backseat and stood by my door. He said, "Out," like I was a truant toddler. He got in and stuck his head beneath the wheel looking for anything resembling a tab, but judging from the amount of grunting I heard, it was a hopeless affair.

The camo Scot was still mowing his yard and doing his best to avoid us. I've had vast experience knowing when an individual would rather not meet your eyes and our big guy was a fine specimen of denial. Trading spaces, I'd done the same thing. No one wants to involve themselves with three idiotic, foreign people roadside, especially if those people start asking to use your restroom, telephone, or for a ride. His biggest mistake had been not giving up and hiding in his house until we left. It's what I would've done. After we had circled the car three times, each of us doing our best to manually force the damn thing open, the guy decided he couldn't take the stupidity anymore and walked towards us.

"Bit of problem, then?" he asked and sighed, resigned to his fate.

Sean explained the engine light and the fact that we couldn't get the hood open to check oil.

"Hmmm," he responded. "A lot of the Fords, the hood latch is beneath the ornament on front, aye? Opened with the key."

We walked to the front of the car and watched as our burly Scot flipped the Ford emblem up and showed us the lock. The three of us uttered, "Ahhh," at the same time and laughed. The hood was opened, the oil checked, as well as the coolant. Everything seemed in order.

I resisted the urge to say, "Told you so!"

Our good Samaritan/ hood specialist suggested we call the rental place and ask for help. He wished us well and walked away knowing he'd helped us, but not knowing that none of us had paid for the international cell phone plan. We got back in the car, deciding to drive down the road and find a pay phone.

We drove another fifteen miles before we spotted a run-down, graffiti littered, public phone. Sean gave me the rental number and I went inside to call. The folding door was stuck in a half-open position, and I was squashed to one side when I slid through, trying not to impale myself through the liver. I picked up the receiver, but there was no dial tone.

I hit the phone several times, listened, and yelled through the cracked glass, "Nothing."

"This is your fault, you know," Sean said, as I came out. "Not paying attention. The odds of this happening were five to one from the beginning."

"My fault? An engine light? The car still runs, moron."

Our father intervened before it came to blows. "Stop. We need to call *someone*."

We couldn't call, but just down the road was a Ford service shop. We decided it was worth a try. We parked and Sean said, "You go. Even in your . . . " he eyeballed me, shaking his head, "ragged state, you have a better chance with some male mechanics." I rolled my eyes, perked up my dirty, blonde hair and walked inside to find a burly man with grease-stained hands standing by a front counter. I told him our problem.

He seemed unimpressed. "You just need to call the rental place."

Well, obviously . . .

I'm going to take a small time-out and illustrate this particular situation as being the legacy of my life—being told by good-meaning people outside work what to do in critical and sometimes stressful situations because they think I have no idea what I am doing. I listen politely and inform them in a very nice way I've already tried that—because although I look like a stupid person, I am, in fact, not a stupid person. Usually.

I smiled. *Be calm,* I told myself. "We tried to call," pointing outside, "but the phone booth isn't working. Maybe I could use your phone to get ahold of them?" I smiled again, but my face was starting to hurt.

"Oh that," he replied. "It hasna worked for years. Yeah, you can use our tele."

He guided me towards a private office and handed me the phone. I pushed it back, showing him the business card. "I'm sorry," I said. "How do you dial that number? In the United States, we have something different." What constituted long distance in the Hebrides? Island to island? Or was the whole area considered local phone call range?

He laughed, dialed it and handed me the phone, walking out to leave me in privacy.

On the fifth ring, a man answered with such a thick accent that it was unintelligible for my American ears. There was so much mechanical background noise, he repeated himself three times before

93

I caught the name of the garage. I told him we'd rented a car and were having problems with an engine light.

"What?" he asked. *Bang, bang, bang.*

"There's an engine light on our rental car?" *The whrrrrr, whrrrr of a hydraulic drill.* I heard a piece of metal falling to the ground, as well as background noise of people yelling at each other.

"What?"

"Engine. Light. On. The. Ford. Rental. Car."

"Hold on," and he screamed a man's name three times. In the next minute, as I sat waiting, I heard a cacophony of garage noises while two men conferred nearby.

A man came on the line. He simply said, "Go ahead and drive."

"Drive the car?" I asked.

"Yes, drive the car."

"With the light? On?"

"My dad says it should be fine," he responded.

I paused a beat. "Fine?"

"Aye. Fine."

"But there's a light."

"He says it dosna matter. He'll deal with it later."

I looked out the window and saw Sean pacing. "You know," I said. "I totally agree with you, but my brother doesn't exactly feel the same way. He's a worrier, you know? Thinks I'm a bit of a slacker and liar. Of small things. Like engine lights. And we have another several days here."

94

"The engine lights come on all the time. It's fine," he reassured me.

I lowered my voice and turned my back on Sean, even though he had never shown the ability to read my lips from two hundred feet. "Listen, the car is losing power when we go uphill. I didn't tell my brother because I didn't want him to worry." Sean was the king of worriers, worse than an eighty-year old grandma before Thanksgiving Day.

"Oh. So ye are a liar," this unknown male said, as the mechanical noises lessened in intensity, as if he'd walked into an interior room for privacy.

"What? No!"

"You just told me you are."

"Oh my God! It doesn't matter. I'm just saying we might have," I peered over my shoulder to see Sean watching me, "a bit of a piston ring problem? Maybe."

"*Who are you?*"

"A girl who drives a piece of crap that knows about fuel intake systems."

"Girls dinna understand intake problems."

"Listen buddy, girls know *a lot* about *intake problems*."

I heard a full belly laugh and a high-pitched snort. It was exactly the kind of thing my Aunt Velma did from time to time after telling a filthy joke.

"Did you just snort?"

"What? Me? No," and he cleared his throat, lowering his voice. "Whatcha plans for tomorrow then?"

"I can't go out with you. I don't even know you."

95

There was a frustrated sigh, similar to one I'd heard many times before. "As in, your plans for travel."

"If we get a spot on the ferry, we're headed to Lewis and Harris. But we're on a waiting list."

"You should've done that reservation months ago."

"*Who are you?*" I asked, hearing him laugh once more. "Believe me, I regret the reservation problem. But if we do get it, I don't want the car breaking down and being stranded in a single room B&B with my dad and brother as bunkmates in Lewis, if you catch my drift."

"Aye. Got it." In the background, music started to play. "How 'bout you drive the car over early to the lot in the morning? We'll switch out, no?"

"That'd be great, but I have no idea *where you are.*"

"*Sheet,*" I heard him mutter. "Ok. You're the folks at the Lochmaddy Inn, no?"

After a moment's hesitation, I said, "Right."

"Leave it in the parking lot. Keys in the visor. One of the guys will pick it up tonight. I'll come get you early tomorrow. We'll drive and get you a new ride and ye can drive back in time for the ferry. Sound good?"

"Can't you just leave another car?"

"All cars out. Some comin back tonight, and in the mornin. But dinna know when." There was a pause. Then he said, "Sorry," as an afterthought, as if it was something he'd been told to do by a well-meaning person.

"Ok. I guess. Do I have a choice?"

"No."

There was silence for a full five seconds. This wasn't working out like the happy Hertz commercials I saw on TV.

The guy said, "Best I can do. Is seven OK?"

"My ferry leaves at nine-thirty. *Is that OK*?"

"Plenty of time," he said, "See ye then."

"Will it be you?"

"What?" he asked, annoyed.

"Will *you* be the one coming?"

"Aye," and he didn't sound happy about it.

"What's your name?" I asked.

"Oh, sorry. Conall."

I thought I heard a click, and he'd possibly hung up. I muttered, "Great," while still holding the phone.

"Great what?" he asked.

"Oh, sorry," I apologized.

"What's your name?"

"Nat."

"Gnat? Like a bug?"

"Nat, as in *Natalie*," I said, exasperated.

"Seven, then," and he was gone.

I walked back to Sean and Dad, who were both looking at a map. "We go back to Lochmaddy. They'll pick up the car tonight. Some guy will come get me in the morning so we can switch it out."

"Can't they just leave one tonight?" Sean asked.

I told him the specifics, including that I didn't think the engine light meant anything. I held back any information regarding the power loss situation.

Sean leveled a look at me. He knew me well enough that he understood I might lie about the phone call to keep us going. There were times I felt my brothers were complete strangers to me, because we hadn't lived together for almost fifteen years. Those childhood years with siblings were like concrete; soft, liquid stuff at first, but eventually hardening till it was a foundation that never fully eroded. Siblings had an extensive knowledge of all your tells and facial glances—basically the TV guide to your inner network. That could work in your favor, or against it, depending upon the occasion. Sean watched me with careful, narrowed eyes as we got back into the car and drove. I pretended interest in the surrounding vicinity.

As far as my family was concerned, I was a pest and annoying, and calculating to get my way. Most often, I was viewed as that single, unmatched sock in the bottom of the hamper. It was stupid to get rid of me, in case I might come in handy, but they didn't know what to do with me in the meantime either.

Limping along in the car, we walked into the ferry office twenty minutes later and the woman working the desk recognized us immediately.

"You're in luck!" she said, waving a piece of paper.

"Really?" I asked.

"We had a cancellation for both days. You just need to pay your money and you'll be set to go."

I paid forty-five pounds, we all high-fived and went back to the hotel to celebrate.

6

Emails:

From Tommie Calhoun

To Natalie Calhoun

Re: Issues

Dear Runt-child,

So very glad your first email to me since leaving on vacation was not the kind that informs me the old man was killed in the line of duty. But instead, I'm supposed to use my military contacts to remove a combatant from your crappy house? Just let him burn the damn thing down and collect insurance. Reset the whole experiment. They do it in the military all the time.

I'll see what I can do. I find it amusing that Trevor has lost his personal Rain Man and is in a real soup sandwich. Even Netflix doesn't entertain me this much. Remember how I suggested rigging a "Trevor-cident" at Xmas? You should have listened.

Tommie

* * *

From Natalie Calhoun

To Tommie Calhoun

Subject: Assassination plots

This is our family, not your day job. We don't OFF people because they annoy us.

Nat

*　　*　　*

From Tommie Calhoun

To Natalie Calhoun

Re: Assassination plots

I bet those gambler friends of his feel differently.

Tommie

*　　*　　*

At seven AM, I stood outside the hotel entrance wearing a jacket and a scarf. Although the mid-day temperatures on the islands were spring-like, the early morning breezes were decidedly chilly. The kitchen staff—which also had been bar staff the night before and occasionally the janitorial staff—was two older women who appeared they could've taken on the English militia in earlier days. They wore no coats and seemed impervious to the morning cold as they sat at a rickety table having a smoke, eyeballing me as if I were an English spy.

"You OK, love?" one of them asked.

I waved dismissively. "Good, good. Just waiting for the rental guy to pick me up so we can replace the car that broke down yesterday."

"Who's the chap?"

"A guy named Conall. His father Alec owns the rental company in Carinish?" I massacred the name, making it sound like Cornish hen.

100

They laughed. "That's right," one said, smoke rolling out her nose. "Alec owns the *big* company," she burst out laughing, "and Conall set to take it *all* over one day." She elongated the word and her friend spit out coffee at the private joke.

Her companion fanned herself, "Handsome bloke tha' one, ma' me wet my knickers," and they cackled, clinking their coffee cups in a mock toast.

They were still having a good laugh when the roar of a beefed-up engine came from around the corner. As I watched, an enormous Ford pickup rattled down the road like a bulldozer and pulled up in front of me. I stepped back, hoping to see some kind of small mid-size car that had been pushed aside by the sheep farmer with an ego problem. The truck didn't move and I was choking on the exhaust. There were two choices: this was either my rental car pick-up or the rendezvous site for a Monster Truck competition. One of the women dramatically rolled her eyes and winked, confirming the first possibility. The truck was a dark blue color, but the passenger door was white, which meant it was possibly scavenged from a junkyard and added. If that wasn't enough to woo my female sensibilities, there were enormous, studded tires to rev up the sex appeal.

I stood on my tippy toes to grab the handle and open the door. My head was only slightly higher than the seat, and when I peered in, the driver was bent down and throwing tools and pop cans in the backseat. Similar to Alec, he was a massive guy with catcher mitts as hands.

He muttered, "Sorry, sorry, I'm Conall," wiping off the seat using the sleeve of his flannel shirt.

"Don't worry, it's fine." I resisted the urge to tell him that I'd lost my virginity in something worse than this, but I didn't know this man and it seemed bad American behavior to enter teenage sex conversations before ten AM.

The altered suspension of the truck made it an incredible step into the vehicle. I grabbed ahold of the door to pull myself in, just like climbing onto a tractor. Knowing I'd be riding alone with a male

Scot, I'd taken some pains with my appearance; putting on my skinny cords, some mascara and trying to look my European best, even though I had no idea what that was.

I was short and starved down due to long work hours, and the constant scavenging off a cafeteria salad bar and eating cellophane turkey sandwiches. Since I usually wore sweats or scrubs, few people had any idea of the actual proportions of my body. I could've hid a good fifty pounds in the clothes I normally wore. The cords were old and novelty daywear for me—they fit like a glove, because they had been washed several hundred times since college. I suppose their stretch capacity had been maxed ten years ago, or I'd eaten too many caramel toffee puddings, because the minute I threw my leg into the truck with the gusto of a farm girl, the stitching in my crotch area called it a day and split wide open. I felt the cool air of Scotland's highlands hit me hard in the privates.

Holy Haggis, I thought, as my petunia was exposed to the cold outdoor elements. I squeaked if I'd seen a mouse, or a Victorian maiden touched for the first time.

Alarmed, Conall said, "You a' right?"

I said, "Sorry, caught my foot," as I pulled myself into the truck and angled my ass was towards the door. I was in full-fledged panic mode, trying to hide that my pants were shredded and underpants were completely visible to the world.

I looked up, and . . . and . . . and . . . and . . . my thought process skidded, jerked to a halt, and flipped sideways like a car out of control on an icy surface. I screamed upon seeing Conall's face. Mental gears grinding, I wedged myself into the corner as I realized the man sitting in the truck was none other than my early-morning, Edinburgh mattress romp.

Conall turned and blurted, *"Jesus, Mary, and Joseph,"* sucking air through his teeth.

I stared out the windshield, saying, "Wow. Unbelievable," my hands moving all over the place. I finally wedged them into my hair. "Well, all right, ahhhh . . . you must be *the* relative of Tannis?"

I let go of my hair and noticed I'd pulled out a few strands. "Cousin?"

"Nephew."

Family relations explained, I glanced to him and away. He stared down, both hands gripping the steering wheel. He sighed and muttered, "shit," like receiving a diagnosis of a venereal disease.

"Yeah," I said. "Yeah," my brain floundering in low IQ status.

"Listen, you need to understand," he said.

"I was there. You don't have to explain."

"Yes, you were . . . But I . . . ye caught me off guard," and cleared his throat.

"Or not," I said.

"Right, I—"

I waved him off. "Don't have to explain."

Conall shook his head. "I do, it's just . . . I don't know, you were—"

"There?"

"Well, yes, but, I was sleeping and, hmmm—"

"Just forget it. All right?" I pleaded and maneuvered myself further into the corner, even though it wasn't possible without throwing myself out the door, which was slowly becoming a sensible solution to the problem. "Pretend it never happened." I avoided his eyes. "A mistake. Never happened. The car. Get me to the car." I couldn't get out of this truck fast enough. With the exposed underwear situation and now a stranger driving me who I'd seen naked, even leaving the country might not take me far enough.

Conall nodded. "Sure. Right, the car."

The women at the picnic table were watching. One of them waved and yelled, "Hey Conall, when ye coming back for supper?" snickering to themselves.

He waved back and smiled, whispering, "Why were ya in my room?"

"Looking for my brother!" I spit out. "We were late. He overslept. I couldn't remember which room it was. Swear." I inhaled and told myself to calm down. "And I . . . well . . .you grabbed and—"

"I know," he said, holding out his hand to stop me. "It's just," he shook his head. "I was asleep and you're . . ."

"What?" I asked.

"I dinna know!"

"You don't know?"

"A girl—"

"A girl?" I could feel my rage escalating. "Just a random GIRL! Is that how it works *in Scotland?*"

"Calm down. You were in my freecking bed!"

"You pulled me in, mauled me and threw me to the floor!"

The women were still watching, some curiosity on their faces. "Shhh," he chastised me. "Keep your voice down. It's a small town."

"Don't tell me what to do. I landed on the floor," I seethed.

"I tried to stop you."

"Oh yeah, thanks. I'll send you the bill from my orthopod."

"What? Orth—"

"Oh, just forget it. I . . ." I shook my head. *Forget the kiss*, I thought, *try to forget the kiss. Oh my God, that kiss.*

"I what?" he asked.

"You . . ." He looked at me expectantly and I saw the deep emerald of his eyes, the patrician nose and the dark wavy locks. He was so Scottish and so very handsome. And, in every way, completely wrong for me. "Dropped me and practically tore my arm from my socket."

"I know." He sighed. "I'm sorry. But you," sizing me up and down, "You are . . . puny."

"Puny! Puny?" That was a new one. I suppose I was puny compared to the giant Scots handing out cars to the wee little people.

But that kiss . . . I'd held onto it like a fairy dream even though I knew I shouldn't have. I'd tucked the kiss into my pocket and pulled it out in secret to wonder over in the last several days. I went over the details as something impossible, but still astonishingly real. It was part fantasy, part true life. But in that moment, as he threw around the word 'puny,' and treated me if I were a Sunday morning tequila hangover, the kiss dissipated, faded, and was replaced by cold air seeping up through my thin panties in a dirty farm truck. Reality was like that—you wanted Victoria Secret's red satin and you got JC Penney baby blue polyester.

"Can you put this thing in gear and drive?" The women still stared on, which was making me nervous. "Before those ladies put you in a fish pie and eat you."

Conall exhaled and did as I asked. We drove past the ladies and out of town. Over the next few minutes, we maintained a deathly silence. The only sound was the loud drone of the engine and the manual transmission sliding into gear as the two of us kept a maximum distance between our bodies. Conall kept his eyes on the road and I attempted to stealthily reach around and navigate the breach in my pants, which was seeping frosty air with every second. I needed to know if the ship had a small hole in the hull, or the whole thing was the size of the Titanic and going down in minutes.

105

Pretending I was scratching my lower back, but lifting my ass in a way that suggested I had hemorrhoids, I reached around and discovered the hole was enormous. There would be no hiding this catastrophe by performing simple subtle angles away from his eyes. My only alternative was to take off my jacket and hide the problem, just like in high school when you got your period in math class.

I unzipped my jacket and immediately felt the glacial temperature inside the truck. Conall wore a fleece jacket, outweighed me by a good hundred pounds and seemed unfazed by the frigid air. With painful resolution, I slid my arms out of my jacket and pretended the non-existent heat of the truck was too much for me in my paper-thin, cotton t-shirt Tommie had given me for Christmas. On the front, in large letters, it said, "Sorry. I'm awkward. Sorry."

With the same sadness a mother might have handing over a child, I took the coat and tied it around my waist. I sucked in air as the cold hit my skin, causing my innards to shrink and my nipples to react in an atrocious way.

Conall gave me a questioning look. I could see his breath as he said, "It's chankin the day."

"Huh?"

"Cold," he responded.

I laughed, saying, "Warm-blooded," as I wrapped my arms around my chest to cover the embarrassing problem occurring beneath my shirt.

"Really? Lil' lass like you? My sister twice your size and barely stan it."

My inner core had already dropped below normal limits and hypothermia was soon to follow. Historically, I wore sweatshirts in the middle of summer to battle the cold temperatures of air conditioning. I had minutes before I would succumb to the elements. I said, "Nah. I'm good. A Midwestern thing, I guess," and scoffed. Truth be told, I'd rather face my OB-GYN for a uterine scraping than face cold temperatures. I resisted the urge to curl in on myself like a fetus.

"I'd turn down the heat," Conall said, messing with the controls, "but I don't have it on."

"You don't say," I said, despondent, rubbing my cords to spark warmth. I peered out the window and attempted to think warm thoughts, checking out the wool on the sheep as we passed. In my cold, deranged mind, I saw myself wrestling one down and pulling the wool from their bodies and stuffing it into my armpits. Conall drove with his hands at ten and two, as I slowly died in his cold cave of a truck. It was possible that when we reached our destination, he'd open the door and some frozen form of myself would fall to the ground—a replicated frozen Neanderthal.

"I dinna ken what came over me," he said.

At full speed, the engine noise was horrendous. "What?"

"The kiss. I should explain," he yelled.

I sighed and curled over, trying to retain heat. "Please don't," I pleaded, as my hands took on a bluish tint.

"But I should," he said, a worried look on his face. "Are you OK?"

"*About the kiss?*"

"Well, no." He shook his head. "I mean yes."

"It's a little late to be worried."

"You're taking this all wrong."

"I don't think so." I curled my hands into fists because I couldn't feel them anymore. "We kissed."

"It was a moment," he said.

"Yup, it was. One moment."

He paused, scratching his forehead. "Ye dinna seem to mind. Ye kissed me back."

I found the courage to look him in the face. "Can we *please* not talk about this?"

"Sure, sure. Sorry." There was an entire second of silence before he added, "And you're not puny. I dinna mean that."

"I *am* puny."

"I was—"

"I know," holding up a hand, bringing the conversation to an end. "Believe me, I know."

We drove into town, past a few quaint shops and a post office. I decided that if I did manage to live through this experience, I was going to take a bath in a vat of coffee and ask for a lobotomy. As we were rolling through town, I saw a small, blinking neon sign advertising coffee.

"Hey, you think we could stop?" I pointed at a cafe called 'The Teacup.'

Conall slowed the vehicle. "There? Now?"

Without thinking, I said, "No. Let's try the hardware store. Just after the apocalypse, when they're giving it away for free."

Conall pursed his lips, displeasure written on his face as he brought the truck to a complete stop in the middle of the street. It didn't make any difference; there wasn't any other traffic. And I refused to apologize when I was freezing to death, showing my underwear, in a vehicle with a man that I'd kissed without ever knowing his name. "If you park the truck, I'll buy." I said, hoping to make peace. I saw the deserted nature of what could only be called a *village*. "Or maybe around here, you can just leave it. What do you want?"

Conall sighed, which had no effect on my compulsion to get caffeine or be warm for five minutes. He reluctantly pulled into a parking spot. "OK."

I opened the door, "So?"

He sat, staring at the front door. "What?" he asked.

"Do you want something?"

"I thought you were getting coffee."

"Yes. But what do you want?"

His forehead creased in confusion. "Coffee."

I couldn't figure out if the guy was slow or deliberate. Everyone I knew used at least three adjectives when ordering coffee.

He shook his head and got out. I followed him by falling out of the truck, almost going to my knees. I ran my hand down my coat to keep it flat and hide to the world that I was wearing lime green underpants.

Conall's head hit a door chime as we walked in and he reached above to silence it, like it was something he'd done many times before. The Teacup was about the same size as its namesake, with some similarities to a little old lady's house. There were some decorative porcelain plates on the wall, small egg baskets hanging from hooks, and little tea sets on precarious ledges. Overall, it was a considerably cozy and warm café, with four round tables and various pastries sitting on the counter.

A woman who was slightly older than Conall and myself with an incredible gravity-defying crown of brown curly hair was managing the place. She had a white apron tied around her substantial body. It had that unfortunate round, oblong shape, heavily endowed with huge breasts, but paired with rod-thin legs. She was stirring something on a small stove behind the counter. From the looks of the menu board, they did a lunch service that included sandwiches and a few soups. I took two deep breaths and

109

felt my body uncoil from itself, the heat allowing my muscles to relax for first time in many minutes. My fingers tingled and I felt my cheeks turn red with the heat.

I was still staring at the menu board and considering my coffee choices, when I heard a high screech and Conall's name yelled out, followed by raucous laughter.

"Ah, Conall, how's you, ya wee scunner! I've missssssed you!"

Holy-high-pitch-wonder, Batman.

At her eardrum-busting-octaves, I resisted putting my fingers in my ears to protect my hearing. Conall and I both took a step back, the two of us accidently bumping into each other. I stumbled sideways until Conall reached down and pulled me upright by the back of my shirt. I was surprised and alarmed that another piece of clothing might meet a bad ending. He quickly let go.

"GAWD! Good to see ya!" Again, the decibel levels were stratospheric, rattling my head.

"Morning, Davina," he said resigned, keeping his eyes on the board in some infantile-middle-school way to keep looking right at her. Davina did not seem fazed at Conall's less than mediocre effort to socialize. She leaned forward and put her sizable goods out for display and I became very worried for the scones that lay in harm's way.

"Wow. It's warm in here." I said and smiled. "Toasty," and rubbed my hands together. Conall saw my smirk and narrowed his eyes. The situation was inflating my low self-esteem, making me feel buoyant. Righteous, that's another word that came to mind. My mojo back, the warmer temperature bolstered my confidence. If I hadn't been flaunting my underpants, I'd been floating in that coffeehouse.

Davina scrutinized me, and she frowned, several crease marks lining her forehead. It was obvious that I did not bring her joy.

110

"Coffee then?" I said to lighten the mood, and held up my money with enough enthusiasm I resembled a customer wanting a lap dance. My American accent threw her and she looked to Conall for explanation.

He said, "Car. Rental," in a way that inferred something closer to 'Girl Rental.'

Wow, I thought, *with that kind of witty conversation, no wonder he kisses strange girls that wander into his bedroom.*

"Right," I said. "You do cappuccinos?" Davina read my shirt, her eyes skimming my right shoulder and hesitating a bit too long as she considered my question. "Or maybe just plain coffee?" I said. "Whatever you got."

"I can do a cap, sure," Davina said, keeping her eyes on Conall and smiling. I tightened the jacket around my waist and walked around the coffee shop, allowing the two locals to have their romantic teatime. There was WiFi and I used the time to check emails and try to take care of the Trevor problem that was hijacking my vacation. As Davina set to work, she asked Conall questions, which he answered like an English pilot captured by a German spy.

"Whatcha bloody been up to then?" she asked.

"Oh, Nothing."

"I haven't seen ye in a while."

"Busy."

Davina wouldn't be denied, "So Saturday, Richie had one roarin gig at his place, but ye didn't mak' it, you naughty boy." Snort, snort.

"Edinburgh."

"What ya doin' there, huh? Huh?"

Conall looked over his shoulder. "Stuff."

111

I wandered further into the café, looking at every object plastered to the walls. Davina's laughter boomed off the walls and hit my ears like shotgun shrapnel on tin. Only when I heard the high-pitch noise of steam heating milk, did I wander back to the counter for coffee. I took out money as she placed two Styrofoam cups on the counter, and said, "I'll pay for whatever he's getting too."

Davina's smile was all graciousness. "Ah, he doesn't pay here, love. Conall gets whatever he wants."

"Wow," I said, all surprise. "*Wow*," repeating myself. I couldn't quite contain my glee. "Conall gets whatever he wants," giggling with the same delight as a school-age kid who has learned school is dismissing early. I picked up my coffee and muttered, "Good to know."

Conall turned away, a sour look on his face. I gave her money, thanked her and told her to keep the change. She made change anyway and put it on the counter.

"Thanks," Conall said, with as much sincerity as a man getting a death sentence. When he reached for his coffee, Davina, quick as lightning, grabbed his wrist before he got away.

"So, Conall," she laughed, high-pitched and throaty. I resisted the urge to slap her on the back to bring it down an octave. "Some folks gettin gether Saturday night. You should come, yeah." She turned her body to create a wall and keep me from hearing, which was impossible.

"Ah, nah, can't, sorry," he mumbled, before jerking his hand back and causing Davina to fall forward. He headed for the door faster than I'd ever seen him move before. He mumbled, "Busy," over his shoulder and tilted his head in perfect timing to miss the door chime. I was still in a stupor from the full-frontal advancements and hadn't even begun to drink my coffee. I held it before my mouth like an Alzheimer's patient who'd forgotten she was holding it.

He stopped and turned. "You comin'?"

"Right," I said, glancing at him, and then Davina, trying to process a few things. I held up my coffee, "Right! Thanks a bunch. Lifesaver," and started a slow death march to the front door and the ice-cold truck waiting for me.

Conall watched my slow steps and whispered, "Hurry up."

"Coming, Romeo," I said, sliding past him. "I'm tripping over your girlfriends."

Conall's meaty hand pushed me and I cursed as I fell towards to the sidewalk. He grabbed my arm and hoisted me up, saying, "Sorry. Sorry," as my coffee almost spilled.

I rebalanced my cup and licked a few spilled droplets on my wrist. "Wow. You treat all your women this way?" I made sure the lid was still on. "Ease up. I'm puny, remember?"

He rubbed his hand over his forehead in dismay, his weight moving back and forth between his feet. He appeared ready to run a fifty-yard dash. From Davina. Or me. Hard to say. He said, "It's just both incidents . . . isn't me, OK?" He held out his arms. "Her . . . me . . ." shaking his head.

I raised my hand in understanding. "Got it. Say no more." I walked towards the truck, saying over my shoulder, "Believe me. Had a few of those mishaps myself."

He said, "What? No. Davina and I . . . no."

"Whatever, Romeo."

"Don't say that!"

I thought I'd steeled myself for the frontal blast, but I was sorely mistaken. It was worse than before. After rejoicing in the heat of the coffee shop, going back outside was some kind of inhumane punishment. I clutched the coffee to my chest and tried to siphon heat from it, as I threw myself into the truck, feeling my pants rip some more. Once seated, I slurped the coffee and tried to think hot, burning thoughts. Conall lumbered after me, sitting there, as I succumbed to the cold all over again.

He stared at the coffee shop. In the window, Davina was wiping down the countertop and putting items away. Conall fiddled with his coffee, and then his keys. Maybe he did care for her after all. Maybe they kissed under the door chime on a regular basis.

He said, "It's not like you think."

It's exactly like I think. "I'm not thinking anything except about you starting this truck," I said, hunched over and freezing.

"What?"

"The truck," and I motioned turning a key with my hand. "Heat?"

"Why aren't you wearing your coat?"

"It's not that warm."

"Fleece?"

"The car? Are we getting my car?"

"Yes," he said, snapping out of his revelry and starting the engine. Tepid heat leaked from the vents that would not have been warm enough to melt ice. He put the truck in gear and looked behind for non-existent traffic, saying, "I never dated her," as if he was apologizing.

"Really? She's into you." I shrugged, drinking half my coffee and wishing I'd ordered two. "Maybe you should."

We started our slow drive down the road, the truck lumbering in first gear, the transmission whining as he slid it into second. He muttered, "That'd be a cold day in hell."

I sighed, took another swallow of coffee, thinking, *well, my friend, I think that day has arrived.*

114

*　　*　　*

Emails:

From Tommie Calhoun

To Natalie Calhoun

Subject: Current situation

Hello? Report in.

*　　*　　*

From Tommie Calhoun

To Natalie Calhoun

Re: Current situation

Dude. Answer your emails.

*　　*　　*

From Tommie Calhoun

To Natalie Calhoun

Re: Current situation

Have you gone AWOL? This email thing is for shit. Respond ASAP.

Just made a few quick inquiries with my friend who's currently working out of a local office. You might want to loosen up your

115

pocketbook and give me a call. We got issues. Or not. Depending upon how much you wanted to clean house, so to speak.

-Tommie

*　*　*

Because of dropping temperatures and calamitous underwear events, I needed to get to the rental car quickly. I wanted to be alone in a small space with maximum-vented heat. But we kept driving and driving, which worried me. The trip was taking too long and I couldn't maintain this charade with my exposed underpants much longer. We drove outside of town, away from the pristine cottage shops and small painted houses. There were unspoiled pastures and peaceful, grazing sheep, which moved at free will, sometimes right up on the road, crossing at their leisure.

"Where's the fences?" I asked.

"Huh," Conall asked, surprised I was talking and the change of subject.

"Fencing?" I asked again. "I don't see any." It was just rolling hills as far as the eye could see. "It seems weird. Everyone has fences."

"Nah, not around here. The animals just graze. This isn't the States, with everything corralled into bloody barbed wire."

I looked out the window and didn't disagree.

After many miles into the country, we took a turn onto a long driveway that dead-ended at a yellow house with a wrap-around porch and a flower garden. Away from the house, I saw where the wife's domain ended and the husband's began; there were outbuildings in various degrees of disrepair, separated from the house by neat line of rose bushes. The repair shop/rental agency was more of an outlaying farm eyesore. There was a large barn, with various livestock and a closely situated shed next door, obviously for repairs, if the number of vehicles sitting around in the field were any indication. A group of men stood around a beat-up pickup, all

116

drinking coffee and talking, wearing coveralls or mechanics bibs. There was small, tiled building where a goat and a smattering of hens loitered and pecked at the ground.

"This it?" I asked. Of course it was, but I had to ask anyway. We'd barely spoken since leaving the coffee shop and the silence was killing me.

"Yup, my dad owns it."

I recognized Alec as the same guy who had met us at the airport. He was standing with the group, talking and motioning with his hands. The red Wisconsin hat was still on his head. Conall put the truck in park and watched the group, not moving.

"So, which one is mine?" I asked.

"Huh?" Conall asked.

"Dude, I got to go. Which car? Ferry remember? American holiday?"

"Right. We'll talk to my dad. He'll know."

I opened the door, but Conall grabbed my arm. Startled, I choked out a scream.

He cringed. "Sorry. Didn't mean to scare you."

"You did."

He still held my arm, his hand like a vice-grip. "You're cold."

"Dude? My arm?"

He motioned to my right shoulder. "How'd ye get the scar?"

"What? Let go."

"The scar."

For Pete's sake. How many times had this been asked? So many times it was impossible to count. Every time, I answered differently. Every single time. It was no one's goddamn business except my own. So I always turned it into a comedic moment. Even Trevor was clueless about its origin, and my family had remained silent on my orders.

"Just interested, no? Can't help myself." He let go and pulled up his shirt, showing me a scar on his lower right side. "We all got 'em, no?"

"Please," I said. "That's an appendectomy scar. Everyone's got those. About as common as a C-section scar."

He gave me a confused look. "How—"

"Was it? Your appendix?" I asked, indignant. I knew it was.

"Well, yeah . . ." he seemed flustered. "What's yours?"

Not now, with a guy I barely knew, whom I would never see again. The scar was superficial, but its roots ran deep.

"Bronco riding. Midwestern thing."

"What?" he asked and laughed. "No, ye didn't."

I opened the door. He reached for me, but I was too fast.

"Wait!"

I jumped out and Conall followed. We walked towards the group, my ridiculous t-shirt broadcasting I was "weird," and my stupid jacket tied around my waist. I don't think I could've done a better job advertising myself as an American geek. The men watched me approach and read my shirt, so I crossed my arms to retain heat.

"She be needin another car," Conall said, sighing. "Which one?"

The men stared, confused.

"Remember," Conall said, frustrated. "The one we picked up from Lochmaddy?"

After a moment of silence, Alec took off his hat, scratched his head and surveyed the surrounding cars. "The Citron then?"

One of the guys said, "The clutch is wonky."

"The newer Focus's fine. Give her that one."

"Red?"

"Brown."

"I could, but dinna the oil needin be changed?"

"Oh, it's fine, just need to find the keys?"

"Aren't they in the barn?"

"Dinna know."

"Last I saw them."

I could have aged another twenty years in this field and these guys would've still been having the same conversation. This was not how I imagined my vacation when I stared at picturesque images on Internet searches. Making matters worse, the hens had migrated our direction in search of fresh ground pickings. Their presence alone was making me nervous. A rusty-looking hen was getting close and avidly interested in my shoes. As the men continued to talk, I shooed her away with my foot, but she came back with a vengeance.

"Wait?" one of the workers said, "The red one had an oil change last week, no?"

"I think so?" another commented.

I said to Conall, "Decisions usually take this long?" as I took several steps to the side, moving away from the hen.

"Always like this, they canna never make up their minds. The tourists beat up the cars on the narrow roads and then they need work. It's a constant patch-work process."

"Obviously," I said. The hen aggressively went for my shoelaces, and I pushed her away. Again. This time she squawked and flapped her wings, distressed and obnoxious. Conall looked over and I smiled tightly back, similar to a beauty contestant who'd been awarded second place. I could feel anger build within me, boiling, but not warming me enough to make a difference.

The men continued, "No, the tires were done last week."

"Nah-uh. Had to go get bloody parts."

"For what?"

No one was making a decision and I was losing time. I said, "I'm freezing, Conall. I need a car," rubbing my arms to keep warm. I kept my eye on the bitchy Rhode Island Red as her head bobbed, strategizing her next move. Keeping me distracted, her friends organized around her; some plain domestic white and a fancy breed with feathers sticking out of its head like a jungle headdress. They always had more courage in packs, those wicked women.

He said, "Why dinna you put on your jacket?"

"How 'bout I get a car?" I spit out.

In the meantime, the hen was not giving up. She could smell the chick genocide on my shoes. She flanked from behind and I turned, catching her in the act. It was apparent this female horde had learned some fancy tricks from the local geese.

Keeping my eye on the poultry, I heard one of the coffee drinkers say, "Alec, the Citron's breaks are a bit wonky too."

"I know, I know."

The chickens circled, constantly moving to keep me confused on their whereabouts.

120

"Then, it's the green Focus, no?"

"I guess. Who's seen the keys?"

How many times could we cover this?

"Maybe the peg board," one said, taking a drink of coffee.

I'd lost the feeling in my fingers and I was now "nipping out." I caught Conall staring. My breasts were distracting him from the fact that we were now being circled by vicious group of hens and his father and his cronies were taking just as long as a chicken to lay an egg.

"OH, FOR FUCK'S SAKE," I screamed, jerking the jacket from my waist and putting it on, the chickens dashing around my feet in a frenzy.

All conversation stopped. I zipped the jacket all the way up to my chin and relished that something was covering my bare arms. I was not going to die of the cold after all. In all crucial moments, there was a time to try to keep a brave face and push on, regardless of casualties, and there was a time to pack it in, hanging out your laundry for efficiencies sake. I'd suffered more than a lime green panty disgrace before.

I turned to Conall; he must have seen my rage because he took a step back. "I'm freezing to death, Conall." I pointed to his truck. "Couldn't you have turned on the heat?"

"You said you were fine! That you were warm-blooded."

"I was lying! Look at me." I held out my arms "What about me says, *warm-blooded*?" The men turned our way and took small steps, eager to hear the conversation. "I hate the cold. Hate it!" I screamed.

"Calm down," he said, motioning with a hand, indicating I should lower my voice.

I bent over and showed him the enormous hole in my pants. I might as well have asked for a kick in the ass. "My pants are ripped. I am wearing green underpants!" I yelled. I pulled at the material, ripping them to the front zipper. This might be a good time to mention that *Let's go back to bed* had been printed on the back. I would only discover this later, adding to my embarrassment.

I pointed at the hole. "I ripped them getting in your absurd monster truck! And had to use my coat to cover my . . .my . . . what's the word?" I screamed.

He smiled. I was too mad to realize it was the first time I'd seen it since the kiss.

He cleared his throat and said, "Knickers."

"Right, my lovely *knickers* are on display." I waved my hand at the onlookers. "For everyone."

The men chuckled under their breath, but I was more concerned with the fact my tantrum had incited something in the chickens. Several had advanced, taking cues from the red, which was landing vicious beak blows to my feet. In one swift, professional move, I picked up the red slattern ringleader, holding her feet and tucking her under my arm so she couldn't make ruckus with her wings, hitting me in the face. I'd done it thousands of times as a kid. Mostly when it was time to butcher them. The key was to be very fast and the cold was making me exactly that.

I held the chicken like a sawed-off shotgun. "Where are the keys to the green Focus?"

They stood staring, mouths agog. One snapped out of his stupor and pointed to the barn. "Just inside the door, on the wall. Take it."

I wasn't an auto thief. I just wanted a car. "Great. It's mine for the next two days." I walked closer to Alec and said, "You need me to sign a piece of white printer paper? Or are we good?"

He nodded, staring.

122

I marched over to the barn, past the men, carrying the chicken, giving everyone a good view of my panties. A northern breeze blew through my underwear and all the way to my core. Several of the men clapped, and I held up my hand and waved with my middle finger. I found the labeled keys, exited the barn and tapped the fob. Headlights blinked on the most atrocious green compact car that had absurd enlarged side mirrors, possibly taken from another vehicle in a salvage yard. Walking by Alec, I said, "Check the piston rings on the other one, maybe the clutch too."

He smiled and said, "OK." As I walked further on, he said, "Do you do mechanical work?" like he was offering a job.

I stopped and turned. "Of a sort, but not this." I pointed to his cap. "And another thing, Wisconsin's a good team, but it's an odd choice for a guy from Scotland." I narrowed my eyes. "Really? The Badgers?" I gesticulated with the chicken, although she didn't seem to mind. "Maybe you should pick Notre Dame or something? For the Catholic connection?"

He laughed, shaking his head and glanced to Conall a split second before glancing back. "I'll stay with Wisconsin if ye don't mind." He took in the rip in my pants, glanced at the chicken, and said, "All right then. Off ye go, wee bear cub," and tilted his head towards the car. "Take the chicken if ye want."

I spoke to no one as I walked to the car and unlocked it. I threw the chicken into the air, where it maintained flight for about two seconds, hit the ground and scurried away. I got in, turned over the engine and blasted the heat. Putting the car in gear, I gunned the motor and roared off. Driving away, I saw Conall waving me down in the rear-view mirror.

I kept going.

7

From Trevor Smith

To Natalie Calhoun

Subject: Deadlines

You need to call me at the number listed below. Had to get a new phone. The landline at the house isn't functional either. For various reasons. So . . . just call.

Trevor

* * *

Emails:

From Tommie Calhoun

To Natalie Calhoun

Subject: Starting to piss me off

Where the hell are you? You're freaking me out. Your phone is going straight to voicemail. CALL. ME. IMMEDIATELY. Use my Watts line. You know the number.

And by the way, how resilient would you rate Trevor? Just Girl Scout cookie prepared or Marine boot camp ready?

-Tommie

* * *

I drove to the inn. I had just enough time to sneak inside, take a quick shower, change my pants and get to Sean and Dad before we left for the ferry point at Berneray. Running into the bathroom, I was seized by panic as I only saw a *bathtub*. Something about it always seemed a bit unsanitary, sitting in dirty water that eventually turned cold anyway. Yes, I know, such posh, privileged American thinking.

The tub had different taps for the hot and cold water, just like nineteenth century plumbing. I sat cross-legged in the tub and mixed the water in my hands, as I attempted to wash out the shampoo. It was a discombobulating affair, alternately scalding my head and freezing me to death. In the end, I filled the damn thing, shampooed my head and submerged, trying to not imagine hairy asses, foot fungus and rotten toenails.

I was pulling on my pants when Sean and Dad bust into the room.

"For the love of . . ." Sean shouted, covering his eyes. Dad tripped, then backed into the hallway.

"Oh my God!" I screamed, jerking on my pants and buttoning them. "I thought you guys were eating breakfast."

"A shower? Why are you changing your pants?" Sean asked.

"It was a *bath*. And I wanted to, all right?" I was out of breath. "Breakfast?" I said to change the subject.

"They don't start serving for another thirty minutes."

"Really?" I asked.

"Do you think we'd be here if it was open?" Sean said with some exasperation.

125

Dad peered in, "How'd it go? Any problems?"

"You changed your pants?" Sean asked again.

I said, "Yes," losing my patience. "Got a bit dirty," running my hands through my unruly hair. "The rental place is on a farm."

"Big surprise there," Sean responded. "Sheep?" he asked.

"No. Not that I saw. A goat."

"Wow. I would have placed even odds on the sheep. Anything else?" Sean asked, raising his eyebrows.

I kept a straight face. "Nope."

We left Lochmaddy, driving through undulating hills with small cottages tucked into the curves and nestled close, similar to small children wrapped into blankets of green. Sheep wandered among the hills and next to the road, raising their heads as our car motored by. We found the ferry pick-up point and cued up with other vehicles already waiting in line. The three of us got out of the car because it was going to be awhile before boarding, and with rising sun, it was a waste to not venture out. I went to a small outbuilding, hoping for coffee, but found only bathrooms. Sean walked to the end of the dike. I watched his profile against the blue water. It was an image straight from a postcard as he stood at the brink of the world, another realm waiting on the other side.

I thought of those first early explorers, Columbus, Delgado, Coronado, who thought they might fall off the edge of the earth or slip off into an abyss where dragons and other sea monsters were waiting. The water lapped at his feet and the eastern horizon lay unbroken beyond him. I took one picture and left it. At some point, you need to put down the camera or device and try to remember. Sean stood there, a lone figure surrounded by ocean and islands, rugged, rocky outcroppings, on a piece of land constructed thousands of years ago in a burst of molten lava that crafted renewal and destruction. I told myself that at the very end of my life, I would still remember this moment and it would give me comfort.

126

Boarding, parking a mere two inches from the car in front of us, we left our car and followed the line of people to an ensconced glass lookout level with a sitting area. The captain opened a small office the size of a broom closet and proceeded to walk around gathering tickets and saying hello to everyone. I've never met a happier person. A woman sitting at a table in front of us pulled an entire tea set from a tote bag. She poured herself and her husband a "spot" of tea and then the two of them talked over a bit of biscuit.

Before boarding, each of us had one cup of coffee. Nothing but vending machine coffee was available on the ferry. Although I love coffee and will take it in almost form, for some reason, I always drew the line at vending coffee. How long does it stay inside in the machine? Especially in far reaching islands in the North Sea? None of us said it, but these traveling hours were the longest any Calhoun had gone in the morning without coffee. If we'd been home, we'd be yelling at one another and thinking about small acts of violence.

An hour later, we docked on the Isle of Harris at Leverburgh and followed the line of cars as we debarked from the ferry to solid ground. I was driving and told Sean about an old church called St. Clement's in Rodel that was built in the sixteenth century and was three miles away. The guidebook had spoken of it in great length and I assumed we'd make it our first stop.

"Why would we go there?" Sean asked, confused.

I stared at him. We were in Scotland and were surrounded by numerous structures that existed before our country had been called a wilderness. This place was in the top ten of the entire area. "Because it's two minutes from here and I want to see it. It's extremely old."

"It's a pile of rocks."

Sean had gone to Brown, eventually earning a CPA. For a moment, I thought he was taking barbiturates and I didn't know it.

"You don't know," I said. "You haven't seen it. We're so close. I came hundreds of miles to see it."

127

"You did not. Keep driving. There's islands to see."

"They talk of it in the book—"

"Keep driving. There's fish to find."

Normally, operating on regular coffee strength, I would have fought and won the battle. I was at the wheel for God's sake, but it seemed too early in the morning to be picking fights and putting everyone in a bad mood. I could see us walking the perimeter of the place while Sean made indiscreet comments, "Oh, look. A bit of rock! Oh, look, there's more! Old rock over here! Can you believe it Natalie? More rock!" We were already on the road that would take us north to the Isle of Lewis and I couldn't garner the strength to fight him.

The Isle of Harris is considered one of the most beautiful islands of the Hebrides and it isn't any lie. It's only twenty-one miles long, but with soaring mountains, it seemed three times that size and had lagoon quality water lapping onto pristine beaches. Every corner brought us to a stunning and unobstructed vista. We stopped numerous times to take pictures, only to realize every upcoming corner had another equally breathtaking view. Sean made me stop several times so that he could get out and ramble about, staring at streams, trying to spot fish. I considered throwing the tour book at him to knock him into the water.

About an hour into the drive though, we had a SERIOUS problem. Careful inspection of our persons would have revealed a certain nervousness blooming within the car—tapping fingers, erratic glances, and a constant repetitive hand motion to grab a non-existent something from a cup holder. To utter the word, to think of the dark liquid would make the problem feel much worse. No one said anything, but we could hear the whisperings in our head. *Coffee, coffee, coffee.*

We fidgeted in our seats and prayed the caffeine headaches wouldn't start, looking with desperation at every small village. Most places only had a few houses, with no businesses of any kind. Where Americans opened shops as early as possible, moving that time forward an hour every year until it became a 24/7 business, in the

Hebrides, they were perfectly fine with staggering in around ten o'clock, if the kids were off and they'd had their breakfast.

About two hours later, we spotted a village with some substance and saw a sign advertising the 'The Temple Cafe.' We turned the corner and sauntered down a small street with cottages on both sides. It appeared deserted, except an elderly woman walking up the middle of the street, boots on her feet and a scarf tied over her head.

I slowed down and pulled close so that Sean could roll down his window and engage her. She was a native; thin, and angular, like she could have been carved out of one of the mountains. As Sean leaned out of the window, I watched him don *the persona*.

Sean can be the most polite and gracious individual, but not necessarily to his siblings. Small children and elderly flock to him and are bowled over by his humor and his way of making them feel important and cherished. As his sister, I have never felt any of this generosity, just watched it from afar and tried to copy it for my own sinister uses. For the record, I've mostly failed; there has to be actual resolve and sympathy to carry it off.

"Excuse me, ma'am," Sean asked.

The woman stopped and bent over to peer in the car window. It took whole seconds for this to occur; her eyes taking in the car, its inhabitants, even the trash on the floor, or it could have been my caffeine withdrawal causing hallucinations. "Yes?" she finally asked.

"We were hoping to find some coffee and was wondering if there was a place in town."

She smiled and said, "Oh, you're over from the States!"

Crap, I thought, *this is going to take forever.* After years working in the hospital, I was used to conversations only containing essential facts. No one wasted time on idle words. Consequently, my conversational skills and patience with friendly banter was limited to almost nothing. I fought the urge to just hit the accelerator and make

129

circles around the town searching myself.

Sean beamed, "Yes, that's correct. On holiday."

"Isn't that lovely! And are you having a wonderful time?" she asked.

"Oh, it's been great," he responded, mentioning several things about the beauty of the area, the majestic mountains and the color of the water. The two of them got on like old war correspondents. I rolled my eyes and my hands gripped the steering wheel in frustration.

The conversation between them droned on and on, and I became more agitated as the seconds ticked by and we were no closer to coffee. Even though he was being monstrously polite, *I WANTED COFFEE RIGHT NOW. RIGHT NOW.* All I could think was, *ASK HER. WHERE IS THE COFFEE SHOP? HOW HARD CAN IT BE TO FIND COFFEE???*

In my semi-crazed state, I overheard Sean saying, "Would you know where there is a place selling coffee in town by chance?"

Thank you, thank you, thank you.

The woman straightened and glanced around, as if she was seeing her hometown, of approximately twenty houses in an entirely new light.

"Well," she said, "I believe there's a place down the street that sells coffee."

Sweet Moses, there is a God. She believes . . .

She kept her eye on the street as she continued, "And I believe they sell other things as well, like pastries." She turned back, "For the visitors and such. Especially in the summer. It's a place where people go."

You build it and they will come.

"It's a building shaped like a boot. At the end of the street."

Sean said, "Oh, that's wonderful." My foot eased off the brake and the car moved forward an inch. He narrowed his eyes at me and turned back. "Great. We'll give them a try."

She smiled broadly. "Yes. Give them a try. And if they aren't open, just walk right across the street and knock at their house. If they aren't open, they'll make you a cup at their house."

We all stared agog. I pictured myself knocking on a random person's door asking for coffee and then getting hit upside the head.

Sean chuckled, "Oh, ok, we'll look for the boot-shaped building then."

She laughed, "Yes, at the end of the street." She wished good luck on our holiday as we drove away.

"Boot-shaped building?" I asked.

Sean laughed, "Well, if that doesn't work, we'll just knock on their door."

We came to the end of the street. There was a building that had a round circular quality that mimicked the toe-portion of an old boot with an attached annex that could have been the leather section that tied up your calf. It was, in fact, similar to a boot on its side, sitting on a beach of the most perfect inlet of perfect blue water. I pulled into the parking lot. The view was tranquil and quiet, with perfect cottage homes lined up in a fairy-tale community.

The coffee shop didn't appear open, but the front door was cracked.

"It looks closed," I said.

"Possibly," Sean said, "but we need to try." When I didn't move, he nodded towards the door, "Well, go on."

"Me? You go."

"I talked to the crazy lady. You get us coffee." *Ah, there's the brother I know and dislike,* I thought.

Desperate times required desperate measures. As I walked to the front door, I could hear the sounds of South American guitar music playing and the distinct aroma of melted, mouth-watering, diabetic-seizure-inducing-chocolate. I almost fell to my knees in prostration. I stuck my head around the door and saw empty tables, with stacked chairs and a counter with a woman behind it, working at a stove. She visibly started when I waved; Ted Bundy probably appeared just as friendly.

"Hi there," I motioned with my thumb to the parking lot, "we're just wondering if you might be open or if we could get coffee."

Her initial look was one of true annoyance. And frustration. It was 10:00 AM in the morning—enough time for any standard Starbucks to have served several hundred cups of coffee—but a sign said they didn't open until 11 AM. She recovered and wiped her hands on a towel, saying, "Well, we really aren't open. I was just doing a bit of cooking for the day, yah?"

Oh, I could *see* and *smell* it, making me ravenous and caffeine crazy. I was surprised that my fingers weren't scratching lines in the wood of the door and grabbing handfuls of my hair and jerking.

"Oh, OK, then, . . ." I didn't finish my sentence, the unspoken disappointment hanging there like an open invitation. I didn't move, hoping against hope, that my presence would somehow move her into action. It's the American way.

She stared at the chocolate, coming to some conclusion. "I guess I could make you some coffee to go, if you really want it. I just don't want the chocolate to burn." She was praying that I would decline; it was a battle of wills, of caffeine hopes, but when coffee is involved, I always ensure that I'm the winner.

"That'd be great!" I shouted and stepped into the house of delectable smells, doing a do-si-do to the counter.

I gave her our order, keeping it simple. She went to work making my latte and two very large coffees. I commented on the beautiful view. She didn't return my enthusiasm, doing her best to get rid of me as soon as possible and not burn the chocolate.

I pulled out my cash and saw some freshly baked scones as she put lids on our coffee. I inquired on whether I could buy three. She hesitated, and I realized that these items were for the customers that would be arriving later in the day with the lunch crowd, not the rowdy Americans who had the gall to show up in the early hours. She agreed and piled three in a to-go container.

I said thank-you three times and bowed like the Queen of England upon leaving. I walked outside and handed out the coffee and scones to the men-folk.

Sean stared at his cup. "Just one?"

"Yes," I said. "She's not even open. I held her at gunpoint to get that."

"No cream?" Dad asked.

"Listen princesses, you both got coffee. Don't be stingy."

Sean took a bite of his scone. "It's a bit dry," spitting dry pieces.

"I didn't realize I was travelling with Paris Hilton and her sister."

"Who?" Dad asked.

"Paris Hilton?" I asked. Dad gave me a queer look. "Pampered spoiled heiress?"

"Never heard of her," Dad said.

"Kim Kardashian?" I asked.

"Nope," Dad replied.

Sean sighed. "Zsa Zsa Gabor."

"Ah," Dad said, nodding.

*   *   *

We stopped at Tarbert; a coastal town with ferry links to Skye and went into the Harris Tweed Outlet store. We wandered the shoreline and found more coffee. We were headed to the island of Lewis, on the A859, when our stomachs started growling. Lunch was becoming a non-spoken issue, just like the coffee. We drove into Stornaway; an interesting wharf town named after visiting Vikings, which translated to "Steering Bay." The city had a one-way street system that had us driving in large circles over and over again to find a restaurant. Sean and Dad craned their heads to see out of the car windows, while I narrowly missed parked cars and pedestrians.

We got in a heated debate about fish and chips vs. decent real food that involved greens or vegetables, of any kind. We argued about eating Middle Eastern food, agreeing it was weird to eat kabobs in coastal European town. The argument wasn't a sound one, but the type of thing that happens among family members who are on the verge of cannibalism and thinking about turning upon one another for sustenance.

"So, fish and chips again?" I asked for the third time, as I accidently missed the side of the sidewalk and tumbled into the street.

"No," Sean said, grabbing my arm and jerking me back. "I need a salad. Vegetables. Something green."

134

I couldn't disagree. In the last several days, there had been a shocking amount of eggs, cooked meats and fish. Some smashed peas and boiled vegetables with not much flavor except the water that clung to them. By some miracle, we were able to find a very nice café, located in a hotel and the three of us ate salads, with appetizers consisting of an enormous plate of olives and a secondary course of onion rings. It was a strange lunch as Sean finished the meal with a sticky caramel toffee dessert as big as his head.

"Dessert?" I asked. "At one PM?"

"Yes," he said, shoving the caramel gooiness into his mouth. "I plan to eat it every day. Maybe twice a day."

Sean weighed about a buck fifty. Up to several years ago, I never knew he had such a sweet tooth. It seemed contrary to his whole personality.

"Every day? Really?" I asked.

"Every day. You want one?" Sean asked.

"No."

"Your mistake," he said, digging into the dessert. "I'm on vacation."

*   *   *

By some miracle, we made it to the Callanish Standing Stones several hours later. Between the wanderings on the island, figuring out lunch and navigating the signs, it was similar to stumbling upon an oasis in the Sahara. If you have no feeling for Scottish tourism, understand this: the Callanish Standing Stones was one of the most iconic tourism spots; every other photo had some version of them at sunset or sunrise, like a Scottish Stonehenge.

We parked in a lower lot and walked up a hill to the tourism building. The stone circle sat in a field that was bordered by farms. Sean mentioned there were cows next door, in a barb meant to bait me that we were going to look at "stones in a field." The tourist

135

center was the precursor to seeing the stones; a bit of history, the lore, maybe a slideshow and then you're escorted outside on a high level of mystic buoyancy.

Sean said, "Where are you going?" interrupting my thoughts.

I pointed. "The tourism center."

"Why?" he asked.

"Why?" I asked, looking at Dad and back in confusion.

"Because it's what people do. That's why." I responded.

"Not us. It's a trap. Let's go and see some *stones,*" Sean said, as if we were seeing a gravel pit on a construction site.

"Are you kidding me?" I asked. "You don't want to spend ten minutes getting some history?"

Sean headed towards a plank fence and said, "Heard and seen it all before."

I said to Dad, "Do you ever get the feeling that we're on the Cliff Notes version of a Scottish tour?"

"I heard that," Sean shouted. "Come on, let's go."

With some reluctance, I clambered over rudimentary fencing and headed uphill. Whatever reservations you might have about solitary pieces of granite, the stones were impressive. They were large and substantial, and someone had taken a very long time, doing an incredible amount of work with no help in the way of modern mechanics to get them erected. The stones were buried deep in the ground and had survived since Neolithic Era; 2900 to 2600 BC for you folks who can't conjure up these numbers from some obscure history class you took in high school. The center stone had an almost perfect north-south placement and there was some suggestion to lunar orientation. I preferred to believe the folklore that the stones were petrified giants who did not convert to Christianity.

136

I circled the outer perimeter and stood at the entrance, working my way inside. A man followed me who had a New Jersey accent and was talking to a woman taking pictures in the small dugout that once contained clay pots. She yelled, "Come down here and let's take a selfie!" Instead of the mystic, the current atmosphere was conjuring the Corn Palace in South Dakota.

Once the husband-wife team moved away, I waved Dad over and had him take a picture of me posing near the stones. I took one of Sean and Dad together. They would not pose in front of the stones, so the picture resembled a family portrait in the backyard of a farm in Kansas.

As Sean wandered off, he said, "Tell me when you've had enough of rocks."

I went back to circle and leaned up against one of the biggest rocks. I said under my breath, "I'm not at work."

Death chuckled, as he stood propped on the other side; his pork pie hat was perched back on his head, his Hawaiian shirt in pristine condition. "You're even more charming on vacation."

I rubbed a hand over my face, realizing I was really losing my sanity if I was having this conversation. "You had to come *here*?"

Death rubbed a foot over the grass and grunted. "Please. Been here a thousand times. This place is regular blood bath," laughing, his eyes full of mirth. "You should feel right at home."

I let the comment slide. There was a pause as the two of us watched tourists migrate in and out of the stones.

"Are you . . ."

Death shook his head, amused. "Heavens no. Trust me, when I come for you," he cleared his throat," you'll never see me coming." He paused. "Just like your mother."

137

A fist tightened around my intestines and squeezed. The campy outfit was amusing, but mere distraction. "So, you're just . . . hanging around?"

Conall appeared, walking around a stone. "No. I'm looking for you."

Startled, I coughed and stuttered, "Sta . . . stalker, much?"

"Please."

"You hang at tourist spots?" I narrowed my eyes, "To meet girls?"

He tilted his head in disgust.

"You need to work on your conversational skills," I said.

"If you're teaching, I'll pass."

I conceded the point and looked over my shoulder. Sean and Dad were watching from afar, wondering if this was some casual, "Hello," or more than that. There was really no way to explain this. Sean, by nature, was inquisitive. There was no way to hold him off for long. "So . . ."

"We want the chicken back," Conall said, with no preamble.

"*What?*"

"Kidding," he smirked.

"Aren't you funny."

"Ye forgot papers," he said casually.

"For the chicken?" I asked.

"*Aren't you funny.*"

As we stood among the stones—the giant and his wee companion—I couldn't deny the connection that floated between us.

I was drawn to him and the language we both understood. Trevor had never understood my cutting humor, nor did anyone else, aside from my own family. I took several steps until I was standing in front of him.

Conall held up a piece of paper. "The car registration, yeh?"

"You just don't leave it in the car?"

"Nah."

I took in in the stones and the surrounding fields. This place was in the middle of nowhere, other than it was a famous Scottish landmark. "Come on, how'd you find us?"

At the mention of *other* people, his eyes darted over my shoulder. "Who is *us* anyway?"

Interesting question, I thought. "My dad and . . ." I couldn't help the rather large sigh. "And my brother, Sean."

"Just family?"

"Yes. Family."

He glanced around and tried to guess which individuals had the sad fate of being related to me. I waved a hand in front of his face. "So, back to the original conversation on the illegal tracking of foreign tourists."

He scoffed. "Please. You're dangerous enough that I'm possibly doing my country a favor." He placed his index finger on my collarbone, and I could feel the heat of it through two layers. "Ye seem a bit . . . erratic," and smiled. He held up his cell phone and leaned forward, until our faces were very close. "All the rentals have a tracker and you said you were takin the ferry to Harris. Most tourists end up here eventually."

"Really? Your low rent, chicken fleet has trackers? I think that's as likely as me winning a congeniality award."

Conall said, "Ya a bit hard—"

"You don't know me," I said with more edge than I should have.

His eyes darted to my lips and back. "Agreed," he said in a low voice. He leaned further, his head dipping close to my ear as he whispered, "But we've kissed, so that counts for something, no?" As he took a step back, I felt the rub of his whiskers against my face and shivered.

"Nat?"

Sean's voice yanked me out of my trance and I tripped as I spun around. Conall grabbed my arm to keep me from falling and quickly let go, bringing his arm back before anyone could see.

"Easy," he whispered.

Sean walked towards us, his eyes narrowing as he took in Conall.

With some reluctance, I did the introductions. "Sean, this is Conall. He's from the rental agency. He picked me up this morning."

Conall cleared his throat.

"I mean," I stumbled, "picked me up for the car. I forgot papers." Conall turned his head, trying not to laugh. "Conall, this is Sean, my brother, and my dad, Martin."

They all shook hands. A very civil affair in a field containing large Neolithic stones.

Sean said, "Super nice of you. Was it necessary for you to come all this way?"

"Well, aye, you'd be needin the papers obviously, but after this morn—"

"The papers," I interrupted. "Where are they?"

Conall's head tilted back, rethinking his previous statement. Sean gave me a nasty look that said, *Quit being so rude.* Dad watched like he was figuring something out, but couldn't quite grasp the scope of the conspiracy.

"Oh, back in the car," Conall said, and pointed to the parking lot.

"Great, let's go," I said, and pulled on Conall's sleeve. He didn't budge. I jerked again and he ground his feet, refusing to move.

"Well, that's the thing," Conall said, pulling his arm free and directing his words to Dad and Sean. "My friend Brian brought me, so I wonderin' if I could catch a ride back to the ferry?" Abashed, he said, "I know, bit weird, yeh, but it would be helpful. Brian's goin to Lewis for the night to see his lass," his face curling into a smirk, "and I'd prefer *not* to hang out with the two o' them." He shrugged. "I need to get back to North Uist. There's a rental car in the parking lot."

Cumulatively, it might have been the most words I'd heard Conall speak at one time. Similar to Sean, Conall had dawned a type of personality to make things sound . . . legitimate. The entire statement took Sean by surprise, but he did his best to hide it. Dad didn't hesitate, saying, "Sure thing," and clapped his hands. "Seems a perfect plan."

I said, "What?" to no avail, the men already turning to walk down the hill. I was forced to catch up with them like a kindergartner left behind. In the parking lot, leaning against a Ford, was one of the coffee drinkers from earlier. Once we were assembled in a group, he introduced himself as Brian and shook hands with everyone. As Conall pointed out a few things on the paperwork, Brian caught my eye and winked mischievously, flapping his arms as if he was a chicken. I rolled my eyes, muttering, "For God's sake."

Brian laughed.

Sean looked up. "What's so funny?'

141

Brian motioned to me, "This wee lassie took one of the chickens hostage this mornin."

"Chicken?" Sean asked, "You took a chicken? At the rental lot?"

"I didn't take a chicken. It wasn't like that."

"Practically," Conall muttered, chuckling. "You held us at gunpoint with the damn thing."

"What?" Sean asked, smiling more than I'd seen him since the vacation started.

"Yes!" I said. "I took a chicken, OK?" I threw up my hands. "But I gave it back!"

"You didn't kill it, did you?" Sean asked. "Even Vegas would be worried about those odds."

Dad burst out laughing and Sean joined him. Brian and Conall just stood there confused.

"Long story," I said.

8

The four of us crammed into a car that was a European compact, something similar to a Toyota Corolla in the United States. It was not meant for three American tourists, plus a giant from Scotland who had to tilt his head so it wouldn't rub against the ceiling. After circling the car and arguing, it was decided that I would drive and Conall would take the seat behind me. Sean would be in the front seat navigating, and Dad would sit in the back next to Conall, who cursed as he ducked into the backseat, his knees wedging against my back.

Most of the islands had circular drives that took you around the perimeter for ocean views if they were big enough. If they were smaller, there was usually one rudimentary road right down the middle. On the way north to Lewis, we'd taken a western costal road through Harris that gave breathtaking views of its mountains and crystal blue-green lakes. The place spoke of forgotten magic, as if those Celtic stone circles could actually transport you back in time.

When plotting our return route, I noticed that there was a non-coastal eastern route through Harris that would take us back to the ferry point, but remembered that the tourist book had stated that this "cautionary road was not recommended for most drivers." The map showed this particular route as small and rudimentary. They had drawn in purposeful curves and if they'd done that, there really was a lot of turns. Most of the roads we'd driven were drawn in rather straight lines, even though there were incredible turns. With Conall in the car, I figured we would stick to the western route and get back to the ferry with plenty of time to spare, maybe time for a beer at the harbor bar. Sean would agree with me. He was cautious, as well as pragmatic, especially when liquor was involved and there was an unknown male entity sitting in the backseat.

As we approached the turn, Sean said, "We should try the other route. For something different. Maybe there's fishing."

"Ah," Conall said, concern on his face. "I dinna ken if that's a good idea."

Sean craned his head. "Why not?"

In the rear view-mirror, Conall give me a warning look. "It's challenging, no? Bit of a head knocker."

"Excuse me?"

"It's just . . . difficult."

"You think I can't handle it?"

Dad mumbled, "God help us."

Conall backpedaled. "Didn't say that. It's just a road that . . ." Conall mimed turning the wheel in crazy directions.

I recited to Sean what I had read in the book; that it might take us a while to navigate the road.

He seemed undeterred. "Take it."

"Really?" I asked.

"Yes. Why not?"

I glanced at Conall. "I don't want to be late for the ferry."

Sean pointed at the map. "We won't."

"I don't think . . ." Conall hastened.

"Take it," Sean said.

Dad said, "Natalie—"

"Ok," I said, swerving towards the exit, tires squealing, "Your call."

I remember thinking, *how bad could it be?* I had driven in the mountains, minimum maintenance roads and in every kind of severe weather, including an ice storm in the Vermont mountains, tornadoes in the Midwest and blizzards at home. Looking at the perfect blue sky, nothing could be so horrific to possibly hinder our way. The other propelling factors were my annoying brother was egging me on, and a Scottish male who'd kissed me and seen my panties alluding to the fact that I may not be up for the challenge. Something about the combined ratio of this male testosterone mania spurned me on, making me rise to the challenge. So, on a whim and a dare, we entered what Frost called "the road less traveled," and what ensued in the next minutes was what I would later call the "Calhoun Formula One Experience."

Immediately upon turning, I hear Dad exclaim, "Oh dear," in something similar to the church lady's voice when the coffee hasn't been made for the AA meeting.

And that, my friends, could have accurately described the entire experience. *OH. DEAR.*

The road was nothing more than a paved golf cart path, essentially one lane by US standards. It turned and weaved through hills and small mountains, rolling through small villages and over streams like a drunken highway engineer had planned it as a joke—a go-cart course for adult professionals. I'd never seen anything like it then or now. No wonder people avoided it. Something about its cautionary turns and dangerous road rating made me feel incredibly reckless. So, I did what came naturally to me.

I accelerated. Hard.

I heard Sean's sharp intake of breath and Conall curse. And I pushed on the accelerator some more.

"Nat," Sean hastened.

"What?"

"Pay attention!" Sean yelled, throwing his hands up to the dash.

145

I sped up over a sharp hill and careened downwards, keeping the speedometer at forty. I cranked it hard through a tight turn and all three men were thrown to the right; Dad giggling as his head knocked against the window. I popped over another hill—the windshield showing nothing but blue sky—and it's possible the front wheels left pavement for a second, as we were blind to anything but the mountains beyond. As our car tilted down with gravity, we met an oncoming car; a desperate game of chicken that had them honking and weaving, taking shelter on a passing point, and flipping us off as we whizzed by.

"Nat, slow down!" Sean yelled. "You're going to kill us!"

"I'm driving offensively."

"Oh," Conall said, jamming his knees into my back. "I'm glad it's been properly labeled then."

With a quick glance in the mirror, I saw Dad relaxed in the back and Conall doing everything in his power to keep his larger body from slamming into—or killing—him. I downshifted on the uphill, accelerated, then popped the car into neutral as we flew over hills, the engine revving and making monstrous noises.

Conall leaned forward and whispered, "And you wondered why all the cars were broken down."

It was a roller coaster ride that never ended. Sean threw his foot into the floor, looking for a brake or an imaginary clutch. When that didn't work, he threw his hands against the dash. The total mileage of the road was thirty-two miles and the posted speed limit was twenty miles per hour. At times, I pushed it to forty or forty-five, just to see if I could keep the car on the road. If Sean had been driving, it would have taken us several painstaking hours.

The ferry back to Lochmaddy was leaving at five o'clock sharp and nothing was keeping me from getting back on that ferry or getting to the bar beforehand. With beer on my mind and sibling recklessness pushing me, I wedged the accelerator to the floor and shifted to higher gears. I whispered to the old girl that she was built for it; her clutch whined in a way that suggested she wasn't.

146

I catapulted the car through small villages built right on the road. They had just enough room to park a car in front of the house, which was a mere inches from the road. It gave a whole new meaning to "door to door." As we rolled through one of these scenic towns, I was forced to the side by an oncoming FedEx van, but sped forward without braking. The van missed my side mirror by several inches and I kept my eyes glued to that exact spot, thinking of the rental. Sean scream out, "Natalie, the parked car!"

"What?" I didn't see any parked car and felt Sean was overreacting. "It's fine." I saw a flash of color to one side and the white of the van as it missed us by inches.

"Slow down! You missed that parked vehicle by an inch."

"It couldn't been that bad." I looked in the side mirror. There'd been some parked cars, but the large FedEx van seemed more important than tiny European cars that were something the size of a Starbucks coffee in the States.

Conall cleared his throat. "It was more like half inch, love."

With Conall's endearment, Sean gave him a strange look and turned his glare towards me, but said nothing.

I laughed with enough force that my side hurt. I was lost to the adrenaline rush and sped up to forty-five. Tears ran from my eyes, blurring my vision. Sean said, "You're out of your mind," as his fingers clutched the seat belt in a death grip. His eyes shot daggers when he wedged his arms into the dash or the door to keep from being thrown around. I rounded a hairpin curve and accelerated through the second half, almost losing the car over the side.

Sean screamed, "You're over the edge. Pay attention!"

"I am."

"You're not!"

I was still laughing. My vision was a bit wonky, so I wouldn't have been surprised if a leprechaun came stumbling across the road.

"I am going home in one piece, Nat," Sean said. "One piece."

Conall muttered, "I'd like to get the car back in one piece," as we rolled through another turn, the tires squealing.

Dad asked, "Is that a common occurrence?"

"No," Conall said, and stared at me in the mirror. "Not yet."

"You don't carry any whiskey, do you?" Dad asked.

"Starting tomorrow," Conall returned.

I continued to treat the whole affair as if it was my last day. With my earlier visitor, maybe it was. There was vast similarities between my life and this car ride; running headfirst into chaos or disaster without regard to personal safety or causalities. And there had been some. My family was used to it, but Sean refused to accept it. There was sweat building in my pits and dribbling down my back as I jerked the car back on the road after hitting a deep rut. I should've been worried, but after a lifetime of navigating frenzied disorder, I was used to standing on the edge and laughing at the abyss.

Forty minutes later, we saw a sign for Rodel, stating we were several miles from the town and the harbor point. Sean heaved a sigh of relief and bowed his head.

I giggled.

He gave me a scathing look. "Go ahead, laugh," he said, outraged. "*Hahahaha.* While you're mucking it up, I've come to the conclusion that you're unstable. *Unstable!* I know this because you just about killed us for the *sheer* fun of it."

"Whatever," I said nonchalantly, "It wasn't all that bad. I used the brakes." I grinned. "Sometimes."

"*Sometimes?*" Sean asked. "Never!"

Conall muttered, "At least you had the option of using of them, while the rest of us were just hoping you would."

Dad said, "She really never uses the brakes."

I lamented that Tommie wasn't in the car to witness the spectacle. He and I'd raced farm trucks on gravel roads until one of them had lost a transmission and we'd been grounded. As we rounded the last corner, I saw St. Clement's—the church that I'd wanted to stop at the beginning of the day. I pointed it out to Sean, driving by to impress upon him the beauty of the place. At that moment, a small wedding party exited the church. The bride and groom created a picturesque romantic scene and a group of people cheered their descent down the stairs to an antique car. Seeing their joy, I was glad we hadn't stopped. I had no desire to witness cheerful couples and their love in the midst of a Scottish countryside.

*　*　*

We made it to the harbor point in record time. I took a deep breath as I parked and noticed a deathly silence in the car. Sean was the first to move; he said nothing, got out, slammed the door and headed to the bar. It wasn't the first time I'd forced family members or friends to drink copious amounts of alcohol or seek refuge. Conall and Dad got out of the car and watched as I pulled myself from the seat. I put my hands behind my back to hide the fact that they were shaking. I smiled at Dad, giving him a wink.

Dad shook his head. "It's not funny, Nat. You shouldn't do that," he chastised.

"Do what?"

"You know what." He motioned over his shoulder with a thumb. "I'm headed into the bar to find the bathroom. Weak bladder in the face of the danger," and rolled his eyes. "You need to get inside," looking at Conall, and then to me. "And buy your brother a beer."

149

I nodded and watched him walk away. The adrenaline levels dropped lower within my system, causing a weakness in my legs that couldn't be ignored. A small giggle escaped.

Conall scratched his head, saying, "Is it funny?"

"What?"

He motioned towards the car. "Riding whatever ledge you're barely hanging onto?"

"Don't worry. Sean's just being a baby."

Conall stared at the ground. He said, "Right. Sure," and turned to walk away. He'd taken off his jacket and there was a thick scar that ran the back of his arm, from his shoulder to just above his elbow.

"You think I'm not?" I yelled, indignant.

He stopped. After several seconds, he walked back, getting very close to me. He bent at the waist, staring. His hands were on his hips, and whether he meant it or not, he was an imposing figure. I fought all my instincts not to take a step back and I think he knew it.

"It's just o' bit of my insight, no? But I keep thinkin that you're trying to convince *everyone* you got things under control. I'm dinna sure that ye do." He paused. "It's a good act, but I'm not falling for it." He raised his arms in indecision, "But what would I know? I've only kissed you." He tilted his head and placed his finger on my sternum, "And that was one hella of a kiss."

I had a decent amount of anger building, but with the mention of the kiss, I felt my rage fall away, which I think was his intention. It made me angry all over again. I was an intelligent woman with a fair amount of competence, but if you threw that, as well as my fears and insecurities into a pot to boil, eventually some combination of it was going to come pouring over the top and splatter all over the place, making a mess. So I did what I always did when forced into a corner to evaluate some hard truth. I sidetracked. "So, how'd you break your arm?"

He seemed confused, so I lifted my own arm, elbow out and pointed. "It took surgery, right? With a plate and some screws?"

Conall shook his head, disappointed, and headed towards the bar.

"Fine," I yelled, "Ignore me. But I'm right. I'm always right."

He stopped and with slow authority, turned around. I saw displeasure in every move. He crossed his arms and surveyed the surroundings, as if every word in his head needed precise thought. "Always diverting and running. Diverting and running. Do ye ever get tired? Must be exhausting."

"Not at all," I said. "And I'm guessing it must have taken some real blunt force trauma to do that."

Exasperated, he said, "Just forget it."

"Or . . . torque." I put it together in my head. "Like wrong angles . . .in . . . " I nodded, "a childhood dog pile gone wrong, . . . or," I pursed my lips, convinced of my greatness, "arm wrestling." I was guessing, but I was very good—many years, many scars, and many stories. It always worked when I needed to distract people.

For a period of time, we just stood there, with nothing but the call of the gulls and the door of the harbor bar slamming. I counted seconds to keep my mouth from opening up and all kinds of extraneous words spilling out. He looked down. "You win, Natalie." He sighed. "I give up." His eyes went all squishy as if the conversation gave him a headache. "Something like that." He took in my scar tissue. "And you?"

"Sky diving. Rope got caught around my shoulder."

"Really?" Conall asked, astonished.

I snorted. "No."

An ugly curse came out of his mouth that didn't bear repeating. "You're a piece of work, you know that?"

"Keep trying."

"Why bother? You don't want people to know you anyway."

I took his arm, making him walk with me towards the bar.

"Why are you like this?" he asked, pulling his arm free.

"I'm not like anything."

Conall grunted. "My dad says you're no different than an angry bear that's just escaped from a deadly trap."

I laughed at the absurd comment. "What's that supposed to mean?"

"Grateful to be alive, but trying to kill everyone in the vicinity anyway."

*   *   *

We entered the tiny bar and Conall hit his head on oars that were suspended from the ceiling. There was nautical theme evident in every weathered, wooden boating item attached to the walls. Sean and Dad were already halfway through their pints, at a tiny round top table that barely fit four chairs. Sean appeared in a better mood with an oatmeal porter in his hand. I sat and scooted close to him and he pushed me away, almost tipping over my chair. Conall sat next to Dad, laying his arms on top. The table tilted and our two beers sloshed and almost spilled.

"Have you forgiven me?" I asked, bumping shoulders with Sean. I pulled out my phone and turned it on. There was no WiFi, so I threw it back into my bag.

"No," he said.

"What about me?" Dad asked.

152

"No one's worried about you. You could die at any moment," I said.

Conall choked on his beer. "Wow. You guys always this endearing?"

"Always," Sean responded, sipping his beer. "Welcome to the family. You'd probably had better luck if you'd hitchhiked." He glanced out the window. "Or swam."

"I found them in the wilderness," Dad said.

I took a drink of my beer and grimaced. Staring at Sean, I asked, "Did you spit in this?"

* * *

The ferry ride was uneventful as we discussed travelling to Skye the next day. Skye was the largest of the islands and the one most discussed in tour books; whole novels had been written about its beauty. Conall gave us some helpful hints, but stressed, "You can't throw a rock without hitting a whiskey distillery or castle."

"Sounds perfect," said Sean, concentrating on some seals that were sunning themselves on a tiny island.

"I agree," Dad responded.

"We were just experimenting with beer," I said. "No one said anything about whiskey."

Dad leaned back and extended his arms. "The beer experiment has gone exceedingly well. I think it's time to move to on." He chuckled to himself, "to whiskey."

"Do you think that might be pushing it?" I asked.

"Like you said, I could die at any moment," Dad said.

Sean said, "I really don't want you to die on *my moment.*"

"Mother have mercy," Conall muttered.

153

Dad motioned to Conall. "I have a bad ticker," using his index finger to dramatically point at his heart.

"Don't be melodramatic. It was bypass surgery and an arrhythmia," I said, eating some stale crackers I'd bought in the vending machine.

"I could die at any moment," Dad said and sighed.

"He doesn't have brain cancer, just a pacemaker," I said.

"Just like the six-billion-dollar man," Dad said.

"It's the six-*million*-dollar man," I corrected.

"Inflation."

"He didn't have a pacemaker. He had bionic legs," Sean said.

"Close enough," Dad replied.

"There might not be enough whisky in Skye," Sean murmured to Conall, "to survive this."

We arrived in North Uist and exited the ferry. When we got to the parking lot, I asked Conall, "You need us to drop you at the parking lot?"

Conall's presence in the car was making me edgy and grumpy. Not only for his sheer size—it was similar to hauling Andre the Giant in a Geo Metro—but because he was scrutinizing my family and calculating my place within it. There weren't equations complex enough to adequately solve my existence.

"Oh," Conall said, "Yeah, guess so."

Dad added, "Well, if you're willing to risk your life further, you could drink with us at the bar, if you want. But we're not much company. Natalie seems intent to kill us off and leave our bodies for the animals."

I craned my head and gave my dad the *look.* For the record, Sean did it as well. At that same time, I hit the curb and the whole car lurched.

"Case in point," Dad said.

"Oh, drinks?" Conall said, "that be grand."

Dad said, "Great. I'll buy."

* * *

We did the single file march into the bar: Sean, Dad, Conall, and myself. The same barmaid from the previous night walked up and told us to take the table by the door. Once seated, she asked about our day and if we wanted beers. Sean and I agreed. Dad said, "No, I'll take a whiskey."

"No. He won't!" Sean and I said at the same time.

"I told you," Dad said. "Today is a whiskey day."

"There are no *whiskey days.* Nobody claims that *today is a whiskey day*," I said.

"I do," Conall said. "It's Scotland. It's tradition to claim it's a whiskey day. "

Dad pointed to his head with a finger, then gestured to Conall, as if the two of them were brothers in alliance.

I said to Conall, "You're a guest at our American table and not allowed to encourage him."

Dad laughed. "He is tonight. I'm the one buying."

I pulled money from my pocket. "How 'bout the distillery tomorrow?" I asked. "Why don't we hold off till then?"

Dad scoffed. "You don't even have enough to buy the first round."

155

The waitress stood confused, but also entertained. She looked to Conall, "The usual, love?"

The familiarity made Conall uncomfortable, but he nodded.

Dad held up a finger, "Your best Scottish whiskey."

"One small mediocre whiskey," I said. "Then no more." I leaned over, "Quit making me the responsible one."

"Don't worry," Sean said, "It happens so rarely, we treat it like a holiday."

There was raucous laughter from another table and a distinctive high-pitched squeal. In a corner, situated at a table full of women, was Davina: our coffee-mistress-busty-goddess-extraordinaire. She glanced several times our direction. Conall sat with his back to them and briefly closed his eyes in pain. The barmaid placed our drinks on the table, using special care with Dad's whiskey.

"There be more where that came from, love," she said, with a wink.

"Water of life," Dad replied, picking up the glass and inhaling.

"Sweet Moses," Sean sighed, slugging down his beer.

The barmaid left and there was awkward silence as we all sat and drank. Dad interrupted the moment by saying, "So, Conall, you've lived in this area for your entire life?" He hissed as he took his first sip and coughed.

Conall laughed. "Mostly."

We all waited, but he said nothing else.

Sean glanced to me, a single eyebrow rising.

"University in Edinburgh?" I ventured.

Sean nodded in approval. I was the master of reasonable guesses.

Conall scratched at his shoulder. "No, I did University in the States."

Our drinks hung suspended as we pondered this. Dad dramatically pursed his lips as he took another sip and Sean's mouth hung open. I just stared. The barmaid watched from afar like it was an entertaining TV show. She giggled and continued to pour more drinks.

"Really?" I asked.

"Really," Conall returned.

"Where?" Sean asked.

"*How*?" I blurted.

"Natalie," Sean warned.

"Sorry," I said, "I don't mean that you're stupid."

"Well, that's grand," Conall said.

"Jesus," Sean returned.

"My mom's from the States," Conall said. "Got dual citizenship." He took a drink of beer. "She wanted me to go and I did."

"You enjoy it?" Dad asked, sipping. His eyes were very narrow as he talked.

"Yes, very much." Conall said, inhaling a large breath of air and letting it go. "Been trying to work my way back, but . . ." I thought about the women talking about Conall taking over his father's *large* enterprise, "things can be difficult."

"Where'd you go?" Sean asked.

157

There was another brain searing laugh that stopped the conversation.

"Wow," Sean said, peering over Conall's shoulder.

I coughed, spit some beer and Conall handed me a napkin. "Thanks," I said, moping at my chin.

"Wisconsin," Conall said, ducking, which did nothing to lessen his large presence at the table. "My mother was from there."

"Ah, your father is the guy wearing the Wisconsin hat, then?" Sean asked.

Conall nodded.

Sean said, "Winters are brutal."

"True," Conall responded, "But I had a scholarship."

Scholarship could mean all kinds of things, I thought. *Academic, sports, financial, physical handicap . . .*

Sean watched my thought process and shook his head, just as Davina screeched like a barn owl across the room, scrutinizing our group between sips of her beer.

"Scholarship?" I asked, "like athletics?"

"Nat, stop," Sean said, "maybe he was a Fulbright."

"Football," Conall said, before it could go any further.

I cleared my throat and gave Sean a nasty look.

"When?" Sean asked, not returning my glance.

"Wow, Sean," I blurted. "Inquisition much?"

"A linebacker?" Dad inquired, going through his whiskey in a way that suggested he'd been sampling before this vacation.

"No, fullback," Conall said, staring at his beer.

I leaned back and thought about the many football games I'd been forced to watch against my will. Even when absorbed in a book or magazine, I couldn't help but absorb the facts and statistics. It was just the way that my brain worked, especially when listening to the incessant chatter of the play-by-play. Trevor would yell at the screen, quoting Vegas bookie lines. One cold weekend, Wisconsin played Michigan State in sub-zero weather. In a last-second moment, Trevor had jumped from the couch and knocked a book from my hands. He yelled at the TV, at the Wisconsin team specifically, wanting an enormous fullback to "run faster." Trevor had money on the game and the first down was imperative to keep Wisconsin in position to score points in the last minutes. He screamed, "You *are not* the Scottish Mountain!" When he looked back to see if I was paying attention, he said, "That Ramsey guy was a freaking monster. Broke all kinds of records." He pointed. "This guy's a cheap imitation."

I said to Conall, "What's your last name?"

Sean threw a napkin. "Are you mentally impaired?"

"I think I'm getting there," Dad said, and we glared. "Joking," he laughed.

"Don't," I said, and turned back to Conall. "There was a Scottish guy named Ramsey that played for Wisconsin, right?"

Conall stared at me as if I was the queerest thing in the joint. Davina laughed in the background, sounding like a soprano with a jellybean stuck in her throat.

Sean scoffed and crossed his arms. "And that has to be him, right? Because he went to Wisconsin?" He waved a hand in the air. "And he happens to be Scottish? Therefore, he is that guy? The odds are like a hundred to one."

Conall said, "I'm right here."

I shrugged, taking a drink of my beer. "Let's place a wager."

159

"Again. Me. *Right here*," Conall said.

"I'll take that bet," Sean said, his finger tapping the table. "Winner pays full tab."

"You're on," I said.

Dad said nothing, eying the two of us.

I laid my proverbial cards on the table; my thoughts directed at reducing Sean to rubble in statistical odds. "Ramsey was a full-back. Big guy, like him," and I pointed to Conall. "I remember Trevor talking about him in the very early days of us dating. When I actually listened to him," and gave Sean a pointed look.

"What's the population of Scotland, Conall?" Sean asked.

Conall rolled his eyes. "About five million, give or take."

"Five million," Sean emphasized. "And you want place money that this guy here, at our table, is the same guy that your ex-boyfriend happened to be talking about five years ago? And played football ten years ago? Five million people, half of which are male. That's 2.5 million males, give or take, and you're putting your money on this guy?" Sean said, looking apologetic. "Sorry, Conall, no offense. This is just about winning."

Conall shrugged. "None taken."

The table went silent. The original question was pondered, but Conall said nothing. There was an uncomfortable moment as we all stared at one another.

"Another whiskey, my fair lady," Dad yelled out.

"No, he won't," I shouted at the barmaid.

She poured another whiskey, as well as three more beers for the rest of us. "Hey, hey!" I screamed, getting her attention.

"Relax, Nat. Let it go." Sean said, drinking a healthy dose of beer. "So, Conall, please relieve the suspense. That you?"

"Huh?" Conall said, hedging.

Four separate languages were being spoken at the table, all of us with different agendas. With impeccable timing that can only be considered divine intervention, Davina's laugh pierced the air, rattling the windows as she screamed, "Oh Mr. Ramsey, get your ass over here. Your body is needed! GIRLS ARE LONELY!"

Well, well, well, I thought. *Conall Ramsey, star full back of the Wisconsin Badgers. Front and center,* I thought. *I am so righteous.*

Sean's fist came down on the table in frustration, his eyes darting back and forth between Davina and Conall. Dad covertly sipped another whiskey and smiled to me. I grinned back. Conall shrugged, something like embarrassment eating at him. He rose to his full height, tipped back his beer and finished it. He placed the empty glass on the table and grabbed the full beer, raising it in a mock toast, but there was no joy in it. "Thank you for the beers. It was . . ." he looked to me, "an interesting day." He took a large drink. "I better make an appearance before I leave. Have a great time in Skye."

We said our good-byes. Conall walked to the table of women and was swallowed whole by their laughter and cheers.

"Nice job," Sean mumbled.

"Excuse me, did you miss your involvement?"

"I was just following your lead. Like following a bulldozer through the timber. And now look at him. He's the kid that's been tossed from the playground."

I sneaked a glance. Although pretty women surrounded him, for all appearances, Conall was a man encased in a female prison.

161

Our table fell into a subdued conversation. Conall left some time later and I watched him go. We spent the next thirty minutes drinking, until Sean told us that we had a long day ahead of us and suggested we head to bed. Previous bets aside, I paid the bar bill, which was the only time it had happened thus far. As I signed the receipt, the barmaid passed me a note with the handwritten bill.

"What's this?"

She grinned. "Conall left that. Told me to give it to you. Said you might need it."

I nodded, thanked her, and put it in my pocket without reading it. I walked back to the table as Dad and Sean clinked glasses in some drunken toast. Later, as the three of us walked down our long hallway, I pulled the note from my pocket.

Bronco rider,

If for some reason, you have any car or catastrophic knicker issues, you can call me for emergency assistance. I can always show up with an extra pair of sweatpants.

--Conall

There was a phone number written at the bottom, but I disregarded it. Not only did I have no idea how to call it, my cell carrier would refuse to make the call. I stuffed the note in my pants and shuffled off to bed.

Dad and I lounged in our twin beds later that night, luxuriating in the fact that for the first time in the entire vacation we didn't have to get up at the break of dawn to catch a taxi, ferry, or plane. I used the sketchy hotel Internet to learn that "Ye Scottish Mountain" had broken all kinds of rushing records as a fullback and helped Wisconsin win a bowl game. Once graduated, Mr. Ramsey disappeared off the radar, even though some professional scouts had been calling.

I was checking emails when Sean knocked at the door, then busted his way through, stumbling into the room.

162

"What time did you say the ferry left tomorrow?"

"I told you, 11 AM."

"Eleven?"

"Yes."

"You sure?"

"Yes," I responded, but something was amiss.

"Tomorrow is Thursday, Natalie."

"Really?" I counted on my fingers, naming off days and what we did that particular day. I came to Wednesday, and Sean said, "Lochmaddy. Here. Lewis and Harris. Almost killing me in a car." Dad followed the conversation as if he were watching a Ping-Pong match.

I said nothing, still doing the math.

"For Pete's sake. The ferry leaves at 7:15 tomorrow," Sean said. "I can't believe you guys. It's like traveling with Abbott and Costello."

"Really? Which one of us is the fat one?" I asked, horrified.

"See you guys at six," Sean said, leaving our room.

I asked, "Did you know that tomorrow is Thursday?"

Dad said, "I hadn't thought about it.

I laughed. Right up to the point when I started reading emails.

9

Emails:

From Tommie Calhoun

To Natalie Calhoun

Re: Starting to piss me off

Never mind the last email. Not that it matters since you're NOT
RESPONDING. Even with careful planning, you can still end up
with a Bay of Pigs. And I think Trevor is definitely the Americans in
this little scenario.

-Tommie

*   *   *

Emails:

From Natalie Calhoun

To Tommie Calhoun

Re: Starting to piss me off

I can't call right now. Not when I have no signal in the middle of
North Sea. In front of Dad. You need to just spell it out. How bad is
this? Like Uncle Tony's funeral wake bad? Or your military
graduation keg party bad? Stop using historical war metaphors that I
cannot understand without looking them up on the Internet.

BECAUSE MOST OF THE TIME I DO NOT HAVE INTERNET… OBVIOUSLY

*   *   *

We boarded the ferry to Skye. It was a much more grand
affair than the one to Harris, with multiple levels, an enclosed third
floor upper deck with a sweeping panoramic view and colorful
couches and large lounge chairs. From this perspective, it was
endless water, dotted islands, and the possibility of slipping off the
edge of the earth.

At the port of Uig, large rocky outcroppings created a niche
harbor point. I imagined young children watching for their sea-faring
fathers, running that coastline, waving their arms, while their white
taffeta dresses floated in the wind. The water was crystalline blue
and the grass a vivid green, clouds clinging to the port, hiding its
presence from the rest of the world.

We exited the ferry and drove the coastline; rugged and
rocky, with spectacular views overlooking the breaking water below.
Dazzling green slopes gave way to treacherous cliffs and
mountainous inclines. It was a land where fairies existed and trolls
peered from behind stony edifices. We skirted sheer drop-offs and
daunting cliffs and stared at strange rock formations called Quiring
and the Old Man of Storr.

We drove into Portree and parked with the rest of the tourists.
It was a coastal village with a city square, quaint shops, and several
open cafes. We stopped in the first one we found, ordered scones and
cappuccinos and strategized our day—some shopping and fishing,

and a visit to the Dunvegan castle just outside of town. We would drive to Sligachan later in the day, for our hotel, dinner and drinks.

We dropped off Sean at his appointed watering hole, praying the fishing Gods would take mercy on his unlucky fishing trip. Dad and I drove on, headed east on unmarked roads until we ended in Claigan.

Did we? It was hard to tell.

We found ourselves in a dead-end parking lot at an inlet harbor. Six feet further the car would have been submerged in coastal water. We were lodged so tightly between cars that Dad opened his door and it immediately collided with another.

"Is this where we want to be?" Dad asked. "The map says Claigan? And . . ." he looked at the map and the surroundings, including the building beside us. "And this the Stein Inn?"

"It's a vacation, do we really have to be anywhere?"

"I thought we were going to a castle. For stones. And gardens."

"We are. But we need refreshments first."

"Fine plan." He threw the map over his shoulder and into the backseat. "I knew you were the smartest of all my children," as he crawled across the gearshift and the seat and fell onto the ground.

"Easy there. We haven't started drinking," I said, helping him up.

*   *   *

We walked into the Stein Inn, which boasted an intimate bar, but still managed to squeeze in ninety-nine malt whiskeys. Those Scots were determined to make the most of limited spaces. We found a table and sat down amongst a healthy group of people for an early afternoon.

166

I asked, "Are we eating?"

"We just ate."

I laughed. "That was three hours ago."

Dad shrugged, "Good enough."

When the waitress came, I ordered a beer. Dad observed the diverse selection of whiskeys and said, "You have any Royal Lochnager?"

The gal smiled, appreciating Dad's knowledge, "For sure."

I put up my hand. "Hello, Captain Fly High, hold on. It's two PM, maybe we should take it easy. And when did you become an expert with the whiskeys?"

"You think you were the only one that did research?"

The waitress nodded. "A fine choice, earthy with a bit o' spice."

Dad cleared his throat, "Well, that decides it, I need a bit of spice."

"He really doesn't need any spice." I said, "Just wait, we'll find you some kabobs and you can do spicy."

Dad ignored me. "I'm spicy. Spicy dad." He opened his arms in a grand gesture. "Bring me a spicy drink, bar wench."

I slapped a hand over his mouth. "Ahhhh . . . he didn't mean that. He had a stroke several months ago."

"I did not!" Dad argued, the words muffled.

The girl laughed and walked away.

"Are you insane?" I asked him.

"I'm feeling lucky."

167

"You're feeling something, but it's not lucky."

"Oh, it's fine. She likes me."

"She thinks you're incapacitated. It's sympathy for the mentally disabled."

Dad drank his whiskey and I had several beers. After the second round, I walked a steep flight of stairs to a bathroom that was the size of an upright bathtub. Upon returning, I found Dad nursing his whiskey and talking up the waitress. There was a very large amount of liquid in the glass.

"You got another!" I yelled.

"What?" Dad asked, feigning ignorance.

The waitress turned her back, her shoulders quivering just the smallest bit.

"I told you no more!"

People were staring. "Hold your voice down," Dad said, shushing me.

"Unbelievable."

I went to the bar and handed the girl money, getting another beer. "I'll give you extra cash not to serve him again."

"He's cute. For an old guy," and her eyes slid to my father.

The woman appeared to be around forty. She was overweight but carried it well. She had green eyes, brown hair and a nice smile. Dad was in his late sixties, but passed for an early fifty-something with baby blue Frank Sinatra eyes and a trim body. It was possible this girl was a "daddy chaser," or just looking to get a ticket to the States. She grinned over her shoulder and waved to my dad with two fingers.

"Listen, you should know that he has a wife and is completely penniless. We're here on a paid charity trip because he has scrotum cancer."

She grimaced. "Really?"

For the record, it's testicular cancer; scrotum is one of those words that always gets caught in the throat and makes people wince. Go ahead, try saying it and keep a normal look on your face. It's impossible.

The waitress leaned over, "So, he's got one of those sacks then?"

I narrowed my eyes. "Excuse me? What kind of *sack* are we talking about?"

"Scrotum cancer. So he can't poop, right? He has to have one of those sacks . . ." holding her hands about waist level in circle that could only mean a colostomy bag.

I bit my tongue to keep from laughing. She was in the general area, but had wrong part. I had no energy for male anatomy lessons inside a bar. "Right, no proper pooper."

"Yeah, that's horrible." Her face scrunched up in sadness. "He deserves a charity trip."

*   *   *

From Tommie Calhoun

To Natalie Calhoun

Subject: Well . . . FINALLY

WHERE THE HELL HAVE YOU BEEN? I thought I was going to have to deploy the Marines for an emergency extraction. To be honest, I'd have better luck contacting El Chapo in a Mexican prison.

Back to the original problem: your house has been tossed and most things of value taken. There is some weird thing going on with your kitchen, like an experiment gone wrong. Trevor not found. At this point, I don't know if that's a good thing or not. Tell me how you want to proceed.

I'd be more worried about your missing underwear than your missing ex-boyfriend.

-Tommie

*   *   *

Emails:

From Natalie Calhoun

To Tommie Calhoun

Re: Well . . . FINALLY

Could you be more specific??? What things have been taken? I know in the military you have little need of personal household items or bodily hygiene but AM I COMING HOME TO AN EMPTY PLACE? Trevor has emailed me and I will contact him for information. For now, sit on the situation until I can figure out what is going on.

How does that FRIEND of yours know about my underwear? Who is this person?

N-

By the time we were driving to Dunvegan Castle, we'd surpassed normal sobriety levels, having spent a full two hours at the bar. I slowly navigated a large parking lot crowded with too many cars and we walked uphill to a castle that was situated upon a high cliff side, surrounded by water—the perfect rendezvous for pirates or a chieftain wanting to keep his family safe. Rising three stories, it was an imposing stone structure with numerous turrets and a manicured walking garden. Once inside, we were met with a vast array of ancestral pieces, period furniture, and historical documents framed on the wall. There were oil paintings of men in tartan with severely famished looks on their faces. We breezed through rooms and read historical documents, but skipped offers of a formal tour.

We observed the mythical "Fairy Flag" that ensured victory in battle and charmed fish from the sea. If local folklore was to be believed, one of the young Lords of the estate had married a beautiful girl that'd been a fairy. She was allowed to stay one year, before returning to her 'fae folk.' She left behind a child, under the condition it would never be left alone or allowed to cry. *Good luck with that,* I thought. On a night of a great celebration, the governess had been lured outside by the music and the child had been left alone. The young fairy mother, hearing her child cry, returned and climbed atop the tallest tower, holding it one last time.

We came upon the glass doors leading to this mythical tower. It clearly stated, "Fairy Tower. No entrance." Dad stopped and craned his head to see up the spiral staircase.

"What are you doing?" I whispered. "Keep moving."

"It's the fairy tower. Why isn't it opened?"

I peered over his shoulder. The width of the stone staircase was so small that most overweight Americans could never have squeezed through the doorway without getting lodged within the first two steps. Added to the unstable structure of the cracked stone, I could think of a million building codes keeping the public out.

"Well, for starters, it doesn't appear capable of holding anyone over two hundred pounds."

"Well, good thing we aren't." And before I could stop him, Dad ripped open the door, pushed the warning sign aside and ran up the stairs.

I stood dumbfounded; my feet rooted into the ground. Historically, Dad was the most reasonable of all people. He worked as a tax accountant for thirty years, sacrificing most personal concerns to take care of three children. He followed all safety codes, once making me wear surgical gloves to clean out the kitchen refrigerator after neglecting it for a year.

My head turned on a swivel, spinning from side to side. Before I could consider the consequences of how much trouble we were in, I tore after him, taking the stairs two at a time to catch up. This was not an easy jaunt to the top of a small knoll. These steps were built for a dwarf wanting a suicidal shortcut. Each step was a different dimension, and I constantly banged my toes or hit my shins. I fell twice and scraped my head against the stone wall, catching my jacket on a rusty chain that served as a bannister. The beer threatened to come boiling out of my stomach. Halfway to the top, I heard footsteps behind me. Seized with panic, I stopped and peered around a corner, only to see three touristy men, gasping and wheezing, as they ran up the staircase behind me.

"What are you doing?" I yelled, as the closest man stopped below me, pushed on my shoulders and urged me on.

"I've been eyeballing this stairwell for the last thirty minutes," he said. "If that geezer is going for it, I'm coming too."

"He's not that old!"

"Older than me," the guy said.

The stairwell circulated forever with no end. Dad's deep breaths echoed from above and I prayed his heart rate didn't reach a level causing his pacemaker to fire. Stranded illegally on top of a castle with a medical emergency would create a whole new level of catastrophic trouble, even for the Calhouns.

Running endless heart-palpitating loops, I bolted out a crude wooden door that belonged in medieval prison. Stumbling onto the roof and blinded by the light, I stopped to gain my bearings and was knocked flat to my knees by the other men boiling out of the staircase. Coming upright, I saw Dad near the ledge. He was bent over with his hands on the balustrade, as he either caught his breath or prepared for thirty-five joules of electricity. I stumbled over and grabbed his arm.

"Are you crazy?" I screamed.

He was wheezing, but laughing. He pointed to the horizon. "Look."

"What?"

He turned my face with his hand, and said, "See." *Cough.* "There."

For the first time since rushing the stairs, I gathered my wits and slowed my breathing, only to have my pulse quickened again. There were endless shades of green and blue of such an intensity that my eyes refused to believe. Placid sapphire water lapped at the rocky shores that lead up to the castle that was surrounded by lush green pastures. The water met with the sky in the far horizon and cascaded on forever. The salty wind blew through my hair and I embodied every one of my favorite fictional heroines: Guinevere, Jane Eyre, Cathy of Wuthering Heights, and Helen of Wildfell Hall. In my novelistic imaginations, I was wearing a green tartan shawl as my eyes sought out a boat coming to shore, or I was a Fairy Queen watching a magical celebration below me, holding my fae child.

Dad and I stared at our surroundings, not saying a word. The three other men did the same; one of them having the presence of mind to click a few pictures with his phone. We stood there in perfect silent harmony, brothers in our little rebellion. That is, until all pandemonium broke loose. The tower door burst open, the large weight of it hitting the castle wall and making a tremendous banging

173

noise. We turned and saw two security guards, hands on their hips, struggling for air and screaming, "There!"

One of our companions bellowed, "Make a run for it!"

We were trespassing tourists, not criminals robbing a bank. But at that moment, the adrenaline kicked in and we all panicked. The three men went one way, Dad and I another. We found a door and descended a staircase, praying it would take us to an exit.

"If your pacemaker fires, I'm leaving you," I screamed as we ran, using my phone to light our way.

"Don't forget who's been paying the bar bill," Dad said from behind.

"Fine, I'll take your wallet, then leave you."

We tripped through another door and fell forward into a brightly lit room. I slid on a rug, caught my balance and managed to grab Dad by the arm. We were in one of the main sitting rooms that we'd toured earlier, containing the Fairy Flag and historical gaming tables. A tour guide stopped mid-sentence and stared, as well as every member of an Asian tourist group. They eyed us suspiciously. I don't know why. We were out of breath, sweating profusely, and I had dark stains on my knees where I'd fallen.

"Right," I said, trying to control my breathing and walking towards the entrance. I said, "Wrong turn. Very dark. Someone should check the lighting."

Dad muttered, "Very dark."

As we approached the doorway, the tour guide said, "Hey! Wait! You two!"

We gave up the facade and made a run for it. For my out-of-shape father, this pushed him past his physical limits as his breathing resembled a man on a treadmill for the first time in his life in the midst of a heart attack.

174

"Hey!" the tour guide screamed again. "Stop! Security!!"

We broke into a sprint, weaving around people reading historical markers and clueless to the spectacle. At the front doors, security did their best to head us off—one man lunging and grabbing my hoodie before I shook him off. I was dragging Dad the entire way and pushing people as I went.

Running to the parking lot, we threw ourselves into the car. With slow clarity, I looked down and found no steering wheel, my hands resting on the dash. I screamed, "Change places! MOVE! MOVE! MOVE!" as we enacted a clown circus act, both of us exiting the car, running into each other in our respective circles, before throwing ourselves back into the car. I started the engine, gunned it and slammed it into first gear, speeding out of the lot.

"The last time I take you on vacation, EVER!" I screamed.

"You didn't take me. I took you. I'm paying for everything," he said.

"What were you thinking?" I yelled as I navigated the parking lot. I couldn't find the exit and we were endlessly circling.

"It seemed like the right opportunity."

I found the exit, or at least, I thought so. There was a large hedgerow on both sides that obscured my view of anything further down the road. "Opportunity? That's a job opening." I shifted to a higher gear and accelerated, "a new move, or a first date," I screamed, looking over. "It's not going off bounds in a historical site and having security almost arrest us."

I was waiting for his explanation when he said, "Oh, oh!"

"What?"

"Twelve o'clock."

"Huh?" I said, turning back. We were headed towards large ornate gates that marked the edge of the estate. In my tirade, I'd migrated off the road. They had placed those reinforced concrete pylons to keep people from varying from the path and hitting their fancy iron-wrought fencing. I was going too fast, the time to correct my alignment was marginal and we were significantly off center. I panicked, jerking on the wheel.

"You're over correcting!" Dad yelled.

"I know." The back end was all over the place.

"Nat."

"It was a Fairy Tower!"

"Nat!" Dad yelled, placing his hands on the dash.

"Shit!"

"Nat!"

"Hold on!"

I hit one of the concrete pylons doing forty miles per hour. There was the grind of concrete as it nicked the bumper, took off a side mirror and finally scraped down the back end of the car. I gunned the motor, causing a heinous metallic noise. Both of us screamed like small children as the sparks flew.

Free of the castle grounds, I slowed the car and drove a narrow country road with no traffic. We didn't talk, both of us trying to calm frayed nerves. Several trips through roundabouts, the bumper was making a horrendous noise and there was the acrid smell of burning rubber. My armpits were saturated with sweat and my knee pounded with pain where it'd hit the center console. We stopped at a nearby pub to survey the damage, and saw the bumper was rubbing against a front tire.

"What do we do?" I asked.

Dad leaned back and kicked it, almost falling over. It left two inches of space between the tire and bumper. If we didn't hit too many potholes, causing the suspension to rattle, we might not burn a hole in the rubber.

"That's what we do," he said, scratching his head.

Without speaking, we walked into the bar and ordered Guinness's. The waitress gave us a sideways glance before filling our glasses.

I said, "So . . . the pacemaker didn't fire, right?"

Dad took a drink. "Am I laying on the ground?"

"Not yet."

He gave me a sideways glance. "Forget my health. We need to call the rental place and tell them we've had an . . . incident."

"You mean we need to call Conall."

"Whatever. The car looks like it was used in a bank heist."

"How long till we pick up Sean?"

Dad pulled out his watch. "We've got several hours." He waved at the waitress and gave the universal sign for another round. "Call the number and see what they want us to do. The car is drivable, but they need to know."

"Right," I said.

"Right," he confirmed.

I took another sip of my beer and pretended interest in the bar signs above the whiskeys.

"So?" Dad asked.

"You want to call?" I asked.

He chuckled. "I think it's best coming from you."

177

"Why?"

"Why?" Dad's head snapped back in surprise. "Nat, I know you think I'm handicapped, but do you think I'm stupid as well?"

"No, your problems have always been heart related."

"Don't divert."

"I'm not."

He held up his hand. "Stop. I'm old, but I'm not dead. I've watched you two since," he mimed quotations, "you met in Edinburgh."

"What?"

"Please, I saw him walking into the B&B after we came back from dinner. I went to the bathroom and ran into him in the entryway. Fate threw him into our path here and the two of you have been doing the dance ever since, constantly sneaking looks at each other like kids at a pep rally. Call the guy and tell him we have issues." He took a drink of his beer and sighed. "Try to dig up any social skills that you remember from a previous life and use them." In his most commanding voice, he said, "BE NICE."

"I am!"

"You're not," and he took a sip of his beer. "See if they want us to drive it and how they want to take care of the repairs. I think all of this will sound better coming from you rather than the old man."

I said nothing, pretending interest in my beer.

"Please, Nat, before I'm forced to exchange notes and ask if you want to go steady."

"Knock it off," I said.

"I will if you'll call him. Tell him we have insurance and that I can get some cash to pay up front."

178

"Fine, but it's not . . . it's not like that. Between us."

He laughed. "Really? Prove me wrong then." He spun a beer coaster on its side. "Call our good friend Conall, who took an entire day to travel by ferry to Lewis just to hand over some stupid registration papers." Dad shook his head. "You know, Nat, sometimes you're the smartest and *dumbest* of my children."

"I think you've just hurt my feelings."

"I hardly doubt that."

A couple of inquiries later, I was in a small office lined with crates containing whiskey and other various liqueurs, using a phone that had a rotatory dial. My call was answered on the third ring by a suspicious, grumpy voice saying, "Hello?"

"Hey," I said, and nothing else, because it's been documented that I am something of a social idiot.

"Who's this?"

"Bronco buster girl," because even when I know I'm being an idiot, I always dig the hole deeper to confirm it.

Silence.

"You there?" I asked.

"I am."

"You should really work on that whole conversation thing," I said, trying to be light.

"Considering your conversational talents, that's the funniest thing I've heard in a while."

I sighed. "You gave me your number."

"I did."

"And I have a slight emergency, although it doesn't involve my knickers."

I thought I heard him say, "Wished it involved your knickers."

"Did you just say—"

"What's happened now?"

"I thought you'd be more pleased to talk to me."

"Why?"

This was worse than anything I had imagined. There was outright hostility in his voice and although that was a common theme with past boyfriends, it usually took a month or so before it kicked in. "Ok, forget it. Nothing. Pretend I never called." I went to hang up the phone, but I could hear him yelling my name. Reluctantly, I put the phone back to my ear.

"Yes?" I asked.

"Talk."

I took a large breath and steeled my nerves. "We kind of wrecked the car. Well, I did. A bit. A few scratches." It was an understatement, but I'd heard the same statement from people who have just been pulled from massive car accidents and almost lost a leg. 'A few scratches' covers a lot of ground.

I could hear Conall inhale through his nose. "I know."

"You know?"

"Yes, I know," he muttered.

"You're something of a sadist. Do you know that?" I stuttered, "Wait? How do you know?"

I heard a frustrated groan, and in my mind, I could see Conall scratching his head behind his right ear. "Because cars have license plates, Nat. I think you have the same system in the states?" He inhaled deeply, "And when you refused to listen to security at a national Scottish monument and take an unstable staircase and roam around on the roof of a castle, then run for it, eventually hitting a concrete barricade, those people in charge make phone calls to the person who owns the car."

"Ahhhhh."

"Yes, *ahhhhh*."

"Alec?"

"Yes."

"Is he pissed?"

"Yes. But it's happened before."

"*Taking the stairs to the Fairy Tower?*"

"Ha-ha," he mocked. "Very funny. Although I am impressed with your pluck."

"It was Dad's idea."

"Then maybe I should be kissing him for his courage."

I didn't say anything because I was holding my breath.

"Nat?"

"Don't kiss my dad. I had to run off the barmaid at the last pub by telling her that he had testicular cancer and was penniless. I couldn't handle having to compete with you. For my dad. Seems weird."

I could hear laughter. "You guys are the weirdest, by far." There was a male voice in the background talking to Conall. He replied, "Yeah, yeah. Sure thing."

"Conall?" I asked.

181

"Where are you?" he asked.

"Just up the road from the castle. Five miles. Small pub, harbor point, looks like a white cottage.

He sighed. "Nat, you just described every place in Scotland."

"Hold on." I walked down the hallway and found a waitress. "Can you tell me the name of this place?"

"Old Inn."

"Very funny," I said. "But the real name."

"Old Inn."

I stared and reminded myself that we were both speaking English. "Really?" I asked.

"Yes," she said, completely at the end of her patience. "Old. Inn."

I had so many retorts hanging at the tip of my tongue that I was rendered speechless. "Ok, thanks," and walked back.

"You there?" I asked.

"Yes."

"Apparently, it's not an old house, but an old inn. Called the Old Inn. You know, I completely understand your language problems now."

"Hilarious," he said. "Ok. Be there in about an hour."

* * *

Conall walked in an hour later. Dad and I were still drinking, but had slowed down, wanting to be somewhat sober when Conall

182

showed up and having to face Sean shortly after that; trial, judge and jury, all in one group.

Conall sat down and motioned to the barmaid. As usual, he got his beer twice as fast as us. He took three very large swallows, set down the beer and wiped his mouth with a shirtsleeve. "I thought you said there were just several scratches."

"Well . . ." I wavered.

"The side mirror is only there because it's hanging off electrical wire," Conall said.

"Yeah, there's that," I replied

"The front bumper is rearranged," Conall said.

"Well, that too," I added.

He leaned towards me and propped his elbow on the bar. "Can you open the back door?"

I inched away. "We attempted it, but it wasn't going well. I thought we'd leave it alone in case it wouldn't ever close again."

"Good idea," Conall muttered.

Dad said, "For the record, we have very good insurance and I can pay the rest."

Conall nodded. "My dad started the process." He took a large drink, appearing to summon patience. "You guys going to Inverness?"

"It's the plan," I said.

"Does it still drive?"

Dad chuckled, "It does now. We re-arranged the bumper."

Conall pushed away a lock of hair that'd fallen into his eyes. "So . . ." and he paused, thinking. "This is how it's going to work.

You're going to drive the car and get it to Inverness, where you can leave it at one of our car lots. We'll deal with the paperwork of salvage or repair there, and whatnot, and they'll get you in another car to replace this one."

Dad nodded. "Sounds fair. We just need to catch a plane out of North Uist in two days time."

We all drank as an uncomfortable silence hung in the air.

Conall said, "There's one small caveat."

"Of course," I muttered.

Dad kicked me in the leg.

"Considering the damage, and the fact that I came here to take care of this," Conall said, "my dad is demanding that I go with you to Inverness to deliver the wrecked car, and then back to North Uist to make sure the new car doesn't suffer any damage. And you don't really have a choice, because my ride took off as soon as he dropped me here."

Dad nodded, his eyes flicking to me and away, as realization dawned that we had a new travel companion. "OK, that sounds . . ."

I slammed my glass to the bar.

Dad waved to the bartender, "Let's get another round."

10

Emails:

From Trevor Smith

To: Natalie Calhoun

Subject: SOS

You need to call. I'm in real trouble. Their threats are escalating.
Can't Tommie help? I fixed his password situation that one time.
That counts for something, right?

Trevor

*   *   *

Emails:

From Natalie Calhoun

To Trevor Smith

Re: SOS

What in the hell is going on? Why has my house been ransacked?
And why is your bookie threatening you, through me??? These are
all questions that need answered IMMEDIATELY.

Fire up that laptop of yours and get talking. Remember that
Guantanamo fallout? That will look like child's play after Tommie
and I get ahold of you.

-Nat

* * *

From Natalie Calhoun

To Robbie Durst

Subject: Interesting thoughts

I believe some items have been removed from my house without my consent. If you had something to do with this, I would appreciate everything being put back. **Immediately.** I am not married to Trevor, or with him. **In any way**. Yes, I have some experience with pain and am also very adept at creating pain as well. I have many tools in my arsenal, if you get my drift. Look up images for the word 'hydrocele.' And testicle. I know EXACTLY how to make that happen spontaneously. The end result makes your balls look like grapefruits.

-Natalie

* * *

Emails:

From Robbie Durst

To Natalie Calhoun

Re: Interesting Thoughts

Interesting visual on the "twisted testicle." You ever think about a career change? We could use someone like you in our employ.

-Robbie

* * *

"YOU DID WHAT?"

Ten minutes after telling Sean of our castle debacle and high-speed chase, he was still screaming. We stood near a large body of blue water, placid and serene, something out of a National Geographic spread. In another life, another trip, we would have pulled out a red plaid blanket and an expertly packed lunch of egg sandwiches from a brown wicker basket. We would have eaten and drank white wine, as we took in the Emerald Isles' best landscape. But in my cursed universe, we stood in front of a deformed car as Sean screamed obscenities and gripped fishing equipment like he might use it as a weapon, swiping his rod through the air. His face bloomed with spots of red as he yelled, "FOR A FAIRY TOWER? YOU DISREGARDED SECURITY AND ALL RULES FOR A FAIRY TOWER?"

"When you put it that way, it sounds less than it really was," I said. "You should really—"

"Shut up, Nat," Sean interrupted.

I flinched. Sean paced, rubbing his head, making his hair stand in erratic ways, as if someone had placed five nicotine patches on his arm.

"Listen, Sean, don't get pissy," I said, trying to calm him.

Sean stopped pacing, murder in his eyes.

Nat . . ." Dad warned.

I continued, undaunted. "We had a little set-back. Conall will get us another car. My insurance will take care of most of the liability. The rest will be covered by Dad and I."

"*Set-back*? Covered by you and Dad?" Sean asked.

"Yes."

"By you and Dad?" Sean asked again with mocking insolence.

187

I paused. "Yes. Why am I repeating myself?"

Sean laughed and doubled over, his shoulders heaving with the effort. When he came upright, there were strange lines around his eyes. He raised his hands, thinking, dropped them again. He opened his mouth and closed it.

After a moment, Sean asked, "How long can you keep this going?"

"I . . . what do you mean, keep going?" I asked. "We had a small accident."

"*Accident?*" Sean said. "*Accident,*" he repeated in a tone that was an octave higher. He scratched at his forehead and pointed to the car. "Accident implies a random act of God, Natalie. A variable not accounted for. This," he gestured, "was not a *random act,* but a disastrous event in which you have full culpability. You, of all people, Nat, should understand the word *accident.*"

Sean might as well have slapped me. I stopped breathing for a full three seconds as I attempted to calm myself, pushing my rage into a small box. Dad blanched and turned away. Conall's eyes slid towards me; I saw the inquiry there but disregarded it. Taking a breath, I said, "Fancy words. But at the end of the day, it's a simple mishap and I'll take care of it."

"OH. MY. GOD. Just shut up!" Sean's shouted, as his flimsy hold on sanity snapped and he completely lost his shit. He pumped his arms in front of him like he was punching a toddler. "You don't have the money for this! Not even close. Not yet. One day, maybe, but not right now. Dad will have to pay. *Every. Single. Cent.*"

"Ok, but—"

"No buts." He pointed at Dad, "He'll have to pay. I might as well start chipping in too."

Dad held up his hands in a peace offering. "It's fine. I can take care of it. The tower was my idea."

188

"*Sure*," Sean said, sounding like an accusation towards me.

I shrugged, "OK, so I might be short—"

"You're short on funds all the time, Nat." Sean interrupted. He took several steps until he was several feet in front of me. "It's not only that your money is sucked into one great pit of education that never ends, but you seem hell bent on living your life in a way that you refuse to rescue yourself. Why is that?" Sean inhaled, shaking his head. "You throw yourself into personal fiasco after fiasco to add chaos to your life. Just be honest, Nat. You enjoy running from the consequences."

"Sean . . ." Dad warned.

I said, "No, it's OK," and turned back to Sean. "Is this one of those self-help talks?" I asked. "Maybe I could get one of those commercial DVD sets and save us all the trouble."

As soon as I said it, I knew I'd crossed the line. Sean's eye started to twitch and his hands fisted. Conall took a step towards us, watching carefully.

Sean leaned forward and when he spoke, it was no more than a whisper. "For once, Nat, just shut your mouth." His words were directed at the pile of scar tissue on my shoulder. "You can keep running, keep adding to the drama, but *we* both have to stop and face what happened," despair clinging to every word. "I would do anything," he visibly swallowed, "*anything* to change that day." He looked to Dad and back, before saying, "When she died, it affected us all. Not just *you*."

After a few dramatic seconds, Sean picked up his bag and walked to the other side of the car. He said, "I'll sit in back," as if he was announcing the end of the argument—possibly the end of everything between us.

Sean grabbed the car handle and tugged. It didn't open. He attempted it again. And again. He pulled so hard that he lost his balance and fell back. He stood there staring.

We all waited. Afraid to move. Afraid to speak.

Dad said, "It doesn't work. We tried." He pointed over his shoulder. "You'll have to get in on this side. With Conall." He cleared this throat. "And climb over."

*   *   *

We drove into Sligachan, which sat at the base of the Cuillin Mountains. Nestled in a pristine valley, with low-hanging clouds, the mountains were a beautiful backdrop to a hotel that resembled a ski lodge in the Colorado Rockies. It boasted a formal dining room with several adjoining drinking rooms equipped with fireplaces, three hundred malt whiskeys and a local brewery. It was the best hotel stay of the vacation. I parked the car and we all got out. Sean fell as he crawled over the backseat. Conall tried helping him, but he pulled his arm away, mumbling, "I'm not a toddler." Standing around the car and organizing the luggage, Conall's large addition to the family seemed outright comical, as if the cross-country team had taken recruits from the NFL. I started to sing the Sesame Street song, "One of these things is not like the other," until Sean hit me on the shoulder and told me to knock it off.

We walked into the hotel and dropped our bags at the front desk. I asked for our reservation, which were two rooms. Sean and I signed papers separately, turned away from each other. Conall asked about a single and was told there was exactly one left. He took it and Dad offered to pay, but he declined. We grabbed keys and agreed to meet in the brewpub in thirty minutes.

Dad and I were the first ones to arrive. We ordered beers immediately.

"Maybe we should wait," Dad said.

"Why?"

"Because Sean is still mad and we should set some kind of good example?"

190

"A good example by *not* drinking? Too late for that. Order up. And stay away from the whiskey."

Conall showed up ten minutes later, a beer already in his hand. Dad spoke once he sat down, "I just wanted to say, thank you so much for saving the day." He raised his glass. "To the Scots and their charity towards American stupidity."

Several men nearby laughed and raised their glasses, saying, "Here, here!"

Dad said, "We're good fun, aren't we? Does that make up for the mess we've made?"

Conall scratched his head, "Well, it's a first. Never had anyone make a run for it at Dunvegan Castle." He paused, "But I've never known anyone to do the Harris Island road in forty minutes either," looking directly at me. "As far as the car," he shrugged, "if it's not totaled, we've got a body guy."

"Really?" I asked. "I want to meet a body guy. I'm kind of a body girl."

He rolled his eyes. "I'm sure you are."

Sean walked into the room and sat at the table, barely acknowledging us, placing his napkin in his lap. He ordered a whiskey as soon as the waitress appeared, but said nothing to the rest of us at the table. She took his order and left chips on the table. I picked one up and threw it at him.

"How long is this going to continue?" I asked. "We still have northern Scotland and Wales. The non-talking thing might be difficult when it comes time to make navigational decisions."

He threw one back and it landed between Conall and myself. Conall picked it up and threw it directly at me.

"Not bad for a full-back," Sean muttered.

"It speaks," I muttered.

"It does." Sean said, his voice all business. "To file a formal complaint."

We all stared.

"A formal complaint? Against everyone," I said, "Or just against me?"

"You." He picked up a chip and took a bite. "She buys tonight," pointing at me. "For everything. And I mean *everything*."

"Sounds great," Conall said, and caught the waitress' eye to order another beer.

I sighed in resignation. "Since that's resolved," I said, "am I *now* officially forgiven for my heinous crimes while on vacation?"

Sean mumbled, "Not by a long shot."

Thirty minutes later, I was eating one of the best lamb shanks of my life and watching everyone else pile into their food. Soon after, we left the dining room and found a private niche by the fire in the bar. We ordered whiskeys, except Dad, who stuck to beer.

When I got up to buy another drink, Sean appeared at my side, tapping his fingers and staring at the various whiskey offerings while whistling a tune. I tried to ignore him with no success. "I guess I'm buying whatever he wants," I told the bartender with some dismay. He looked at the two of us, making mental calculations.

"Well, if she's buying," Sean said, "Make it a double of the Laphroaig."

"Wow," the bartender said, "Classy guy."

"I know, right? Expensive guy," as I pulled out more money.

"Smart guy," Sean said and wandered off.

The bartender raised his eyebrows, as if to say, *You're with him?*

192

"My brother," I said.

"Ah," my Scottish mate said, with a ghost of smile. "Say no more."

I stood at the end of bar. The bartender walked away to rinse glasses and restock liquor. I saw the bright color of his shirt before I heard his words.

"That's a motley crew," Death said standing close, both elbows propped against the bar, a glass of whiskey in his hand.

I inhaled and let the air trickle out.

He tilted his head towards the mirror behind the bar. "Not surprised *that one* ended up your group." Together, we observed the men in the mirror's reflection, in which I noticed, Death was glaringly absent.

"Don't know what you mean," I said, keeping my voice low.

He shook his head and chuckled, rotating the glass in a way that the solitary ice cube moved in a perfect circle. "You humans," he said in a tired voice, taking a large drink. "You collect your grief like chains around your neck." He peered over his shoulder to a couple who were having a serious conversation, and not a happy one, by the look of it. "Every year, you add more and more, until the weight of them pull you to the ground." He sniffed. "By the time I get there, there's no need to dig a grave." He turned and stared right at me. "They're already there."

"Screw. You," I said, with real venom.

The bartender stared with concern.

Death smiled to himself. "Like to like," he said, as I walked away.

* * *

Later, the conversation turned to aliens and Stonehenge, and we migrated beyond the point of sober discussion. The octave of our voices increased and people around us—nice couples wanting peace and quiet—started to stare. Conall took up an entire loveseat and leaned back at such a precarious angle, I thought he just might fall over backwards and land on the floor. Dad fell asleep in a spot close to the fire. It was the point in the evening where a spouse, if any of us had one, would've told us to hold it down and take our father to bed. Stifling a yawn, listening to Sean's and Conall's discourse on alien invasion, I told them we needed to head to our rooms. Dad was snoring and it'd been a long day.

"What time are we leaving in the morning?" Sean asked.

"We need to make it to Loch Ness, then to Inverness and the B&B." I said to Conall for confirmation, "And the rental place for the exchange?"

Conall nodded, but seemed disappointed that the evening was coming to a close.

"Then Culloden the next day, before heading back," I responded.

"Sounds good," Sean said, "I say six AM."

"What? Absolutely not."

"Six AM," Sean said, giggling. He reached down, tapped Dad on his shoulder to get him to rise.

I sat by the fire, my body a lax pile of skin and bone. "I'll see you at 7:30."

Sean said, "Six-thirty," and mouthed the word *key* to me.

I found the card in my pocket and threw it at him. He caught it at his chest and pulled Dad to his feet. Sean said, "Seven," as Dad waved over his shoulder to say goodnight.

"Seven-thirty," I yelled.

Someone nearby shushed us. I gave them a rude look.

Conall said, "Easy slugger—don't be the wicked American."

I replied, "I am the wicked American."

*   *   *

Emails:

From Trevor Smith

To Natalie Calhoun

Re: SOS

I know this all looks very bad. But I have a plan. I needed some money to take care of escalating problems, so I took a few small cash advances from you. It will all be repaid, I promise.

Trust me ......

Trevor

*   *   *

And then there were two of us.

My Scottish friend sat across from me, taking up an enormous amount of landscape.

I squinted.

He squinted back.

"You are a very large man."

195

"It's the whiskey," he responded, holding up his glass, as fiery notes danced within the amber liquid. "Makes everyone look big."

"Really?" I sat up and puffed out my chest in a mock exaggeration, slurring my words. "How 'bout me?"

"You, my wee American, are still very puny," he said and snorted. "Like a wee sprite running through the heather."

"Hmmm." I leaned back and took a drink of my whiskey. In the dim firelight, with the whiskey warming my insides, it was hard to deny that Conall was a handsome man; dark wavy hair, piercing green eyes, and a large physique of a Scottish warrior straight out of a historical fiction book. I'd always been a girl that went for the life-of-the-party-huge-man-holding-the beer-tap-maintaining-order, and it had always been my horrific downfall. Dating these men had the same results as trying to keep the fraternity party going at 4 AM when the keg went dry—everyone left as soon as the fun ran out. These guys always disappeared at the first sight of commitment. That's why I thought Trevor would be the answer. He would be the antidote to my poisonous male tendencies; a computer geek who wrote code and worked the numbers of college football instead of participating within it. A year into the relationship, with nothing but weekends of TV college football and couch sex, I knew I'd made a mistake.

I watched Conall through slotted eyes. I said, "So the Ye Ole Scottish Mountain goes to school, breaks some records, breaks some hearts, has a possible chance at the NFL and disappears off the radar."

Surprise flittered across Conall's face. He nodded, sipping his whiskey. "You've done your homework."

"What happened?" I asked.

He pondered this and leaned forward, the couch groaning in protest. With his elbows resting on his knees, he was the image of a great king sitting upon the throne making a decision. The only thing he lacked was a sword and a crown, and a bloodied soldier kneeling

196

before him, begging for his life. Out of the corner of my eye, I noticed several women at a corner table watching, trying to determine our status, since we'd all arrived as a family. This guy was obviously not my brother and attracting attention.

The mountain of a man smiled and I imagined a boulder cracking, changing its whole face, from an impervious craggy surface to a smooth grassy knoll. Conall raised a hand and pointed at me, just like a king making his royal judgment. "What happened to me?" he laughed, his head rocking back. He shook his head in disbelief. "You think I can watch that spectacle between you and your brother today and not get answers in return." He flopped back into the sofa. "No way. You first."

I raised my hands in ambivalence and smiled, a small hiccup sliding out. "No real secret. You don't have to be a genius to figure it out." I shrugged. "My mother died when she was only thirty-eight and my father was suddenly in charge of three very young children, with no support. End of story." I attempted to keep eye contact with him and failed. I took a large sip of whiskey.

"Right," he said. "Sure. End of story. Give me a break."

"It was a long time ago. Dad has . . ." I mimed quotations in the air, "a friendly companion. Her name is Eve."

Conall surveyed our surroundings and paid zero attention to the women who were now openly staring. "Ahhhhh," he rolled in his thick Scottish brogue, "I believe you. But I also believe that would be the start to a very lengthy story, if given the chance to tell it properly, no?" and stared right at my scar.

My hands itched to reach up and cover my shoulder, but I kept them still. "There's nothing lengthy about it. It's a story like any other." I closed my eyes briefly to gain focus over the whiskey. "If there's one constant Conall, it's horrible stories that end with destroyed people and lost lives." I gave him my best *what are you going to do* look. "No one enjoys a sad ending."

He shrugged. "I don't mind," interest shining in his eyes. "What happened?"

197

I said nothing.

"Oh come on," he said in a commanding voice. "We've had whiskey, it's just the two of us . . ."

"Don't try to be intimidating," and I grinned. "I've eaten larger men for a snack."

He chuckled. "Oh, I have some idea," and waved me off, almost spilling his whiskey. "No girl that wanders into the wrong bedroom and ends up kissing a strange man in a foreign country is easily intimidated." His tone was too loud for a room made for whispering. An elderly woman gave me a look as if I was a hooker wandering into a church. I toasted her with my glass.

Conall continued, nonplussed. "I'm not trying to bully you. I'm just on a fact-finding mission to understand what drives strange, puny," a smile bloomed on his face, "*cantankerous* Natalie."

"Aw, you make me blush."

"So, what happened?" he asked, all seriousness.

I thought about my small, beautiful mother, whose face had faded from my memory, no matter how hard I tried. I kept her picture in my wallet and reprinted every several years to keep it familiar. I thought of her blonde hair and small body, and the hearty laugh that stopped us all in our tracks—the perfect mother who had one simple imperfection.

In my long timeline of never-ending academia, I'd learned that the heart was a tough, resilient system with elegant parts, just like my mother. While my mother's heart had been perfect, her aorta had not. It came with one weak spot, one genetic anomaly; one discreet place over time that had thinned, with no one the wiser. A sleeper in the night. A bomb waiting to ignite.

The heart is an organ that refuses to quit, even against the most catastrophic conditions. Several things can trip it up; electrolyte imbalance, electrical problems, blockage of the coronary arteries or a simple hole in a closed system—like cupped water in your hand. The heart doesn't understand holes and keeps pumping, trying to appease a system that is crying for blood and oxygen and beats faster until there is no blood left to pump. This was exactly what happened to my mother.

Thinking about the crafted biology and my mother, I said, "My mother had an aortic aneurysm. It's a small weak spot in the vessel that expands, until one day, it bursts. She had intense back pain for several days, but ignored it. She was young and healthy, so no one ever suspected it. It's very rare for a woman, especially her age. It's one of those things that just sits there, until . . ."

"Yes?"

I inhaled a healthy amount of air. "Think of a dam under pressure. Eventually, it just gives out." I mimed an explosion with my hands. "Blows actually. You can bleed out over several days or in several minutes." I rubbed my finger along the scar on my face. "That's all."

Conall narrowed his eyes and said, "That's all?"

"And you?" I asked.

"Me?"

"You."

The boldest of the three women got up and walked toward us. I watched her out of the corner of my eye, her perfect shape coming into view.

"Oh no, you don't," Conall said. "You—" The woman approached and laid a hand on Conall's shoulder. It was a practiced move, done with precise, fluid grace. Conall stared at it like it was a dead fish. His eyes followed a course from her arm, to her shoulder and then her face.

When their eyes met, she said "Hi," turning on a full wattage smile. "Don't mean to interrupt."

I rolled my eyes.

"Looks serious over here," she said, "but my friends and I have placed bets on something and we just can't leave it alone." She laughed and it came out as what I would call a coquettish chuckle. "I was wondering if you guys could help us out." She straightened, placing her figure at his full viewing advantage. "So, are you guys . . . related?" motioning back and forth with a glass of white wine in her hand.

Of course they did, because the similarities were so vast.

This woman was slim and tall and perfectly put together in a way that I hated. Even with help, even if I really tried, I couldn't compete with her. She was the perfect choice for Conall; tall enough to match his height and proportioned to fit into his side. I, on the other hand, was Tiny Tim's cousin who looked like she'd been shot out of a five-car pile up on Interstate 80.

I winked at her, relieved to escape this conversation, even though the thought of them together made me physically ill. I stood and did a dramatic arm sweep towards Conall. "You're in luck. This is the Ole Scottish Mountain, who played football for the University of Wisconsin. He was an All-American and All-Academic his senior year."

Conall stared, appearing hostile.

I took a step back, tripped, and regained my balance. I filtered through facts that I had learned online and vicariously through Trevor. Taking one last long drag of my whisky and placing the glass on a table, I said to the woman, "He played against Oklahoma's Jason White. It was a tough game, but he helped them to pull out a win anyway. Set a Wisconsin rushing record that day."

"Who's Jason White?" the woman asked, confused.

Conall gazed in disbelief. I wanted to laugh out loud and remind him that no one played this game better than me.

"Heisman trophy winner," he muttered.

200

The woman's smile could have lit up a Miss Universe Contest. "We thought we might've seen you before," which was a lie. There was no way anyone on these islands was watching American football with any regularity except Alec.

Conall grimaced and attempted to stand up, but he couldn't quite do it with the woman in such close proximity.

I backed away another two steps. My work here was done. "He's all yours," I said. "And in answer to your question, we're cousins."

Conall said, "Cousins? What—"

"Well," I interrupted, thinking about the two of us together, side by side. "Second cousins once removed." Another step. "I'll take my leave." I inclined my head and gave him a sinister smile. "Good night."

I hightailed it to the hallway and up the stairs to my room on the third floor. I pushed my small legs as fast as I could, but there was no mistaking the sound of a heavier body behind me with long legs taking the stairs two at a time.

"Nat!"

One more flight. It was just like the Fairy Tower, which had caused me to fall twice, bang my knee, bruise my shins and stub my toe.

"Nat, slow down."

I hit the top of the staircase, tripped and caught myself, continuing to run down the hallway. I was David being chased by Goliath. About six doors from my room, I felt his hand on the back of my shirt, tugging, like a defender taking down a running back.

"Let go!" I yelled. He grabbed my arm and turned me in one professional move. "Are you crazy? This isn't football."

We were both out of breath. He said, "Then quit running."

201

"I'm not."

"I just chased you up three flights of stairs!"

A door opened and a woman with a pink bathrobe that barely made it around her midsection stuck her head out. "What's going on?"

Conall tugged me to his side, which knocked my head painfully against his sternum. I put on my happiest face and spoke in my sorriest English accent. "So sorry, just messin' about."

She stared at Conall, then me, giving us a queer look. "Well, go mess about somewhere else. People are sleeping."

We backed away and Conall bowed slightly. "My apologies, so sorry, ma'am."

When the woman shut the door, he grabbed a hold of my shirt and continued dragging me down the hallway.

"Let go."

He pulled a hotel key from his pocket. "Come here," he seethed.

"You idiot. You're going to get us tossed out of here. And Sean won't talk to me for weeks."

"Shut ye trap, Nat. You're goin' to listen."

I was trying to work myself free by pushing on his ribs when he opened the door, shoved me inside and closed the door behind us. It was very dark, the only light coming from under the door.

"Really?" I asked. "Locking me in a room? This isn't college game day anymore, Conall. You can't pull these kinds of stunts and get away with it," making light of the scenario.

Conall said nothing.

"Conall?"

There was a large pause in which my eyes adjusted and I could make out the dim outline of him against the door.

"My mother was diagnosed with pancreatic cancer my senior year. That's why I left right after school."

The words were spoken in a dry monotone voice, but ignited like sparks from a fire. I reached for them, grabbed on and silently repeated them. And repeated them again. My head dropped a few inches as I thought. We were a pair of physical extremes, but twins in our disaster. Both of our mothers deceased—my mother dead in minutes, gone except some residual agonal breathing that could not save her. His mother had slipped away over months, her frail body sinking into itself until there was nothing left. The whiskey bubbled in my gut, a sour taste coating my mouth.

Genetic anomalies, cancer, heart ailments and catastrophic accidents made sure no one got off easy in the game of life. Roll the dice and take your chances. One day everyone was peacefully sitting down at dinner, complaining about cooked carrots, and the next, there was an empty spot at a table that left people so despondent that family meals were put on sabbatical for an entire year—kids grabbing food from a refrigerator and disappearing into their rooms.

"When'd she die?" I asked, my eyes slowly adjusting, allowing me to make out his facial features.

"I never said she died."

I rubbed my hands up into my hair, grabbed some curls and jerked. Sometimes it helped to ground me. "Pancreatic cancer?"

"Yes."

"There are very few people that make it past a year after diagnosis. Even Steve Jobs couldn't escape it."

Conall sighed. "*Who are you?*"

"Someone who tries to fix people." I shook my head. "But you can't fix that."

203

"She died within the year."

"But you were there. At the end."

"Yes," he said.

"And been here ever since?"

"Yes."

I'd witnessed it many times before; a loved one moving home or putting their life on hold to take care of another, then struggling to get back on track after the death. The interruption caused a crack that was difficult to mend. I nodded, although he couldn't see it. It took all of my resolve, but I took several steps until I found his body, and then his chest, and wrapped my arms around him and squeezed. I don't know why I did this. In my other life, I rarely touched anyone. It was contrary to my whole personality. My head came to his chest and I laid it there and tried to breath evenly. His arms come around me and held me close, and I fought the instinct to pull back.

"I'm sorry," I said.

"Me too."

We stood that way for a full minute. I know, because I counted every second in my head.

Conall asked, "How old were you? When your mother . . ."

Deep breaths. "Ten," I said. "I didn't take it well." That was an understatement. Basically, I'd taken residence up in the barn with the horses and refused to come out for a month.

His hands came up and curved around my head. In the dark, I could see as his face move towards mine. I felt his lips, as he kissed me beside my right nostril.

"Wow," I said. "That was . . ." I laughed. "So unromantic."

I reached behind him, trying to find the door handle. "Listen, we've both had a lot to drink. I illegally ran a Fairy Tower. Resisted security and crashed a car. On that catastrophic total, I should head to my room."

I heard his deep grumble of frustration as Conall picked me up and carried me over to the bed. He sat me down and then walked to the bathroom, turning on a light. He dimmed the intensity by closing the door, which softly illuminated the room, leaving the corners in darkness.

He sat next to me, neither of us saying a word, but I needed to explain myself before things got too far. I said, "Conall . . . I don't think that I—"

He put a hand over my mouth and shook his head. Then sat down next me. "We're not."

I grabbed his hand and pulled it into my lap. "I'm really sorry about your mom." I turned his hand over and traced the lines on his palm with one finger, thinking about time and distance and the intersection of those lines.

After several seconds, he asked, "Do you trust me?"

I looked up and saw the sincerity on his face, but shook my head. "Listen, it's not personal. I don't trust anyone."

"I know," he said. "I think I understand."

"No. You can't." I let go of his hand and sighed. "I'm a bit of a mess, Conall, an idiot really, unless it involves work."

"Work?"

"Yes, work. I can bury myself in it. Be good at it. With the rest," I waved my hand dismissively, "I'm really bad. Catastrophically bad."

"You're not bad." He paused. "I think you just confuse chaos with normality."

205

I laughed. "I think you're no head shrink."

"Ok. Fai' nough. I don't know you. How 'bout we correct that?" He shrugged. "Test things out a bit, no?"

"Excuse me?" I asked. "A test? Of what?"

"Courage." One eyebrow lifted and there was a hint of a smile. "Trust."

"*Courage*," I said, mocking him. This felt like a trap and I told him so.

"No, I promise, it's not." He reached out, his finger tracing my scar as it ran along my neck. "How about we trust each other . . ." his finger continued its path until it stopped at my shoulder, "to show our scars?"

"Our *scars*?"

"Yes."

"Are we talking physical or metaphorical?"

He tapped at the junction of my scar tissue. "Physical."

How original. "Forget it," I said and stood, but he grabbed my hand and hauled me down.

"What are ye afraid of?" he asked.

With as much courage I could muster, I said, "Nothing. Scars are nothing. Just tales of our lives," repeating the same words that Tommie had used many times.

He grinned. "That's the lass I know." His finger pulled on my shirt. "Then let's see the scars."

I laughed, sounding like a frightened schoolgirl. I slapped at his hand. "Uhhm, I don't—"

206

"Come on, Nat. It's just a game of truth or dare. You can handle that."

"Is this the game 'whoever has the most wins?' Because I'm going to tell you right now you have an absolute zero chance of winning."

"You don't know that. I played football."

"Conall," and shook my head. "Actually, I do."

I barely heard him as he said, "Come on, let's see, wee chicken."

Those stupid chickens always working their way back into the conversation. Why couldn't they just leave me alone? I'd never backed down from any kind of dare and the amount of whiskey I'd drank was emboldening me. With no sense of self-preservation, I strangled out, "Fine."

We turned until we faced each other and he pulled off his shirt with no hesitations. If I'd had his body, I would have paraded shirtless around town on a regular basis. With both of us entering our thirties, we were no models of fitness, but Conall was still rocking it. No beer belly in sight. Past the finely defined abs and the bit of flesh creeping over his pants, I saw his appendectomy scar and another angry scar near his left shoulder. He brought up his arm so I could see the surgical suture line, which we'd discussed previously at the harbor. I traced them all with my finger and contemplated their length and their history. The scar on his chest was jagged and vicious, as if he'd been cut with a serrated knife. I laid my hand over it.

"Got between two teammates at a kegger. The whole group of us went through a window."

I'd always believed that physical perfection was too easy. I'm sure there are handfuls of lovely models that would argue with me, disparage me with tales of discrimination and stereotyping, but if forced to spend time on the other side of the marred dime with an amputated leg or clef palate, would quickly flip back to their

207

attractive side of life. Beauty is allotted without payment and flaunted like a personal right. I didn't resent these individuals for their loveliness, with their flawless skin and straight teeth, but I always felt life's passage was deserving of a little gift-wrapping courtesy of that humble passenger called experience. My eyes always went to the scars—their length, contortions and intensity— and the bodies they were attached to. There was a story with each one—a daring passage through time and a physical badge given— making each one more lovely to me than perfect, porcelain skin.

Without thinking, I leaned over and kissed the scar left by a jagged piece of glass. I heard Conall's intake of breath and felt his chest rise in surprise. I leaned over and placed my lips on his midsection near his missing appendix. He flinched and goose pimples appeared, which made me smile. Tucking my legs, I rose and kissed his sternum at the third intercostal space and then left three inches, where his heart lay, beating a fast and steady rate. My lips lingered here in a silent prayer. I moved towards his neck, placing caresses as I went. There was a scar by his ear that was thin and white, and very old. My lips traced his topography, the timeline of his life. I migrated over to his mouth and lay a chaste kiss there, nothing compared to our first kiss in Edinburgh. I pulled away and regarded him.

His eyes were closed, his mouth slightly open in surprise; an exposed picture of chiseled skin and stubble. Slowly, his eyes opened and a grin tugged at the corner of his mouth. He nodded and said, "OK. Fair's fair. Your turn."

Gut instinct had me pulling away. Faster than I could see, his hands grabbed my wrists and held tight. He moved forward until our noses almost touched. "Trust me? OK?" A shake of his head, "There'll be no judgment. I promise."

I took a breath, commanding my heart to slow. My virginity card had been punched a long time ago, but I'd always kept my nocturnal affairs a strictly "lights off" physical event. I kept my scars hidden in daylight around Trevor, dressing in the bathroom and keeping the door locked. He never asked and I never told. Tracking my scars with a man was a first, even for me, and that was saying something. And Conall, whether he knew it or not, was in for more than he could ever imagine.

He grabbed the bottom of my shirt and paused. I nodded. As Dad would say, *this was where the rubber hit the road.* I realized too late that having sex would have been much easier. Conall pulled up on my shirt and I reluctantly raised my arms. When the shirt finally cleared my arms, he threw it to the floor and stared.

And stared.

And stared.

And stared.

I was back in Edinburgh, tracking his eyes, watching his movements, attempting to read his mind. I counted the long seconds as his eyes couldn't quite encompass everything he was seeing. Air left my lungs and I tried to use my arms to cover myself. Conall grabbed my wrists; I was strong, but no force against his strength.

The general public was privy to the simple scar that started by my ear and trailed down to my shoulder. It was straight and clean—a simple white line, a latitude or longitude on a map. From there, the scar migrated to my shoulder, where a pile of scar tissue sat like a lumpy piece of meat; discolored and crisscrossed with different running suture marks. It was the work of a country doctor in a small emergency room that did what he could with his limited training to stop the bleeding. What lie beneath that shirt line was a whole different affair. The scar tissue at my shoulder was just the peak of the mountain, the beginning of the geography. Beneath my shirt, running below my shoulder like fissures in the earth's crust, my right side was covered with wide crisscrossing scars that looked similar to jagged red burns that been tattooed into my skin. The longest ones branded their way to my hip and buried themselves below my pant line, just like a map of the world.

I closed my eyes to Conall's investigation and let my head roll back. "It's gruesome, I know. Let's just say, I don't accept many invitations to bikini swim parties," and laughed out loud.

209

Conall said nothing and I opened my eyes. He let go of my arms and reached out to trace the thickest of the group; a wide boa constrictor of a scar that ended in a dense knot of tissue at my hipbone, like a bow on a present. He touched that gruesome ending and applied pressure, as if he could push it beneath my skin. He couldn't. Other men had found that spot in the dark, hesitated and quickly moved on, embarrassed for themselves and me. They were always overly anxious in their attentions after that, desperate to prove that it didn't matter. Conall left his hand there, his fingertips memorizing its surface. After the incident, some of the tissue had remained numb to the touch—the nerve endings severed and destroyed—but his fingers sizzled and caused cold bursts beneath my skin.

Conall traced the lines on my body, circling the scar tissue at my shoulder, pushing away my bra strap. When he spoke, his Scottish brogue was thickly accented and I listened carefully to understand him. "The Scottish have many stories concerning the fae and other mystical creatures. It's a part of our heritage and goes back to the first Scottish descendants, no? My great-grandmother used to tell a story of a Fae princess that stood with the Macleod clan when their enemies came to sack the castle and burn it to the ground. The princess loved the oldest son and would not allow him to be killed. So she fought and killed many in her love for him. When her father, the Fae King, found out, he became so incensed that he disfigured her beauty; long, dark tattooed lines that ran across her face and body. As the tale goes, it became her symbol of strength and beauty and she was beloved by both the humans and Fae alike. A true warrior."

I shook my head, feeling myself relax for the first time in many minutes. "You made that up."

He shrugged, grinning. "Maybe."

"You shouldn't think I'm any kind of warrior, because I'm not."

"No way o' telling, no? They hide in many disguises. Even in puny American bodies."

210

He leaned over and kissed the scar where it started at my ear. And slowly, he worked his way to my shoulder, his fingers feeling their way before his mouth. His lips took a meandering path as he tracked the winding lines, their curved outlines, sharp turns and knotted endings, until he migrated the entire course. When he found my lips again, he laid me down and pulled me in a tight embrace. We kissed like we had in Edinburgh, maybe for minutes or hours, lying scar to scar, his large body encompassing my own until I was vaporized within his heat. And when we finally slept—Conall wrapped around me like a blanket around a child—I felt my heart pulse and vibrate, pushing away the scars and tethers that had held it hostage for so long.

11

Emails:

From Tommie Calhoun

To Natalie Calhoun

Subject: PISSING ME OFF

Hello?

Hello?

HHHHHHEEEEEEELLLLLLLLLLOOOOOOOO

What the hell is going on? I've heard nothing from you. And it's starting to piss me off. Anytime you feel the need to engage, be my guest. I got more important things than wonder about your house of ill repute.

*   *   *

The next morning, I bolted upright at 5:00 AM, internal alarm systems going off in my head. Confused, I reached out and my hand grazed the chest of a mammoth man who lay in a single bed with me. There was a kink in my back and my shirt lay on the floor. I tasted the sour residue of whiskey in my mouth and remembered the game of sneak a peek." I groaned and reached for my shirt, almost rolling Conall onto the floor. His arm encircled my waist and he drew me back to his side.

"Conall, let go."

"Stay," came the rumble, and he tucked me closer.

"Can't. Got to go," I sighed.

"Yes. You can."

I didn't disagree with him, but I didn't want to do the walk of shame in front of family in light of recent events. My head was buried in his chest and I tilted it back, smiling at the large slumbering giant that barely fit in the single bed.

Through slotted eyes, he said, "Ahh, she does smile. It's so rare, I wonder if it existed."

"I got to go," I whispered.

He sighed and released me. "Go on then, but we're not done. Not by far," kissing me.

I threw on my shirt and tucked it into my pants, trying to convince myself that looking presentable was going to save the day if I ran into my family. I whispered, "Catch you downstairs in a couple," but Conall's eyes were already closing.

I stumbled out the door and tiptoed down the hallway. Rounding a corner, I made my way to our rooms, praying Dad was still asleep. The hotel was quiet and the hallway floor popped beneath my feet. I carried my shoes; my shirt barely buttoned to presentable levels.

Fumbling with my key, I heard the soft click of a door across the hallway. I turned and was surprised to see one of the women from the bar standing in a doorway. As she was leaving, an arm reached out and grabbed her around her waist, pulling her back. She

213

laughed and turned towards the dark figure, the man's face coming into the light.

Blinking twice, I cleared my eyes. Unless I was hallucinating, the person holding the woman was Sean, who was passionately kissing the woman in a way that suggested a lot of previous practice. There was a shocking amount of tongue and I groaned in disgust. The woman turned in surprise and gasped. I paid her no mind; she was no concern to me. My eyes were locked onto Sean, who had gone deadly pale, seeing me.

Nothing was said for a full three seconds as Sean and I took stock of each other, like prizefighters before the big event. The woman glanced back and forth between us, horrified. "You guys know each other?"

We continued to stare, assessing each other's weaknesses before battle.

The woman was in full-fledged panic mode. "Hold on." She held up a hand. "If this is your husband, I had no idea . . . he was in the bar . . . he bought me a drink . . ."

Oh. My. God.

Of all the times to have Sean confused as my husband. I righted my shirt where one side of the collar sat higher and shimmied my hips to hitch up my pants. I smiled, saying, "No worries," and looked directly at Sean. "He's my brother. And by the way," I pointed, "he's engaged."

Thinking back, there was probably a sounder plan of action. But in social situations, I've always been a bit careless, just like a general that decides to shoot off the biggest cannon before the first soldiers have advanced out of the trenches.

The first thing that happened was the woman turned and slapped Sean hard across the face. The sound ricocheted down the hallway and Sean's head jerked as he stumbled back against the door.

214

Did I laugh? I think it's possible.

"You arsehole," the woman screamed. "You cheat!" the tenor of her voice raising an octave. "You said that you were single!"

"Well, he lied," I said, as I took a step closer. I was fully invested, stoking the fires, throwing on diesel fuel just to see what would happen. I was blind to my rage, even if this was Sean. I knew I was sworn to protect him, but I also felt the need to see him punished. And the more public, the better.

Sean had ahold of the woman's arm; an endearing touch two minutes ago was now a heat-scorching insult. She pushed on him, saying, "I'm going to kill you."

"Listen. Listen to me!" Sean pleaded, "It's broken off. We aren't going through with it."

"What?" the woman and I both screamed.

"I'm single!" he yelled.

The woman let loose with a caterwaul, like she was being attacked. I was worried about any hernia issues she might have and if anyone in the vicinity would call the police. A tug-of-war ensued between her and Sean, and he let go at the same time as she pulled away. She came careening at me, the two of us colliding and bouncing against opposite wall, landing in a heap.

While the two of us wrestled, she called out Sean as a leper and a cheat. When she stood, she pushed her foot into my rib cage, crushing me into the carpet.

"Sean!" I wheezed. "Get. Her. Off!"

"Screw you," Sean yelled.

The woman turned, scathing. "No, not you!" he backtracked, his face blanching. "Her!" pointing at me.

There was the sound of doors and feet appeared in the

215

periphery. A man said, "Is there a problem? I got kids here."

Another voice said, "Hey. It's five AM! FIVE!"

The woman marched over and hit Sean with a sound kidney punch that doubled him over. His voice was breathy as he raised a conciliatory hand. "Sorry. No problem. Just a misunderstanding."

"Like hell!" the woman screamed. "I should have stuck with the good-looking football player."

"Got that right," I said, up on my knees. The woman smacked me upside the head with a shoe and Sean laughed, still holding his side.

"Ouch! You bitch," I said.

She hit me again before walking away, incurring the gods to strike down Sean with all kinds of dreadful diseases. Her imagination was quite varied, including syphilis and scabies.

I got up from the floor, and the people who'd come out of their room, slipped away, disappearing behind their doors.

"What in the hell do *you* think you're doing?" I said.

"And you think you're in a position to judge?" Sean said, looking at my clothes.

"I'm not engaged. No one gave me a ring." I shrugged. "Officially, anyway." I stood upright. "And I certainly didn't vow my eternal love and put a down payment on a banquet hall. So yes, I think that gives me some maneuvering room."

Sean saw the wrinkled state of my shirt and the fact that my hair was plastered to the side of my head. "Considering that you've possibly come slinking out of Conall's room, I don't think so."

"Is this conversation really about semantics?"

Sean surveyed the hallway, as if he still expected to see her.

216

She was gone, possibly halfway to Ireland by now. He dramatically exhaled, let his knees buckle and slumped to the floor, leaning against the wall. He said, "You know, I was forced to come on this trip," he said with hostility. "I was forced to come with *you*."

I laughed because I couldn't help myself. I knew my brothers often felt the need to watch over me, but chaperoning me on this trip seemed beyond that. "Excuse me. No one held a gun to your head and said, '*Book that ticket. Take your irresponsible sister and elderly father on a trip and keep them alive.*'"

He shook his head, considering. "No. Nothing like that." He scratched at his scalp, mumbling to himself, then hit the floor with a fist.

"What?" I asked.

"Nothing."

"*What?*"

"It's over. Ok?" Sean said.

"Over?"

"*Over!*" raising his hands in emphasis. "Everything's over." He groaned and banged his head twice on the wall. "The wedding. The relationship. *Everything*. Liz made me come because she wanted me gone while she moved out of the house. Ended the whole thing a month ago and got back our deposits." He sighed. "Except the wedding dress. Apparently, that's not returnable. A whopping two thousand dollars down the drain."

I had an enormous amount of anger built against Sean. It was solid, forceful thing that I fueled with great care like a fire in the night. But in that moment, my anger slipped away from me, crumbling bit by bit, the ashes of it distasteful in my mouth. And that made me angry all over again.

"What? Why didn't you just tell me?" I sputtered.

"How?"

"*How?* Oh, I don't know. Anytime in the enormous amount of time we've spent together *on vacation?*" My eyes bugged out. "We've sat and drank large amounts of alcohol. Don't people usually blurt these things while *intoxicated?*"

Sean stood there staring, saying nothing. I held up my hands in a *What? Say something!* He said, "It's not that easy," in a tone eerily similar to ordering a burger at McDonalds.

"I think it is. You say, Liz's left. Pretty easy to me."

"Please," he said. "It would've just complicated things further."

"Further?" I narrowed my eyes. "Further how? Before or after I told you about Trevor? If there ever was an opportunity, I think that was it. Cannons were going off for Pete's sake."

Sean looked down the hallway, thinking. "Couldn't. This whole vacation . . ." he shook his head, "it's nothing short of a disaster." He pointed between us. "We're *total* disasters. Just admit it."

I didn't disagree. None of us were married or had kids; none of us could stay in relationships, often choosing people who were ridiculously wrong for us. Tommie was the worst of the group, picking women like cheap convenience store watches—knowing they were going to work for a while, but just waiting for the day when the time ran out. Sean was the consistent, solid middle child, appearing to date no one.

When Liz showed up with Sean one Thanksgiving, we were all wowed by her sheer normalcy. She wore pearls and a cardigan for God's sake. Eve practically peed herself having a woman around that had some experience cooking and just didn't just sit around drinking glass after glass of wine, excusing herself outside to smoke, shooing away the dogs with her feet. I thought maybe someone had broken the curse and cleared new ground. I took notes, watching carefully. Tommie scrutinized her with suspicious eyes like she was

218

a terrorist in disguise. Dad scratched his head and poured another drink.

When I didn't say anything, Sean sighed. "Jesus, Nat. Look at you."

"*Me?*"

"Look at your life. At your choices. Sometimes you and Tommie are wrecking balls, plowing us all down in your path."

I rubbed my hands up and down my face, trying to focus. I didn't want to talk about this. Not now. Nothing was going to get accomplished in this hallway, while on vacation. We simply had to get through it without killing one another.

I held up my hands. "Forget it. Forget this whole . . . " and motioned to the hallway. "We need to get ready." I pointed over my shoulder to the door. "I'm going take a shower and pretend that I haven't been sneaking around with a large Scotsman and being berated by my brother. The same brother who I thought was engaged, but was in fact, shagging a woman from the bar." Sean was in a pair of boxers, his cowlick causing his hair to stand at weird angles. "I would suggest the same for you. Unless you're going for the tribal look today."

Sean muttered, "Right, sure thing," standing and rubbing at his shoulder, a nervous tic he'd had since childhood. There was something bothering him, but I was too tired to care. I pretended I saw nothing. Pretended that we weren't related and turned towards the door.

Out of nowhere, he said, "Jesus Nat, are you ever going to forgive me?"

I stopped, making sure I'd heard him right; my feet concreted themselves to the ground as a cold sweat formed along my forehead. I told myself to ignore it. I'd avoided this conversation for years and I had no plans to give it up now. I considered my options for escape, but there was none—just endless shag carpeting and closed doors. Regaining my composure, I turned and smiled. "Quit talking

219

nonsense. There's nothing to forgive. You shacked up with a woman on vacation. It's practically a requirement on those Carnival boat cruises."

"Stop it. I won't let you joke this away."

"OK, great," and grabbed the doorknob. "See you in a bit."

Sean said, "How long does this go on?"

I sighed. "Nothing's going on, except the two of us sabotaging our sex lives."

"That's exactly my point!"

A woman walked through the hallway, holding a cup of coffee. She looked at the two of us and quickened her pace, looking twice over her shoulder.

Sean leaned forward, whispering. "Mom . . ." He inhaled and paused, appearing to build his courage. "Nothing could have saved her. She was dying . . ." He threw up his hands, "I don't know why we can't—"

My anger heated up a notch. "You don't think I don't know that? I'm a doctor, remember?"

"I . . . It's just . . ." His body seemed to collapse as he stuttered, "I know, I know, I should've—"

"*Sean.*" I shook my head in warning. "Don't. Just *don't.*"

I had no intentions of letting this conversation go any further; it was a foreign territory with unknown boundaries. None of us had spoken of it, of her death, or of the incident that followed for so long that it'd become hallowed ground. By stepping foot there, we were entering something holy and unbidden. Left untouched for years, it was no different than dusting off a precious relic that was lost and forgotten and was supposed to remain that way. Yet, here we were, in Scotland, talking in a public hallway of a hotel in the wee hours of the morning and admitting that neither of us had truly recovered; that the entire incident still hung around our necks like nooses, strangling us with words that were never spoken.

"You don't understand, Nat." He peered down the hallway and looked back. "You and Tommie. You guys are . . . and I'm . . ." There was pleading in his voice. "It's lonely out here."

"Sean," I said. "We'll do this later." I swallowed. "With drinks."

"That won't make it better."

"It might," crossing my arms.

"It won't."

"How do you know?" I asked.

Sean sighed in frustration. "You still miss her?"

"Of course I do."

"It's been a long time."

"Funny," I said, rubbing the scar on my neck, "Doesn't feel that way."

Even as I said it, I knew how cutting the words were, but it still didn't stop me from saying them. I saw the blow hit home and the hurt in his eyes, and cursed myself inwardly for being such a bitch; it was a muscle reflex that I couldn't turn off.

Embarrassed, I turned towards the door and fumbled with my key. I heard Sean say, "I just need to . . . I should have—"

"Stop. Don't say it," holding up my hand. I refused to have this conversation. "It wouldn't have made a difference."

"Bullshit," Sean said, with outright anger. "That's exactly what people say when they know you're guilty."

"Sean . . ."

221

"I knew. *I knew*. But that day, I just . . . I couldn't think. She was dying."

Any residual positive energy from the previous evening seeped out of my body and drained into the floor. I felt a deep weariness as I remembered the grisly details of that day. Sean was frozen in panic against the wall as our mother gasped for air, dying, her arm outstretched as her horrible moans echoed in the small kitchen. We'd both been panic-stricken, but Sean sat hyperventilating with a dull, glassy-eyed look about him. I'd made the decision to run for help and had fallen twice as I stumbled out the back door to find Tommie.

But I never made it.

That been twenty years ago and I was still running, still trying to make things right. And it was never going to happen.

There was a defeated look on Sean's face, as well as lines around his mouth and the early traces of gray at his temple. When'd we get so old? I remember wanting to grow up so badly and now look at the shape of us—bruised and beaten to hell. Our soldier faces were still intact, but our souls were frayed and tattered. Maybe it was time to admit that by constantly looking over my shoulder to the past, that I'd been running into enormous potholes of the present, right under my feet.

I whispered, "Sean?"

"Yeah?"

I took a moment, inhaling, feeling something akin to wild magenta hyacinths blooming in a place that was once a barren wasteland of my soul. Eve used to place large arrangements of them on the kitchen table, saying, "Sadness and forgiveness. With a dash of sincerity."

I said, "I'm glad it was me."

Confused, Sean said, "What?"

"I'm glad it was me." When he stared in confusion, I panicked, resorting to my usual derision. "Let's face it, even scars can't ruin my perfection."

He shook his head. "Stop it. The joking—"

"For you and Tommie," I interrupted, all seriousness. "I'd taken worse."

Sean opened his mouth to speak, but I cut him off. I had get through this, or I never would. "You two," I said. "You've all I got." Sean blinked twice but remained silent. "The only ones who . . . get me." I whispered, "I'd be *the one*, over and over again. And again."

He dumbly nodded, and before he said anything in return, I walked into my room and shut the door.

*   *   *

Emails:

From Natalie Calhoun

To Trevor Smith

Subject: Out of your mind

Small advances? What does that mean? How can you take small advances from me in my absence? You better not have hacked my account. You are talking like a crazy man. I'm calling the cops. The statute of limitations on our "whatever" has just run out.

-Nat

*   *   *

From Natalie Calhoun

To Tommie Calhoun

223

Re: PISSING ME OFF

OMG. Just hold on. You can't believe the stuff going on.

-Nat

*   *   *

From Tommie Calhoun

To Natalie Calhoun

Re: PISSING ME OFF

You asked me to help. Remember?

Back to business: My friend says that he's spotted a guy going into your place at night, through a window in the back. It sounds like Trevor from the description. He leaves in the morning carrying small appliances. I guess he's resorted to petty theft?

It's your call. What do you want me to do, call the cops? It's a no brainer for me, but it's YOUR sex slave we're talking about.

*   *   *

Entering my room, I found Dad comatose and snoring loud enough to rattle the nightstand. Small miracles. I took a nap until seven and then showered. When I left the bathroom, Dad was awake and sitting upon the bed, folding clothes. Together, we packed our bags and waited for Sean to come to our room, which never happened.

Again.

So I went to his room.

I knocked.

Nothing.

I knocked. Again.

Nothing.

I wanted to kill Sean with my own hands. Slowly.

I knocked a third time.

"Hello?" from inside the door.

"You up?" I asked. "Ready?"

A groggy, "No." A pause. "Not ready."

"Get ready!"

Nothing.

"Hello?"

Nothing.

"SEAN. GET YOUR ASS OUT OF BED!"

I banged at the door and continued to yell, until I noticed that someone was standing next to me.

"Hey," Conall said, sleep lines around his eyes.

I said, "Hey."

"Problems?"

"That depends." I pointed at the door. "He said six-thirty. I said seven-thirty. It's now almost eight." I yelled, "SEAN. I AM NOT JOKING!"

A couple from next door stuck out their heads, giving us a nasty look. The wife was a scrawny thing with shellacked hair that surrounded her head like a football helmet. She said, "We have children you know. That you woke this morning. At five AM. And now you seem convinced to do it again." The husband seemed embarrassed and ducked back into their room.

"I am so sorry. About earlier," and motioned to the hallway. "That was a misunderstanding. This," and I pointed to the door, "is just my brother being an idiot."

"Oh, I think your brother was being an idiot this morning. As well as you." She crossed her arms and gave us a smug smile, like she knew all about our late night histories. Conall raised an eyebrow in her direction.

"Excuse me?" he asked.

A small child appeared at the door, grabbing the mother's leg and whining, "Mummie," while sucking on her thumb.

"Well," she said, and placed her hands over her child's ears.

"I think you are both noisy, rude and inconsiderate."

I gave her a questioning look. "You didn't swear."

"What?" the mother asked, confused.

"Why are you placing your hands over your child's ears when you aren't even swearing?"

The woman's face turned red and she pulled the child back inside, slamming the door.

Conall narrowed his eyes. "Five AM?"

"Nothing. A misunderstanding."

"At five?"

"Yes. Small one."

"You left my room at five."

"Yes. Someone else was leaving Sean's room at the same time."

Conall's eyes slid to the door, then back. He whispered, "Really?"

"Yes. One of your admirers."

"What? No way!" he laughed.

"Way."

A conspirator's grin appeared on Conall's face. It was so like a man to congratulate another man on his sexual conquest.

"Wipe that look off your face," I said in my most admonishing tone.

Conall screwed up his face. "What's the rub?"

"Up till five this morning, I thought Sean was engaged."

Conall eyes widened. "Ooooh."

"Yes, oooooh."

"Wait? He's not?"

"Guess not. Not that any of us knew. I found out right after I made a scene in front of the woman about him being engaged."

"Oshhht, that's nasty work."

227

"You're telling me. I still have her tread marks on my back."

*   *   *

Fifteen minutes later, Dad was going through the room making sure he hadn't left anything. I was thumbing through emails, trying to keep a straight face and not yell out in frustration. Conall sat on the bed watching TV. There was a knock on the door and I opened it. I saw Sean standing in the doorframe, clutching a newspaper to his chest, his eyes half open and a ridiculous smile on his face. His hair was completely flat on one side, standing straight up on the other.

I said, "I can't believe you," and slammed the door.

I heard his laugh, right before another knock. This time Conall opened the door and Sean stepped into the room.

"Six-thirty?" I asked, indignant. "Why do you keep doing this?"

"What?" Sean said, laughing. "I'm up. I'm ready to go."

"Yeah, and now it's eight-thirty. We all could've slept later."

"Hardly. You were—"

"It's time to go." I pushed him into the hallway as I grabbed my bag. He was wearing the same clothes as the day previous. Even the wrinkle-free Gore-Tex pants managed to look slept in and his shirt was hanging askew.

I said, "I've never seen anyone more NOT ready for travel. You're wearing yesterday's clothes."

He pulled up on his collar and sniffed. "Smells fine."

"Yeah. If we were on a survival trip in Moab."

*   *   *

We settled our bills at the front desk. Sean and I took the luggage to the car, while Conall promised to help my dad find coffee to go. Sean and I rotated the bags into a new system, like a jigsaw puzzle to make room for Conall's small duffle.

"Jesus," Sean cursed, pushing on my bag. "Carrying that around Scotland is like carrying a dead relative."

"Please. It's not National Lampoon's Vacation."

"Isn't it?" Sean asked, mumbling, "Feels that way."

We slammed the trunk twice to get it stay locked. Sean stood staring at some kids with fishing poles walking down the road.

"So you guys, you and Conall . . ." Sean asked, watching the kids.

"What?"

"You . . ." and he motioned out with his fist.

"Had sex, you mean?" I asked, as an elderly couple walked by.

Sean winced. "Just once, could you act appropriately?"

"Me? Act appropriately? Like you?" I scrunched up my face, mimicking deep thought. "The person who picked up a woman in a bar, who just a mere hour earlier had been flirting with a guy that I messed around with later in his room? But had sex with anyway? You mean that kind of appropriate behavior?" The woman gave us a face that could have singed the hair off a squirrel.

"Keep your voice down," Sean seethed.

"I was just trying to get all the facts straight. That's all."

"Forget it. Forget I asked."

I waited a beat, and said, "For your information, we didn't."

229

"What? Really?"

"Nope."

"Oh."

"Don't act so surprised. I can be something of a prude," I said.

"You are nothing of a prude."

"True."

"So . . .?"

I threw my hands up in ambivalence. "Uh, we just kind of talked." When Sean's eyes rolled, I emphasized the word, "talked," again.

Sean gave me a look that I'd seen thousands of times as a kid, basically calling me out as a liar and double-dog daring me to tell the truth.

"OK, OK," I said, "We did some other things too," being vague. "But nothing else."

"Bullshit," Sean said and laughed.

"I wish it was, my friend."

"Really?"

I nodded. "Really."

"What about the scars?"

"Up close and personal."

"Wow, no wonder it took up most of the night."

I tilted my head at him.

He had the decency to appear contrite. "Sorry. That was mean."

I scoffed. "Hardly."

"You tell him? How it happened?"

"Sure," I said, enthusiastically. "Nothing better than telling a morbid story about how your body ended up looking like a road map to incite lust in a man."

Sean sighed. "So that's a no."

Dad and Conall walked out the front entrance, each holding two coffees. They were laughing at something like they were old chums.

"Why not tell him?" Sean asked.

"No point. He won't be around that long."

Sean shook his head and turned away. "There's the Nat I know and love."

12

Emails:

From Natalie Calhoun

To Tommie Calhoun

Subject: OUT OF CONTROL

Sorry, things going on:

Like random women coming out of Sean's hotel room.

Did you know that Liz threw Sean out and called the whole thing off?

And Sean had sex with a woman from the bar?

And is eating dessert for every meal?

And is sleeping in EVERY SINGLE DAY?

Call the cops. Give them my email. Tell them the details, including Trevor's name.

-N

P.S. Who has my underwear?

P.P.S. I can't believe the stuff I am being forced to write about in these emails.

* * *

We motored down the road, impressed by the change of scenery. Rocky outcroppings and blue water turned into soaring mountains. We crossed the Kyle of Lochalsh, left the Isle of Skye and entered mainland Scotland. We pulled to the side of the road near the Eilean Donan Castle, which sat on a tidal island where three lochs met. It was situated in lagoon water and ensconced behind towering stone walls. Conall explained it was where the movie 'Highlander' was filmed. There was a large pause as we all considered this.

"What movie?" Sean asked.

Conall said, "You know, the Scottish movie with a swordsman who's immortal? And fights for a prize?"

We all stared, confused. "Was this made in the 90's?" I asked.

Conall said, "No, 80's. I think. The main guy was tall with long brown hair and weird accent. Sean Connery was in the movie as well."

"Oh," I said, "Was it the same guy that played Tarzan in that other movie?"

"What movie?" Sean asked. "Oh, you mean where they take him from the jungle and try to make him an English Lord or something?"

"Hello? Yes. The *Tarzan* movie."

"All right," Conall said. "Forget it. You guys are the worst," shaking his head.

I said something about visiting the castle, but Sean muttered Loch Ness, water and fish, and we motored on. Again, the fish pushing us forward, even though we had barely seen them and I was becoming alarmed that they might not exist in Scotland. Maybe it was like Nessie; lots of rumor, no substance. I realized that if we had been on one of those survival trips where you had to hunt for everything you ate, we would have been dead days ago.

233

We drove another hour to Loch Ness. I imagined a small, picturesque lagoon, something you could easily swim across. I don't know why, but I did. A petite body of water, comparable to one of the farm ponds I skated upon as a child. Except this one had a large dragon-looking-amphibian thing at the bottom that popped his head out from time to time for historians and photographers.

I was surprised to find out that Loch Ness was HUGE; a body of water that was comparable to the great lakes in Minnesota. We stopped at the Urquhart Castle and viewed Loch Ness from the tourist center. Conall saw my confused face and explained that experts had never really been able to navigate its depths. It was so deep, that they'd never seen the bottom and that's why the Loch Ness monster tale continued to thrive.

"So, let me get this right. We can send astronauts to space, but can't see to the bottom of this thing?" I squinted. "That seems ridiculous."

He shrugged, "Some things should stay a mystery. And some things shouldn't."

"Mystery is overrated."

He looked at my lips, then a bit lower, and said, "I'll agree to disagree . . . about the Loch. But not about other things."

* * *

We drove into Inverness.

And out.

If we'd been on one of those organized tours that spanned two weeks, we would have visited every single castle and distillery along the way. We would've spent the entire day, navigating the city center and taken tours of historical structures. But this was the Calhoun Formula One experience, taken at breakneck speed, reduced to a crazy schedule that included the entire northern section of Scotland in a whirlwind seven days. We could only lean our heads out the window of the car and snap a picture from the bridge or at a stoplight.

Sean held out the map to me. "Where the hell is this place?"

"In the country," I answered, pushing the map back and peering out the window. Dad laughed from the backseat.

"Don't encourage her," Sean said.

"Oh, no worries," Dad responded. "It's not like she ever needs encouragement."

Sean was driving and I was not helping. At all. I pretended avid interest in the never-ending countryside. Conall reached out and snagged the map, looked at it, and turned it in his hands, reconsidering. This was not a good sign.

My childish behavior was stemming from the fact that just a mere ten minutes earlier, Sean had broken some interesting news regarding what he called his *reconfiguring of our travel plans.*

"What do you mean reconfiguration?" using my fingers to emphasize quotes. It was a term that I'd use when the simple outpatient procedure had accidently morphed into a massive invasive surgery.

Before the vacation, we'd spent an entire day texting back and forth about costs of hotels in Inverness. We had not been able to find a place in the Inverness city center within our price range, so Dad had agreed to pay for a "castle" experience in the country. I'd gone online to see breath-taking images of a looming, eighteenth century castle with luxurious, tapestry lined rooms, walking shrub mazes and a sprawling countryside filled with wildflowers. With the eagerness of a child on the doorstep of Toys R Us, I'd given up my reservation at the cheap place in Dingwall—which sounded like a hotel for your third cousin when they show up for your wedding unannounced. It wasn't until that day, I'd learned that Sean had decided that the family had to be more financially responsible, cancelled the castle experience and booked a more reasonable bed and breakfast that included trout fishing as one of its amenities. He did this all over coffee without asking any of us.

Of course, I thought, *the fish win out once again.* I was incensed and picking for a fight. If I could not be Claire and find my Jaime from *Outlander,* I'd hoped to embody the spirit of Elizabeth Bennett and think about my Mr. Darcy. I was being foiled at every turn to experience my literary romanticisms and holding Sean responsible for it. I was going to *Rochester* his ass.

"You need to help, Nat," Sean said. "We're lost."

"I don't have to do anything. I was promised a castle, not a sickly small pond holding genetic modified trout prisoners."

Sean sighed. "I didn't tell you because I knew this was exactly how you would react. I thought you would be happy considering the *car situation* and our extra expenditures."

"I wanted a castle."

"I wanted to drive a car that didn't look like it was involved in a three-car pile-up."

I said nothing.

"This B&B was very pleasant on the website," Sean said in a consoling voice.

"I don't want pleasant. I wanted GRAND!" I screamed.

"It's overrated," Conall said from the back.

I turned in my seat. "What do you mean? Why are you taking his side?"

Conall rolled his eyes. "Some of the castles are the barest of the word. They take guests to pay the bills. The electricity is shite, the plumbing no' trustworthy and whole place is a fierce gale from falling into itself."

"Really? Because the pictures of Kincraig Castle were spectacular. Nothing like it was *falling into itself* and turning off the lights right after dinner."

"Oooch, that place? Yeah, that place is great. Supposedly Brad Pitt and Angela Jolie stayed there one night."

I slapped Sean on the shoulder and incurred the fishing Gods to strike him down.

*   *   *

"So, you kind of know, or don't know at all?" Sean asked Conall, regarding the fact that we were completely lost.

"I've been to Inverness, of course, but never spent much time here, much less at bed and breakfasts," Conall said.

I said, "I bet if we'd been driving to a castle, every person on the road would have heard of it and there would have been those nice tourist destination signs to guide us every step of the way."

"Shut it, Nat," is all Sean said back.

Five minutes later, we found ourselves on a remote countryside road with little markings or signs. The road meandered like a snake, rolling through woody hills and sharp turns. Dense trees and thick underbrush surrounded us on both sides, hiding small estates and cottages, some with wrought iron fences, installed for privacy and security to keep people like us out.

We drove for miles and saw no indication that we were going the right way. If we'd ended up in the Shetland Islands, I wouldn't have been surprised.

Sean said, "We need to stop. Turn around."

I said, "Where? This road is six feet wide. I've seen hallways wider than this. We keep going." Conall leaned forward, "I agree. We're close. Besides, the bumper will end up wedged in that hedgerow."

237

Sean shook his head, "You're just agreeing with her to keep her happy, like everyone else."

We traversed through a heavily forested area, on a road that ran helter-skelter according to tree lines. Sean threw up his hands, saying he wanted off the joyride. I told him to keep his mouth shut unless he wanted his wish. Dad gaily looked about and smiled. After what seemed an eternity, we saw a road sign that indicated that we might be in the right area. We pulled into a long driveway that ended in a quaint house, with large side-addition. Wooded expanse surrounded us and there was a sizable pond sitting at the bottom of the acreage with one elderly man sitting on a chair, napping as he held his rod.

"Yeah, they're really biting here," I said to Sean, getting out of the car.

There was a very large outbuilding that had been built right on the edge of the property, with the continual sound of barking dogs. A large sign posted said, "Kennel Inn."

"Did they mention the dog kennel on that website when you booked this place? Or is that just part of the fishing experience? To have the dogs barking in the background?" I asked Sean, as we pulled bags from the trunk.

Sean jerked on his bag, "No, no dog kennel."

"Shame. It might have been helpful information when making the decision between here and the grand Scottish *castle*."

A woman came out of the house and walked towards the car. We introduced ourselves, and she told us that she had been expecting us all afternoon.

"Navigational issues," Dad said.

She took a good look at the car and said, "Obviously."

She escorted us to the main house, where she went to a desk and pulled out paperwork.

238

"Small problem," I said. "We have an additional person," and pointed to Conall. He gave his best smile and waved with a hand. "You wouldn't have an extra room by chance?"

Our hostess was shorter than me, which was saying something. To see Conall's face, her neck arched back a full five inches. Small lines creased her face. "Not really. We're full up, no?"

Conall spoke in his thickest Scottish accent, "No worries. I be good finding a place up the road if ye just point me in the right direction."

She regarded him. "So you're from . . ."

"North Uist."

"Right," she said and sighed. Taken as a whole, we were a confusing group. She was used to seeing romantic couples escaping to the countryside for the weekend. We were the Simpson's after a nasty divorce and a foreign exchange student addition.

"Well," she said, tapping her pencil on the paperwork. "There's a lil cottage in the back, for the guy who tends the dogs, no?" She chewed on her lip, thinking, "But he's on holiday. It's not much, nothing more than kitchenette and wee bedroom. You could have it, I guess."

"That be grand," Conall said.

She handed out keys and pointed us down the hallway to our respective rooms.

"So," I said, "the dog kennel? They make much noise?"

She smiled in a way that told me that she found this question irksome and tedious. I was sympathetic; I often walked in a patient's room and was asked to empty the urinal and bring breakfast.

"Most people worry about that," she said. "They only make noise when they're bein' fed and cages bein' cleaned. You shouldn't hear a thing at night, unless there's something that wakes them."

239

We settled into our rooms and Conall was taken to the supervisor's cottage. Sean tried the fishing and found it as dismal as it appeared. With great reservations, we drove back to Inverness for dinner and were surprised how little time it took when we knew where we were going. We settled on a place called the Castle Tavern. Sean turned to me and said, "See? You get your castle experience after all!"

I was not amused.

The noise inside the restaurant was a decibel akin to a Viking celebration—boisterous and catchy. After the first round of drinks, we were all laughing and telling personal war stories, except the one that mattered the most to anyone who might want to understand the sadness that lurked on the edges of our family. Several times between the laughter and the clink of dishes, Sean would glance across the table and our early morning conversation would bubble up, to mingle in the merriment like a red maraschino cherry floating in a martini.

Despite that, Sean laughed more than anyone. The words spoken that morning had loosened something deep within him. He ordered multiple whiskeys and told a childhood story about how I made the entire family come outside so I show them that I could ride a bike without training wheels. Instead of it being my great moment, I crashed the thing in the back of a pickup, bust open my lip and almost knocked out my front teeth. Conall laughed, spitting beer from his mouth. I looked at Sean and smiled, knowing that he'd been the one to pick me up and hold a towel to staunch the bleeding. He'd always been the softie, the one who mended wounds, whereas Tommie had laughed and walked away; a future war commander in the making.

We ate rib-eye steaks and washed it down with endless bottles of red wine. At the end of the meal, Sean ordered bread butter pudding and I conceded to Conall's demands that I order a cranachan. It was a surprisingly lovely dessert made of raspberries, oatmeal soaked in whiskey, topped off with whipped cream. Dad insisted that he pay for the whole dinner, which was an apology to Conall for tethering him to our obnoxious group.

Conall sat to my left, with my dad and brother across from us. It was a seating arrangement staged by Dad once we were shown to our table. Conall took the opportunity to touch my back several times during the meal. With the dim lighting, excellent food and courteous service, the whole thing was similar to a date, if the male contingency of my family hadn't been watching from the sidelines like it was a recreational sport. It'd been a long day and we all wobbled as we made our way back to the crumpled, disfigured car. Conall drove, and Dad and Sean fell asleep in the backseat.

*   *   *

Emails:

From Tommie Calhoun

To Natalie Calhoun

Subject: Huh?

Sean isn't getting married?

Really?

Wow.

How can he even pull his head from his ass to consider this?

I really didn't think he had it in him. Cracks me up to think that he went on vacation with his family so that he could have sex for the first time in five years.

*   *   *

An hour after everyone went to bed, I snuck out of my room like a high school delinquent on Saturday night and went into the

241

dark night to find Conall's cottage. A thousand times as I stumbled along the narrow path, I asked myself what was I doing. Those reservations fell on a deaf, alcohol-addled brain, even as I fell down the stairs, jerked the front door shut and fought through pitch black to the back property where a single light was burning in the cottage window.

The walk to the cottage was further than it looked by daylight. I had no flashlight and navigated on sheer instinct from what I remembered. There was horrendously uneven footing and more than once I almost fell, my foot getting lodged in some unseen hole. I screamed and caught myself, the noise causing the dogs to start barking. In my drunken giddiness, I shushed them, which only incited them more, the volume increasing twofold.

Failing to navigate the dark terrain, I tripped over a bush and laughed at my stupidity, falling to my hands and knees. When I pushed up, the loose sweater I wore caught on something and snagged. I pulled back, but couldn't get loose, so I reached out to find what was holding me hostage. My fingers grabbed something sharp and wicked, and I screamed, only to snag my shirt again, much higher on the neck. Behind me, the dog's volume increased to a full crescendo, the noise conjuring images of a posse of rabid animals biting at my heels. It fueled my moderate anxiety into full-fledged hysteria. I fought, turning from side to side, and managed to get my hair caught, tearing my scalp.

Something brittle and ancient snapped inside of me; the force of it unlocking a door to a dark place that I thought was buried and long forgotten. These fears set free screamed their presence, shredding what little courage and sense I had left. My cool sanity said goodbye and transitioned into a panicked frenzy. I fought to get loose, like a crazed animal caught in a trap. I only succeeded in making it worse. My jeans were now caught and small razors bit into my bare skin at the ankle. I heard a guttural noise and realized it was coming from me.

A light came on outside the cottage; a beacon in the night. From my position on the ground, I saw Conall come running from the small building. As he approached, he laughed, saying, "You silly

242

wee lass," but upon seeing me crying and savagely ripping at my clothes, sobered immediately.

"HELP ME!" I screamed.

"Nat, calm down."

He tried to get ahold of my arms, or any kind of leverage to keep me still, but I lashed out with wild abandon. "OH MY GOD. HELP ME. GET ME FREE."

"Nat—"

I was sobbing, large tears freely running down my cheeks and grabbed at him like he was a life force that would save me. "PLEASE CONALL. GET IT OFF."

"Shhhh. It's ok. It's ok. I got it."

"No, you don't. Get help. GET TOMMIE. GET TOMMIE," I said, making no sense. My hair was tangled and I tore at my scalp with my frantic efforts. Conall grabbed my arms to stop me. When I fought him, he physically shook me, rattling my teeth. "Nat! Stop it. Look at me, Nat. LOOK. AT. ME."

His hands were manacles on my forearms. With some effort, I stopped flailing. My brain was a chaotic spectrum of wild colors, like peering through a kaleidoscope as a kid. Everything was out of focus and twirling, winding, sliding away from each other.

He got very close to my face, his arms holding me still. "I am going to get you free. You understand?" He shook me again. "Nat, understand?"

I sucked in air, hiccupping as I continued to cry.

"Just hold still. Can you do that?"

I nodded.

He laid his hand on the side of my face. "Just keep your eyes on me, OK?"

I felt my whole body shake and grabbed a hold of his shirt.

"That's right. Just hold on, love," he said, wiping tears from my cheeks.

Carefully, he let go of my arms and pulled my clothes free of the barbs. Several times, he ripped my clothes to get me loose. In my mind, I saw those twisty, metal spikes, their vicious ends and the blood. I felt the metal tearing into my skin and the searing crisscrossing path. There was an uncontrollable shaking that rattled through my body.

"Almost there, hold tight."

My hair was snagged and Conall just pulled at my hair and left some behind. I didn't care. He was slow and methodical, telling me the entire time, "Yup. There's another one, love. Just a few more. Almost there," till I was free.

Finally, the job finished, my clothes and hair free, he pulled me upright. Without saying a word, Conall drew me to his side and walked me into the cottage, kicking the door shut. It was a tiny place, with nothing but a bed, a small kitchenette and a tiny round dining room table. In my confused mind, I thought maybe it was one of those miniature gardener huts that had been decorated into a home. He sat me in a chair. I shook so badly that I almost slid off and onto the ground; I'd seen drug addicts three days without a fix with better composure than myself. Conall squatted before me, holding onto my knees, not saying anything until the worst of it seemed to pass.

"You OK for just a sec?"

I nodded, but it was a lie. He turned and put a kettle on the stove. When that was accomplished, he placed a mug next to me. He went into what had to be a small hidden bathroom. I heard the rattling of a cabinet, the water turned on and then off. When he came back, he was holding a wet towel, a bottle of antiseptic and some Band-Aids.

He put the supplies on the table, grabbed the kettle, which was just about to boil, and poured some hot water in the mug. He threw in a tea bag and sat down. He leaned forward and surveyed me, grabbing one of my arms. "You OK?" he asked again.

"Quit asking that," I said with more bite than I wanted. I hated when people felt sorry for me. After the accident, when my neck was a fresh patchwork of gruesome proportions, people in town would either look away or give me uncomfortable glances of sympathy. It would send me into a screaming rampage until Tommie ushered me away like a special needs kid out of control. Later on, I would teach myself how to put those feelings away in a box—tuck those emotions far below the surface of my skin, where they laid buried and away from prying eyes. That is, until some rangy Scotsman came along and started excavating a hole and hitting at it with his hands.

"Right," he said, "let's see those cuts." He extended my right arm and dabbed at paper-thin wounds that were leaking small drops of blood.

My arm jerked and Conall looked up, and then went back to work. I was embarrassed and mortified. I wanted nothing more than to hide under the table. Or anywhere. Away from here, from this very nice guy, who if he had any sense at all, would run far, far away from me. "If you will just give me some of those bandages," I said, glancing towards the door, "I'll be on my way. I am truly sorry to have bothered you like this." I couldn't meet his eyes, but focused on the mug.

"Bothered me?" Conall said. "*Bothered me*? Jesus, Nat, stop saying that. And look at me."

I met his eyes and turned away. "I am very, very sorry. I don't know what came over me."

"Stop it!" He bounced my arm as he said it. "Quit talking like you accidently spilled a drink in my lap. What the hell just happened?" When I didn't say anything, he said, "Nat?"

I opened my mouth, shut it, glancing at the front door, pondering. Conall waited, his grip on my arm tightening. "Don't even think about it," he said, reading my mind.

Balling my fists, I asked, "Was it . . . is it . . . barbed wire?"

His eyes narrowed and confusion crossed his face. "Barbed wire. *Barbed wire?*" He rubbed at his forehead, his fingers threading through his hair in frustration. "This is Scotland, Nat. A bed and breakfast. Not the high plains." He cleared his throat. "There's no bloody barbed wire."

"No?" I asked, amazed.

"No."

"What, ah—"

"It was brambles."

"Huh?"

"You know. Brambles."

I stared on, confused.

"Those wicked plants that grow barbs. There's a nasty nest of them outside."

I swallowed, as thoughts ping ponged around in my head. "I got caught in brambles," calming myself and pushing away bubbling fears. "Brambles," I repeated, my hands gripping the table.

Conall's head tilted in thought as he stared at my scar tissue. He stood and bent over the table, lifting up my shirt to see the quagmire of scars. "Shit," he muttered, as he stepped back and a

246

chair scraped across the floor. "No way," and shook his head. "Are you kidding me?"

What would I be kidding about?

"That?" he pointed. "Ya got caught up in bloody barbed wire?"

Did I say that?

"Thought it was car accident or something."

I stared on, not saying anything.

As Conall paced, his fist pounded against his forehead. Once, twice, three times. "Please tell me some bloke didn't lead you into that American nastiness and leave you?"

"No."

"No," he repeated. When I said nothing more, he stopped and raised his hands. "What then? How'd you end up wrestling barbed wire?"

My mind bounced in chaotic manner like droplets of water in a hot oiled pan. Random thoughts of my childhood trickled through as if moving on a conveyer belt; my Shetland pony named Lady Bug, Eve's strawberry-rhubarb crisp, the Chesapeake named Charlie Brown, Rufus, the rooster that would attack from behind and Dad's precious sweet corn in the garden. "The raccoons," I said, unable to pull thoughts together correctly. My mind grasped at loose ends like a frayed rope just out of my reach.

He took a deep breath and placed his hands on the table, lowering his voice. "Raccoons?"

I said, "Well, maybe some dogs and a possum as well."

He sighed, "Natalie . . ."

I grabbed the mug to warm my hands. I hated tea and had no intentions of drinking it. "My mother had a garden. But hated it. Because of all the work. Dad loved green beans and sweet corn, so she did it. Every year. For him."

Conall nodded and sat. Sometimes remembering a painful memory is a slow meandering path to the truth. Even if you know how the story ends, even if you've sat in that spot a thousand times, eyeing the landscape, breathing the air, wondering if you could have changed it, you still have to mentally walk the entire way to face it once more. It's more about the trip itself than the final outcome. Conall dabbed at a cut with the towel and some antiseptic. "Keep going," he said, letting me talk. He took a Band-Aid and put it between his teeth as he continued to clean wounds.

"My mother complained that animals were eating everything. All her hard work was for nothing, except to feed them. I remember her yelling at Dad to do something about it." I cleared my throat. "Raccoons love sweet corn."

Conall looked up and said, "I dinna ken," then corrected himself, "know." I watched him tend my wounds. There was something very soothing about it and I felt so tired. I closed my eyes for just a second.

"Nat," Conall said quietly. My eyes popped open. "So, ye Dad put up barbed wire, dinna he? To keep out the animals?"

"Huh?" I shook my head. "No." I knew I wasn't making sense, but my reasoning abilities were beyond my grasp for the moment.

"He didn't?"

"Ah . . ." I paused, distracted. "My dad loved my mom so much." And he had. Their love had been a constant that bathed the house with light every day. When my mother died, someone might as well turned off the electricity and condemned the place. Dad would never marry again, even though Eve was deserving of it.

"So he put up barbed wire."

248

"No."

"No?"

"He made Sean do it."

Conall froze.

"Sean?" he asked.

"Huh?" I was walking through the memory, seeing the garden, just outside the south window. I thought about Conall's poor mother, dying over months, with cancer. Long days to talk, to say good-bye. "My mother was in the kitchen that day. I was upstairs with Sean. My Dad was at work. Tommie was at a friend's house next door."

Conall took a breath and grabbed my hand. "Yes," he said. "Go on."

"And her aneurysm, well . . ."

Conall dropped my hand and sat back—the air deflating out of him. "That was *this* particular day?" he asked, his face losing color. "The day of barbed wire and your mother were the same?" I nodded and he muttered a Gaelic curse.

I traveled back to that pristine day. I was upstairs reading *A Wrinkle in Time*, enjoying my summer vacation, ruminating over the fact that Tommie had called Sean and I brats because he was being forced to work for my uncle and we weren't being forced to do chores around the house. He called us both spoiled babies, right before walking out. It was a June day out of the storybooks—cornflower blue skies, mild warm breeze, and the sound of sheets snapping on a clothesline just outside the window.

"I heard a noise," I told Conall. "Something very loud hitting the floor and my mother . . ." I inhaled, "when Sean and I found her, she was just lying there, holding her mid-section, taking breaths that weren't really breaths. Not the kind that really take in air. She couldn't talk she was in so much pain. We didn't know what to do and were so young. She was . . ." I sucked air into my lungs and sputtered, "We panicked."

He blinked several times. "Right. Anyone would've."

"I tried to help her, but it was apparent that . . ." I ran a hand over my face, my finger glancing a spot that stung. I had sensed Death for the first time that day. He watched from across the room, his pork-pie hat pushed back on his head, a surprised look on his face.

"So I ran out the back door to find Tommie. We needed help. And Tommie always fixed things." A nervous laughter bubbled out of me as I tried to see out the window, only to see the room reflected back.

Conall looked at me. "And Sean?"

"Sean, he . . ." How could I explain the pivotal moment when Sean had taken several steps back and stood against the wall in a frozen state of panic? He had not helped, even when I yelled at him to do exactly that. He'd been catatonic, with glazed eyes and his small, shaking hands clutching his t-shirt. He'd never been built with sharp edges and quick tempers like Tommie and myself. Consequently, he'd been the one we'd protected from playground evils. Until this day. Afterwards, we'd left him to face his demons alone, deserting him in light of this one event. As a child sheltered, Sean had no defenses against the real-world brutality—we might as well have sent him into a snowstorm without a winter jacket.

"Sean was incapable of helping." I shook my head. "In that moment. It all happened so fast. He was . . . inconsolable, seeing her in that condition."

Conall's eyes narrowed. "You were *kids*. Most adults would've been in the same state."

I inhaled, thinking about choices. I used to think it was just one bad decision had decided our fate that day, but my mother's death was simply the momentum that plunged us into the hundred missteps that we allowed to happen afterwards. I shook my head at the thought.

"I took a short-cut through the back yard and . . ."

How was I to know that Sean had put up the fencing the day before? He'd done a horrible job, but with no guidance, how could he have known better? It was curled and loose; a limp circle of horrific barbs hidden amongst overgrown plants. I hadn't seen it in my blind hysteria to get help. Afterwards, there'd been conjuncture among family members, but only discussed when Dad and Sean wasn't in the room. *What if Dad had done the job? What if the fencing hadn't been so loose? What if he'd chosen to use electric fencing? And what if Sean had come with me.* All kinds of thinking that didn't matter anyway. The truth of it was, I hit the fencing and fell into it and then the whole thing curled and caught around my right side.

"I hit the barbed wire at a full sprint. Never saw it coming." I took a breath. "And then I *panicked*," letting the air seep out of my lungs. Panic didn't even describe the mania that overtook me in that moment. "I tried to wrestle my way out of it . . . pulling, jerking . . ." I saw the grimace on Conall's face. He understood how brutal barbed wire was in that kind of situation. I stared at my hand, where small white scars were visible on my palms. I waved it off. "Well, you know."

He nodded.

What he didn't know—what no one knew, what would make most people think that I was insane, and maybe I was—was that I had watched Death walk outside after finishing his business with my mother. He sat down next to me in patch of green beans. He eyed me curiously, sympathetically, pulling his notepad from his pocket. A job was a job after all. I'd been screaming for help but was losing blood and energy reserves fast. He wrote my name with some resignation, carefully dotting the "I." I remembered crying and reaching out, grabbing onto vines when I heard Tommie's voice. I opened my eyes to see his panicked face hovering above mine. He used both hands to stem the blood coming from my neck, while

251

saying, "You're OK, you're OK, I got you." For the first time I could remember, Tommie was panicked and it scared me. He screamed, "DON'T YOU DARE DIE ON ME!" as he pushed with so much pressure that I screamed.

Death glanced up surprised, his notepad still on his knee. He scratched out my name, winking as he rose. He'd disappeared into the house, taking my mother with him. I only mentioned this entire scenario to one person—the emergency room doctor. He'd smiled sympathetically and said that large blood loss could cause hallucinations and patted my arm with a genial smile. I never mentioned it again.

"Tommie found me. Heard me crying. I was bleeding out, just hanging on. Dad rushed home and was the one to find Sean and my mother, who was already dead." I looked away, "I suffered a large amount of blood loss." I rubbed my neck in the spot that had almost secured my death. "The wire punctured my jugular. Not my carotid. I was lucky. Tommie held pressure as Dad drove. A county doctor stitched me up and stopped the bleeding."

Without thinking, I picked up the tea and took a sip, spitting it out, spraying it all over. Conall stared at the mess, including tea spots on his own shirt. A grin curled at his lips. "That good, huh?"

I wiped at my shirt and noticed blood spots on my sleeves. I said, "I really hate tea. I don't understand the purpose of tea when coffee is in the world. Seems kind of pointless."

Conall tried to contain it, but burst out laughing anyway. "You are so American. Right down to your barbed wire scars."

I smiled. "Thanks. I guess." Evaluating my arms, I saw most of the cuts were superficial. I would survive, but Conall might want to be put out of his misery. "So, after telling you of my bloody past, I need to get going." I rose. "A girl can take only so much humiliation in one day. In one week for that matter. Spending time with me is like attending an AA meeting at a fraternity keg party."

Conall laughed, then sobered when he saw that I was serious. He reached out and grabbed my arm. He said, standing, "I ran

252

headfirst into swearing, three-hundred-pound blokes that wanted to throw me down and grind ma' balls under their feet." He paused. "I think I can handle you."

"You haven't seen me on the job."

Conall laughed. "Well then, I've been warned. About everything." Conall took a step forward. He took my hand, intertwining our fingers; my small hand engulfed by his. Whispering, he said, "Please. Stay," and pulled me into his arms.

I said nothing as his whole body came around me. He carefully maneuvered me backwards until the wall was against my back. I took stock of my emotions and realized that the internal shaking had stopped. His body was a barrier that could keep away the world and a ragged breath escaped my lungs.

There were a million reasons why I needed to walk away, to find my way back through the dark and close the door on this right now. As I was about to voice those concerns, Conall leaned down, slid his arm around my back and pulled me closer. He whispered, "*Tá tú go h-álainn,*" in my ear, nipping, and moved over to my jawline, migrating to my lips. For the record, a bunch of gibberish in a sexy foreign language can make all those reasons slip away. He could have been speaking Icelandic; it wouldn't have made a difference.

"What was that?" I asked, standing to my tiptoes, my lips brushing his. Without thinking, I helped him take off his shirt and watched as he kicked off his shoes. He took a hold of my ripped sweater and pulled it over my head. Bending, he kissed my neck beneath my ear, his finger tracing a path beneath my bra strap, pulling it down and continuing over my arm, following a scar.

I laid my hand on his chest, feeling the warm skin there and pushed, just the tiniest pressure, until he took a step back, confusion written on his face. My hand continued to move of its own accord over his sternum and then to his heart, my fingertips tracing a path. I ran my palm from his heart to his smooth clavicle, the skin perfect and unblemished. My fingers finished their path when I grabbed one of his hands and turned it over. There were callouses along his fingers and a small scar along his thumb. "Cleat mark," he said, right before he gently lifted my chin. He leaned forward and kissed me, just the merest hint of lips. His arms wrapped around me and he lifted me to my toes as his kisses became more urgent. He pulled back and asked, "Trust me?"

I nodded.

Conall reached behind me, to pull me close, as his hand slid over my ribcage, finally resting on my hip, his fingers rubbing small circles that burned through my skin.

"What did you say before?" I asked, as he kissed me once, twice, three times like small prayers.

"Trust me," he replied, as I grabbed his shoulders, pulling him closer to cover my scars in the bright light of the room.

"Before that," I said.

Conall reached up and slowly disentangled my hands from his shoulders. Moving slowly, he brought them above my head and held them against the wall. He took his time to survey every inch of my body—his eyes travelling from my shoulders, to my breasts, and finally my legs. He smiled as placed a kiss on my shoulder, my entire body bending towards him. His hand meandered down my side, running the length of my scars.

"It means, 'you're beautiful.'"

13

Emails:

From Natalie Calhoun

To Tommie Calhoun

Re: Huh?

We should cut Sean some slack.

Maybe we should do a lot more of other things.

Like talk to him.

-Nat

*   *   *

From Tommie Calhoun

To Natalie Calhoun

Re: Huh?

Are you going soft on me?

Beef up, cupcake, I was just going to suggest to my commander that you be our medical support in a spontaneous meet-and-greet group going to Kandahar, for a little extra cash flow. But if you're

255

seriously worrying about Sean's caramel toffee pudding intake and sex life, I'm rescinding the offer.

-Tommie

* * *

I'd agreed to accompany Conall to the car lot first thing in the morning to exchange the car and figure out paperwork. I'd been the one driving and my name was on the agreement, such as it was. Dad and Sean didn't argue, just nodded and told me fill them in with the details. At dawn, I meandered back to the main house, staring at the innocuous nature of the bushes in broad daylight. Slipping into my room, I showered, dressed and met Conall outside within thirty minutes.

When he pulled up, I opened the door, and said, "Feels like old times. We got to quit meeting like this," and threw myself into the passenger seat. He laughed, threw the car into gear and we took off towards Inverness.

We drove in silence; the windows cracked an inch, allowing cool air to circulate. He put on the heat for my comfort. We said nothing of the night before, even though several small scratches were still evident on my hands and forehead. I sipped coffee that the B&B owner—still in her robe and pajamas—had slipped me while standing outside.

When we arrived at the car lot, a burly man with the tightest curly red hair I'd ever seen stumbled out of a small building. He hiked up his pants twice as he walked towards us.

He waved, "Conall, good to see ye, ole man."

The two of them shook hands and slapped each other on the back. Conall said, "Angus, this is Natalie. Nat, this is Angus. He's our contact for replacement vehicles and," Conall cleared his throat, "repairs that go beyond our scope."

256

I raised my hand, "That would be me, Angus. I am the girl that caused *repairs that go beyond the scope,*" and motioned to the vehicle behind us with a thumb.

Angus said, "That's what I hear," and clapped his hands. "OK, then. Let's take a gander, shall we?" He walked down the side of the car that had the most damage and paused mid-inspection to say, "How's the old man?"

"Aye, good." Conall frowned. "Grumpy."

"I bet," Angus said, laughing, "especially when rentals are . . ." he ran a finger down a large dent, taking in the mirror and the destroyed bumper. "Sideswiping other cars?" and peered at me with a questioning glance.

"Nah." I waved him off, tucking my unruly hair behind an ear. I adopted a sassy pose. "Just storming fairy towers, trespassing in formal gaming rooms and running from museum cops. All in a day of tourism for the Calhoun family."

A toothy grin appeared on Angus' face that made him look ten years younger. He stood to his full height and patted down the bumper. "Impressive." He put his hands on his hips and hiked his pants once more. "Ooch, you get away? Or they place a spike strip on the ground to keep from making ye escape?"

"I'm a professional, Angus, no one got anything on me and my driving," and I mimed shifting at a high speed.

Angus bellowed in a way that was most likely heard in the Shetland Islands. He said to Conall, "You got a live one here, no?"

Conall scratched at his forehead. "Ye have no idea."

Angus and Conall talked over the small details. It was decided that the car could be repaired and Angus would do the work there. The bill would be submitted to Alec, my insurance company would be informed, and the proper authorities would fight over what was owed and how much would come out of my pocket. Angus

257

threw us the keys to a Vauxhall Corsa, which was about the same size as a Ford Festiva.

"OK, kiddies, have fun," he said, pushing Conall towards the car. "Don't do anything I wouldn't."

Conall looked around. "You got anything larger?"

Angus said, "Are ye kidding me? No. Ye spent too much time in the states with those gas-guzzlers. Besides ye want your Bonnie here taking out anything larger than she already has?"

* * *

On the way back, we stopped for coffee and muffins. I ordered a double shot cappuccino. With full-drip caffeine circulating within my body, some of my mojo returned. The night before had been a roller-coaster ride, leaving me unmoored, but my feet were back under me, along with my confidence, so I dived headfirst into unknown territory.

I turned in my seat, watching Conall drive. His enormous body behind the wheel of that small car gave the impression that someone had used a crowbar to slide him in and it would take a crane to get him out. "You once said . . . that first morning, when you picked me up," he nodded, urging me on, "you said that you were trying to get back. To the States."

Conall smiled. "You mean the morning you ripped your trousers? Or the one when you stumbled into my bed and kissed an unknown stranger?"

"Right," and I laughed. "My checkered past. But you kissed me!" I said indignantly. I cleared my throat, "I'm talking about the underwear incident morning."

"Ahhh, I remember it fondly."

"Of course you do. They were fine lime-green underpants."

258

"Knickers."

"Right. Knickers." I shook my head. "So, you're thinking about it? The States?"

Conall glanced from the road to me, and back again, grinning. "Why, perchance, Miss Natalie Calhoun, would you be interested in that?"

He was being glib, but it grated like sandpaper against my skin. I shouldn't care. *I didn't care, right?* Men usually chased me, until, that is, they really knew me. Then they ran. This thing between Conall and myself was strange, unchartered territory. He'd gotten a big, heaping portion of me and my secrets in a very short amount of time, and for some uncanny reason, he was still sitting at the table, asking for seconds. A part of me was entranced; the other part was mortified.

I shrugged as if it was nothing, but my stomach churned on the coffee as if I had a cement grinder inside of me. "Dinna know," I said, in my best Scottish accent, "Ye a wee scunner, but kina like you. No?"

Conall didn't say anything for the longest time, possibly disregarding me and choosing not to answer. It wouldn't have been the first time a man had treated me in such a way. Having him do it was making the grinder inside me halt and seize, the concrete expanding within my intestines and solidifying.

"It's very hard, ye know?" he said. "My dad is used to me being around. I help with the business. Have for a long time now."

I nodded.

"But I can't keep doing this. Not working at a used car rental lot and farm. Before . . . at school . . . I had plans. Maybe get my MBA." He shrugged. "My mother got sick. Things got put on the backburner. Things I left behind." Maybe he was talking about professional football, maybe not. He looked out the window towards

259

the horizon. "Anyway, it didn't work out. And the islands, they're just so small. And not just in a distance kind of way."

"People like Davina?" I asked.

"People just like Davina," he said and sighed. He considered the countryside as he drove. "I love this place, it's my home." He paused. "But it's also my prison."

I thought about being stuck in the hospital for hours and the lack of sunlight or fresh air. "At least it's beautiful," and pointed at the lush, green landscape.

He snorted. "What's the word? Gilded cage?" He shook his head in dismay. "It's why I end up in Edinburgh sometimes."

Neither of us said anything for several miles and I thought the conversation was over. Turning into the driveway of the B&B, Conall put the car in park and said, "I've reapplied to schools again. But my dad . . . he dosna know."

"Oh boy," I said.

Conall muttered, "Yes, oh boy. Hell hath no fury like Alec's temper, trust me."

*　　*　　*

We picked up Dad and Sean, and drove to Culloden, where the Scottish Bonnie Prince gathered the clans and rallied them to fight to win their freedom from the English throne. Lacking the gun power and canons the English held in their arsenal, the Scottish men were slaughtered and the clan life destroyed forever. From the beginning, I wanted to see Culloden. I told Dad this and he never questioned it, thinking I'd simply become a history buff. I wasn't. I was just following the trail of Death's most prominent and famous work.

My first impression of Culloden was that it would have been an ideal place for a picnic, and then I was embarrassed for thinking it. It could have been Gettysburg; the hallowed ground a sweeping landscape, preserved for its bloody history, but unabashedly tranquil in its beauty. The horrors of another time existed in the whispers within the grass, as sunlight bent through tree limbs and there was the call of the birds in the distance. The view was unobstructed by any building, other than the museum itself.

Unlike the other small exhibitions and castles that we'd seen, the museum at Culloden was like a miniature Scottish Smithsonian. There was visual effects and an audio tour giving both sides of history from the English and Scottish viewpoints, and military relics and digital aerial reenactment that showed exactly how the English charged and how the Scottish fell in grotesque numbers. Conall was engrossed in the details, listening to almost every video clip, as Sean, Dad and I skipped a few and kept going at our own pace.

Towards the end of the exhibit, I rounded a corner and stepped into complete darkness with another group of people. We all stood confused and blind in a pitch-black room with Scottish bagpipe music playing. I was about to leave, not understanding the purpose, when the lighting increased, similar to the sun coming up. Growing in volume, as if they surrounded me, were the voices of men as they prepared for war; readying rifles, making small talk and officers giving orders before the great battle. Horses came in and out of the shadows, like they might run me over.

I felt him before I saw him.

Death said, "Regular meat grinder, that day."

His skeletal profile was exaggerated in the low light. I sighed, "I'd think you'd need a vacation from the place."

His teeth flashed. "You know how it goes, Nat. Your best work is when you're knee deep in the blood. Hard to stay away."

We stood as a couple as the skirmish came alive; there were hair-raising screams of the men and the first sounds of gunfire. Gruesome conflict played out on all sides. Shadows of the soldiers circled and moved, running right at us, yelling orders, as cannon fire became louder. The violence increased ten-fold, as well as the horrendous shrieks of men as they fell to their death.

261

I felt the cold tang of his breath as he leaned in, "Men will always murder and I will always exist, rolling in after fate and catastrophe throw the dice. But sometimes," there was the wet sound of a bayonet hitting tissue and a man's groan, "an innocent slips our arms." I saw his eyes slide towards mine. "What's eternity without some entertainment?"

A shadow of a horse falling made me flinch and I stepped back. Intermixed within the ghastly video soundtrack were the first cries of children. Parents ushered their kids out, holding hands over their ears and eyes. I stood paralyzed. The disconcerting authenticity and ear-splitting volume levels made me lose my balance and I tripped, almost falling. Holding down my panic, I turned to find the exit when I felt a large hand come about my neck, solid and comforting. I leaned into it and took a deep breath.

Conall's voice was soothing, as he whispered, "Let's go, no?"

I nodded.

We walked out into the sunlight and the blue skies of a perfect day. I held up a hand to shield my eyes. The field was solitary, quiet, unassuming—beautiful in its serenity. We walked its perimeter and read the names on rock markers where whole clans fell, died and were buried in mass graves. MacGregor, MacKintosh, Fraser, Boyd, MacIntyre, Cameron, MacClachlan, Maclean. Mass burials, unclaimed bodies; fathers, sons, husbands, brothers. Stone markers were worn with age and covered with lichen and moss. Dad and Sean wandered aimlessly, standing in the sun and conferring about battle strategies. I lingered behind with Conall.

He took my hand.

I let him.

We finished our tour in a café lit by large glass windows overlooking Culloden field, drinking cappuccinos and eating scones. I leaned my head back against the booth, my shoulder rubbing against Conall's arm. Through slotted eyes and a pastry-sugar overloaded brain, I glimpsed a familiar figure walking through the

262

food line in a plaid shirt, surveying muffins, but told myself I was imagining things and to forget it. About the same time, a nice Scottish woman touting the local tourism walked up and encouraged us to download a Scottish tourism app for our smart phones. She gave us the directions to local spot called the Clava Cairns that was a few miles away. With several hours still to burn, we decided to make it our next stop.

My head was doing a slow migration towards Conall's shoulder when the sound of dishes crashing to the floor raised everyone's attentions. I raised my eyebrow and made a small joke about the scones not being up to par. A woman screamed for help and another woman yelled back in Gaelic. Before I knew what was happening, Conall was standing up, alarmed, like the quarterback was refusing to get up after being taken out by a lineman.

"What?" I asked, perturbed.

"Someone's got a problem."

"What kind of problem?"

"Dinno. Medical something."

I inhaled, closed my eyes and tried my best to ignore the entire situation. As appalling as it sounds, it was the truth. I had cappuccino, a warm chocolate croissant and a decent fluttery romance vibe going on, and I didn't want my lovely diabetic high being ruined by a medical snafu. Generally speaking, there were two kinds of medical providers out there; those who eagerly waded into public medical emergencies outside of work, and those of us that only interceded if forced, like someone else wasn't around. I'll give you one guess what club I was solidly a member.

Sean looked over. "You going to sit there?"

I took a large breath. "I'm in another country. On vacation. Weird logistics," and took a sip of coffee.

"Nat, don't be an ass."

263

"Always taking the high moral ground. Well, except for—"

"The *emergency?*" Sean said, interrupting me.

I groaned and stood up, wiping crumbs off my shirt as I scooted by Conall, saying, "Excuse me."

Conall grabbed me by the arm and said, "What are *you* going to do," like I was car mechanic running towards a house fire.

I said sheepishly, "Helping."

Word of advice: When you wait to help and had the potential to assist all along, you do look like a bit of an ass when you finally do.

"*You?*"

For the record, Conall's face is one I'd seen many times before. Whenever I entered a patient's room and started talking about the possible statistical outcomes of a loved one's coronary bypass surgery, people peered at me as if I'd grown another head. Since I have the appearance of a twelve-year old human relations secretary, I was used to seeing full-fledged panic bloom on people's faces. For this reason, I never took off my long white medical coat like some of my male colleagues. There was an adjustment period as people came to grips that I was an interventional cardiologist mid-way through her fellowship, specializing in cutting-edge coronary stent placement. For some elderly grandmothers though, they still saw Little Debbie from the Oatmeal Crème Pie boxes. As soon I finished talking about the complications of cardiac stenting, they would politely say that they wanted someone older, but what they really meant was someone *male*.

I walked behind the food counter to find a very large, overweight man collapsed on the floor. I took in the sight of him and my mind rattled off the list of possible ailments that were hijacking him at the moment—diabetes, hypertension, coronary artery disease and possible alcohol cirrhosis, observing the color of his skin and rotund belly. Several women fluttered around in hysteria, raising the panic levels. I knelt next to him and felt his carotid artery, but found no pulse. I groaned and added possible ventricular tachycardia leading to a full code to the list. There was no heartbeat and he wasn't breathing.

"She a nurse?" one person in the crowd asked.

"Dinno," someone answered.

"Geez," I muttered. "Why do they always assume a nurse?"

Behind me, Sean muttered, "Nat . . ." warning me into better behavior, as a woman chanted Gaelic prayer.

"Right then," I said, turning to a woman standing close. "You call the ambulance?" She stared as if I was speaking gibberish. "Go, go, go," I said, shooing her off. "And tell them to bring Epinephrine and that it's a full cardiac arrest."

I said to another by-stander. "You work here?" She nodded vigorously. "Go look for a medical kit. Something with an ambu bag," and mimed a big bag and placing something over my face, "and an AED!" I screamed the word, hoping someone in the vicinity would have one. Did they have them in Scotland? I had no idea. She stood there staring, and I screamed, "NOW!" She shook out of her trance and took off running. I heard Conall curse under his breath.

Sean leaned in and whispered, "Easy on the hired help. You're scaring people."

"You wanted me to help," I said as I ripped open the man's shirt. I pushed up my sleeves and started CPR, holding off on the rescue breaths, just trying to get some blood pumping. *One, and two, and . . .*

Conall said, "Does she know what she's doing?" with real worry in his voice.

"Yes," Sean said.

"Do I?" I said, joking.

265

"Shut up, Nat. Concentrate," Sean said.

Six and seven and eight . . .

"Trying," I said, continuing my compressions and counting to thirty. "Sean, get in here." *Fifteen and sixteen, staying alive, staying alive . . .*

"What?" he asked.

I gasped for air, "Breaths. Do the breaths." *Twenty-one, Twenty-two . . .*

"I want compressions," Sean said.

I wheezed, "You get breaths."

Conall whispered, "Should this be a debate?"

"He needs to spend more time with our family," I said.

"NAT!" Sean seethed. "Concentrate and act appropriately."

I gave the guy two slow breaths, cringing; his breath smelled of burnt coffee and cigarettes. "Uggggh, you're right. Get the ambu bag immediately!" My voice was labored as I began the second set of compressions on the rib cage of a two-hundred-and-eighty-pound man. I used enough force that several ribs broke, the sound similar to cracking a stick in your hands.

"What the hell was that?" Dad asked, leaning around Conall and trying to stay as far away as possible because he thought of death as a communicable disease.

Puffing air, I said, "Ribs. I don't usually do this. Just give orders."

"Orders?" Conall asked. "What?"

Sean was on his knees next to me, but saved by the woman showing up with a decent medical kit that contained an ambu bag.

266

Small mercies. "Seal it with your fingers around his mouth," I said, pointing at the mouthpiece. "Tilt his chin up. Squeeze the bag fully. Not too fast. Make sure the chest inflates fully before you give another breath."

"You're a doctor?" Conall asked.

Sean and I glanced up. Sean gave two slow squeezes of the bag and I started compressions again. "Ah, yeah," I said, using my best fifth-grader language.

Conall swiveled to Dad, who shrugged, using a *'oh gosh, I guess so'* kind of look.

Conall said, *"Really?"*

At that moment, the ambulance showed up and someone threw an AED that landed at my feet. I guess credentials of any kind were not needed in Scotland.

"Family doctor?" Conall asked.

"God, no," I said, slapping electrodes on the guy's chest. I hit the power button and listened to the motor whine to life. The computerized voice rattled off instructions and advised an electrical shock. I told everyone to stand back because it was going to hit him with two hundred joules of electricity.

I leaned back, preparing to hit the button. "No way. Too much small talk. People expect you to *really* involve yourself."

I raised my hands and yelled, "Clear!" and hit the button. The man's body jerked, as well as everyone in the vicinity. A woman started to cry.

Conall stood staring, confused.

I sat back on my heels. "I'm a cardiologist."

14

Emails:

From Natalie Calhoun

To Tommie Calhoun

Subject: Suck it

SOFT? Don't even start. Just broke three ribs on a cardiac arrest patient inside a cafeteria, while yelling at the locals. Saved the patient, but they took my coffee. Still pissed.

-Nat

*   *   *

From Tommie Calhoun

To Natalie Calhoun

Re: Suck it

Impressive. Once you've finished your pity party about the locals falling down and ruining your breakfast, you need to wrap your head around the fact that Trevor has been detained by the authorities. Apparently he was trying to take money out of your account by using an old debit card left at the house, and he's now being housed at the local pokey awaiting arraignment. I'm thinking there won't be any more correspondence from that area.

As a parting gift, I'm attaching some pictures of the damage to your house. Be forewarned, you might want to find a bottle of decent

Scottish whiskey before viewing. Or snog a local boy. (Sean's been emailing as well. You animal!!!) It's a combination of serious boyfriend stupidity and your gangsters' intervention. Look closely, my friend got some images of the guys taking stuff from your house. I leave it to you to decide what you want to do.

-   Tommie boy

* * *

From Natalie Calhoun

To Robbie Durst

Subject: Gonads

Please observe the attached images. I believe these individuals, breaking into my house and taking my possessions, are your acquaintances. Or employees. Since Trevor has been detained by local authorities for fraud and theft, and my possessions have most likely been sold on the black market in re-payment of his debt, I am expecting full cooperation of you and your employees in the rebuilding/restocking of my house. I assume you know friendly local contractors who would be more than willing to help with this endeavor. Free of charge. It's either that or I submit photos to law enforcement for criminal charges. Trevor could always use some friendly company.

-Nat

P.S. For your viewing entertainment, I also included an image of a fully engorged, gangrenous testicle. The end result of a hydrocele. Good stuff for dinner parties and family get-togethers. A "how-to" on emasculation.

* * *

"Quit looking at me like that," I said.

270

Conall said, "I can't help it."

"What'd you think I did for a living?"

"I dinno ken. But not that. Maybe a nurse?"

"That's completely sexist."

He backtracked. "OK, maybe a medical secretary of some kind."

"Wow. It gets worse."

"It's just . . ." he scraped his foot around in some dirt.

I filled in the gaps. "That I'm somewhat of a spaz and a social idiot, right?"

"Well," he ran his hand through his hair. "Yes," and he laughed.

"They're both requirements for medical specialists."

"Well—"

"Don't worry," I held up my hands. "I'm good at what I do." I shrugged. "It might be the only thing I'm good at."

After the medical episode in which I did CPR for fifteen minutes and used the AED to zap the guy twice into normal sinus rhythm, the ambulance carried the man away to the local hospital in Inverness. In the following minutes, in which people stared at me and I stared back, I stumbled back to our table to find that my coffee and scone had been cleared away and the table was completely clean of debris. For some reason, this upset me more than anything. No one helped with the CPR, but they had the time to clear away my coffee? At that exact moment, the manager of the museum introduced himself—Roger Lee, a robust man who appeared to have some medical issues of his own and had been strangely absent during our time of need—and gave me a firm handshake and year's

271

free admittance to the museum. I would've preferred a complimentary latte.

We now stood several miles away, staring at local cairns, which were burial sites that were about four thousand years old. Normally, I would have been intrigued, but the fact that I'd just performed CPR for twenty minutes and listened to Sean convince Conall that I was a cardiologist had the day feeling surreal. My wrists hurt from manually busting the guy's ribs. Between Culloden, CPR, and now the cairns, I was officially proclaiming it, "The Day of Death."

Afterwards, we drove down a picturesque country lane so Sean could look at streams. I was too tired to fight him. At regular intervals, we stopped and Sean stood and stared at the water, looking for fish. One of our last stops was at a large bridge that had distinct similarities to some Roman cousins I'd seen in northern Spain. There was old country estate nearby with inconspicuous rental cottages built right up to a tranquil stream. Sean scouted the Internet later to find that the entire place was a getaway for trout fisherman, complete with your own housing and fishing guide.
"We stayed at the wrong place," he said.

"Yes."

"I was stupid booking that B&B."

"Yes." I cleared my throat. "But I won't hold it against you, because I've been known to make questionable choices from time to time."

We leaned over the bridge, letting our arms dangle like we were small kids. The sunlight made iridescent colors bounce on the water and warmed our backs. Conall and Dad walked down the winding road, discussing something that had Dad inclined towards him in great interest. I remembered a time when Tommie, Sean and I would ride our bikes into the country to an old plank bridge, throw rocks over the side, and then wander down to the river to catch crappies or sunfish with a piece of fishing string and a bobber. Tommie would throw us in the water, but we never minded much. Our mother would give us hell about the state of our clothes

272

afterwards, making us leave our dirty tennis shoes outside and undress in the laundry room. I would be in my pink floral underpants, the boys in their white boxers. She would chase us up the stairs and we'd all be a ball of elbows and knees, giggling as we ran to our rooms.

Sean looked down the road. "Trip almost to an end." His eyes focused on the two men. "What are you going to do?"

"Go back to work. Take some extra call. Make money for the rental I buried in concrete pylons."

He leaned against the bridge, shaking his head, "Nat. Stop it."

I threw another rock. I counted six ripples before they disappeared. "Nothing to do. He's here. I'm there."

"You could."

"I'm not."

"Long distance?"

"With my schedule?"

"Phone sex?"

I laughed. "With my imagination?"

"Move to Scotland?"

"With all my money?"

Sean sighed. "OK, pen pals it is.

* * *

Emails:

From Robbie Durst

To Natalie Calhoun

Re: Gonads

Your love notes make my heart sing in joy. If I'd known when I saw you, (working betting lines, crunching numbers for possible statistical outcomes on the Oklahoma-Arkansas game,) that you were a woman with such "moxie," I might have tried harder to warn you about your gambling-infantile-philanderer boyfriend.

We operate many services. A diverse company with many opportunities for growth. We would love to see you for possible interview and employment. Please leave your military friends/relatives at home.

R-

*   *   *

Our trip came full circle. We made it back to North Uist at six o'clock. After dinner in the hotel bar and polite conversation, Conall convinced us to walk down the street to a local pub called the "Smoking Toad." It was a white, stone edifice flanked by several groups of kids smoking outside as the thumping bass of a band inside vibrated two small, fogged windows. A large sign hung over a red wooden door, displaying a fat amphibian lounging on his back against a rock, holding a cigarette while drinking from a tankard of beer.

When we walked inside, the full force of a four-piece Scottish band hit us like a wall. The music reverberated around the small pub that was decorated with reused plank boards, faded black-and-white photographs of past bands, low ceilings, red leather booths and tightly packed tables. There was a long bar along one wall and a small stage on the other. People were shoulder to shoulder, and the sheer volume of humanity was overwhelming. Out of instinct, I took a step back. Conall placed his hand on my shoulder, smiled and took the lead, clearing a path for us to the bar. People greeted him as he went. He shook hands and patted people on the back, moving along at a slow pace, maneuvering us through the throng. Conall found a table in the back with just two people. He talked to a man who seemed to know him and pointed back to us. The guy turned, then nodded. Both men rose, took their beers and joined a group of friends at another table with a couple of free chairs. Conall sat down and motioned us over.

I shouted, "You sure this OK?"

He yelled back. "It's fine. They come every week."

Once seated, Conall motioned to the bartender, holding up four fingers. The guy nodded, pulling out four glasses from behind the bar.

Sean leaned over to be heard. "You should get out more. No one seems to know you here."

Conall grinned. "The islands are small. Usual crowd. I went to school with the guy that owns the place."

The band was playing a fast Scottish ditty that had the younger crowd standing close to the stage and bobbing their heads. They had pints in their hands and cigarettes dangling from their lips, leaning into one another and talking over the music. There was a high whistle as the bartender slid four full pints towards us. Conall stood and retrieved them. He leaned over and said something to Dad, who looked perplexed and tapped his ear, smiling.

I touched Conall's shoulder. "It's no use. He can't hear you with this kind of ambient noise. His hearing is shot. Too many afternoons with a chain saw or other loud engine."

Conall nodded and placed an arm around my back. Sean made notice of it, but his eyes darted away. I didn't like crowded bars, or music so loud you could barely talk, but tucked away in a small corner, the Scottish music soothed us all into a contented lull as we drank our pints. When the band took a break, Sean stood to go get us another round. The silence was a pervasive thing that left a jarring hole in my chest. Dad yelled, "WHERE'S THE BATHROOM," in a voice that carried across the bar.

275

I laughed and motioned with a hand to bring his volume down.

"WHAT?" he asked.

Conall pointed across the room to a sign that said, 'Laddies and Lassies.'

Dad nodded and headed in that direction.

Secluded at a corner table, the crowd a physical barrier, my dad and brother away, it was one of the few times I'd been alone with Conall outside a bedroom. It felt illicit, as if I was a sixteen-year-old on my first date. Conall bent down and put his lips right near my ear.

He whispered, "I'm going to pretend that I am saying something important so that I can," a small kiss, "keep doing this," and another kiss, "and this," as his lips travelled to a spot beneath my jaw.

I leaned into him, whispering back, "Well, Dad might be gone for a while, but Sean won't. He's usually fast with the beers."

Conall navigated the contour of my neck, muttering, "Large crowd, long lines, they may get lost."

I giggled. Actually giggled.

We exchanged kisses, until without warning, Conall abruptly stopped. A small vibration of alarm shot through me. Looking up, I saw Davina and her unruly planet of curly hair standing right next to the table. My first thought was, *Crap, now you've done it. You've poached on another's hunting ground and she wants retribution for bringing down the largest elk.* Without thinking, I moved away from Conall. It didn't help. We appeared guilty enough that Conall might as well have had his hand up my shirt.

"What going on, Conall?" Davina asked, hostility lining her face.

276

What an interesting question, I thought, *with an infinite amount of answers*. I wanted to ask for clarification, but I didn't feel that was the most prudent of actions. After a few more beers, I would have done exactly that. Conall's eyes slide to me and I knew he was thinking the exact same thing.

Conall said, "Celebrating."

"Celebrating? *Really*? How so?" Davina screwed up her face and eyeballed me as if I were a piece of rancid meat.

Conall said, "Nat saved a life today."

"Oh, it's Nat, is it?" She narrowed her eyes. "She saved a life? How *interesting*."

I shook my head. If there was something worse than actually having to do CPR and swap spit with an unknown male smoker to resuscitate him, it was talking about it and rehashing the moment. The entire situation required a certain amount of pleasantness and decorum, served up with a heaping plate of gratitude that went, *"No really, it was nothing. I was happy to be there. To be helpful. It's my job."* It made my skin crawl. I would have just rather people said, "You were lucky," and walked away.

I pretended interest in the last dregs of my beer while Conall explained the horrendous episode at the museum. I searched the bar and found Sean watching the scene with great amusement. One of the four beers was already gone and he was working his way through the second. I mouthed the word, "traitor," and he laughed, saluting me with his pint. Dad sat on a stool next to him, drinking a whiskey. God help us all.

Davina asked, "She's leaving soon, right?"

I nodded, assuring her. "Yes. Vacation almost finished. Going to Wales tomorrow and home after that."

Conall's face went flat and emotionless. We had not spoken of timelines, or rather, the ending of mine in Scotland. And I certainly hadn't spoken of Wales. It was not anything we could have

277

ignored, but in his cross look, I could tell that we had done our best to try.

I held up my glass to Sean, hoping that he would bring me a beer and save me. Instead, the bartender acknowledged me, poured another pint and sat it next to Sean. He grabbed it and placed money on the bar, ignoring me outright and talking to our father.

Cursing, I turned back to the conversation. Davina caught my eye and put her hand on the back of Conall's chair. I told myself to relax and look away and think positive, rational thoughts. But in the back of my mind, I was making mental calculations—myself, Conall, Davina, the distance to the door, and how many bodies in my way. Davina outweighed me by a good forty pounds, but careful instruction by Tommie had taught me how to bring down larger individuals using their weight against them. The thought of physical retribution made me smile.

Davina caught my inner thought process. "Conall, love, I thought you and I could go to the music festival next week." Her eyes never left mine. "Spend the night, do the whole weekend, no?"

"Right," I said, finding the situation so uncomfortable that I needed to leave. When you boiled everything down to hard truths, I'd had a self-serving fling with a guy I'd met while on vacation, who'd I most likely never see again. Now a local girl was claiming him as her own. Rising, I said, "I'll go find our beers." I gave Sean such a nasty look that he burst out laughing. He hit his head on some hanging glasses and Dad started giggling. I'm glad everyone found the whole situation hilarious.

Conall grabbed my shoulder and shoved me down, saying, "You can stay," as if I was an insolent child.

My temper radiated like a nuclear blast; the heat of it expanding into my face. "Excuse me," I said, pushing his hand away. "Don't tell me what to do. Talk to her. I'll give you space."

"I don't want space," he muttered.

Davina said, "Leave her be, Conall. She's going back to the States, no?" She gave me a malicious smile. "It's all colonized trash there anyway."

I stood and laughed in such a manner that people turned our way. I knew I was attracting attention, but couldn't contain my unleashed temper. "Colonized?" I said to Davina and scoffed. *"Colonized?"* Without thinking, I stepped towards her. The term 'trash' I could deal with. I'd heard that plenty of times. The word 'colonized' sent me into a crazed stratosphere. I wasn't exactly sane, but my historical knowledge was up to snuff. The United States had been a wild territory while still tethered to England, that is, until we gone through the paces of a war to come out on top.

"Yeah, sweetheart, go ahead and take it back to the English and the Revolutionary War," I said, pointing a finger into her blanching face. Conall's lips twitched with the urge to laugh. "At least we had the fortitude to get rid of them and send them packing." I narrowed my eyes and tilted my head in thought. "But let's see, you guys still can't shrug them off, right? They got full *reign* around here. Whereas we're an *independent country.*" A man at a nearby table whistled and gave me a cautious look. I threw it right back. Conall put his hand on my shoulder to calm me, but we were past that.

Tommie had once described me as a junkyard mutt—undersized, underestimated and of no breed, but given the opportunity, I would chew off a piece of hide if you got too close. I never fought off the description because there was a fair amount of truth in it. I took a step past Davina, appearing as if I was headed to the bar. Swinging my elbow, I knocked out Davina's arm that she was using as leverage to lean down and talk. She lost her balance, fell over and landed on her back. There was a high-pitched scream, followed by, "You wanker!"

I watched her fall and then gave Sean a look that had been forged between the three of us since we were kids hiding in the tree house from Eve. It was time to rally the troops. Sean chugged his beer like a frat boy hearing the police sirens down the street. Dad was trying to do the same with his whiskey, but sputtered and

279

coughed. Conall helped Davina to her feet, grabbing both of her arms and pulling her up.

There was laughter, even a snort or two, and I thought that might be the end of it, until a large man with a red, angry sheen to his face stepped in my way, keeping me from the front door. His nose had been broken once or twice, considering the crevice, and his hair was the consistency of pubic hair—wiry and frizzing out of control. There wasn't enough gel in the world that would ever calm it to a respectable shape. Taken as a whole, he had the appearance of an Irish prizefighter past his prime.

Conall cleared his throat and said, "Peter, nice to see you."

"Nice, my ass, you shite. What's going on?" He gave Davina a look-over to see if she was all right. There was no doubt in my mind that these two were siblings. The gene pool that carried this particular hair type needed to be rebooted.

Conall pulled back his shoulders, which gave him three inches on Peter. It would have been reassuring if Peter didn't outweigh him by fifty pounds. In the background, Sean was pushing Dad towards the door and finishing off the third beer. He walked towards us, adopting the goofy brother guise.

Sean said, "Yo, sports fans, ready to go?"

And that was exactly when Peter swung at Conall.

Conall saw it coming and stepped aside, causing Peter to stumble into a table. Davina came careening towards us—screaming and lashing out—but Conall pushed her away and in one fast move, swept an arm around my waist, picked me up and sat me down on the bar.

"I don't need saving," I told him.

"I know. But humor me." He looked over my shoulder. "Danny?" he said to the bartender.

"Conall," he said. "Take it outside. I'll watch—"

The rest of the words were cut short because Peter came roaring back. He grabbed Conall around the shoulders, and before I could think about it, I slapped both my hands hard into Peter's ears. Peter went stumbling off, holding his head.

Conall gave me a quick kiss. "Get going. Meet you at the hotel in ten." Conall turned away. I heard him say, "Now Peter, no use bein dafty."

Peter screamed, "Whit a knob man!"

Patrons turned towards the action; a group of men surrounding them in a circular ring. The bartender left his station, grabbed a few guys and headed out to diffuse the action. The band continued to play, a scene straight out of the Titanic. I crawled down the bar like a small child—my dignity counting for nothing. I inched my way over beers and mixed drinks with floating fruit, my head low to miss the hanging glasses. Sean and Dad were standing at the door, urging me on, but keeping a careful eye on the melee.

I was almost to the end of the bar when I saw Sean's eyes go very large. His lips formed a very large O and he screamed the first part of my name. Someone grabbed my leg and pulled. Remember the horror movies when the teenager is climbing their way up the stairs to freedom after being stabbed several times? Similar to that same idiotic person, my initial reaction was to kick out as hard as I could.

I connected with hard flesh. When I looked back, Davina was lying flat on the ground, her hand on her boobs. I yelled, "Face or chest?"

"Chest," Sean screamed. "Let's go."

I jumped down and saw Conall in the midst of a large group of men, but not fighting. He waved me on. I ran through the door, the menfolk on my heels like the English had come raiding and were intent on burning everything to the ground.

15

Emails:

From Natalie Calhoun

To Tommie Calhoun

Subject: Possible employment

Do you think I would cut it as a mob interrogator? Is my personality/DNA/psyche *that* suspect?

You know what? Don't answer that.

Trip almost done. We're out of here in several days. I've got a plan for the house and it doesn't include me doing much of the work. The only problem I need to worry about is state officials dropping by and possibly condemning the place and leveling it to the ground.

-N

* * *

Back at the hotel, I said, "I don't think that's what Eve envisioned for this trip." I pursed my lips. "Any of it." Sean shrugged as if fighting the locals was nothing of consequence. He didn't look like a man coming from a brawl, but a guy returning from a spa weekend. He'd stolen a bottle of oatmeal stout and was still drinking it.

Dad said, "You should see the bridge nights Eve and I have occasionally," and winked.

We stood in an uncomfortable silence as the sounds from the bar—deep laughter and a man yelling, "I'm telling you, it was at least sixteen inches,"—rolled down the hallway and hit us in waves. I said, "I'll be upstairs in a bit. I need to tie up some loose ends," as if I was an assassin getting rid of an eyewitness to the crime.

Sean rolled his eyes and said, "Right, sure thing," as he took a final swallow of the beer and threw it in the trash. "Tell lover-boy good-bye for me," searching his pockets for the room key. "Thank him for the transportation. And"—he found the key and waved it in the air— "tell him we're sorry how we treated them." He laughed, Dad joining him. Sean looked up the staircase. "How about we meet here? 7 AM?"

I nodded. "Don't be late."

He scoffed. "Yeah, yeah. Such a worrier. You'd think we'd just started a fight at the local bar by bringing up three hundred years of English colonization." They climbed the stairs. I heard Dad say something about "poor Scottish humor," and Sean whistled the Darth Vader theme song.

We were flying out of Benbecula and headed to Manchester the next day. Wales was the last stop. My *Roman Holiday* would officially be over. If there was ever a reason to sit down and order a whiskey, I think this was it. I found a table in a corner away from the smattering of couples and fishermen. We'd eaten dinner here and the waitress was the one to mention the band. When she put my drink upon the table, she asked, "The band goo' then?"

I mustered some weak enthusiasm. "Quite the scene."

About fifteen minutes later, Conall arrived, spotted me and walked my way. Every single person in the place turned their heads, and glanced away, trying to hide their curiosity. Conall sat with his back towards the room. There was a red mark on his forehead and his collar was stretched. Other than that, he was unscathed.

I reached across and rubbed a finger over his forehead. I was leaving in twelve hours and allowed myself this one weakness. His eyes fluttered shut and opened. I said, "I don't know if I should be apologizing or not."

He grabbed my hand and smiled, taking our conjoined hands and placing them on his knee, beneath the table and away from prying eyes. The waitress walked over and handed him a whiskey. I pretended interest across the room. He took a long sip. When the waitress left, he said, "The Davina thing has been brewing for a while." He shrugged. "I should've stopped it, but never had the energy." He leaned back in his chair. "Peter, her brother, has always been a huff-n-puff. But he's a no show. Never has been."

"No damage?"

Conall put down his whiskey and rubbed at his forehead. "Nothing that my skull can't take. Man's got remarkably poor aim."

He raised our conjoined hands and placed them on the table, grazing a thumb over my upturned hand. The waitress looked over and her eyes dipped to our hands.

"I leave," I said. "Tomorrow."

"I know," he replied. "Wales," staring at my hand like it was a map to the future.

"Maybe this was stu—"

"Don't." There was an edge to his voice I'd never heard before.

I succeeded in removing my hand and told myself to get firm, remember who I was, which was the woman who had successfully foiled and ruined every relationship previously. I was not going to let the pressure get to me in the final inning. "Hello?" I said, "Remember me? I'm the social idiot from the states. That little skirmish you just came from?" I pointed out the window. "That follows me on a regular basis. You have no idea the mess I'm involved in. You are the Scotland hunk. We," I gestured between us, "as a whole, do not add up. Not in any kind of scenario."

284

He narrowed his eyes. "Why do you do this?"

"What?"

"Discount yourself and run?"

"It's worked wonders in the past from saving innocent men from peril."

He took a long drink of the whiskey. "You sound like some demented romance novel."

I emptied my glass. The waitress walked over, but I shook my head, warning her off. "Listen," I said. "In an alternative universe . . ."

"Yes?" Conall asked.

I shook my head, dismissing it. "No . . ."

"No? No what?"

"Disaster isn't an adequate word to describe me, Conall." He opened his mouth to disagree. I stopped him by putting up my hand. "Besides the whole mother-dying-messing-with-my-head—"

"There's an amazing amount of us with the same issue . . ."

"—I have a job that takes up most of my waking hours, the sleeping ones as well, a fellowship to finish and an ex-boyfriend with a gambling problem who owes money to some unsavory individuals who have been breaking into my house and stealing all of my stuff." I threw in the clincher. "There are mobsters emailing me at this moment, handling my underwear."

His eyes narrowed. "Is that really true?"

"Yes. Possibly." I shrugged and scratched my neck. "I don't know. You've seen my underwear—"

"Knickers, you mean," he said, grinning.

"Panties," I volleyed.

"Drawers."

"Bloomers," I giggled and caught my breath. Beneath my skin, there were layers of hardened steel that I had meticulously welded with precise care, year after year, until I created an impenetrable shield to hold off all others and protect myself. I felt a piece crack, leaving a small hole, in which fresh air rolled into a place normally devoid of light.

"Hey," Conall said, tapping on my forehead with a finger. "You were saying something about *panties?*" A couple of fisherman looked over from the bar, smirking.

I inhaled, "Well, right, everyone seems to have seen mine, so it seems to be a common problem." I leaned back in my chair, saying, "I don't even know if I have much of a house to return to."

The waitress disregarded my warnings and came over with two more whiskeys. "You two are the sorriest couple in the place. Cheer up. Maybe go back to the Smoking Toad. Heard there was a roarin' tumble down there," and stared at the stretched neck of Conall's shirt.

We said nothing as she laughed and shook her head. "I'll leave you two in peace," and walked away.

I took two large sips and poured the rest into Conall's glass. Good-byes were terrible things and whiskey never made them better. I pulled out a pen and wrote my phone number and address on a napkin, as well as my email. "You OK with getting home?" I asked.

Conall nodded, but seemed confused at the amount of information that I was putting on a thin piece of paper. I pushed the napkin towards him. He leaned away like I was handing him a dead cat. "Have your dad call me or email. About the car, when it's squared away. The phone number won't work till I get back home." I pointed. "I've got no international phone service."

He tapped the napkin. "That's it?" irritation biting at his words. "You? Me? Paper napkin? Just . . . done?"

Finished is the right word, I thought. *Finished. Why was I always having this conversation?* My breath caught as I felt my heart pause and pick up the beat again. My brain was telling me to run and my heart was anchoring barbs into my chest. I felt the force of them puncture my lungs. It sent shots of pain up my spine. *Oh God, I can't breathe,* I thought, as my brain whispered that I might be having a heart attack. "I'm no good at these things," I said and looked away. "I've got to go home. Finish things. You've got . . . here."

I cringed at the sound of my ridiculous words.

"Really? That's the best you've got?" Conall said. "*I've got here?*" repeating me. His index finger tapped a fast beat on the table. He concentrated on the window, where the sun was just setting, even at this late hour. I glanced down the hallway, pondering how I could remove myself without looking like an ass. It was the theme of the night, the music of my life, removing myself from hostile situations, donning the guise of the girl that operated with no heart, which I thought I was.

Without warning, Conall stood and grabbed my arm. "Come on. I've got something to show you."

"Huh?"

He placed money on the table to cover the tab, and said, "Come with me." He took me by hand and pulled me down the hallway, my shoulder bumping against the wall.

The waitress yelled, "Conall, what about your change?"

He waved her off and kept us moving at a rigorous pace, my short legs complaining.

"Conall, hey!" I said, laughing. "Slow down."

He marched us out of the hotel and over to the car. Opening the door, he pushed me inside, shut the door, kicked the bumper for good measure and got behind the wheel.

He looked over and smiled.

"Where are we going?" I asked, some alarm rising.

"I want you to see something."

"It's late—"

"Not too late for this."

We drove for several miles, the car bumping down something that only vaguely resembled a road; narrow and pitted with potholes, it reminded me of tractor lanes next to cornfields in the Midwest. The sun was setting, casting an orange-pink hue in the west. He said nothing, but sped along the lane, the suspension rattling and groaning in protest, until we finally found ourselves in the middle of the open country, surrounded by heather at a dead end. A large loch sat in front of us, civilization behind us like we were the last two people left on Earth.

Twilight approached. "This is great. Lovely." I said, confused.

"Just wait," he said.

"Wait for what? I get it. It's pretty, but I've been here for a week, remember?"

"Come with me," he said and tilted his head towards the door. He got out and grabbed his coat from the backseat. Taking my hand, we walked together through patches of heather until we found a spot near water that was like staring at a liquid mirror reflecting the sky. Conall laid down his coat and the two of us sat. I left some distance between our bodies, but he reached across and grabbed my hip, pulling me close and tucking me under his shoulder.

The quiet minutes ticked by and the world turned deep violet, then black velvet, the first stars popping in the vast sky. The barbs released their hold in my chest, and I inhaled air to the lowest part of my lungs; the freedom of the open country and the security of his solid presence freed a tension that might have been there for years. I leaned against Conall and he tugged me closer as if he knew that I was a floundering child drowning in a large swimming pool. In the far corners of the horizon, I saw faint flickers of green, similar to a light show displayed in Technicolor. Conall reclined onto his elbows and I tucked closer to steal his warmth.

The emerald hue weaved a braided path above our heads, with yellow tungsten licking at the edges like a gas flame. The combination of colors migrated across the sky as a magic carpet ride of electrons. I watched, saying nothing. I wanted to reach up and feel it sweep through my fingers, like a child reaching for fireflies. "My mother used to love the Northern Lights," Conall said after many minutes of silence. "Used to drag us out of the house to see them. After she died, for two years, we weren't north enough to view them." He shrugged. "It was as if she'd taken them with her."

I watched the flow of luminesce; it spun above our heads and melted into the far horizon like a Christmas ribbon set free from a present. It was breathtaking and heart wrenching.

I leaned over, saying, "You're lovely," and kissed him.

Conall eyed me suspiciously and backed away an inch. "I get the feeling there's a *but* just waiting to be said," kissing me once, twice on the corner of my mouth.

"I don't know how this can work," putting both hands on each side of his head.

He groaned and said, "It might," using his weight to push me back onto the coat.

I nuzzled my nose into his neck, hiding from his eyes ann from my own fears. I pulled myself into his enormous shelter. I could have set up a tent there and never left.

"Natalie . . ."

I took a deep breath and inhaled his scent, trying to remember and infuse it with my own. "I'm letting you off the hook, take it. By some chance, you make it to the States, come find me."

He murmured into my ear, "Divert and run. Divert and run."

I sighed, almost wishing I'd never stumbled into that bedroom, just to make my life easier. Without Conall, it would've been a regular vacation experience, with a few decent photos to give to Dad at Christmas as a memento.

I said, "Early flight out of here," like I was a travelling salesman.

"Really? You don't say," he said, his weight settling on top of me, as if he could keep me from getting away. "I think I could find all kinds of ways for you to *love* Scotland," pushing his hips against mine, reminding me of the first morning we were acquainted.

I laughed as his hands started to roam, moving of their own accord. "I already love all those things. They should put them on tourist posters." His hand slid inside the edge of my jeans, undid a front button and then skirted to the back.

"I just want to see if your knickers are still in good shape."

I laughed. "I don't wear the same pair every day. Even on vacation." Conall inched his way down my chest, unfastening two buttons with slow precision, staring at several freckles that lay on my sternum like they were constellations in the sky.

"That's too bad. I really loved that particular pair of knickers," laying a chaste kiss in the middle of chest.

"So did your dad's staff."

Conall chuckled and leaned back to look at my face, his hand reaching out to touch my cheek with his forefinger. The way he looked at me left me feeling exposed and I couldn't help but shivering in response.

"We really need to do something about you getting cold," and he pulled me into his arms.

"It happens a lot with you," I said, wrapping my arm around his neck and kissing him.

"All you needed to do was say something," as his hand found mine and secured it within his own.

"Like what?" I asked, my insecurities drifting away in the heat of what was here and now.

Conall pulled away several inches and adopted a very serious tone. "You just say, *my trousers are trashed and my knickers are a fabulous lime green. And I need some warming up.*"

I smiled, laughing at our ridiculous conversation. "And what would you have done?"

He kissed with such intensity that my lungs burned with the need for air. My heart skittered a fast beat and my brain whispered, *closer, closer.* His lips migrated to that sensitive spot at my neck, which had been ravaged in a previous life. The touch caused me to shiver for other reasons. He said, "I could have done many things," tracing kisses up over my jaw and upon my chin. "I wanted to do so many things," and kissed me on the nose and each eye in turn, "to these lips, to this scar," a small peck on the side of my face, "to those underpants." He stopped and I could feel his mind working over the details. "Where do you go in Wales?" the neon green of the sky like a halo over his head, making his eyes glow in the darkness.

"Are you using your lips to maneuver me for answers?"

"Whatever works," he said, as his hand inched down my thigh, grabbed my ankle and pulled it around his back.

"Some place like . . ." I felt one of his hands slide up my back and settle on my neck. "Betsy in a corner."

291

Conall stilled, his lips a hair's breadth from my own. *"What?"*

"Ah," I shrugged, as well as I could while being held by a bear-man, "Betsy in a corner?"

He burst out laughing; his body heavy against my chest, his forehead on my shoulder. He snorted through his nose and his gut clenched with the effort of a belly laugh.

When he didn't stop, I said, "OK! OK! I don't know. Obviously. But it's something like that. I swear."

"That makes no sense."

"It's Wales! *Have you seen their language?*"

Conall placed his forehead against mine. We stared eye to eye. "You, Natalie Calhoun, are one crazy lass. And complete shite when it comes to understanding language."

I drew him close and kissed him until we were both gasping for air. When I pulled back, I said, "I understand the most important ones."

16

Emails:

From Tommie Calhoun

To Natalie Calhoun

Re: Possible employment

I think you would be the Andy Warhol of the mob interrogation team. But you'd be wasting your efforts with them. Let's face it; the government would pay you more. And it'd be legal.

Well, sort of.

Tommie

*   *   *

    We rose early. Again. I'd come on vacation to get rest, and sleep deprivation was following me around like a disease I couldn't shake. Sean was on time, awaiting us in the lobby with hot coffees to go. Either he was trying to end the vacation on a positive caffeinated note or he felt sorry for me. As we packed the car, I surveyed the parking lot, hoping to spot a beefy football player that might be retrieving a rental car, or possibly me, but it was empty save for the three of us. Conall had dropped me off the night before, kissed me and promised to see me soon. He didn't elaborate and I didn't have the courage to ask for details. I was attempting to prove that I didn't care by keeping a brave face, which was a total lie.

    I was a liar to myself, and my family. And some habits were very hard to break. I told myself that the vacation was over and I needed to move on. We caught the early flight into Manchester, got the last of our rental cars and drove into Wales.

Wales was our last-minute addition; a postscript, a secondary thought, a while-we-are-here-we-might-as-well-cross-the-border kind of thing. In hindsight, it could have been the entire book, the main event, let's-just-stay-here-and-never-leave kind of place. It was the hidden treasure, the unexpected gift, the small miracle on Christmas Eve. It took us all by surprise and left us breathless. In an area in north Wales called Snowdonia, we were surrounded by lush mountains and eternal green, curvaceous roads lined in trees. We rambled over ancient bridges with placid water running beneath. Sean stared agog. It was the antithesis to the Hebrides, but perfect in its own kissing cousin way.

We headed towards Betys-y-coed, not 'Betsy in a corner.' *Close enough,* I thought. Similar to the east coast, the towns had a way of running into one another. You had to carefully watch storefronts to decipher exactly where you were. Out of nowhere, Sean yelled, "Gwydr Hotel," and I turned the vehicle on its wheels, swerving into an alleyway the size of a sewer line, bounced into a postage stamp-sized parking lot and threw on the brakes. I backed our tiny European vehicle into a spot with barely a foot on each side. It was masterful piece of driving. No one seemed impressed since we could barely exit the car.

"Seriously, Nat," is the only thing Sean said, sucking in his gut and inching his way out, trying not to ding the door.

We grabbed our suitcases and entered through the back, near a kitchen that smelled of garlic and beef, and into a front reception room. The hotel was a grand stone edifice, complete with gables, bay windows and old-world charm. We checked in, got our room keys and were told to have a drink in the bar area, which was exactly ten paces from the reception desk. The hotel had no rooms with two single beds, but several rooms with just one single bed. Since the price was reasonable, Dad and I both got our own room for the night.

My single bedroom was exactly the size of my walk-in closet in the States. Getting my bag into the room required me to back myself in while hauling the suitcase, until I was seated on the bed, and then reach out with my leg to shut the door. There was a bedside table, a bed, a wardrobe and a door that led to one of the smallest bathrooms known to man that still managed to squeak in a shower. To get to the bathroom, I would have to step over the bag, miss the bathroom door by turning sideways and then close the bathroom door once safely inside. It conjured images of an Olympic skating routine.

Miniature room aside; it was one the first times I'd been alone the entire trip. It felt good to be in my room and do whatever I wanted. Farting and gastric noises aside, I gloried in the confined space with a tiny window that gave me a view of the parking lot and the dumpsters.

We all met downstairs and had drinks and dinner in the hotel. The same guy that checked us in and owned the place, ran the bar. The girl that served us drinks upon arriving, brought us our food entrees. One sweaty, overworked kid ran from the bar to the kitchen, back to the tables and then repeated the process over again twenty times to get food and drink out in a timely process, which wasn't timely, but no one seemed to mind. Sean started a conversation with a local guy who ran the outdoor store. While we drank beer, Sean obtained a fishing permit and the guy drew a map on a cocktail napkin to the fishing location the next day. Whiskey and beer all around. Since it was going to be the last full day of vacation, we agreed that we'd sleep in the next morning. Sean would go fishing, Dad and I would putz around town, later departing for Manchester, to spend the night and fly home the next day.

I went to bed early. Sean and Dad continued to drink. Around midnight, I awoke to an incredible ruckus outside my room; booming voices that ricocheted down the hallway, like men working construction. I sat up in bed and stared at the light seeping beneath the door, which was blocked intermittently by numerous feet. There was laughter and the sounds of horseplay, and several bodies bounced up against the door, the hinges creaking with the weight of heavy men. This was not an American hotel with a strong locking mechanism and a security arm on the door. This was a centuries old hotel with paper-thin doors and a small door lock that my grandmother could have broken while sitting in a wheelchair.

The door rattled and bowed with the weight of bodies, which was followed by more laughter. Alarmed, I got out of bed and stepped towards the door at the same time an incredibly heavy body fell against it. The lock made a popping noise, the door swung open, hitting me in the head and causing me to fall over my suitcase. A man fell on top of me like a prizefighter going for his last swing.

We lay there as the large throng of partygoers stared on, utterly silent.

I was sleep-deprived, cranky, romance-stricken and questioning every motive that had brought me on this ridiculous vacation. At that moment, the sum total of all my insecurities and fears came bubbling to the surface as I completely lost my shit.

I screamed, "GETOFFGETOFFGETOFF," until the guy fell backwards and crab-legged to the door. I stood, rubbing my head and squinting against the hallway light. The intoxicated men stared at my t-shirt and underpants, and the radiator heat made the room feel like a greenhouse.

I was a feminist, voted Democrat, toured Europe on my own for three weeks and once fought off the center for the Dartmouth football team when he grabbed my tits and thought he could score. But for the first time in my life, I wanted a male counterpart, a defensive lineman to take the lead, a bodyguard, a large Scotsman to beat the crap out of them. Fighting the feminist battle had made me brave, but it had also made me incredibly lonely.

The men stood frozen staring, until the same idiot that came stumbling into the room, took a drunken step back and fell on his ass. One of the guys giggled and the rest joined in. It was hysterical.

Everyone laughed. And laughed. And laughed.

It was so funny.

Until it wasn't.

Maybe saying I *lost it* isn't quite full summation of what happened. I started screaming in a decibel of a mother who had just lost a child in a shopping mall. I pushed at the men, frenzied, until people in nearby rooms came stumbling into the hallway. Management came running and someone called the police. Within minutes, the entire occupancy of the hotel was looking at me in my panties and the young men in their intoxication, now sobered by the mortification of hysterical thirty-something yelling obscenities.

Tears streamed down my face, and the police, who had arrived five minutes before, were unable to calm me. I overheard one of them say something about mental instability.

"Go ahead," I screamed, "call the medics." Wiping away some snot that was leaking from my nose and rubbing it into my cheek. "That's really, really awesome."

Sean pushed through the crowd, wearing gym shorts and an old Oingo Boingo t-shirt with a faded skeleton face. He said to the police officers, "It's OK. I got it. I'm her brother."

"What?" I screamed, clearly out of my mind. "You've got *nothing!"*

He sighed, resigned to my terrible behavior as if it was something that happened every day. He reassured them as I stood laughing like a mental patient off her drugs. The police officers glanced between us, obviously not convinced.

One of the officers said, "You sure?"

Sean panicked, saw my tears and snot, and was possibly worried about mental health and medical personnel being called. Without thinking, he blurted, "She's being treated for manic chlamydiosis."

Everyone stopped and stared.

I screamed, "What?" and shook my head in disbelief. "Oh my God! You got to be kidding me!"

In slow motion, the crowd of men turned, their eyes grazing over my purple underpants. They all took a step back.

"Really?" one of the guys snorted.

"Not *chlamydia*," I yelled, "you idiot. Chlamydiosis."

"Whatever," the guy said and mumbled "STD," to his friend.

I lunged and swung at him, and Sean pulled me back, putting me in a headlock. Dragging me back like I was an unruly child, he thanked the police and said that he would take care of the situation. Sean jerked me into my room and kicked the busted door several times to get it to stay shut.

The two of us fell onto my bed and sat there for several minutes until the voices quieted from the other side of the door. "I do not have parrot fever, you moron," I whispered, pushing at Sean, while wiping away my tears. "Seriously? That's the best you could come up with?" It was an infection that got into the chickens when we were kids that caused them to lose weight, pull out their own feathers and secrete a nasty green substance out their beaks.

"Sorry! I'm not a doctor." He threw up his hands. "I don't have a plethora of diseases handy at my fingertips. If you didn't notice, I did manage to get rid of them."

"By suggesting I have an STD!"

"You don't?" he said, laughing.

"Oh my God." I said. "They think I'm an American whore."

"Dude, you are."

"Look who's talking?!"

"Fair enough, but I had to do something." He stared at my red eyes and snotty nose. "Besides, you do have green stuff coming from your nose."

I wiped at the snot and attempted to pull it together, but I was sitting in my underpants and crying, and the picture as a whole lacked any sanity.

"OK, OK," Sean said, leaning into me. "A bachelor party breaks into your room and causes havoc. There were crazy men, singing bawdy songs and tripping over your luggage. The Natalie I know had this happen all the time in college." He scratched his head. "And sometime after?" I pushed on his shoulder. "My point is, normally you would have invited them in." He crossed his eyes. "Do you have advanced syphilis?"

I laughed. And because he was my brother and we were in a room that measured eight by twelve feet, requiring him to sit next me in my underpants, I took a deep breath and spilled everything. I described my rental-car-underwear incident and the encounter with the chickens. I told him about Trevor's money problems, the destroyed house and possible mob debt, and the fact that I'd asked Tommie to help. The only thing not confessed was that my heart had attached itself to a large Scotsman.

"You involved Tommie?" Sean asked, with real concern. His doubts were not unfounded. Tommie had once sent a Marine colleague to the house of one of my classmates who had made the unfortunate mistake of making unwanted sexual advances towards me. I'd told Tommie I could handle it and he'd told me that the guy needed to understand true male aggression up close and personal.

"Who else was I going to ask?"

Sean was aghast, as if I'd kicked him. "Well, *me,* for starters!"

"You weren't liking me much."

"Well, quit running concrete pylons, wrecking cars and running off the women I meet and *I'll like you more!*"

We both laughed until tears leaked from our eyes. With some sadness, I realized it was the last night of vacation and we'd finally come to some understanding of each other. Both of us sobered around the time the radiator made a clanking noise and the room's temperature inched towards sauna levels.

Sean shook his head. "You make my breakup look like child's play. I can't believe it. You *always* upstage me." He used a delinquent's kids voice as he said, "*Natalie this, Natalie that. Natalie almost dies. Natalie knows mobsters. Natalie has no house. Natalie has no underwear.*"

I giggled, but with my plugged nose, it came out as a snort, along with a substantial amount of snot.

"Gross."

I grabbed a Kleenex. "I think I've made a mistake."

"I have as well. Too many to count," he said. "But you, Nat, you're on a whole different playing field. Starting by bringing that rabid tomcat into the house, achieving monumental, insurmountable college debt and finally," he rubbed at his forehead, "the pinnacle of your hairbrained idiocy when you left Tommie's office to find the lower war zone of the Pentagon." He shook his head. "Could you be more specific?"

"A large Scottish one."

Sean's eyes widened and he laughed so hard he choked. "Ah, yes, *that one.*" He laid his hand on the radiator and pulled it away, cringing. "That is a rather large one. I didn't realize we were talking sheer size over catastrophic state." He shrugged. "I don't see how he's a problem." He counted off points on his fingers. "You know his address, his phone number." He rolled his eyes, "and I know that he's very interested in you. That's more than most people have. That I have. You even held his chicken hostage for God's sake." He cleared his throat, announcing he'd come to his final important point. "To be honest, I think the public should be more worried about your future career as a mobster torturer." He looked at me. "It might be your true calling."

"Stop it," I said.

He laughed. "Hey, you think they'd do tuition reimbursement?

"Shut. Up!"

The radiator belched and hissed like a reptilian creature. I turned and punched Sean hard in the shoulder. He stared. "What in the hell was that for?"

"It's me, saying I'm sorry."

He narrowed his eyes. "Punching me? To say you're sorry?" He laughed, leaning sideways and accidently touched the radiator with a shoulder. He flinched, muttering, "Ouch!" rubbing the spot. "Well, you're terrible at it. Apology not accepted."

I exhaled, thinking. "After Mom's death, after . . ."

Sean let his arm drop and straightened. "Nat—"

I laid a hand over his mouth. "Just let me talk, OK?"

He nodded, his eyes moving back and forth.

"I should have said it a long time ago." I shook my head, thinking. "It . . . we . . ." I blurted, "It wasn't your fault." I gave a moment for the words to sink in and said them again.

I dropped my hand and the two of us stared. There was a bubble of silence that hung heavy as he said nothing. *A single accident that had culminated in a hundred missteps.* I continued, "No one could've known. She was so young. And that barbed wire? What were the chances? Tommie and I, we kind of just . . ." Sean stared at his hands. "We were stupid. You were an easy target. But we shouldn't have been so . . ." I shrugged. "It was no one's fault."

Sean sat.

Just breathing in and out.

Sweat formed under my shirt, from the intense radiator heat or my nerves, it was impossible to say. It was worse than I thought and I began to fidget, saying anything that came to mind—ridiculous babble to fill the space of silence. "And maybe I'll use my new acquaintances to put a hit out on Tommie, although the military has made him into some kind of spook, but if you want, I could take out another loan to truly bury myself to even the score. But to be honest, Trevor just might get the job done anyway. My credit—"

Sean walloped me on the shoulder so hard it stung.

"OUCH!"

"You guys were idiots," Sean said with hostility.

"OK. Wow. Glad that's clear."

He hit me again. "And mean."

"OK, stop—" Another solid wallop. "Hey—"

"I want back in."

"What—"

He hit me again.

"OK, STOP. I mean it!" I put up my hands. "That really hurts."

"Back in the Calhoun club. I want in."

"OK, OK," I said. "Back in. Sibling truce," and I held up two fingers like a scout's honor. "Just please, quit hitting me."

Sean lowered his fist, and tentatively, we both laughed. When Sean spoke again, it was in a tone that brokered none of the recent humor. "But I should have gone. . . with you. That day."

"Sean—"

"I should have gone." He rubbed his hands over his face. "To get help. I knew about the barbed wire. *I knew.* I've replayed it so many times," and shook his head. "I want a different ending." He sighed. "I *wanted* a different ending."

I nodded, thinking. "Yeah. Me too."

The radiator *clunked, clunked, clunked,* and *hiiiiisssssssed.*

"So . . . we good?" I asked.

He brought back his arm and walloped my shoulder with enough force that it bent me sideways. "No. Now we're good."

*   *   *

The next day we departed from the Manchester and landed in Chicago by mid-afternoon. We debarked and followed the signs pointing towards the domestic concourse and luggage claim with all the other wearied travelers. I turned on my cellular roaming and my phone repeatedly chimed for the first time in nine days with incoming texts. Many were from work, reminding me of call/work obligations for the upcoming weekend. One was from Robbie, telling me that the house was being fixed and suggesting a possible meet time, and a final one was from Trevor, using a phone number that I had never seen before. It said:

It's Trevor. I am going to jail. Hope you had a nice vacation.

Sean was headed towards the parking garage, and Dad and I would go through security and enter it all over again for one final flight. This time, we had four hours. It was an eternity; an entire vacation compared to the last adventure here. Since we'd now completed this process eight times over the last week, we'd become experts of removing shoes, electronics, metal on our body and telling personnel about Dad's pacemaker.

We stood in the middle of the concourse as people walked around us. Good-byes were as awkward as gastric noises in church for the Calhoun family. There were strange silences, uncomfortable pauses and stiff farewells. No one touched or hugged, but bumped shoulders and muttered insincere goodbyes. We held our arms close, warding off surprise attacks from distant relatives who thought they could sneak in a friendly hug. Friends enjoyed watching the spectacle because it resembled a group of severely autistic children trying to avoid social interaction.

I don't know the exact words spoken, because I was trying to avoid being touched. But it went something like this:
Sean: (Rocking on his heels a bit.) So that was . . . fun.

Me: (looking away) Interesting.

Dad: It was fabulous. Well, maybe the whiskey. Thank you for taking it with me.

Sean: We can do it again. Another location?

Me: Sounds great. How about the Palestine border?

Sean (shaking his head, muttering): Never serious.

Me: Or Haiti. Tourism on the turn-around.

Dad: I'm game.

Sean: I'm sure you are.

Sean said, "Alright, then." He did that one-arm-around-one-shoulder-lean-into-it-but-don't touch kind of hug. He did the same with our Dad. Sean held up one hand in a salute, told us he would call later and raised his eyebrows to me in a silent gesture, mouthing the words, *Call him.*

Dad and I walked down the concourse, found a Chili's with open tables and sat down. There could not be a more appropriate final signpost that the vacation was officially over. I normally wouldn't eat at Chili's, but stranded in an airport, you do all kinds of things you wouldn't normally do, like squeezing out a twelve-year-old for that docking station you desperately need. Dad and I both

304

ordered beers and nachos, which were soggy and cheese laden—just another reminder that we had re-entered the States.

There was a moment of silence, then Dad said, "You know, Natalie, the worst part is, that I'll go home and people will ask about my vacation, and I will tell them about some of the places we saw and what we did, but . . . they'll have no idea."

"I know," I said.

"A photo album won't do it justice." He sighed. "Even talking about it doesn't do it justice."

"I know." I grabbed a chip and threw it back on the mess of salsa and sour cream.

"How am I even going to explain it all to Eve."

I was barely paying attention. "You'll find a way."

"For Pete's sake," Dad said. "Quit your moping."

"I'm not."

"You are!"

"Just call him."

"What?"

"You heard me."

"I didn't." I bugged my eyes out in a look of annoyance. "Because it sounded distinctly like you told me to contact a sane, honest man that I've known seven days who lives in another country while I finish one of the hardest fellowships known in the academic world and still maintain my thin line of sanity."

Dad laughed. "Life's short."

"Believe me, I know," I said. "No one knows better than me," folding my hands and placing them on the table. "But I think in this case, you really don't know what you're talking about."

He gestured with his beer. "Yeah, you're right, because I've never known what it's like to love and lose anyone.

17

Texts:

Unknown number: Hello?

Nat: Who is this?

Unknown number: Hey

Nat: Get lost creeper

Unknown number: ;\

A large industrial work-site dumpster was sitting in my driveway and five guys were methodically taking my house down to the studs, removing drywall, carpeting and everything that had been ruined in what I was calling the "Trevor-disaster." I was taking all remaining foodstuffs and utensils from the kitchen, storing it in boxes and moving it to a corner of the house not destroyed. Most of my "livable space" was in my bedroom and I'd built a full campsite there, including a hot plate and dishwashing station in the bathtub.

I walked out of the kitchen my third day home to see a strange, leggy redhead standing in the living room, talking to the hired help. She was wearing a pair of tight jeans and black t-shirt, with a leather jacket. She wore lace-up boots and was devoid of any jewelry. My initial reaction was that she was taking the biker chic look too far. She wasn't a traditional beauty, with round eyes that overtook her face and masculine line of shoulders, but a woman that turned heads by her solid presence and rigid steeliness. As she talked, I noticed a slight accent and that the hired guys barely made eye contact and deferred to her in all things.

"May I help you?" I asked.

The woman turned, gave me a head-to-toe appraisal and extended her hand. "Natalie?"

"Ahhhh, yes," I said, trying to catch the eye of one of the workmen, but he turned away from me. "And you are?"

"Robbie."

It took a second for the information to compute. *"Robbie?"*

I'm embarrassed to report that after years of being stereotyped—of putting shoved into a certain shaped box, of fighting tooth-and-nail against men who thought I didn't belong, of white-knuckling my way to the top—not only was I dumbstruck to this announcement, I was unbelieving.

I continued to stare.

"Well, formally, I'm Roberta," she said, "but that name never had the right tone in the gambling dens," in a way that suggested that this conversation was the usual tedium of her day-to-day existence. She waved a hand as if disregarding a small inconvenience. "No one appreciates testicular removal like another woman, would you say?"

I burst out laughing and when I didn't stop, she joined in. When I finally controlled my outburst, I said, "It's a pleasure to meet you."

"Same. I can't say that I meet many women willing to go another level, if you know what I mean. Your emails were a delight."

After that initial meeting, Robbie stopped by on a regular basis. She contacted her local guys to get my house fixed, as I worked out a way for Trevor to pay her back over time. I realized that this particular arrangement wasn't allowed to most, but I'd been given some maneuvering room because she either found me amusing, entertaining, or had some other sinister plans. I tried not to think about it too much and reminded her repeatedly of our agreement.

A week into construction, I'd come home from work to find all copper stripped, my new washer and dryer gone and my camping gear, stolen. I'd immediately called Robbie and within a day, I'd had all gear returned and two guys working on the copper. I'd never had it happen again, and for the first time since living in the neighborhood, I'd felt it safe to leave front door unlocked. I told her in no uncertain terms there would be no "medical intervention services," and she grudgingly handed back some of my personal belongings, including my underwear in a garbage sack. She said, "The guys kept pawing through them. It was weird." Friendships had been built on less.

Robbie stopped by one day, and said, "You should still think about our arrangement," as she handed me a beer and waggled her eyebrows. I was in the final stages of my fellowship and had three months to go before taking the boards. Several days previous, one of her men had used a nail gun on his hand. I'd removed the three-inch nail, sutured the wound and bandaged it with some meager supplies that I had at home, including super glue.

I took a long drink of my beer and said, "I'll stick to my original, legal plan for medical employment."

"Women are rare in my particular line of work," she hinted.

"Whatever *that* is exactly," I said. "Interesting prospect. But I'm an albino leopard where I am right now."

Robbie sighed. "Point taken. But it's a shame."

Trevor received two years jail time and would be serving two years' probation after that, which included teaching IT classes at the city rehabilitation center and penitentiary. This worried me, but it was now up to the government to monitor him. I was interviewing for cardiology positions, one of which had been conducted over Skype for the Royal Infirmary of Edinburgh, which hosted an impressive cardiothoracic department. They asked several times about my intentions, wondering why I was looking to move abroad. I kept my answers vague, stating a wish to change my life. Conall and I emailed regularly, but the correspondence was a poor excuse to a real relationship. I told myself that missing him was something I couldn't afford.

Tommie showed up one day, walking into the house unannounced, unceremoniously pulling me into a headlock and lifting me off the ground in the closest thing the Calhoun's could call a hug. He dragged me around by my neck while investigating the damage. The workers watched horrified—several wondering whether to mind their business or call Robbie, like I was some kind of battered wife. Tommie appeared sleep-deprived and fatigued, with wrinkled clothes and deep bruises beneath his eyes. When I pulled away, he gingerly held a hand to his left side before he caught me watching.

"Why are you here?" I asked.

He said, "meetings," and mussed my hair, his hand sliding down to brush my scar. I knew there were no *meetings*, but Tommie did this from time to time, showing up like a mother hen concerned over her chicks.

"You should've come to Scotland," I said, and pulled two beers from the fridge.

"I should do many things," he said, grabbing the beer and leaning against the wall, "but don't." He paused. "No matter. It sounds like you kept things . . ." he tilted his head back and forth thinking, "comical."

"Campy, you mean," and I took a drink.

"More like crazy."

I mimed the bird sound, "Cuckoo," and fluttered my hands, imitating birds rising to the ceiling.

His smile reached all the way to his eyes, which was a rare treat indeed. He reached across and we bumped knuckles. He said, "I am truly sorry that I missed it."

"Yeah, me too." I sighed. "With you around, I could have actually looked normal."

Robbie walked in at that exact moment and said, "That's hard to believe," and stopped in her tracks. She and Tommie stood staring. Tommie's eyes narrowed, as if he were tracking prey. Robbie stood her ground, but muttered, "Well, maybe not."

"Tommie," I warned, intoning my words very carefully. "*Be. Nice.* She's a friend."

Tommie never took his eyes from Robbie as he took a long drink of his beer. He said, "That remains to be seen," his hand sliding into a pocket.

I gestured to the new flooring and the fresh paint on the walls. "She's fixing the house." When he finally looked my direction, I added, "For free. It's a good arrangement."

Tommie relaxed and shrugged, a silent message of truce. Robbie took a breath and said, "Remember, Gomer Pyle, your Polaroid camera will be useless against my power tools."

Tommie's eyes dipped in amusement, but he said nothing in return.

Robbie left as soon as it was polite, lingering to talk to the workers and giving the impression that she wasn't fleeing the scene, but neither Tommie nor I were fooled.

The entire scene reinforced Tommie's unnatural presence in the general public. In my eyes, he was still my rangy teenage brother from our youth, with long arms, swimmer's body and a disarming, one-sided grin. But as an adult, he should never have been let out to wander amongst regular civilians. His blonde hair was trimmed to his scalp and he had a scar that ran through his left eyebrow causing his eyelid to droop; there was no disguising the looseness of his body that spoke of corded strength and the way his eyes always seemed to be assessing for things that the rest of us did not. Tommie was a gray wolf spotted in the distance—by seeing him in the light of day, you knew something was amiss and your first instinct was to immediately vacate the premises.

*   *   *

One day later, Tommie and I were pulling out the destroyed dishwasher when one of the drywall workers ran in to tell us a strange guy had wandered into the living room, looking like he might steal the copper. Tommie, who had been severing lines between the dishwasher and the wall, stood up and moved towards the living room in a prowl.

"Tommie," I said, "Hold on," grabbing his shirt. "Wait," I yelled.

Tommie didn't listen, but instead engaged the guy by using his shoulder as a battering ram to his midsection, causing the hulking figure to bend at the waist and curse as the two of them banged against a wall. My first thought was, *For God's sake, don't hurt the drywall.* Tommie was the smaller of the two, but quicker. The other guy made up the difference with his larger size. When Tommie went for the tackle, the man reared back and threw a punch, landing it to the top of Tommie's head, which was similar to hitting your fist on a concrete wall. Tommie laughed out loud.

When I saw the dark hair, the big hands, and an unmistakable "BUGGER" come roaring out of the giant's mouth, I screamed, "STOP!"

They went tumbling across the floor—a solid mass of arms and legs, knocking into a chair and cracking a window. "For God's sake, *STOP!*"

Robbie walked in and stood staring. "I was on my way over when I got a SOS call about men fighting." She grimaced as Conall landed a knee to Tommie's ribs, who in turn, caught Conall on the chin with a fist. "This is good. You think they'd be interested in some cage fighting?"

"Do something!" I pointed. "He's a friend."

Robbie cringed as she watched Tommie maneuver to the top and use his arm to keep Conall in a chokehold. "Not to your brother apparently."

"Robbie," I pleaded.

She walked away, muttering, "*Robbie do this. Robbie do that. Robbie save the day.*"

Conall flipped Tommie using his massive legs as dead weight, but Tommie was a wiry monkey—when you combined the government training with his penchant for pain, sometimes even breaking his bones barely got his attention. I ran over and grabbed Conall's ankle, just as Tommie kicked and knocked me sideways. Tommie found enough maneuvering room to land a sharp kidney punch. Conall wheezed, lost his hold and Tommie rolled to the top. I grabbed Tommie's collar and jerked, but Conall heaved with gusto of a Sumo wrestler and the dog pile flipped, almost landing on top of me.

Robbie grabbed my arm and pulled me back. "That's enough," she muttered, "They're about to ruin the paint." Robbie was hauling a nail gun; maneuvering the tool in such a way that left no doubt she'd used it before. She placed her foot on Tommie's head and an explosive noise ricocheted around the room; the nail embedding in the carpet two inches from Tommie's nose.

"Hey, losers," Robbie said, leaning over, grinning. The men lay frozen in a wrestling tableau. Conall's head was jammed into Tommie's armpit and Conall was pushing Tommie's elbow in an unnatural direction. Tommie's eyes slide to the nail and back to Robbie's face. She said, "Are you listening?" and pushed harder with her foot.

"Gorgeous," Tommie said in an exaggerated English accent, the words muffled beneath her heel. "We're just waiting for you, love."

"The next one goes in your skull," Robbie said. "And I'm not joking," pulling her foot away. "You're a thick-headed bastard, but I'm willing to place money on how far it will go."

313

Tommie burst out laughing; the noise so strange that I had to make sure it was coming from him.

Conall grunted. "Who the hell are *you?*"

"Get up," Robbie said. "We'll do introductions. Including you two jackasses."

The men separated themselves, going to their arms and knees and then fully upright. Conall had a cut on his forehead and dabbed at it with a finger, blood on his hand. Tommie pushed him, saying, "It's OK Barbie, we'll get you a Band-Aid. Try not to cry."

Conall smashed his size sixteen foot on Tommie's right insole, which caused him to bend over and cough. Conall gasped air as if he'd run a race. He smiled at me and said, "Hey."

I said, "Hey" back, mimicking an infantile middle school conversation. We stood staring. I couldn't contain my silly grin, or the nerves causing me to clutch my hands like a nervous schoolgirl.

Tommie—always the wrecking ball to any significant moment—came up to his full height and slapped Conall on the head. "So, who's this pansy?"

Incensed, I grabbed Tommie's arm. "Tommie, this is Conall. He's from Scotland. He's . . . he . . ." I stuttered, because I wasn't quite prepared to make family introductions. *Rental car agent? Bar brawler? Coffee acquaintance? Bramble rescuer?*

Boyfriend?

Redness seeped into my face. "I . . ."

Tommie stared.

I blurted, "We had sex. Multiple times. OK?"

Conall groaned, "For Pete's sake, Nat!"

314

Tommie snickered. "Awwweesome. And now he's here. That's some good—"

"She's my girlfriend," Conall announced.

There was a pause as Tommie's eyes shifted to Conall, then back to me. As a rule, the Calhouns were not used to pronouncements of love. Endearments of any kind were looked upon with suspicion; something used as distraction right before you stole the electronics.

Tommie said, "Are you *pregnant*?"

"*What*? She is?" Robbie asked, alarmed.

"I AM NOT PREGNANT!" I screamed.

Conall appeared visibly distressed. I caught his eye, shook my head in exasperation and whispered, "Girlfriend?"

Conall nodded, rubbing at his forehead, saying, "I mean, if you'll have me."

"Wow," Tommie whispered, loud enough for everyone to hear. "Is this an episode of *The Bachelor*?"

Robbie bit back, "Can you not ruin everything?"

"I don't ruin *everything*," grinning her direction.

"*You sure?*" I mouthed.

Conall nodded, motioning me over.

I'd taken a single step when Robbie grabbed my arm and pointed at Tommie. "I know this one is your brother, but remember that one specific *medical* thing that we corresponded about in length? That you're very good at?"

"That's your *brother?*" Conall asked, aghast.

315

"I lied," I said. "There's no way to cause a testicular hydrocele spontaneously."

Tommie snorted. "Yes, her brother. I know, seems impossible since Sean looks like he was made in a Korean experimental laboratory.

"What? You said you could!" Robbie whined.

"I was being intimidating," I returned.

"You're really her brother?" Conall asked.

Tommie laughed. "Well, I guess there's a chance—"

I interrupted, regaining control of the conversation. "Conall, this is Tommie, my *brother*."

"It's *Thomas,*" Tommie corrected.

"He's been hit too many times in the head and is mentally impaired," I said. "He had to wear one of those protective caps as a baby for six months because his head was soft."

Tommie reached across and slapped me in the forehead.

Robbie held out her hand to Conall. "I'm Robbie, part of a specific group trying to recruit your girlfriend to take off other guy's balls," and tilted her head suggestively at Tommie.

Both men stared confused. Conall asked, "Huh?" about the same time Tommie yelled at Robbie, "Wait a sec. I know you!"

Robbie laughed. "Course you do. I'm a regular in your nightmares."

Tommie shook his head. "Nah uh. You're—"

Robbie shot another nail, which implanted just two inches from Tommie's left foot.

"Christ!" Tommie yelled. "OK, that's it!" and took a step towards her.

I grabbed his arm and jerked him back. "OMG!" I yelled. "OK! ENOUGH." I swallowed, and it felt like something was stuck in my throat. I said to Conall, "Why. Are. You. Here?" I was two parts terrified, one part excited and hundred times frightened beyond reason. And if I didn't find out immediately, I was going to lose my mind.

"Well," Conall said, looking at each person, including Robbie's workers, who were pretending to paint a windowsill. "I imagined this going down a bit different." Everyone stood waiting, cashing in on my personal moment. "I thought it'd be just the two of us—"

"Tick-tock, Conall," Tommie blurted. "My Tinder account just notified me that six women are waiting for me at the hotel bar."

"You need to quit mistaking hotel staff for women interested in you," Robbie muttered.

"I'm just down the road at the University of Kansas now," Conall blurted.

"Like you, possibly?" Tommie laughed.

"What? Really?" I asked.

"No. Like the hookers you pay," Robbie responded.

"STOP!" I screamed. "JUST STOP!" I jumped in the air and slammed my fists against my side. I hit myself hard enough it hurt. "I am trying to have a moment. ONE MOMENT." I looked at Tommie. "Can I have *my moment*?"

Tommie rubbed a hand over his cropped hair. "Sure. Sure. Knock yourself out." I held out my hands to show my impatience. Tommie shrugged, asking, "What?"

317

I turned to Conall, "At University of Kansas?"

Robbie fired the nail gun and we all jumped.

"Sorry," she whispered, widening her eyes. "Accident. Continue."

I grabbed fistfuls of hair and said, "Maybe we should just—"

Conall blurted, "I thought you could use an extra hand." He cleared his throat. "Or maybe more." He glanced at Tommie and back to me. "That we . . . could . . . we could be more."

Conall looked pleadingly at me. I stared back. Tommie narrowed his eyes and turned to Robbie in accusation, while Robbie stared at Conall, confused. No one said a word for a full five seconds as the words hung in the air.

I expelled air and whispered, "More," repeating the words. Conall nodded. "More," I said again, as a slow smile bloomed on his face, and he nodded again. I took one step, then another and threw myself at him. I hit him with enough force that we fell back against the wall. He held me, my feet hanging mid-air.

"I missed you so much," I whispered, dangling from his neck in the height-disadvantaged situation. "I tried not to. But I did," hitting at his chest with my forehead. "I applied for a position in Edinburgh, you big lug."

"Well, for God's sake, tell them that ye changed your mind," Conall said, hoisting me higher and kissing me on the lips.

"Really?"

"Really," and he kissed me again.

I was willing to stay there for the rest of the day, but behind us, Tommie cleared his throat. With some reservations, I slid off Conall's body. He took my hand, refusing to let go.

"Well, I'm glad we've clarified the whole boyfriend thing," Robbie said, sighing, "I just hope you fare better than the last one." She squinted at Conall. "Weird question. Have we met?"

"No."

Robbie considered. "You sure? You're familiar."

"So are you," Tommie said to Robbie.

Robbie inhaled, "It's like one of those toys that doesn't shut off."

Tommie held out his hand, and he and Conall shook hands, tentatively. While leaning in, Tommie pressed his leg to the side of Conall's left knee. Conall tried to step back, but Tommie kept a firm hold, whispering, "How's the knee these days? After that misstep with Michigan State?"

Conall gave me a confused look. I shoved Tommie aside and said, "Behave yourself. This isn't your day job." I said to Conall, "He grows on you. After about ten years."

"Day job?" Conall asked. "You said he handled customer complaints for a large corporation."

Tommie's sharp laugh ricocheted around the room. "That's awesome." He placed a hand on Conall's shoulder. "I'm going to use that later when going through security."

Robbie muttered, "Like he goes through security," and glanced out the front window. She went still, surveying the street. "How'd you get here, sport?" muttering *sport* under her breath and taking a sideways glance.

Conall said, "Flight. From Scotland."

Robbie sighed. "Right. Of course. But . . . today?"

Conall shrugged. "I drove."

We all peered out the window. The only visible cars were my depilated Subaru, Robbie's pickup, Tommie's rental and a few banged up trucks that belonged to the hired hands.

"Really?" I asked. "You buy something?"

Conall untangled himself, taking a step closer. "A brand new red S-10 that was sitting in the driveway only ten minutes ago."

I saw no such vehicle. "And the keys?" I asked.

"I left them in the visor," Conall said, as if it was a dumb question.

Robbie's face pinched. *"Who does that?"*

Conall said, "The Scots."

Tommie sniffed. "Sometimes the military."

Both men smiled conspiratorially, which made me more nervous than their fighting.

Robbie said, "I doubt it. I don't think *anyone* does it, except maybe guys who look like you." She shook her head. "It never stops," sighing. "I'll start making phone calls," and walked away.

Tommie, Conall and I exchanged silent glances. After several seconds, I grabbed Tommie's arm and pushed him towards the kitchen.

"All right, all right," Tommie said, "I'll go make myself useful." He pointed. "Just. *Over. There.*"

I could still hear him laugh as he walked into the kitchen, saying to Robbie, "Call your goons, Nikita. We'll go on reconnaissance."

Conall exhaled, saying, "He's entertaining."

"Never a dull moment."

"Is he around to eliminate *all* threats? Or just threats concerning you?"

I inhaled and felt it all the way to my toes. Something light rebounded, bubbling back up through my body, into my fingers, and fizzing into my head. "Tommie is the one . . . who . . . that . . ." I stopped. Conall waited. It felt strange to talk about it. Out loud. To someone who might understand. I took another breath and stepped into new waters. It was an alien world, full of danger, but maybe it was time that all of us took some chances. "He kept me from dying. That day." I tilted my head, thinking. "It changed something in him." I shrugged. "It changed something in me." More than anyone knew. "He feels responsible. For all of us. You know?"

Conall nodded. "I know."

Clearing my throat, I said, "So, you're really here," unable to keep out the emotion.

He smiled. "I'm really here. Accepted and enrolled in a MBA program." He took a step towards me. "With housing. Just down the road." He took another step. "It's a new beginning. Of many sorts." He pointed between us. "This, us, needs a real chance, yeah? And I intend to do just that."

"Alec must be beside himself," I said, trying to calm my nerves.

"Furious," Conall replied, taking one last step.

"He's probably worried about the damage I might cause. To you and your truck," pointing to the vacant space.

"No. I think his exact words were that ye might be the only thing to keep me alive." He surveyed the dismantled house and kitchen, where Robbie was talking on her cell. "What's she mean about ye taking men's baws?

"*Baws*?"

Conall laid a hand over his package, saying, "Testicles."

"Don't worry," I said, "That only concerns the men who try to steal my underwear. And my goods."

"*I'll* be trying to steal your underwear. And your *goods*."

"Yeah, but I know where to find the keys to your truck."

He reached across and grabbed a fistful of my shirt, pulling me closer. He whispered, "About that first truck ride, I thought . . ." he looked over his shoulder and saw Tommie talking to Robbie. "I thought we could reenact things. Maybe get it right this time."

"I think that could be arranged," I said, sliding a finger down his chest. "If you manage to get your truck back."

Made in the USA
Monee, IL
01 September 2023

41757658R00187